THE WEAVER'S GLORY

Also by Donna Baker

The Weaver's Daughter
The Weaver's Dream

The Glassmakers Saga
Crystal
Black Cameo
Chalice

THE WEAVER'S GLORY

Donna Baker

HEADLINE

Copyright © 1992 Donna Baker

The right of Donna Baker to be identified as the Author of
the Work has been asserted by her in accordance with the
Copyright, Designs and Patents Act 1988.

First published in 1992
by HEADLINE BOOK PUBLISHING PLC

10 9 8 7 6 5 4 3 2 1

British Library Cataloguing in Publication Data

Baker, Donna
Weaver's Glory
I. Title
823.914 [F]

ISBN 0–7472–0523–X

Printed and bound in Great Britain by
Richard Clay Ltd, Bungay, Suffolk

HEADLINE BOOK PUBLISHING PLC
Headline House
79 Great Titchfield Street
London W1P 7FN

To Valerie Hutty,
longtime friend and favourite librarian . . .

ACKNOWLEDGEMENTS

For information on the transportations to Australia and the conditions there, I am indebted to Robert Hughes' *The Fatal Shore* and to *A Faithful Picture* – a collection of letters written by Eliza and Thomas Browne from 1841–1852.

REBECCA

Chapter One

March, in the year of Our Lord 1837, and the daffodils were opening their golden trumpets as if in silent fanfare to the spring. But for Rebecca Pagnel, sitting in the drawing room of her house at the top of Mount Pleasant and gazing down over the rust-red roofs of Kidderminster, it was winter still. And for ever would remain so, she thought as she watched the pale sunlight gleam through racing clouds. For winter had come into her life, and no bright sunbeam, no golden flower, could ever melt the ice that had frozen around her heart.

Below stairs at Pagnel House, much had changed since Rebecca had first come there as scullerymaid, almost twenty years ago. Polly, who had gladly relinquished her job at the sink, washing an endless supply of dirty dishes, was now housekeeper. Mrs Hudd, who had taken Rebecca on because of a fondness for the child's mother, had retired with her savings and a pension to a small cottage on the outskirts of Kidderminster. Mrs Atkins, the cook who had supplied Rebecca with most of those dirty dishes, had died making bread one morning, clutching at her pillowy bosom as she slipped sideways to the floor. There was a new butler, Mr Bessel, who held sway in much the same manner as his predecessor. Billy the Boots had risen to the heights of Odd-job, and a new footman and two new maids giggled and flirted whenever they thought they could get away with it.

And Rebecca, who had married Francis Pagnel, was now mistress over them all.

'Poor soul,' Polly commented that morning in spring as the

household prepared for the saddest day since old Mr Pagnel had died. 'She looks as if she don't rightly know where she is. It's hit her real hard.'

'Not as if she weren't expecting it, is it?' the cook remarked. She slapped a huge wad of pastry on the table and began to roll it out, muscles knotting in her bare forearms. 'Bin sickly for years, 'adn't 'e? Like to pop off any time, from what I 'eard, and he's never looked right all the time I bin 'ere.'

'It still hits you hard when someone dies, all the same,' Polly said. ''Specially when you think as much of 'em as Beck – Mrs Pagnel – thought of Mr Francis.'

The maids were listening, wide-eyed. They had been up even earlier than usual that morning, scrubbing, sweeping and polishing, and had only just finished their breakfast. In a few minutes they would be sent about their work again but for the moment it seemed there was a chance of a short respite.

'You knew 'em when they was young, didn't you, Mrs Barlow?' the kitchenmaid asked. 'When Mrs Pagnel worked here, in this very kitchen.' She looked around the cavernous room, awed. 'Coo, it seems funny, don't it, to think of her working here, just like one of us? And then marrying the master.' She sighed sentimentally. 'Childhood sweethearts, they were, and never had eyes for nobody else. It was a real love story.'

'Tell us about it, Mrs Barlow,' the parlourmaid begged. 'I likes a nice love story, 'specially when it ends up sad. Is it true they used to –'

'No, it's not, whatever it is,' Polly said sharply. 'And I'll thank the two of you to remember just what day it is. The master's going to be buried today, and it's no time to be gossiping about him and the mistress. It ent fitting – and there's too much to be done. I don't know what you think you're doing, Meg and Annie, lolling about here as if it's Christmas. Now get out on with your work or you'll have more to think about than love stories. You'll be thinking about how to get yourselves new jobs without a character, that's what you'll be thinking.'

4

The two girls scuttled away, one to the scullery to peel vegetables, the other to the butler's pantry to help with polishing some of the family silver brought out for the occasion. Polly looked after them grimly and then turned back to the cook, who was slapping her pastry into a row of pie dishes.

'Girls today! I don't know what would hev happened to me and Becky if we'd dared take liberties like those two do. We never had more than a minute to ourselves all day. But there, we had to work hard and I suppose that's made the difference. She remembers what it's like.'

Mrs Bentley nodded. 'It's not often you finds a mistress like Mrs Pagnel. Most of 'em don't even seem to know where their own kitchen is. As for what goes on there, they don't care a tinker's cuss so long as the work gets done, not even if the servants has to stay up 'til four in the morning and get up again at five. Why, there was one I worked for in London, before I come 'ere, I swear she didn't even know she '*ad* servants. Thought the 'ouse swept and polished itself and the meals got theirselves ready, she did.' She scooped veal and ham mixture from a large bowl, distributing it amongst the pies, then looked at Polly. 'Mind, it do seem a bit like a story,' she said. 'The master marrying the maid, I mean. Was it really like that?'

'Except that Mr Francis weren't the master, I suppose it was,' Polly said. 'He was a cousin then, you see – nobody knew he was Mr Jeremiah's son. Of course, it all come out later – caused a lot of talk at the time. But there, everyone respected Mr Jeremiah, and Mr Francis was grown up by then, and somehow it all seemed to come out all right. And Mr Jeremiah never went back on his word to make Mr Vivian the heir to the carpet business – that was agreed when he wed Mr Vivian's mother. But that's why he left Mr Francis the house.'

'So Mrs Pagnel come back 'ere as mistress.' The cook sighed, much as young Annie had. 'And now he's died, and she's a widow. And two little boys to look after, an' all. An' only – what? Not thirty yet, I'll be bound.'

'Just over,' Polly said, forgetting that she'd thought gossip ill fitting. 'Still, she won't hev it hard like her own folk would've done. She'll be well off. Her boys won't want for nothing, not the way Becky and her family did when they fell on hard times.'

She stood for a moment lost in thought, remembering the skinny waif who had come to stand on a box at the scullery sink, scrubbing all day with only a breath of fresh air when she had to go out to the rubbish heap with scraps. Who would have thought that she could have become wife to one of the brightest young carpet manufacturers in Kidderminster? Or that she would, just a few short years later, find herself his widow?

In the drawing room, Rebecca sat alone, gazing into the fire. Outside, the sun shone from a sky of tender blue, lighting up the daffodils in the garden, bringing a shimmer of silvery green to the winter-bare branches of the trees. But here in Pagnel House, the air was chill with death and loss and sadness, and Rebecca shivered and drew her fine wool shawl more closely around her shoulders.

There had been so much death in her life. Her parents, perishing in the poverty of a weaver's hovel. Her sister Bessie, dying slowly over the years of the dreadful disease of her life in London. Her little son, Geoffrey, his bright, eager life extinguished by the muddy waters of the Stour. Jeremiah, Francis's natural father, who had shown her kindness and welcomed her into his family; and his brother, old Geoffrey, who had brought Francis up as his son.

And now Francis. Francis, her husband, her first, her only sweetheart, who had given her his love, who had accepted hers and cherished it. Francis, her other half.

Rebecca rose to her feet and walked restlessly about the room, as if activity could shake off her grief. But it would not be shaken away. It bore down upon her like the weight of all the world, crushing her, a relentless pressure on heart and mind.

I can't, she thought desperately, I can't live with this misery for the rest of my life. For how many years? Thirty, forty, fifty? Alone, bereft, suffering this incessant clawing torment until the grave claims me at last? She shook her head. It was not possible.

And yet what other course was there for her? Her body would not die simply because she willed it. And she could not will it yet, anyway. Not until the boys grew up. Not until they needed her no longer. Not until their own children . . .

No! Again, she shook her head. No, she would not look ahead so far, she would not think of Daniel and William grown, with children of their own. Children who would call her Grandmother, who would have called Francis Grandfather . . .

She thrust her hands forwards, palms outwards, her arms stiff as if pushing uselessly at some powerful force. But the pain, the grief, the bewilderment of loss, all stayed with her and she could see no end to any of them.

The door opened and she turned slowly, wearily, as if all her strength had been used up in the struggle.

'Tom.'

Her brother came into the room. He closed the door behind him and crossed the room to take her in his arms. She looked up into his face and saw the compassion there, the concern, and knew that she had to answer it with strength. Tom too had suffered his loss.

'Oh, Tom,' she said, and let her head fall against his chest.

He stroked her hair, murmuring softly but saying little, and she knew that there was little for him to say. The same thoughts, the same futile questions were in both their minds. The same useless railing against nature, against the inexorability of life and death.

'It was London,' Rebecca said, as if he had asked the question aloud. 'London killed Francis, Tom, just as it killed Bessie.'

She felt his arms tighten about her. Nobody ever talked about the cause of Bessie's death. Everyone knew that it was because of the life she had led – been forced to lead – when she and Tom had first fled to London. Everyone knew that if

Bessie had not been compelled to earn her living in the only way left to a woman when all else fails, she would not have wasted away so terribly before their eyes.

But Francis had not suffered from the disease that had ravaged Bessie. His death had been brought about by an even more insidious agent, one that struck at rich and poor alike. And the cough that had troubled him during the past few years, sometimes almost disappearing, at others bringing a lump of fear to Rebecca's throat, had finally won. With one last gush of bright, pulsing blood, the life had soaked away into the white pillow, and he had died as he loved best to live, in Rebecca's arms.

'They say that living in cities is dangerous,' she said bitterly. 'I knew it too. When we came back to Kidderminster, I thought everything would be all right. But it was too late, Tom – too late for Bessie and too late for Francis. Too late for any of us,' she added brokenly, and wept against his coat.

'Time's getting on, Becky,' he said at last, and she raised her head and looked at him with drenched brown eyes. 'The hearse'll be here soon. D'you want to take one last look at him?'

Rebecca closed her eyes and her body trembled under the black shawl she still held about herself. She nodded slowly and they turned towards the door and went down the stairs to the library.

It was in this room, where they had first met, that Rebecca had asked that Francis should lie. A fire burned in the hearth where she used to come to clear the ashes in the early mornings and on the shelves were ranged the books that Francis had slipped down to read while the household slept. The bier stood in the middle of the darkened room, the coffin as yet unsealed, and Rebecca released Tom's hand and went slowly towards it.

Francis lay as if sleeping in the silken shroud. His face was pale as marble, yet without the two spots of hectic red that had so often shown like warning flags in his cheeks, and his eyes were closed. His hair had been brushed and lay like worn gold on his brow, and his long, thin hands were folded over his breast.

Those hands would never touch her again in the loving they had shared. Those lips would never again brush hers, that golden hair never twine between her fingers. Those arms would never hold her, and the voice that had whispered in the night would never again speak of the love he bore her.

Francis's body lay here still, but Francis himself had gone. His body would be buried, but his spirit had departed. And she could only pray that wherever his new journey had taken him, he would wait for her there.

Tom touched her arm and she turned. His face was grave.

'The undertaker is here, Rebecca,' he said quietly, and she knew that this was the final moment, her last chance to look upon her husband's face, for soon they would nail on the lid of his coffin and take him away from her for ever. And she moved close to the bier and touched his face with her fingers and bent her lips to his, cold as they were, and knew that this was her last goodbye. From this moment, she was alone.

Tom led her away from the library where she had seen Francis for the first time and the last. He led her back to the drawing room, back to her chair by the fire. And there, he knelt beside her and took her once more into his arms and let her weep.

The funeral over, Rebecca was composed and calm as she moved among those who had come to the house to pay their last respects to Francis Pagnel. She moved quietly, only her pallor and a slight heaviness of the eyes betraying her grief. Now and then her eyes would seek those of her brother and when Tom caught her glance they would exchange a look of understanding, and Rebecca would feel comforted.

But her sorrow was never far away and after a while she felt the need to escape from the gathering. Quietly, she slipped out of the room and went to the library where Francis had lain until such a short time ago, and there she sat down in his favourite chair by the fire and rested her head against its strong back.

It was here that Vivian found her, her eyes closed. He stood for a moment, regarding her thoughtfully, and then she stirred and her eyelids lifted. She met his dark, brooding gaze and felt a moment of unease, almost fear. Then, quickly, she dismissed it. Had Vivian not proved a good friend to her in recent years? Could there really be either need or reason for remembering the dread he had inspired in her years ago?

'You look weary,' he said quietly, and she nodded, then made to rise.

'I'd better go back. They'll be wondering –'

He put out a hand. 'Stay there, Rebecca. Nobody will wonder where you are or why you've left them. You're a widow, you've suffered, you're entitled to want to be alone. Nobody will think it strange.'

She hesitated, then sank back with a little sigh. Perhaps she could just stay a little longer. The thought of facing them all again, knowing that she might break down in tears at any moment, was more than she could bear. 'I must confess, I'd rather not go back. Everyone's very kind but –' her voice shook a little '– somehow that makes it all the harder to bear. It makes it seem more real. I know it's real. I know Francis is dead, but somehow I seem to want to pretend he's not. Just for a little while. Just until I've got used to the idea.' Used to the idea! she thought with bitter incredulity. How could she ever get 'used to the idea'?

Vivian nodded. 'I know. I understand.'

She looked up at him, ready to refute his words. How could anyone understand what she was suffering now? But something in Vivian's face took her back over the years and stopped her words.

'Of course, you would. You've suffered it yourself.' But even as she spoke, a part of her wondered just how true that was. Vivian's wife, Maria, had died in childbirth many years ago, leaving him with six daughters. Yet Vivian had never seemed as heartbroken as Rebecca felt now. Nor had he ever seemed to feel the same deep love that she had felt for Francis. The marriage of Vivian and Maria had always been

10

one of convenience, one intended to produce sons to inherit the business, to carry on the Pagnel name.

It had not been Maria's fault that no sons were produced, but Vivian had always seemed to blame her for not giving him his heirs. And that resentment had deepened when old Jeremiah had died, leaving the business to his adopted son as he'd always promised – but Pagnel House to Francis.

Rebecca would not have been surprised if the rift, sometimes deep, sometimes shallow, that had always existed between the cousins had not become a gulf during the years that had followed. To see Francis and the wife who had once been the lowliest of scullerymaids, now master and mistress of the house he had always believed would be his, must have been galling in the extreme. And Vivian was not a man to take such a rebuff lightly. For a long time, Rebecca had treated him with caution, certain that beneath his apparent acceptance must seethe a turmoil of hostile envy.

But Vivian, after the first shock, had shown little of this feeling. From time to time, she had caught a strange look in his eyes as they rested upon his cousin – a term tacitly accepted by all, inaccurately though it described the odd relationship between them. But although he had never been warmly friendly, preferring instead to continue with the patronising condescension with which he had always treated Francis, he had kept any animosity to himself. And Rebecca, after her early hesitation, had continued to look after his daughters as she had done ever since their mother's death.

Yes, Vivian was a past master at hiding his feelings. So perhaps they ran deeper than anyone realised. Perhaps he had indeed suffered when Maria had died, and did understand exactly how Rebecca was feeling now.

'It doesn't seem possible that he's gone,' she said, looking into the fire. 'Just last week he was here, sitting in this very chair – feeling better, he said. And I hoped – I *tried* to hope – that perhaps he would get well again. People do.' She looked up at Vivian, her dark brown eyes almost black. 'People have recovered, with care. And I did try to take care.' It was hard to speak through her aching throat. 'I tried so hard to keep him well.'

'Nobody could have tried harder,' Vivian said. He took a chair from beside the long table and drew it close so that he could sit beside her. She could feel the warmth of his body as he took her hand in his. 'Nobody ever had a better wife than you, Rebecca. Frank must have known that. Indeed, I heard him say so, many times.'

'A selfish wife,' she said in a low tone. 'I wanted to keep him well so that he would stay alive for *me*. I couldn't bear the thought of losing him. And now . . . he's gone anyway.'

Vivian stroked her hand gently. 'It's a sad time. A sad and bitter time. You'll grieve for him – it's right and natural. But you're young still, Rebecca. One day the skies will seem brighter and you'll begin to live again. And when you do –'

He paused and Rebecca looked up at him, startled. But his eyes told her nothing. He smiled slightly and continued, 'When you do – until you do – I'll be here. As your friend. I hope you'll always think of me as your friend.'

She nodded. 'I do, Vivian. You've been a good friend to me, even if you and Francis didn't always see eye to eye. I've never forgotten your kindness when Geoffrey –' But the memory of her dead son, coming at such a time, was too much for her and she broke down completely, burying her face in her hands and weeping without restraint.

She felt Vivian lay his arm about her shoulders and draw her close. Almost instinctively, she turned towards him, accepting the comfort he was offering.

'He was a good husband to me,' she said brokenly. 'He never passed a day without thinking of me above himself. He helped me when my mother died, you know. He brought her here to Pagnel House and told Mrs Hudd she was to let her stay in the kitchen – she was almost dead then and many people would have left her where she was, in the hovel with my father's body. But it was so bitterly cold that day in the snow – she would have died even sooner and in even greater misery. And Francis brought her here and defied his aunt to keep her here.'

She stopped abruptly, remembering that the aunt Francis had opposed was in fact Vivian's mother. And neither Isabella nor Vivian himself had been in the least sympathetic over that episode.

But Vivian had apparently forgotten his own attitude. He nodded. 'I remember it. And he would have done more, but for the trouble over Isabel. Poor child, she was deluded – she thought Francis loved her and when she found that he didn't, she lost her mind. It was very sad.'

'Yes,' Rebecca said a little doubtfully. She didn't recall the incident in those terms, remembering instead that Isabel, the youngest of the Pagnels, had gone into a decline which nobody had been able to halt. From her first refusal to eat, she had become apparently unable to swallow even a morsel, so that when she finally died her body was as thin as a stick and unable to perform any of its proper functions. It was as if she had given up living; as if, unable to have Francis, she had decided there was nothing to live for.

Perhaps Vivian was right; perhaps she had lost her mind.

Icy, skeletal fingers clutched at Rebecca's heart. Would this happen to her as well? Would her body, deprived of her husband's love, decide that there was nothing left to live for, that it might as well die? Would she too find herself unable to eat, unable even to drink . . . ?

But I do have a reason for living, she told herself with sudden urgency. I have several reasons for living. My children. My family. Tom and Nancy. The co-operative. Even – she glanced up at the man who held her close – even Vivian's children. They need me, even as much as I need them.

The door opened and she turned her head to see her son, Daniel. Her eldest child, her first-born, conceived on the first occasion when Francis and she had made love together. The child she had once doubted if she would live to bear, and had believed would never see his father.

'Daniel.' She stretched out a hand. 'Daniel, come here.'

He came slowly across the room towards her. He looked more than fifteen years old today, she thought sadly, seeing the sombreness of the dark eyes so much like her own. His mourning clothes deepened the pallor of his cheeks and there were traces of his own grief in his taut expression. But he held himself upright and there was a new air of responsibility about him, as if the many people who had told him that he was now the man of the family had persuaded him that it was true.

I shouldn't have allowed it, Rebecca thought with sudden regret. He's too young for it. He's still no more than a child, and he's already had too much taken away from him. He'll never learn to laugh now.

But her tears began again all the same, as if there were an inexhaustible supply, and she bowed her head over his hand and sobbed at the thought that he and his brother William were now fatherless.

'Don't cry so, Mamma,' Daniel said in a low voice, not far from tears himself. 'You'll make yourself ill.'

Rebecca caught at his hand and gripped it hard as she struggled to control herself. To weep like this in front of her son! But the thought of all that they had lost, she and her sons, was too much for her. Francis – Geoffrey – Jeremiah. Even Enid and old Geoffrey, who had been as extra grandparents to the children. No wonder Daniel was more like a man of forty than a fifteen-year-old boy.

The door opened again and her sister-in-law Nancy came in. As pale as the rest, her light brown hair drawn tightly back from her small-featured face, she looked nevertheless as if she at least had everything under control, including her own feelings. She came swiftly forwards and took Daniel's hand.

'Come on, Danny, it's time you and William was back in your own quarters. Your ma's got enough to worry her.' She gave Rebecca an anxious glance. 'I told you I didn't think the boys oughter come down. It's upset 'em both and young Will's playing up already.'

'We've always shared everything with the boys,' Rebecca said wearily. 'Good and bad. And I shan't stay here any longer, being sorry for myself. I'll come and say goodbye to everyone and then I'll go up to the nursery myself and have tea with

14

them. Daniel, you can take William and change back into your everyday clothes and go out into the garden for a while. You've been cooped up in the house ever since – for days now.'

'In the garden?' Vivian said, scandalised. 'Rebecca, do you really think –'

'That it's fitting?' She stood up and her swollen mouth twisted a little. 'No, Vivian, I don't suppose it's at all fitting. But then, Francis and I never did do what was *fitting*, did we? And I don't suppose I'll start now.' She gave her son a smile. 'Don't look so solemn, Daniel. Go out and enjoy the fresh air for a while. And don't be afraid to play your games. Your father wouldn't have wanted you to be miserable.'

She watched as the boy went uncertainly from the room, and stood for a moment quite still, struggling within herself to gain the release she had offered him. But for her, it was impossible. Her wounds were still too raw, the pain too severe.

All she could do was act. But that, at least, she could do well. For hadn't she been doing it all these months, as Francis's disease gripped him ever more tightly in its harsh grip? Hadn't she forced herself to go calmly through the days, pretending there was nothing wrong, never letting her own fear show? Hadn't she been determined to keep the full horror from him, so that he could live without fear, without dread?

And if she could do all that, couldn't she now go back amongst her friends with her head held high, her eyes dry and her manner calm? And if her strength had indeed left her, couldn't she at least pretend it was still there?

The day was over at last. Vivian had gone home to the house Jeremiah had built for him when he married Maria, to the daughters who had each been a more bitter disappointment to him. His sisters Jane, Enid and Sarah had departed with their husbands, their going no less a relief to Rebecca than it was to them. And those whom Rebecca and Francis had counted as true friends – Tom and Nancy, the men he worked with in the co-operative, some of his friends from schooldays – had left more reluctantly, each aware that this moment was

15

the end of an era, the beginning of a different and unwelcome life for Rebecca.

There was one friend, however, who had not come, and it was he whom Rebecca would have welcomed most. Matthew Farrell, bright-eyed and laughing yet serious enough when the occasion warranted, who had been Francis's best friend through their schooldays, who had disappeared to travel the world and turned up on their doorstep one windy March morning and become as one of the family.

She thought of him now, sadly, remembering the times she had walked with him, talked with him. That first morning when he had entertained her and Edith with wildly exaggerated tales of his adventures abroad. The day she had gone to inspect the foundations of his new house; the day he had gone out with Francis to celebrate Lawless Hour, when she had begun her labour with baby William, an ordeal that had nearly killed them both. The day he had been injured in the riots of the Great Strike, and the horror of the night, when he had accidentally shot and killed Bill Bucknell . . .

And the grimness of the weeks that had followed. Matthew, thrown into prison, awaiting trial while poor Bessie, the unwitting instrument of the accident, had died in her own squalid cell. The trial, with its constant attendant fear that he would be judged guilty and hanged. The mixture of emotions – relief, dismay, dread – when he had been sentenced to transportation.

And now he was in Australia, having survived the voyage. Occasionally a letter would arrive from him, telling of strange sights, of animals it was difficult to imagine, of savages who ranged in wild, untamed country and killed any convict desperate enough to try to escape. Of long, hard days spent clearing the forests, cultivating the land, scraping a living from a country that seemed reluctant to provide it.

What would Matthew feel when he learned of the death of his boyhood friend? But she would have to write and tell him. For Matthew was her friend as well, with a bond between them that distance could not sever.

'I don't like leaving you on your own,' Tom said as, last to go, he and Nancy had stood by the door. 'Why don't you let us stop a few nights, just 'til – 'til –'

''Til I get used to it?' Rebecca supplied wryly, and shook her head. 'Tom, I don't think I'll ever get used to being without Francis. Just as you'd never get used to being without your right arm. But I have to learn to deal with it, and I may as well begin now. Tonight, next week, next month, in a year – it will be just the same. There has to be a moment when you go out of that door and leave me here.' She smiled. 'And I'm not alone. I have the boys here, and Polly. She's not just a housekeeper, you know that. She's my friend.'

'Aye, I know. All the same . . .'

Rebecca looked at her sister-in-law, and Nancy touched Tom's arm.

'Becky's right, Tom. And she's had just about enough, you can see that. You'll go to bed now, won't you, Becky – try and get some sleep?'

Privately, Rebecca thought she would never sleep again. Whenever she tried, images of Francis rose before her eyes. Francis as he had been in their youth, so bright and strong, waiting for her in the library. Francis, following her to London, searching for her in the teeming streets. Francis, working hard at his own business, setting up the looms with Tom and old Samuel, his fair head bent over the designs he and Rebecca made together for new carpets.

Francis, coming back to Kidderminster, fighting to set up his co-operative, working as a partner rather than a master with his weavers. Francis, striving to make his dream come true, the dream he had always had of weavers raised from poverty and respected as the craftsmen they were. Francis, supporting the Great Strike seven years ago, arguing their case with the other manufacturers, opposing his cousin Vivian with a quiet strength nobody but Rebecca had suspected.

And Francis, growing more fragile as the years passed yet scorning the illness that was slowly gnawing at his lungs.

Growing thin as a wafer, his frail body racked by the terrible cough, beaten at last by the ravages no man could withstand.

There were other images too. Of herself and Francis together in the library, she afraid all the time that she would be discovered and dismissed. Of that afternoon in the woods when she had lain in his arms and tasted the exquisite delights of love. Of her terror when she had realised she was pregnant, her certainty that Francis would help her, her despair when she had been turned out of the house and found herself in London, alone, friendless, without hope.

Her thoughts still circling in her mind, she hugged Tom and Nancy and saw them out, assuring them that they mustn't worry about her. Polly would come and sit with her for a while before she went to bed. They went at last, Tom still doubtful and Nancy repeating her advice to go to bed at once and have a good night's sleep. As if sleep were something you could simply order, like a cup of chocolate, Rebecca thought ruefully as she went back to the drawing room.

She sank down on a chair by the fire and gazed into the flames. So it was over. Her life with Francis, finished. Fifteen years of loving, of being a part of each other. All the years of her adult life, finished. And now she must start again.

How would she ever find the strength to drag herself through the rest of her days? How to decide this, attend to that, how to take an interest in matters that seemed so unimportant now, so trivial?

The door opened quietly and Polly came into the room. She crossed to the fire, put on a few extra coals and sat in the chair opposite Rebecca. For a few moments, they regarded each other in silence.

'How things have changed, Polly,' Rebecca said at last. 'Do you remember when we were maids here together? Creeping about the house early in the morning with our housemaids' boxes, making the house shine so that everything would be in order before the Family got up. And always terrified one of them might see us – as if we were elves, doing our work secretly in the night, and not human servants at all.'

'Aye, I remember.' Polly looked down at her hands, smoother now than they had ever been in those days, one adorned with the wedding ring that was her only right to be called 'Mrs'. Polly had had her times as a young girl, but had never found a man she wanted to marry. But when she became housekeeper to Mr Jeremiah, she had taken the wedding ring and the title as part of her job.

And she certainly looked matronly enough. From a wisp of a maid, almost as skinny as Rebecca herself had been in those early days, she had grown and filled out into a buxom woman with quite as much majesty as befitted a housekeeper. Her black dress added to the impression and she wore her bunch of keys with pride. Enough to intimidate any impertinent tradesman, Rebecca thought with an unexpected glimmer of amusement, and certainly enough to strike terror into the heart of any maid or bootboy.

'Did you ever think you would become a housekeeper?' she asked. 'I remember that first morning, when Mrs Hudd took me down to the kitchen and handed me over to Mrs Atkins. I looked at that huge pile of washing-up in the scullery and vowed there and then that I wouldn't spend my life scrubbing. There were better things in the world for Rebecca Himley! And I made up my mind that I'd be a housekeeper one day and wear a black dress and carry keys.'

'And here you are, mistress of the whole house,' Polly said. 'Aye, things change in ways we can't foresee – and mebbe it's just as well. No, I didn't reckon I'd ever make it this far. I just took one day at a time, always did. I reckon a parlourmaid was as far as I ever looked. Or head housemaid. And then getting wed to some handsome young footman, mebbe. Well, it all happened, bar the footman. And I'm not too sorry about that – footmen aren't much, after all.'

'Perhaps you had the best of it,' Rebecca said. 'A good position and no one to cause you pain. No husband or children to die and leave you alone.' Her voice wavered and she stopped and bit her lip. 'No. I must not start feeling sorry for myself again. And I still have so much – Daniel, William, Tom and Nancy. You.'

'But none of us enough to fill the gap *he's* left behind,' Polly said quietly. 'It's all right, Becky. I know. And if you can't feel sorry for yourself today of all days –'

'Oh, I know. One must mourn. But I also have to be strong, for my boys and for myself.' She was quiet for a few moments, then said slowly, as if working it out in her own mind as she spoke, 'You see, Polly, I know that if I allowed myself I could just sink into a decline of misery and stay there. I wouldn't have the strength to pull myself out of it – I wouldn't even want to. And I can't let that happen, for the boys' sake.'

'Nonsense,' Polly said robustly. 'You're not the sort at all.'

'Oh, I am. I can be. I'm human, Polly, just like everyone else. I don't have an endless source of strength. I know this could happen to me, because it almost happened after Geoffrey was drowned. I sank then and almost didn't rise. I can't let that happen again.'

'Don't be too hard on yourself. You've been through a lot. You're bound to feel a bit shocked to begin with. In a few months –'

'A few months! Polly, I can't afford to sit idle for months. I've told you, there is this part of me that would sink back, let others take over and never come to life again. No, I have to start again at once. I have to find something to do, something that's important to me.'

'The boys –'

'The boys are well looked after. They go to school, they have their friends and their games. I see them in the mornings at breakfast and in the evenings before they go to bed – what am I to do with the hours in between?' She shook her head. 'And Vivian's girls are just as occupied, with their governess and their lessons. I see them most days, as you know, and I help Vivian with their needs, but they really take very little time.' There was a tinge of despair in her voice as she went on. 'The days are so long, Polly, so full of hours. And I can't spend them as other women in my position do – by calling on friends, leaving my card, holding "At Homes" two afternoons a week. I've never done that.'

I've never been able to, she thought, imagining the reaction of the other wives when she had first come back to Kidderminster as Francis's wife. A former scullerymaid, sitting in their drawing rooms sipping tea and nibbling at little cakes! And she had never wanted to pass her time in that way. Since the age of eight, when she had first begun to draw for her father, she had been accustomed to hard work. Living a life of idle luxury, delightful though it might sound, had never suited her.

'You had your Wives' Group during the strike,' Polly said. 'Helping the weavers through their hard times. And there's the school you and Mr Francis set up, you go there a couple of times a week. There's plenty for you to do.'

'Yes, those things.' She gazed broodingly into the fire. 'But I need more than that, Polly. I need a purpose in my life. Something that will drive me on, give me something positive to live for. And, of course, the answer's easy.'

'Is it?'

'Yes. Don't look so bewildered, Polly. It's right there in front of our eyes – or perhaps I should say, under our feet.' She looked down at the carpet, at the rich colours blending in one of the designs she and Francis had worked on together. 'The co-operative. I shall take Francis's place with that.'

'The co-operative? But Tom looks after that.'

'Tom and Francis together. And without Francis, Tom will find it difficult – he never liked to deal with customers. Francis and I did the designing and Francis dealt with suppliers and customers, leaving Tom and the weavers to produce the orders. It worked well but Tom won't be able to do it all himself.'

Polly stared at her. 'But *you* can't do that! Go travelling to London and Halifax and such, buying wool and getting orders like Mr Francis did.'

'And why not?'

'Well – you just can't. I mean, ladies don't. How could you go and talk to people like – well, like Mr Broom and the

21

others? They'd think there was summat queer about you. I don't suppose they'd even let you in the factories.'

'I won't be going to factories. I'll be going to the big London stores and to private customers who have always bought our carpets. The wool-buying and dyeing side, I'll employ someone else to do. But if you're a customer looking for a new carpet, you can't do better than talk to the designer. And as I shall still be doing that –'

Polly shook her head. 'But it'll be a year before you can even think about these things, Becky. What'll happen in the meantime?'

'A year?'

'For – for your mourning,' Polly said hesitantly.

Rebecca tightened her hands in her lap. She felt the familiar ache in her throat. How easy it would be to agree with Polly, with everyone else, to take that year of mourning. How easy to sit back in her widow's weeds, refusing to venture out, sending away callers. How easy to let the waters of grief close over her head as the waters of the Stour had closed over Geoffrey's, to drown in them, to let life go by without her . . .

'No,' she said, and although her voice was low there was no doubting the iron determination that strengthened its tone. 'No, Polly. My mourning will be my own affair, not a public spectacle. I shall set my affairs at home in order, and then I shall begin. Francis and I had a dream which we worked together to achieve. And I shall go on working towards it.' She lifted her chin and looked Polly in the eye, and her own eyes glittered with tears and with resolution. 'I shall turn the dream into a glory.'

Chapter Two

'You can't be serious.'

Rebecca looked up at Vivian. He stood before the fireplace, legs straddled, hands behind his back. His head jutted forward a little, his brows were lowered and his face dark. She felt a small qualm. Vivian could be as determined and as stubborn as a prize bull when he felt like it, and as unstoppable.

'You can't mean this, Rebecca,' he repeated. 'You're still upset. You're not thinking clearly. It's a madcap scheme and in your heart you know it.'

'I know nothing of the sort,' she answered. 'And I've thought about it a good deal. Even before Francis died. I know quite as much about the business as he did, and I've been designing carpets ever since we were married. Who better to go on running the business than I?'

'Who better? Who *worse*, you mean! Rebecca, you know perfectly well that women in your position do not go into the marketplace. And there's no need for it. You've got your brother to run the factory itself, you can employ someone to do the selling. You surely don't intend to jaunt about London with an order book in your hand! It would be totally unfitting.'

Unfitting. That word again. But hadn't her entire life been *unfitting*? Wasn't it unfitting that Francis had married her at all? Wasn't Francis's own existence unfitting? Isabella, Jeremiah's wife and Vivian's mother, had certainly thought so.

'I don't think I can take that into account,' she observed. 'I seem to have lived my whole life so far being involved in unfitting events. Perhaps I'm fated to go on doing so.'

Vivian stared at her. Then he dropped into the chair at the

other side of the fireplace and ran his fingers through his dark, curling hair. It was beginning to recede a little now, she noticed, and wondered if he minded. Vivian had always been vain about his looks.

'Rebecca, we had better talk about this. I hadn't intended to do so – I thought you might still be too grieved. But if you are, it seems like to have turned your mind and clearly something must be done before you start to act foolishly instead of simply talking about it. Now, I've been thinking about this a good deal and what I want to propose is this –'

'I'm sorry, Vivian,' she broke in. 'But I've been thinking a good deal too – I told you that – and I've made my decision. I really can't see what we have to discuss.'

'Nor will you unless you listen to me,' he said sharply, and she inclined her head, acknowledging the truth of his words. Perhaps she ought to listen to him? After all, he'd taken the trouble to think about her position and come here to discuss it. And he had been kind to her, according to his lights.

'All right,' she said. 'What do you want to say?'

Vivian sat up and looked at her intently but didn't speak at once. Now that he had her attention, he seemed to be taking careful consideration over his words.

At last he began, speaking slowly and thoughtfully and without any hint of the condescension he was often accustomed to use. He spoke, she thought, as if he had at last forgotten she was a woman and recognised her as an intelligent being. And she immediately felt herself respond and open her mind to him.

'It's been clear for a long time,' he said gravely, 'that Francis was seriously ill and unlikely to recover – I think you saw that for yourself.'

Rebecca bowed her head. It had been all too plain for months. Francis had virtually faded away before her eyes. She had known that there was no hope.

'But I couldn't speak before,' Vivian went on. 'I had no idea what arrangements Francis might have made, what his wishes were. Of course, I would have been only too pleased to have

discussed it with him if he'd wished it – but you know Francis
has never been wholly easy with me. I hesitate to speak ill of
him now he's gone, but it has to be said that he was always
jealous of me.'

Rebecca stared at him. 'Jealous? Francis? Of *you*? Vivian, I
don't think –'

'Yes, jealous,' Vivian repeated. 'Oh, it was natural enough.
I tried always not to allow it to affect our relationship. But
ever since he discovered the truth about his birth – and,
quite honestly, I think it would have been better if Father
had kept that to himself – I was aware of his bitterness. He
always felt that he should have been acknowledged as Father's
true son and taken precedence over me. Even though I'd been
adopted and it was always understood I would be heir to the
business!' Vivian gave a short, unamused laugh. 'He played
on poor Father's feelings towards the end, of course, and that
was why the house was left to him. But there was never any
question of his inheriting the business.'

'Nor did he ever want to,' Rebecca said in a firm voice.
'Vivian, you're quite wrong about Francis. He was never
jealous of you, nor of any other man. He hadn't a jealous bone in his body. And he never, at any time, tried to
manipulate his father's feelings. He was as astonished as
the rest of us when he discovered that he'd been left Pagnel
House.'

'I'm sure you believe that,' Vivian said smoothly. 'You're
a good, loyal and devoted wife. But perhaps I saw a side of
Francis that you didn't suspect. We grew up in each other's
pockets, after all.'

Rebecca was silent. She did not believe Vivian, but the
thought of arguing with him was too painful. It would be
like fighting over her husband's grave. She simply shook her
head and looked into the fire.

'Well, we needn't worry about it now, anyway,' Vivian said
after a pause. 'I didn't come here to discuss Francis's nature.
What we have to decide is what you are to do now, and what
is to happen to the business.'

'I told you,' she said in a low voice. 'I've decided what to do. And if you'll forgive me, the business is –'

'Not my business,' he finished for her. 'Well, of course I understand that. But you'll surely allow me to talk to you as a friend, Rebecca? As I hope you'd talk to me – as indeed you have talked to me, during these past few years since my dear wife died.' He leaned forward a little and she glanced up at him, meeting his dark eyes. 'I've accepted so much help from you,' he said softly. 'Won't you at least let me offer a little of my own?'

Rebecca felt ashamed. It was true that she had taken over a good deal of the upbringing of Vivian's daughters. And she had enjoyed doing it. It had made her feel useful, wanted, and had helped to repay the debt she'd always felt to him over the way he'd supported her when her own son had died.

Wasn't it churlish of her to spurn his offer now – and even more churlish to refuse even to listen to it?

She reached out to touch his hand.

'I'm sorry, Vivian. Please go on.'

'Well, as I said, I've given this a lot of thought. And it seems to me that you have several problems. The business, of course. Your own life and how you are to lead it – though that's something that can be left for a while, since you must observe deep mourning for at least a year. And your sons.'

'Daniel and William are not a problem,' she said quickly. 'Francis and I were both happy with the way their education is progressing. They will continue with it, of course.'

'Of course,' he agreed. 'But to what end? For what sort of life are you preparing them? Have you given any thought to that?'

'Vivian, they're children still.'

'But not for long. Boys have a habit of growing up, Rebecca, and they do it very quickly. Daniel is – what? – fifteen years old. It isn't too early to be thinking of his future, especially in the circumstances. William, I agree, can be allowed to continue for the time being, but you should be giving very serious thought to Daniel's future, Rebecca.'

'But why? He'll almost certainly go into the business. Which Tom and I will build up between us,' she added with increased firmness. 'Vivian, you must know that I have no intention of becoming a recluse for the next twelve months. I should go mad.'

'There may be some,' he said quietly, 'who think that you have already done so. Now –' he held up a hand '– you said you'd hear me out, Rebecca. I have a definite proposal to make – one that will help both you and your son.'

Rebecca watched him. She felt a tiny slither of fear inside her, like a worm moving.

'Well? I'm listening.'

Vivian lowered his hand. He looked at her very gravely, and the worm lifted its head again. She wanted suddenly to stop him, knowing that what he was about to suggest would be abhorrent to her. But even as she opened her mouth, he spoke, and his words chilled her into silence.

'I want to adopt Daniel as my son,' he said. 'It seems to me to be the best solution to all our difficulties. He's a sensible lad and biddable enough – if he joins my household now he can be trained into my ways. I'll educate him and bring him up, and when he's ready I'll teach him the carpet business. His future will be assured – I'll make him my heir. And you'll be relieved of the responsibility of him, and only have young William to worry about, and I daresay we'll find something equally suitable for him when the time comes.'

Rebecca gazed at him. She found it difficult to take in what Vivian was saying. Adopt Daniel! Take him away from her, bring him up as Vivian's own son? She shook her head numbly, unable to comprehend the idea.

'But why?' she asked at last. 'Why should you want to do such a thing, Vivian? What benefit is it to you?'

His mouth twisted a little, wryly.

'Does it have to have some benefit for me? Couldn't I be doing it simply because – well, because I care for you, Rebecca, and want to help you?' He smiled and then went on, 'But you're quite right, of course. There would be some benefit for

27

me. You know that I've always wanted a son, to carry on the business, and that Maria – God rest her soul – was never able to give me one. And somehow I've never found another woman I wanted to marry.' There was an odd, dark shadow somewhere deep in his eyes as he said this. 'And here is Daniel, a Pagnel by birth and by name, with no father to bring him up . . .'

'He has me,' she said quickly, but Vivian shook his head.

'A boy needs a father, Rebecca. Petticoat government is no good for any boy who wants to grow up to be a man.'

'But you could help me, as I help you with the girls,' she persisted. 'They have no mother but I try to fill that place as well as I can. Couldn't you do the same for Daniel? And there's Tom as well,' she added. 'He's here most days. He and Nancy will give me any help I need.'

'Tom!' There was no mistaking the dismissal in Vivian's tone, and Rebecca felt herself bristle. Had he forgotten Tom was her brother? 'Forgive me, Rebecca, but fine man though Tom is, he still displays his origins. He's still a common weaver at heart. Whereas you –'

'Whereas I am a common weaver's daughter,' she cut in quickly. 'And proud to be so! And Daniel is a weaver's grandson, and will not be allowed to forget it. If he were to come to you, Vivian, would you let him remember that? Would you let him honour his grandparents, or would you want to pretend they had never existed? No,' she said, shaking her head, 'I thank you for the offer, Vivian, but I'll not let you have Daniel. He's Francis's son, and mine, and so he stays.'

'You're making a mistake,' Vivian said, and she lifted her head proudly.

'Then at least it will be *my* mistake, and no one else's.'

Vivian sighed, with the air of a man who had expected trouble and now must try again.

'Rebecca, you haven't given yourself time to think about this. Try to understand what I'm offering. Daniel will have a good home with me, but of course you'll be able to see him whenever you wish. You can come to him or he can visit you here. He'll also have a fine education – better than the one you're providing for him at the local grammar school, good though that might be. He'll live close to me and so grow up understanding the ways of the carpet business. And he'll be heir to one of the finest manufacturing firms in the country. How can you refuse him these things? How can you say no to such opportunities?'

Rebecca felt a helplessness creep over her. How, indeed, could she refuse these things on behalf of her son? What would he say to her when he was grown and perhaps wished she had decided differently?

'But there's already a business for Daniel to inherit,' she pointed out. 'His own father's business – the co-operative. He'll grow up beside Tom and me, hearing our discussions, learning our ways.'

'And how often have you and Francis told me that no one *inherits* a co-operative?' Vivian cut in. 'Doesn't it belong to all, as much to the lowliest draw-boy as to the manufacturer? Isn't that the fine principle by which you and your brother live?' His dark eyes flicked over her. 'Have you looked at the accounts of your co-operative lately, Rebecca? Have you seen just how well it pays its way, what fine profits are made? Have you ever considered that it may have been bolstered up, subsidised, by the money Francis earned in *my* business and the money that the rogue Farrell put into it before he was transported?'

Rebecca stared at him. 'Of course it makes a profit! Francis and Tom were very pleased with it. Francis told me how well it was doing the last time he –'

'A business may be said to be doing well when its losses are below a certain limit,' Vivian said smoothly. 'Provided it can be expected to stop losing at some specified future date and the losses can be borne until then. But that isn't the case now, is it?'

'I don't know what you mean,' she said after a silence.

'And that's one reason why your own scheme is so fool-hardy. You're chasing a dream, Rebecca. You haven't even begun to look into the reality. The co-operative was never more than a dream – a fantasy. With the money that was being poured into it, it might well have given the appearance of being a success. But it could never have been a real success – it could never have stood on its own feet. And now that it's lost that support –'

'How do you mean?' Rebecca interrupted. Her skin felt cold, as if the blood had left her cheeks, leaving them pale and cool as marble. 'How has it lost its support? Why should it not go on to be successful? People are buying our carpets – orders are still coming in – our customers are standing by us –'

'And will they continue to stand by you when it is known that Francis is dead? I doubt if the news has reached all your customers yet. What do the Duke of this and the Lord of that care for the demise of one insignificant carpet manufacturer? But your suppliers may hear sooner, and they may hesitate to send you their wool and their dyes when they know that Pagnel of Pagnel & Himley has died. They may want to be more certain of being paid.'

'They will be paid,' Rebecca said stubbornly, and Vivian gave a short laugh.

'And with what will you pay them, Rebecca my sweet? With the money that Francis is no longer earning from his work with me? With the money that Matthew Farrell can't contribute now that he's in Australia and likely to spend the rest of his life there? Those rivers have run dry, Rebecca, and what is to take their place? I tell you, the co-operative is not strong enough to stand alone. But there –' he shrugged and began to turn away '– you don't have to believe me. Ask your brother.'

There was a long silence. Rebecca looked ahead and saw that the future could indeed be a bleak one. That Vivian spoke the truth, she had no doubt. He would have made sure of that before coming to see her. And she knew that he was right about the co-operative. It had not yet begun to pay its way, confident though Francis and Tom had been that it soon would. All it needs, she thought, is a little more time. Just a little more time . . .

She rose to her feet and touched Vivian's sleeve. He turned and looked down at her and she searched his dark eyes, trying to find the kindliness that she believed must be there. Vivian would not stand by and watch them starve. He could not.

'Please, Vivian,' she said in a low voice, 'could you not help us? Make a small loan, enough to keep us going until the business begins to make a profit? It can't want much now. A year or two – no more. It would mean so little to you, and so much to us.'

A small muscle moved near his mouth. 'So little?' he said. 'And how do you know, Rebecca, just what it would mean to me?'

There was a strange force in his tone, and she hesitated and drew back a little. Surely she had not made him angry? But before she could speak his expression changed, softened a little. He shook his head.

'No, Rebecca, I will not make you a loan. Why should I? Without Frank, the co-operative will fail, however much money is poured into it. He was the driving force behind it. I should be throwing my money away.'

'No! Surely not.' She gazed up at him, her eyes as dark as his. 'Don't you have any belief in my abilities, Vivian? You know that many of the new designs are mine – and they're as successful as Francis's. I've sat with him, discussing the business side of the co-operative. I know how to reckon the accounts, he taught me all that. Why should I not carry on with it? Yes, *and* make a success of it?'

He flicked his fingers. 'Because it simply isn't that easy, Rebecca. Francis had the contacts, the people in Halifax and in Scotland, wool suppliers who had known him for years. Are they going to deal with his wife? They'd laugh in your face. And your customers in London and the country houses where you've been finding a market for your exclusive designs – are they going to believe in you? Of course not! It isn't a question of *my* believing in you, Rebecca – nobody else is going to take you seriously. And no loan is going to help you there.'

She stared at him, then turned slowly away. She stood at the window, looking down over the town. Kidderminster lay below, the tumbled roofs leading down to the river, the factory chimneys laying a pall of smoke over the sprawling buildings.

'So you won't help me?' she said in a low voice, and Vivian sighed.

'Rebecca, I've offered you help. But you don't seem to want to take it.' He paused, then went on, 'If you don't allow me to help, the entire responsibility will rest with you. I've tried to point out the problems you'll have in building up your own business – this so-called co-operative that Francis and Tom were so pleased with, and which is now doing no more than staggering along. I've tried to show you that it will never do more than that, if indeed it manages as much. That's all you'll have to pass on to your sons. And if it fails, what then? Weaver's hovels for them both? The loom again and poverty, like the grandfather you want them to honour? Wouldn't it be better to swallow your pride and allow me to help in my own way?'

She swung round on him, her eyes suddenly aflame.

'Help? Is that what you call it? Robbing me of my son? Taking away one of the few people I have left to live for?' Her voice trembled. 'And what would happen to the co-operative then? You believe it will fail anyway. What is to happen to Tom and Nancy, and to me? And to William? Are we all to be reduced to the gutter while you take what's left of our business?' Her voice was bitter. 'You wouldn't even have to pay me for it. It would just fall into your pocket.'

Vivian shook his head. 'You know I would never let that happen to you, Rebecca. But if you persist, what choice would I have? Listen to me. If you allow me to adopt Daniel, your own future and that of William will be assured. Of course it will. And I'll be only too glad to assist with the business of the co-operative if it should run into difficulties. Perhaps even merge it with my own – now is that so unfair, considering that I'm taking on the expenses of your entire family? Does it seem so unreasonable?'

'My entire family? William, as well as Daniel? Tom and Nancy too?'

'William, of course,' Vivian said steadily. 'There should be sufficient money in your business – particularly if I am permitted to have a say in its running – to provide him with an education and set him up in his own career. You, of course, would always be provided for. But as for your brother –' he shrugged '– he's an able-bodied man and had more advantages than most. I can't see how I could be expected to provide a living for him. Nor do I think he would be willing to accept it.'

Rebecca was silent. Vivian was perfectly right – Tom would never accept help from him. He had never trusted Vivian, ever since those days when he and Bess had been forced to accept his help in their flight to London. The debt had rankled ever since, and the fact that Vivian had refused to accept repayment when Tom had scraped it together and offered it, had made it no better. 'I'd rather know it was paid back,' Tom had said to Rebecca then. 'He'd hev no power over me then. And he knows it, too.'

It was power Vivian had always wanted, she thought. Power over Tom, over Francis, over his weavers. Power over Kidderminster itself. Wasn't he even now working towards attaining the position of Mayor? And now, power over herself and her family . . .

'So,' she said, 'I am to betray my brother and see him on the streets, without a job.'

Vivian made a sound of exasperation.

'Rebecca, why must you dramatise everything so? Your brother won't be on the streets. He'll not want for a job. He's a fine craftsman, he's been running a business. Every manufacturer in Kidderminster will be willing to employ him. I'd employ him myself if he'd accept it – my point is that he probably won't. I'm well aware of how your brother feels about me, but it's his own obstinacy that prevents him from seeing the truth, Rebecca, and his own stubborn pride that stands in his way. There's nothing I can do about that.'

He came swiftly across the room and took her hands in his, looking down earnestly into her face. 'And it's that same pride that prevents you from thinking clearly too. Let me say again what I am prepared to offer you. A secure home and living for the rest of your life. A secure future for your son – for both your sons. Nothing to worry about, ever again. And all I ask is that you allow me to adopt Daniel. For God's sake, Rebecca, I'm robbing you of nothing. He'll be here in the same town, you'll continue to see him, he'll be your son still. Is the favour yours or mine?'

She looked at him doubtfully. It sounded so reasonable. And yet . . . She thought again of all Francis had worked for, of the dream he had fought to turn into reality.

Slowly, she shook her head.

'It's kind of you, Vivian, but I can't let it all go so soon. I must at least try. I owe it to Francis.'

'Rebecca, Frank's dead.'

She flinched at his brutality but answered steadily, 'But his dream is alive, Vivian. And so am I, and so are Daniel and William. And Tom. And the weavers who are also part of the co-operative. They have their rights too. I can't just give it all up. It isn't even mine to give.'

'Nobody's asking you to give up anything, Rebecca. I'm not even suggesting you should change things at the co-operative. Just let it go on in the same way, if you like. You'll soon see if it can carry on.' His tone told her what he thought of its chances. 'I came here to offer help, to offer security for your son. Do you have any right to refuse that help, out of hand, on his behalf? Have you even given it real consideration?'

'I could consider it for months and my answer would be the same. Daniel is my son, mine and Francis's. I can't give him up.'

'Rebecca, you're not giving him up. He wouldn't even have to change his name –'

'No,' she said again, and this time her tone silenced him. They stood without speaking for a few moments. Then she turned away and sat down again, her forehead resting in her palm. 'I'm sorry, Vivian. Perhaps this has come too quickly. You're right, I haven't had time to think.' She looked up at him, raising trembling fingers to brush away a wisp of tawny hair. 'Give me time, Vivian. I don't believe it will alter my mind at all – but give me time. And I promise I will think about it.'

She saw his eyes move over her, assessing her words, and then he nodded slowly. 'Very well, Rebecca. There's no hurry, after all. And perhaps a closer look into the affairs of your precious co-operative will convince you that it will never stand on its own feet. You'll realise then that my offer is not to be sneezed at.' He paused. 'It means security, Rebecca, security for you and for your boys. You, of all people, should understand the value of such a promise.' He drew his watch from its pocket and looked at it. 'And now I must go. I've stayed overlong as it is. No, don't ring for the maid – I'll see myself out.' He lifted her hand and touched it briefly with his lips. 'You're a strong woman, Rebecca,' he said quietly. 'I've always admired that in you. But there is a limit to what a woman's strength can achieve, and few women are able to survive without a man to support them. Remember that, won't you?'

The door closed behind him and Rebecca heard his footsteps descend the stairs. Below, she heard the sound of the front door and then all was quiet.

Was it true that a woman could not survive without a man? But there were plenty of widows who did.

Yes – but those were widows who were provided for, whose income came steadily from their husbands' businesses. Widows who had the means to bring up their children, educate their sons and see them start in those same businesses, or perhaps in some new life, able to earn a living and support families of their own.

There were others who did not. Who had no easy income, no fortune, who saw their homes crumble about them, removed by failure and bankruptcy. Who ended destitute, thrown on the mercy of their families. Or worse . . .

Was this what could happen to her and her sons?

Never! Rebecca thought with sudden determination. Vivian is just trying to frighten me. He says himself I am strong –

he doesn't know how strong. I helped Francis build up the business, I helped him dream his dream.

I can continue it.

Vivian let the door swing shut behind him and strode away from Pagnel House. Halfway down Mount Pleasant he paused and looked back at it, his eyes narrowed.

A slap on his back caused him to turn sharply, and his expression relaxed.

'Ben Messinger! You old rascal – where did you spring from?'

His assailant grinned and fell into step as Vivian resumed his walk down the hill. 'Oh, I've been here and there. Edinburgh, mostly. I've more or less taken over the business at that end. Thinking of building a house there.'

Vivian stopped and looked at him. 'In Edinburgh? You're doing so well?'

Ben Messinger nodded complacently. 'The Scots are good workers, Vivian. More hard-headed than the Kidder manufacturers, and the weavers aren't so lazy. They've seen hard times up there before – the Clearances may have happened a long time ago, but they remember. They'd rather eat than have that happen again.'

'Ours want to eat too,' Vivian growled, 'but sometimes I think they want the food put into their mouths to save lifting their arms. Except when there's a strike, of course. They've plenty of energy then for posting pamphlets and raising riots.'

Ben gave him a sideways glance. 'You sound out of sorts, Vivian. Don't tell me you're missing that so-called cousin of yours? I heard he'd died.'

'That's right, consumption. It's been hanging around him for years. I wondered the cholera didn't carry him away a few years ago when it was rife here, but that wife of his took as much care of him as if he were a baby. I'm surprised she let the consumption have its will in the end – the way she's been these past few years, God Himself would have thought twice about taking her precious husband before his time.'

His tone was a mixture of bitterness and grudging admiration, and his friend hesitated before remarking, 'That was the little serving wench, wasn't it? You make her sound quite a character.'

'Oh, Rebecca has character all right. Rather too much of it, if truth be known.' Vivian scowled and then added forcefully, 'Truth to tell, I never really understood what a woman like that could see in my cousin. Even as a housemaid she had fire in her – and he was as studious as a schoolmaster and as insipid as my mother's lapdog. And yet he managed to seduce her, God knows how! And put a brat in her belly for her first time, if either of them's to be believed.'

Ben laughed. 'It sounds as if you envy him his fortune. Are you telling me you tried and failed? Turn you away, did she?'

Vivian's scowl deepened, but Ben Messinger was one of the few people not afraid of his temper and after a moment or two he grinned wryly. 'Well, it's a long time ago now and – yes, I did try as a matter of fact. After all, she was a maid in my mother's house, it was more or less expected of me. And none of the others . . . anyway, she fought me, the little minx.' There was a touch of admiration in his voice even now. 'Kicked, scratched, bit – it was like tussling with a tiger. Sharpened up my appetite, I don't mind telling you. Most of them were all too ready to give in for a sovereign or two. But Rebecca . . . yes, I can easily see what attractions Frank saw there, though I'd not have thought they were his dish of tea. Those dark eyes held a deal of promise.'

'So what happened?' Ben asked. 'You didn't give up, did you, on account of a few bites and scratches?'

'Not I! I simply let her go with a promise to come back for more. I was rather enjoying the fight, you see – and the more she spat at me, the more I looked forward to the final conquest. Only young Frank got there first, and without a mark on him – must have cuddled up to him like a kitten. And before I knew it, she was dismissed – sent out of the house, and disappeared to London.'

'Where Francis found and married her. A romantic story indeed. And you've never made your mark with her since? Even though she's no longer a serving girl but one of the family?'

Vivian shook his head. 'I've more sense than that, Ben. Though I don't mind admitting, I've sometimes been tempted – given her the odd glance, you know, just to see if the old fire's there still. But now . . .' He turned again and looked back up the hill at the house that could still be seen above the roofs and the trees, and his eyes narrowed again.

'Now she's a widow,' Ben said softly. 'And well-to-do.'

Vivian laughed shortly. 'That's what everyone thinks. Up there in her grand house, where once she came to scrub dishes. Ironic, isn't it, Ben? She, a weaver's daughter who grew up in a hovel, living in one of the best houses in Kidderminster. The house that by rights ought to be mine.' He moved restlessly. 'How did he do it, Ben? That by-blow of my father's – how did he get to possess everything *I* wanted, everything that should have come to me? The woman, the sons, a business of his own – a share in *my* business, as if that weren't enough – and then the house I grew up in? Just what did he do to deserve all that? What did *I* do that I didn't get it?'

Ben shrugged. 'Nothing, I'd guess. It's just life, Vivian. Did anyone ever promise it was going to be fair?'

Vivian made no reply but his mouth set in a way both his mother and his wife would have recognised, and somewhere faintly in his memory he seemed to hear just such a childish cry: *'It isn't fair!'*

Isabella would have hastened to make sure that it was fair – in other words, that Vivian got what he wanted, because to her that was what fairness was. And Maria would have hastened too, in much the same way, though from different motives. In Maria's experience, if her husband didn't get what he wanted, she was likely to suffer for it.

There was no one now to give Vivian what he wanted. But he had long been accustomed to take it for himself.

Ben's words sounded again in his mind. A widow now . . . and well-to-do.

Except that Rebecca wasn't well-to-do. She was facing disaster.

'But she's as stubborn as ever,' he told Ben as they began to walk down the hill again. 'You'd think, wouldn't you, that she'd see this as an opportunity for her son? But she seems to think I'm trying to steal him from her! My God, I'm offering the boy my home – he's already got my name – and an inheritance. What more can she ask? How many men would be willing to do that, especially with his background – father a bastard, mother out of the slums. Why, he only just escaped being illegitimate himself! But he's a Pagnel and I'm offering him the best chance he'll ever get. And is Rebecca grateful? Not she! She turned me down flat. And if she thanked me at all, it was only for the look of it. Well, she'll be sorry when that precious co-operative of theirs begins to fail. As it will, Ben, as it will.'

He nodded. 'Of course it will. Damn silly idea in the first place. Anyone could have seen it wouldn't work, after the first flush of enthusiasm. But young Francis was always an idealist.'

'Trouble is, he never lived to find it out,' Vivian growled. 'That man died happy, Ben! He had it all – wife, sons, business, house, and even his blasted Dream seemed to be coming true. And he died believing it. I think that's what sticks in my craw most of all.'

Ben grinned. After a moment, he said, 'You'd still like to best him, wouldn't you, Vivian? Even though he's in his grave, you'd still like to think you had those things that he prized so much. The house. The boys – or one of them at least.' He paused, then added idly, 'It's a pity you can't marry her. Then you'd have it all, just with one kindly action.'

Vivian stopped. He caught at Ben's arm, turned the other man towards him. His dark eyes glittered suddenly.

'Can't marry her? Who says I can't marry her?'

'Well, you can't, can you?' Ben said reasonably. 'She comes within the proscribed relationships, surely. "A man may not marry his brother's wife." Francis was old Jeremiah's son, so –'

'But I wasn't,' Vivian said. 'I wasn't Jeremiah's son. And Frank was never formally acknowledged so – he was adopted by Geoffrey and Enid. There's no blood relationship between us, Ben, and no paper one either, except as cousins both adopted. There isn't any reason at all why I can't marry Rebecca.'

'Except for the lady herself,' Ben said slyly. 'She fought you once, remember? The bites, the scratches, the kicks?'

'I remember very well,' Vivian said slowly. 'I remember how they whetted my appetite for more. And I told you, the fire's still there – I've seen it in her eyes.'

'Well then,' Ben said, 'perhaps it's time you went courting again.'

'You mean to go to all the carpet masters in Kidder and ask 'em for money?' Tom pursed his lips and shook his head. 'They'll never lend us any, Becky. Why should they? Stands to reason – they don't want the competition. And there's not a man amongst 'em wouldn't be pleased to see Pagnel & Himley go to the wall.'

'Tom's right,' Nancy said. 'No manufacturer is going to help another business on its feet – 'specially not a co-operative. It's a dirty word to them.'

'They'll be glad to see us in Queery Street,' Tom said. 'And like to hev their wish too, before any of us is much older.'

Rebecca looked at him with sudden fear. 'What do you mean?'

'Why, only that Vivian's right, blast him. Business ent good, Becky, you must know that. Seems to me it never has bin, ever since Boney's wars was over. We ent never got over them. Even the Jacquard ent really bringing in the money, and it cost a

40

mint to instal them high looms. Done better to hev stuck with good old Brussels, we would.'

'There are other methods,' Rebecca said doubtfully. 'The new Tapestry carpets . . . and I've heard talk of something that looks very like velvet.'

'Tapestry!' Tom snorted. 'Nobbut cheap gaudiness, flaunting all its colour like the river on dyeing day. You know what Francis always wanted, Becky – the best quality weaving to the best designs. Tapestry's for them as don't mind heving the same carpet as the folks next door and knowing just what they paid for it. Our customers don't want summat you'll see in every parlour in the street.'

'I know.' Rebecca sighed. 'And we've got a good clientele now – people who know what we can produce and will come to us again and again, and recommend their friends. So why are we in such trouble?'

'Well, it ent that we're in *trouble* exactly,' Tom said, frowning. 'Like you say, we got the customers and they're good customers too, ready to pay for what they wants. But mekking carpets the way we does is expensive. We uses the best materials and they costs money. Money we has to pay before we gets paid for the carpet.'

'And we have to pay the weavers too,' Rebecca agreed. 'And because it's a co-operative, we have to pay them a proper share of the profit – not just the basic wage that most manufacturers pay. Yes, I see what you mean, Tom. Once the business is properly established and making a good profit, all this can be done and money put aside for future expansion. But until that time –'

'Until that time,' he said, 'we're still living on what was put into the business in the first place, to get it started like. Money from Francis, money from Mr Jeremiah, money from Matt Farrell. And that money's just about all gone, Becky. And none, so far's I can see, to tek its place.'

'And we're not yet making a profit?'

He shook his head. 'At the present rate, it'd be another two years before we can say that, Becky.'

They stared at each other. Rebecca's heart grew cold. Another two years! With expensive wools and dyes to buy, looms and machinery to be maintained, new designs to be transferred to the big Jacquard rolls. With rents and weavers to be paid, her own and Tom and Nancy's living expenses. The boys to be clothed, fed, educated . . .

'But we are still making carpets,' she said, knowing that she was clutching at straws. 'Those carpets, when we deliver them, will bring in good money.'

'Which won't be enough,' Tom said grimly. 'Not to do all it has to do. I tell you, Becky, blasted Vivian Pagnel's right. The co-operative can't go on. Not without someone gives us a lot of help.'

A lot of help, Rebecca thought. A lot of money, he means. Enough to keep us going for another year, two years, maybe three. Enough to pay all our expenses and keep us all for as long as that. And even then, we'll still be struggling. We'll only just be making enough.

Or I could agree to Vivian's suggestion and let him adopt my son. Daniel, conceived in love between me and Francis the first time we ever lay together, in the woods on a Sunday afternoon.

It felt more like selling him. Selling her own son, for the sake of a business.

The Dream she and Francis had shared was rapidly becoming a nightmare.

Chapter Three

'It ent going to work,' Tom said gloomily. 'We're set for disaster, Nance. And I can't see naught we can do about it.'

Nancy laid down her mending and looked at him. He was sitting at the table where she prepared their meals, where they ate, where Tom did his figuring, where they sometimes played a game of cards. He had papers spread out in front of him, a pile of shavings from the quill pens he had kept sharpening all evening, a pot of ink. Some of the ink had transferred itself to his fingers, from where it had reached his face so that he looked as if he had some virulent disease. And if he had, he could not have looked more anxious.

'Is it really as bad as that?' she asked.

He nodded. 'I think it is. See – we've got a lot of wool to pay for, wool we haven't even started to use yet. And orders are going down. Folk hev heard about Francis and they don't see us carrying on without him. They're looking for other manufacturers to mek the special carpets they wants. Manufacturers like Vivian Pagnel,' he added bitterly. 'And masters like him aren't going to turn away orders, are they, not even if they knows they're rightfully ours?'

'But he could tell them,' Nancy said. 'He could tell them we're still working.'

'And do you think he will?' Tom asked, and she was silent. 'No, Nance, if Vivian Pagnel sees a chance to tek away our customers, he'll grab it with both hands. It's in his nature. He's that sort anyway, and when it's us . . .'

'But he's fond of Becky. He's bin helping her – up there three, four times a week, he is, asking if she got any problems,

43

anything she wants done. Takes an interest in the boys – and Becky's bin looking after his girls ever since Mrs Vivian died. I know Becky wouldn't let him take young Danny, but he wouldn't do nothing to make things worse for her.'

'You sure of that?' Tom asked sceptically. ''Cause I ent. He's deep, Vivian is, allus has bin. He don't do nothing like what you'd expect a bloke to do. He got his own ideas and he don't talk about 'em, neither.' He leaned forward, looking at her intently. 'Know what I think, Nance? I think he still means to hev young Danny. He don't give up that easy and once he's made up his mind he wants summat, he don't give up till he's got it. And he's allus wanted a son to carry on his name.'

'So why didn't he get married again?' Nancy asked bluntly. 'Mrs Vivian's bin dead a long time now. Why ain't he found someone else to give him his son?'

Tom shrugged. 'Couldn't find a good breeder, mebbe. Looking for proof – like some strong young widow who's already got a few boys to show she can do it.' He stopped suddenly and stared at his wife, and after a moment or two Nancy said what was in his mind.

'Like Becky.'

'Like Becky,' Tom said slowly. 'Nance, you don't reckon . . . ? But she never would. She'd never tek Vivian. She never, never would.'

'She might,' Nancy said quietly. 'If she was desperate enough.'

The letter came one chill November afternoon, thick as Matthew's letters always were, and Rebecca caught it up with an eagerness that surprised her. Had she really been waiting for it with such longing? But it was the first since Francis had died, the first since she had written to tell Matthew the news, and she looked at it with sudden foreboding. Whatever Matthew said, it was bound to bring back the pain she had been fighting all these months. Was she strong enough to bear it?

She stood for a few moments turning the letter over in her

hands, then glanced up as Polly came into the room. Her eyes went at once to the letter.

'From Mr Farrell? What do he say?'

'I haven't opened it yet. To tell you the truth, Polly, I'm a little afraid to.'

'Think it might be upsetting, do you?' Polly said. 'Well, it's bound to be really, ent it? Him being Mr Francis's friend and all. And he'll be worried about you.'

'I suppose so.' Still holding the letter, Rebecca walked to the window. 'It seems such a long time since Matthew was here, Polly, that sometimes I can barely remember what he looks like. Yet we were all so close – and when I read his letters he seems to be beside me again.' She looked once more at the package, soiled from its long journey. 'He lives in another world now,' she said sadly. 'And he seems almost to have settled down there. I don't believe he will ever come back to England.'

'Rubbage! Of course he will,' Polly said stoutly. ''Specially now. He'll want to see you're all right – look after you, like. I bet he's working for his pardon this very minute.'

'It'll be another three years before there's any chance of that – and where will I be then?' Rebecca gazed down through the darkness of the winter's afternoon at the town, the spreading roofs. Even though trade was bad in the carpet industry, new factories continued to sprout like weeds and there were other, smaller industries besides – the tanners, coachbuilders, wheelwrights, brewers and blacksmiths – that any town of size could boast. And there seemed to be more and more people too. Even the great cholera epidemics of a few years ago, wiping out so much of the population as they did, had failed to have any noticeable effect. It was as if Nature had doubled her efforts to keep the human race alive.

'Well, where d'you expect to be?' Polly asked. 'Here, won't you, same as now? 'Less you gets wed again, and that's as likely as not. You don't look a month above twenty-five.'

Rebecca smiled. 'I look as old as I am, which you well know is two years above thirty. I am an old widow with two boys to bring up, Polly, enough to put off any man.'

'This must be your day for talking rubbage,' Polly remarked, and went to make up the fire. 'I'll hev that young housemaid's skin for a bedspread, see if I don't. Hevn't she bin in here at all today to mek up the fire? As for putting off men, they're only waiting till your year's up and then they'll be round here in droves. You'll hev your pick of Kidder, see if I'm not right. Oh, not the young shavers, I'll allow, but you wouldn't want them anyway, would you? No, there's plenty of good, well-set-up bachelors and widowers will be glad to hev another –'

'Polly!' Rebecca spoke sharply, aware of a sudden distaste for the conversation. What was she doing, talking like this with Polly, and Francis not six months in his grave? 'It's all right,' she added more quietly. 'I'm as much at fault as you. It's this letter, it's unsettled me. It reminds me of so much – of happier times.' Her voice quivered and broke a little. 'So many gone, Polly, and Matthew's so far away, he might as well be dead too. I'll never see him again.' She looked at the familiar, sprawling handwriting, and felt an ache in her throat. 'If only he hadn't gone out that night. If only he hadn't been persuaded to take his pistol.'

'And were "if onlys" flagstones, the world could be paved,' Polly observed. 'You might as well say "if only he hadn't helped with the strike". Or "if only Bessie hadn't followed him and grabbed his arm". Or even "if only Bill Bucknell hadn't bin stood in the way". Except that if it hadn't bin he, it'd hev bin some other body. And Mr Farrell, he was never one to stand aside. And he's still a hero with the weavers, you knows that.'

'And much good that does him,' Rebecca said bitterly. 'Kept on a hulk for six months, enduring that dreadful voyage, treated as a slave at the end of it all ... Well, at least he's not kept in a cell or a dungeon as he would have been if he'd stayed in an English prison. At least he's out in the air, doing real work.'

'That's it.' Polly finished making up the fire and straightened up, brushing the coal dust from her hands. 'Now, you set yourself down here, comfy by the fire, and read your letter.

It'll do you good. And what's it matter if it makes you cry a bit? Crying's good for you. Ask me, you ent done enough.' She made her way towards the door.

'I didn't ask you,' Rebecca said, sitting down where she was told nevertheless and taking up a paperknife. 'Not that that stops you ordering me about. Just remember, Polly, I'm the mistress here – you're just a housekeeper.'

'Coo!' Polly jeered. 'And you nothing but skin and bone when you first come, and scullerymaid under me.' She paused at the door and turned, her grin reminding Rebecca suddenly of the saucy kitchenmaid Polly had once been. 'I'll send you in some tea. I daresay you'll be wanting it.'

The door closed behind her and Rebecca smiled, but there were already tears in her eyes. What would she have done all these months without Polly? She sometimes felt that the housekeeper, so stout and majestic now yet still revealing the odd glimpse of the skittish girl who had giggled and grumbled as she swept floors and brushed out hearths, was her only friend.

That wasn't fair, of course. She had Tom and Nancy too. But Tom, although her brother, had been torn from her life when she was only ten years old and not come back into it until she found him in London, when she was pregnant and penniless. It had been Polly she had grown up with, Polly who had shared her days, Polly who understood.

Rebecca looked down again at the package, half open now in her lap. With a sudden firmness, she ripped it open and drew out the closely written pages. Matthew had been her friend too. And although she truly believed she would never see him again, he was still her friend – even across the thousands of miles that lay between them.

The looms were already clattering when Tom arrived at the co-operative, and he paused to listen to the sound that, to him and his weavers, meant life. A noisy loomshop meant food in bellies, roofs over heads: a silent one meant doom.

Tom had experienced enough poverty in his life and it

showed in the stoop of his shoulders, once so straight, in the anxiety that was never far from eyes that had once held a spark. And although for the past dozen years and more he had enjoyed regular work and a growing business of his own, he was always aware of the disaster that could be waiting round the next corner. He never trusted his good fortune to last.

And now it seemed he was right to have doubted. For Francis, on whom the business had depended, was dead. And Rebecca, strive as she might, could never take his place. For she could never overcome the one great handicap that would always hold her back – the fact that she was a woman. And women were simply not taken seriously in business. Without a man to run the co-operative as Francis had run it, it was doomed to failure.

He opened the door to the small office where Francis had kept the business accounts, and stopped dead.

'Mr Vivian!'

Vivian Pagnel glanced up. He was sitting on the high stool usually occupied by Browning, the ledger clerk. His dark eyes moved slowly over Tom, taking in every detail of the rough trousers and waistcoat, the collarless shirt, the battered hat. Tom felt suddenly diminished, at a loss. To cover up, he stepped forward, his chin jutting.

'Here, what do you think you're doing in here?' he demanded aggressively. 'This is my office. You ent got no right to come prying in my books. And where's Browning? I ent give him no time off.'

'*Your* office, Himley?' Vivian's voice was smooth and relaxed. 'I'm sorry, I thought Rebecca had some part in this concern. And isn't everyone here equal? Doesn't the office belong to your weavers as well?'

'You knows what I mean,' Tom retorted, feeling his neck flush hotly. 'It don't matter who has the right to come in here – you ent one of them. And who said you could look at our order books? Where's that clerk?'

Vivian reached out and closed the book he had been studying, lazily as if he were folding an uninteresting newspaper. 'I told him to slip out on an errand for me. As it happens, Rebecca herself suggested I might cast my eye over a few things. But if you have some objection . . . Naturally, I'd never go against the wishes of a master in his own factory.'

Tom kept his temper with some difficulty. He said, 'You knows I'm not master here. And if Becky said you could look, I suppose I has to agree. But I'd hev thought she'd hev said summat to me first.'

'Then you'd better check with her.' Vivian stood up. He seemed almost to fill the little office. 'By the way, I see you've an order there from Sam Truman, for his daughter's new house.'

'Suppose we hev,' Tom growled. 'What's it to you?'

Vivian shrugged. 'Nothing, nothing at all. Only that it seems rather strange he should be ordering carpets from us too. He came in yesterday – wants all the bedrooms done, the dining room and the drawing room. Odd, isn't it?'

Tom stared at him. A cold sensation crawled across his skin. 'But . . . that's what he ordered from us.'

'So I saw.' Vivian's fingers drifted down to touch the order book lying on the desk. He opened it, flicking the pages back, scarcely glancing at it as he did so. 'Odd, isn't it?'

There was something in Tom's throat, something hard that prevented him from speaking clearly. He cleared it with difficulty. 'D'you mean he's decided to hev his carpet made by you – he's going to cancel his order with us?'

'How would I know? Perhaps he means to have two sets for each room – winter and summer, maybe. Or weekdays and Sundays.'

Vivian smiled but Tom shook his head disbelievingly. 'It ent no joking matter, Mr Vivian. It's clear as paint what he means to do. He's going to cancel his order with us. But why? Why go to you the very day after he bin here? And why don't he have the decency to come and say, if he ent going to buy? Why, I might hev already ordered the wools. Stuff I couldn't use for naught else. We only wants one or two like that to finish us.'

'So I can see.' Vivian glanced down again at the ledgers.

'Well, as you say, it's none of my business. And until you've made sure Rebecca's happy about my being here, I'll not bother you any further. But I'd make sure soon if I were you, Himley. From what I saw, the situation isn't good. And if you're losing orders . . .'

He lifted his hand in farewell and sauntered out of the office. Tom watched him through the little window, then turned back. He picked up the order book and looked through it.

The door opened and Browning came in, breathless and disconcerted to find Tom there instead of Vivian Pagnel. Tom turned on him at once.

'And who give you permission to go out on errands? Vivian Pagnel ent no master here. Or did you think he was? Is that it? Mebbe I'm the last to know when someone else takes over my own business – the co-operative me and Mr Francis set up. Mebbe I'd better come to you for me orders in future, since you knows so much more'n me about what's going on.'

The young clerk shook his head helplessly. 'I'm sorry, Mr Himley. Mr Pagnel told me to go and see one of his young ladies to Mrs Rebecca's – Miss Lucy it was. He said it'd be all right with you. I couldn't say no, could I? And Mrs Rebecca seemed pleased enough.'

'I'll lay she did,' Tom growled, but it was clearly useless to say more. The clerk had been in a difficult position and wasn't to be blamed. And no real harm had been done.

He was more worried about that order from Samuel Truman. It had been a good order, that one. Not only was it for a good amount of carpet – enough to keep the shop in work for several months – but it would have brought others in its wake. Sam Truman was a wealthy ironmaster and had wealthy friends, many of whom had marriageable daughters or would be thinking of refurbishing their own homes. That order could have been the turning point for Pagnel & Himley.

Browning settled down on his stool and began to work on the ledgers. And Tom, feeling suddenly uneasy, left the office and the loomshop and set out to walk up Mount Pleasant.

* * *

'He told you I'd said it was all right?' Rebecca's forehead creased. 'I think he must have misunderstood me. It's true he offered to look over the books and make any suggestions that he thought might help us – and I did say that it might be a good idea, sometime. But I never actually agreed . . . at least, I don't believe I did.' She thought for a moment, then shook her head. 'No, I'm sure I didn't. And yet – well, you know Vivian. He talks so reasonably and so persuasively, sometimes you find you've agreed to things without even knowing it. And I suppose he must have believed I did agree, or he would never have done such a thing. Why should he, after all?'

'I wonder.' Tom thought again of Vivian, casually flicking over the pages of the order book. He wondered whether to tell Rebecca about the Truman order, then decided against it. She had worries enough. She was still grieving over Francis, that was plain to see, and Nancy had told him that young William was being troublesome. Not doing his schoolwork properly, sulking and even answering his mother back at times. I'd give him answer back if he was mine, Tom thought, but Rebecca wouldn't have either of the boys beaten. She'd seen enough of that when she was a girl, she said, and she was surprised that Tom didn't feel the same way.

'I heard from Matthew this afternoon,' she said suddenly and Tom brought his attention back to her. 'The first letter I've had since – since Francis died. Such a warm, affectionate letter.' He saw that her eyes were filled with tears. 'It seemed to bring him right here into the room with me for a while.'

Tom didn't know what to say. Sometimes he was aware of a huge gap yawning between him and his sister. Try as they might to deny it, they lived in different worlds now – she in her big house, him in his plain cottage down in Church Row. And she'd learned a lot from Francis: how to talk, how to behave, as well as things like reading and writing. Time was when she'd still been able to talk to him and Bessie as if they were all at home in the weaver's hovel. But Bessie was dead and those days were too far away now. Now, she talked like a lady almost all the time.

It didn't mean she wasn't the same old Becky, of course. But even as a little girl, Becky'd been different from the rest of them. That was why their mam had been so set against her going into the carpet shops and insisted on putting her into service – that and what had happened to him and Bess.

He realised that Rebecca expected some sort of response, and muttered, 'Ah, he was a good friend, Matt Farrell.'

'The best we had,' Rebecca said, but before she could say more the door opened and Vivian's daughter Lucy came in, followed by Daniel. 'Hello, you two. What have you been doing?'

'Just playing a game in the schoolroom,' Lucy said. She came over to Rebecca and sat down on the floor, leaning against the chair. Her fair hair lay spread on her shoulders and her lowered eyelids were almost transparent, shadowed by the blue of the eyes beneath. She's growing up, Rebecca thought, looking at the skin, pale as creamy rose petals. Seventeen . . . too old to be playing schoolroom games with her cousin.

'What have you been playing?'

'Daniel's been teaching me chess.'

'She's very good too,' Daniel said, taking a cake from the plate that had not yet been cleared after tea. 'Better than most of the boys at school.'

'And what was William doing? Didn't he want to play?'

Daniel made a face. 'He sat in the corner and sulked. But it's his own fault. He doesn't really like chess. He never plays properly, like Lucy does.'

He sat down on a small stool and munched his cake. He had grown lately – surely he was almost two inches taller than when Francis had died? And although he was nearly two years younger than Lucy, he looked older with his serious expression and thoughtful eyes. Too serious, Rebecca thought, too grave. It made her heart ache sometimes to look at him and think of how much he had suffered, how he still suffered over his brother's death. Even then, as a little boy, he had blamed himself and she sometimes wondered if he blamed himself still. And now he carried the responsibility of being the elder son, the 'man of the family'. It was too much.

'Have you finished your schoolwork?' she asked, and Lucy laughed.

'Daniel's never finished his schoolwork! Even when he's done all the tasks his masters set him, he'll still find more to do. I had a task myself, to persuade him to a game of chess.' Her eyes dancing, she leaned across and touched her cousin's arm. 'Shall I challenge you to a return match, Danny?'

Daniel's face relaxed into a smile, but he shook his head. 'Not today, Lucy. I have an essay to write.' His voice rose above her laughter. 'I do! And no, you can't help me write it. I can just imagine what marks I would get if you did.' He finished his cake and began to brush away the crumbs, but before he made any other move the door burst open again and William erupted into the room.

At twelve, William was almost as tall as his brother and very nearly twice as broad. He took after his grandfathers – both Jeremiah Pagnel and William Himley, for whom he was named. His build was that of Will Himley, stocky and muscular, but his features those of Jeremiah, already strong. And he had the determined will of both men.

Strange that they never met, Rebecca thought, and wondered if they might have been friends, one a carpet manufacturer and one a weaver, yet with these two grandsons in common.

'William!' she exclaimed as he came to a skidding halt before her. 'You'll have everything over.'

'Well, there shouldn't be so much furniture,' he retorted, grabbing a cake. 'All these knick-knacks . . . Hello, Uncle Tom, I didn't know you were coming to tea. How's that loom, has the fault been corrected? Is that a letter from Uncle Matt?'

Rebecca retrieved the letter from his hands. He missed nothing – and to think how slow he had been as a baby, slow both to walk and to talk so that they had all feared his difficult birth might have caused some permanent damage. Yet now he was as bright as his brother and twice as lively – though he seemed reluctant enough to put his brains to as good a use.

You would never discover William taxing his mind with extra schoolwork!

'It's from Uncle Matthew, yes, and it's for me, not you,' she said firmly, and pushed the letter into the pocket of her skirt.

'Oh, come on, Mamma,' William protested. 'Surely he has some news you can tell us. Has he been hunting? Has he shot any kangaroos? Have there been any fights with the savages? Oh, I wish I could go to Australia – it sounds a fine country.'

'It sounds a very uncomfortable country,' Rebecca said grimly. 'Matthew says that four convicts escaped one day and set out to walk to China – *China*, if you please. Apparently there have always been stories of a way to walk there from Botany Bay, and the poor wretches who believe such tales wander off into the jungle.'

'Bush,' William interpolated. 'They call it "bush".'

'Bush. And lose their way, of course, and starve to death. Every time a new area is cleared, their skeletons are found. Or . . . worse.'

'Worse? What could be worse than dying?'

But Rebecca glanced at Lucy and would not answer, and William was forced to subside, with a dissatisfied glance at the pocket where the letter had been hidden. He sat down on the floor, an untidy jumble of arms and legs, dropping crumbs as he stuffed cake into his mouth.

'It's a good thing your father isn't here to see this,' Rebecca remarked to Lucy. 'He'd take you away at once, fearing that you'd grow up with the same rough manners as these boys. Not that you're any better yourself,' she added, 'sitting on the floor in that way. Anyone would think we had no chairs.'

'Chairs are uncomfortable,' Lucy observed carelessly. 'You have to sit so straight in them. That's what I like about coming here, Aunt Rebecca – you don't fuss about being straight-backed all the time. My other aunts never stop talking about it – yet you're as straight as any of them. And you never had to spend hours strapped in a backboard.'

'No, I didn't. I stood at a loom instead. Perhaps that's just as good for you.' Rebecca spoke lightly but instantly regretted her words, for William sat up at once, his eyes bright as he looked from her to Tom.

'Mamma! Does that mean – have you asked him? Have you talked to Uncle Tom?'

'Asked me what?' Tom said, and saw Rebecca's quick look of annoyance. 'Ent I supposed to know? Don't tell me – I don't want to get caught up in a family quarrel.'

'There's no quarrel,' Rebecca said with a frown at her son. 'It's just William being impatient. I told you, William, there's no question of it. You must wait.'

'But what am I waiting for? Mamma, I'm almost thirteen years old – that's old enough to begin work. Nearly twice the age lots of children start in the factories. Why can't I start too? Not as a draw-boy but with Uncle Tom. He can show me the business, I can learn from him, and in a few years I could take over the ordering and accounts, all the things Papa used to do. It's so *silly* for me to be at school when I could make myself useful.'

'William, we've had all this out before,' Rebecca said sharply. 'You know I want both you and Daniel to stay at school as long as possible. You'll never have the opportunity for education again. After that will be time enough to learn the business.'

'And by then we might not have a business for me to learn! Don't look like that, Mamma, I'm not a fool, nor a baby. I can understand what you and Uncle Tom say and I understand what Uncle Vivian says too. And everyone's expecting the co-operative to fail now that Papa isn't here to run it. Well, I can learn to take Papa's place, so why not let me start now? You know I hate being at school – and I'm not learning anything there. It's such a waste of time.'

'You could learn,' she said. 'You need only the will. Your masters all say you're clever enough but you just won't apply yourself.'

'Because it's all so dull! And so useless. Greek, Latin . . . what use will they be to me when I'm working with Uncle Tom?' He jumped up from the floor, his eyes stormy. 'I'm *tired* of being "educated"!' he burst out. 'It's all so stupid

55

– I'm learning nothing that will be of any use to me. What help will I be because I've done another few months' Latin? Did my grandfather know Latin? Or Greek? Did he ever need to use them in the factory? We're not making carpets for Romans or Ancient Greeks, Mamma, we're making them for people in Kidderminster and Worcester and London – even America. And I've had enough schooling to teach me how to do accounts and make out an order book. What I need to learn now is how to tell a good sample of wool, how to make a dye to achieve a certain colour, how to design – and how to introduce new weaves. Improve the looms. Bring in steam power. It must come, someday.' He had begun to pace up and down the room and now he wheeled and faced them. 'Mamma, we're standing on the brink of a new age. We have a new queen on the throne. It's time to show everyone what a co-operative can do. *And you're making me stay at school!'*

There was a short silence. Rebecca stared at her son. Never before had she seen such fire in his eyes, heard such passion in his voice. And he was right. What use, after all, were the subjects he was learning at school? What use to a carpet manufacturer who was determined to make his business succeed?

But Vivian had warned her against letting either boy leave school too soon. He had insisted that they needed their education. 'Great changes are coming in industry,' he had told her only a few days ago. 'Don't let them miss their chances now, or they may miss more later.'

She sighed. What was the right thing, the best thing to do? If only Francis were here to take these worries from her shoulders. If she could sit and talk with him, as they had done so often of an evening. If she could turn to him and lay her head against his shoulder, feel his arm warm and comforting around her . . .

But Francis had gone where she, it seemed, could not follow. And she must deal with all these things alone.

'I shall have to think about it,' she prevaricated. 'It's not something I can decide in a moment.'

'But I've been asking you for weeks! Please, Mamma, don't just *think* about it. Do something about it. Ask Uncle Tom what he thinks – ask him now.' He turned to Tom. 'You agree with me, don't you? You think I ought to leave school and start work with you? I can learn so much – and I'll help too,' he promised. 'I'll work hard. And it won't be long before I know enough to be really useful.'

His whole attention was transferred to Tom, but his uncle looked uncomfortable. He shook his head.

'I told you, don't get me mixed up in your squabbles.'

'It's not a squabble! It's serious. I want to work in the business – I *know* I'll be useful to you, if you'll only give me the chance. And I should be there now, learning all I can. Schoolwork is no good to me, not like it is to Dan. I know all I need about reading and writing, I can reckon in my head faster than most of the other boys can do it on paper – what else do I need? I understand how a loom works and how to make a Jacquard design. Those are much more important.' He dropped again to the floor in front of his uncle, gazing at him with impassioned eyes. 'At least let me work with you during the Christmas holidays, Uncle Tom. At least let me show you how useful I can be.'

Tom stared at him, then looked at his sister. Rebecca shrugged helplessly.

'I can't see how we can refuse him that,' she said. 'And it will keep him out of mischief. But will he be in your way, Tom?'

William sighed with exasperation, but before he could expostulate Tom said, 'He'll not be in my way – I'll mek sure of that.' He spoke to William. 'You'll hev to do the same hours as everyone else. Aye, and the same work too. Start as a draw-boy and learn it all. That's if you really mean to do it.'

'Of course I mean to do it,' William said impatiently. 'Haven't I been telling you that?' He leapt to his feet. 'And I really can come every day all through the holidays? And learn it all?' His face was alight, his eyes like flames. He really does mean it, Rebecca thought. He really wants to go into the factory and learn the business. And I believe he will.

I believe he'll work harder there than he ever has, or ever will, at school.

But what of Daniel? What of his future? She turned her eyes doubtfully upon her elder son.

Daniel and Lucy were sitting close together on the carpet, looking into the fire. They seemed to have lost interest in the argument that raged above their heads. They were talking softly, their faces glowing in the heat of the flames, their eyes reflecting the brightness. And there was something in their attitude that caught at her heart and caused it to falter.

Schoolroom games . . . such things were all very well. But when the players grew out of the schoolroom, what then? And she remembered that other childhood friendship, between Francis and his cousin Isabel, which had ended in such tragedy.

It was much later, when she was alone in her bedroom, before she was able to think over all that had happened that afternoon. There had been so much – Matthew's letter, Tom's arrival with his disturbing news, William's outburst, and her sudden disquiet about Daniel and Lucy. It was difficult to know which to think about first.

It ought to be the business, on which all their livelihoods depended. Or the boys, one so full of fire and determination, the other so grave and quiet – although there was fire in Daniel too, she knew, smouldering until some tinder should set it aflame. Even Lucy, rapidly growing to womanhood yet content as ever, it seemed, to spend her time in the schoolroom with a cousin two years younger than herself.

Any one of these should demand her attention. But as she sat by the hearth, wrapped in a loose gown, and warmed her toes at the fire that had been lit there earlier, she found her mind turning again to Matthew's letter. And she took it out of its packet and read it once again, feeling herself drift through the dark mists of the November night and across the thousands of miles to a land where the sun blazed relentlessly down, where men and women toiled to wrest a living from dry, harsh soil, where strange animals roamed and trees shed their bark instead of their leaves, and where savages waited with spears in the jungle for any misguided convict who strayed on a hopeless quest to walk to China.

'It isn't like being in prison here,' Matthew had written soon after he had first arrived in Australia. 'There are no cells, no dungeons. Here, our punishment is to work at certain tasks to get the colony established – so most valued are those who have experience of building or agricultural work. Here is where my travels in America are proving of great benefit! I know how to look after cattle, how to breed them and round them up and do all the things required to turn them into milk, meat or leather . . . As well as my other accomplishments, which as you know are many, though as yet there seems little prospect of setting up my loom to make carpets . . . Some ticket-of-leave men do very well and hope to be assigned their own land at the end of their sentence here and become respectable farmers themselves – an opportunity that would never exist for many of them in England.'

He had made it sound quite idyllic, Rebecca thought, and as though he had ideas of staying in Australia himself, once his own sentence came to an end. And why not? He could send for his money from England, be assigned land in Australia and live the life of a rich man. He could marry, found his own dynasty . . .

It sounded a good life. Why should he want to come back to Kidderminster?

She looked down at the letter in her hand. There was less news of Matthew's own life in this one; the pages were mostly taken up with expressions of his sorrow at Francis's death and concern for her. 'Francis was my best friend from the moment we met at school,' he had written, and had gone on to recall some of their escapades as well as fond memories of Francis's foster parents Edith and Geoffrey – revealed later as his aunt and uncle. 'Edith was always so very kind to me, knowing that I had no parents of my own. And Geoffrey was the best of schoolmasters – not nearly strict enough, he scarcely ever beat a boy and then never very hard. But he instilled in us a love of learning that I am afraid I allowed to lapse but have never entirely lost.' And then he had recalled his first meeting with Rebecca herself, one windy March morning as he knocked on the door of the house in Unicorn Street and Rebecca, pregnant then with William, had come stepping up the hill towards him. 'It was like a breath of that fresh March breeze itself to see you coming towards me,' he wrote. 'And to discover that you were the wife of my best friend – well, I hardly knew whether to be glad or sorry. But I know this: that you made Francis's life a very happy one, to the very end. And, short though it may have been, it was a more fortunate life than most men achieve even though they may live to be a hundred, because it contained you. So never reproach yourself, my dear Rebecca, that you did not do all that you could or should for him, for you gave him a joy that shone from his eyes for all to see and sounded in his voice for all to hear.'

Rebecca's eyes were wet with tears as she laid the letter down, the words blurred and dancing, and for a long time she gazed into the fire, unable to read more, thinking instead of the memories Matthew's words had conjured into her mind. Yes, she could remember that spring morning when she had first caught sight of him, his auburn hair flowing in the gusty wind as he stood at the door. She remembered his wild tales of travel in outlandish places, living an outlandish life. Working as a trapeze artist in a circus – feeding elephants with buns – riding horseback across the wide American prairies, driving cattle for hundreds of miles . . . Some of his stories true, some blatant fabrications, and all told with that same cheerful gaiety that had brought such dazzling life into her and Francis's lives.

Would she ever see him again? Would she ever look into those bright, dancing eyes, listen to that laughing voice? Would he come back one day with tales of kangaroos and savages and stars that hung in different constellations?

'Write to me soon,' Matthew had begged her. 'Write and tell me how you go on now that you are alone. I think of you so much, and wonder how you are contriving to bring up your boys by yourself, how you are managing the business. For I am certain that you won't leave it all to Tom. And I know that if you try to manage it yourself, you will find great difficulties standing in your way . . . If only I could be there to help you. If only I could stand at your side.'

If only he could. But it would be years before Matthew could return to England, and if he were never to achieve a full pardon – which was by no means certain – he would never be able to come back. Even if he wanted to.

No. She could not depend upon Matthew to come back and help her. He was a world away; he might as well be in a different time. And if he did one day receive his pardon and come sailing back across the oceans – well, by then both William and Daniel would be grown men and able themselves to manage the business. Her need for Matthew or any other man would be over.

William and Daniel, grown men. And before that?

Rebecca sighed. There was no escaping it. She must give serious thought to the problems of her boys and their futures. To Daniel, who worked so hard at his books and must be given the opportunities he deserved. To William, who cared nothing for school and wanted only to be in the factory beside his Uncle Tom.

What was right for one was not, perhaps, right for the other. But how was she to know? How to be sure of doing right for them both?

'But you gave me express permission to look at the ledgers and order books,' Vivian said. 'Don't you recollect? When we were discussing business matters a week or so ago. I didn't rush to look, naturally – I wanted you to have time to reconsider. But when you said nothing more I assumed . . .' He studied her face, noting the tiny lines that were beginning to appear, lines that told of sleepless nights, of worry, perhaps even of fear.

'Well, let's not go into it all again,' Rebecca said a trifle wearily. 'It's done now. And I daresay you're right, Vivian – I've been forgetful lately, I don't know why.'

'You have too much on your mind. Too many worries. That's

why I'd like you to let me shoulder some of them. Let me work with your brother to sort out the problems at the co-operative. And let me help with your boys' upbringing – just as you've been helping me with my daughters.'

He saw her breast rise and fall with her sigh, and felt again the almost unwilling admiration she had always been able to inspire in him. She was, he reflected, like no other woman he had ever known – able to reason almost like a man, yet at the same time passionately determined on her own way. A woman who threw out her own challenge; a woman it would be worth taming.

She must know well enough that it was almost impossible for a woman to try to undertake the work Francis had done, dealing with woollen suppliers, dyers and all their other suppliers as well as the customers for whom they made carpets. Yet she was reluctant to give in. It was as if the idea fired her blood. He could see that she wanted to do it. She wanted to prove that it could be done. She wanted it very badly.

But she also wanted to provide her sons with a good, sound future. She could not take risks with that. And here lay his own power.

'What do you think I should do?' she asked. 'There's Daniel, with a brain his masters say is brilliant. They think he should go to Oxford University to study and I know he longs to do that, though he won't say so. But if he does, it will be years before he can come into the business – even if he wants to. Perhaps he *won't* want to. Perhaps he'll take after his Great-Uncle Geoffrey and be a scholar.' She sighed. 'And then there's William, fretting to leave school and start working with Tom, convinced that in a few years' time he can take his father's place. He can't, of course – the hard-headed wool merchants of Halifax aren't going to place much reliance in the word of a young man. And William's only thirteen – it will be seven, ten years or more before he can really take his place, and by then he too may want something different.'

'By then many things will have changed,' Vivian told her. 'Not just the whims and fancies of young men who ought to be taking notice of their elders, rather than trying to decide their own futures. Why, Frank and I had to do as we were told. The business was there and we had to come into it, willy-nilly – and grateful for the chance. You're in danger of spoiling those boys, Rebecca, letting them have so much to say. Yes, even young Daniel, in his quiet way, is twisting you around his little finger. Oxford University! Does he have any idea what that entails?'

'I told you, he's said nothing about it himself,' Rebecca pointed out. 'It's what his master tells me . . . and the look I see in his eyes. But what do you really think, Vivian? Do you think he should be made to forget such ideas and come into the business? It does seem a pity, when he so much longs to study, and with William so keen.'

Vivian stared thoughtfully into the fire. They were sitting in the library, which held so many memories for Rebecca. But they were less deeply aware of those memories now. Her immediate concerns were more pressing.

'Perhaps you're right,' he said at last. 'Perhaps both boys should be allowed their way. In a modified form, of course,' he added quickly. 'I see no good in letting boys think themselves capable of making their own decisions. But you can allow them a little rope, while not letting them go too far for safety.'

Rebecca sat forward eagerly. 'What do you mean, Vivian? What do you suggest I should do?'

He lifted his eyes and regarded her gravely. She was looking especially fine this evening, still clad in the deep black of full mourning, with a jet brooch gleaming at her breast. Her eyes, brown as mahogany, were darkened further by the sombreness of her gown, and the only colour about her was the rich chestnut of her hair. Tightly drawn back as it was, a few tendrils had managed to escape and curl around her pale cheeks, and he felt a sudden desire to touch them, let them twine about his fingers.

'Let them think they are having their way,' he said slowly. 'For the more I think about it, the more I believe that they've hit – accidentally, of course – on the best way. But they must realise that there are conditions – as you must realise that too, Rebecca. Times are changing for all of us. None of us has what we most want out of life. All we can do is make the best of what we have.'

He paused, thinking over his words. They were of just the philosophical turn that might appeal to Rebecca, influenced as she had been over the years by Frank's unnecessarily scrupulous principles. Having grown up with an increasing impatience towards those same principles, Vivian knew that it was important to tread carefully. He felt confident that Rebecca, like some wild and timid creature, was almost in his hand. A wrong move now could send her scampering for cover.

But Rebecca was nodding, as if his words chimed exactly with her own feelings. He felt his confidence grow.

'I understand what you are saying, Vivian,' she said. 'But how should I let them have their way? And what conditions do you think I should impose?'

'Let's take William first.' Vivian leaned forward. 'I've been watching that boy, Rebecca. He's bright, there's no doubt about it. And he's not using his brains at school – that's clear from the reports his masters give of him. Well, if he wants to learn the business and work in the factory, let him – but on condition he works at his books as well.'

'I don't understand. How can he –'

'Hear me out, Rebecca.' Vivian paused. He was enjoying himself now, ordering someone else's life, arranging and controlling. 'Take William away from school. Give him a tutor instead. And let him spend some of his time at the factory, so that he can learn the business as he wants to do, and continue with his education at the same time. And make sure he works well by insisting that if his tutor's reports are bad, back he goes to school. I think you'll find that will solve the problem of that young man.'

'A tutor?' Rebecca considered the idea. Yes, it might well work. If someone could be found who was willing to agree with this unconventional approach, who would be prepared to work unusual hours so that William could spend part of his days at the loomshops. Yes, it might well be the answer. 'And Daniel?' she asked. 'What about him – should he go to Oxford? Or should he too have a tutor and learn carpet-making at once?'

Vivian shook his head. 'No. Daniel must be allowed to come to carpet-making in his own way, his own time. As you say yourself, he's like his great-uncle. He wants to study.' He waited a moment, choosing his words carefully. 'I believe that when he's had his opportunity to do that, he will be a great asset to the business. But not to your business, Rebecca. Daniel will never be a co-operative man. No – Daniel needs to look ahead to bigger things. Daniel could take over from me, when the time comes.'

Rebecca stared at him. He met her eyes steadily, and saw understanding slowly dawn.

'You – you still want him to be your heir, don't you,' she said at last. 'You want to adopt him as yours.'

Vivian's eyes were intent, persuasive. He reached out and took her hands.

'Rebecca, I don't want to take Daniel away from you. But think of what I can give him. I'll pay all the tuition fees necessary to get him into Oxford. I'll see that he has enough money to live there as a young man should. He'll need books, clothes, all manner of extras. I'll attend to all that. And I'll make sure that he's ready to take over what will be the finest, most successful carpet business in the country. What more could any young man ask? What more could any mother want?'

'No more,' she whispered. 'But –'

'There are no "buts", Rebecca,' he said. 'You know it. Give Daniel the future he deserves – by letting me make him my heir. Is it so very much to ask?'

She shook her head. 'You're being very, very generous, Vivian. I hardly know how to thank you. It's just that . . . Daniel is *Francis's* son. Somehow, I don't want to change that. It – it's like a betrayal.'

65

'And will it not be a betrayal,' he asked quietly, 'if you refuse both William and Daniel what they most want and then don't even have a business for them to work at? If you can offer them no future at all?'

She raised her eyes to his, mutely questioning. He returned her look and said, 'Tom's told you about Samuel Truman's order, Rebecca. It could be the first of many. It wants only one customer to lose confidence . . .'

She bowed her head. He was right, she knew it. The co-operative was in trouble, and the trouble was growing deeper. And only Vivian could rescue it.

And he had made his conditions quite plain. He wanted Daniel.

He wanted her son.

Chapter Four

Christmas came and went, and Rebecca stood at the brink of a new year. It was no longer 1837, the year in which a king had died and a young queen come to the throne – events which she had barely noticed, wrapped as she was in her own grief. It was no longer the year in which Francis had died.

As she sat alone on the last evening of that year, watching it blend with the first morning of the next, Rebecca found herself strangely reluctant to let it go. It seemed in some way to be a final severance of the links that had bound her to her husband. A year ago, they had been together, watching the fire die and listening to the pealing of the church bells as they clamoured to the stars. A year ago, he had sat beside her, his arm about her and her hand in his. She could feel his warmth, look at him and touch him, know that she had his love.

And now he was gone. And so was the year which had been his last.

In the church tower below, the bells were ringing again, muffled in mourning of the death of an old year. It was a poignantly appropriate sound, that dulled chiming that went with partings and sorrow. She listened to the sad, slow music that they made, hearing the tumbling melody that was peculiar to the ringing of bells. Gradually, it formed a steady fall, from the highest note to the lowest, and then it stopped. Only the heaviest bell, with the deepest voice, spoke on, tolling the twelve strokes of midnight. And then, after only a brief pause, came the joyous, open-throated hullabaloo that heralded a new year. New life. New hope.

And what new hope do I have? Rebecca thought sadly. What

new life can I look forward to? Only years and years like this, stretching away into a grey fog. Years and years alone, without Francis beside me. Years of worries that nobody can share – worries over the business, over my two sons, over Vivian and his daughters, over Tom and Nancy . . . And nobody to worry over me, nobody to give me the comfort I crave.

Those dreadful bells! Shouting to the skies, crying out their lies about hope and joy, when everyone who hears them knows the truth. That life is just a cruel joke, a tease. A 'now you have it, now you don't' game such as children play when they want to make another cry. A trap from which there is no escape.

She moved suddenly, as if physically to shake away the despair that threatened to overwhelm her. But as the fire died, so the shadows crept thicker and darker from the corners of the room, and wrapped themselves about her like a stifling cloak. She shrank from them, hugging her arms around her body as if to give herself the warmth that only another loving touch could truly impart.

The sound of the bells hammered on her skull, sharp on the clear, frosty air. Would they never stop? Didn't they know the truth, that there was no hope anywhere? Didn't they know that their joyful message was all lies, at best a terrible mistake? Did they really believe in the faith and trust of which they spoke? Were they really so sure of the future as their eager voices proclaimed?

She leaned back in her chair, with no choice but to listen. Never, she thought, had she heard the bells so clearly, never been able to hear each separate chiming voice, never realised that they rang a definite melody, the different notes repeated and then separating, wandering off in an ever-changing harmony before returning to sing again, briefly, the changes that had caught at her attention. At her attention and, she realised slowly, at her heart.

It was as if they were speaking only to her. As if they held a message for her.

But what message could it be?

The bells pealed on, and Rebecca stared into the embers.

The room was growing cold. If she did nothing about the fire soon, it would be completely out and there would be nothing for it but to go to bed. The sensible thing to do, she knew, for what use was it to go on sitting here alone, haunted by memories? Memories that should have brought joy, but gave her pain instead, a pain that twisted and gnawed and stabbed at her frozen heart.

But was her heart so frozen? After the first agony of Francis's death, she had tried to close her mind to the memories of his love and their life together. It had been difficult at times – there were so many reminders, large and small, tormenting her day and night. But gradually she had managed to force them into the deepest recesses of her mind, closing the door on them with as much struggle as if she were closing a door against a gale. And for a time now, she had believed them to be buried and had gone through her days with a capability that was cold, remote but effective.

People admired her, she knew, for the recovery she had made. Others, less charitably, remarked that she was fortunate not to have suffered deeply. None knew of the battles she had fought against the memories, the thoughts, that would have brought her to her knees if she had only allowed them to push the door open. It needed only the slightest crack to bring them all pouring through.

And now, with the passing of the old year and the birth of the new, with the clamour of the bells demanding that she listen to their message of hope and new life, she could feel that crack appearing at the edge of the door. She could feel her defences crumbling as the door opened wider. She could feel the ache in her throat, the stinging in her eyes, the pain that clutched at her heart as it gave way and the memories flooded through like the waters from a broken dam; a wild medley of sensation, of pictures of herself and Francis together. Here in this very library in the early mornings when she had come, a shy housemaid, to clear the hearth. In the streets of Kidderminster, half carrying her dying mother through the bitter cold of a blizzard. In the woods, making love for the first time on a carpet of spring flowers, a carpet more beautiful than anything that could be woven by man. In London, in the first years of their marriage. And back in Kidderminster, bringing up their family, mourning together over Geoffrey, drifting apart after William's birth and then together again when Matthew was standing trial in Worcester . . .

The memories rose like a wave before her terrified eyes, then crashed about her, engulfing her with the pain of her loss, with regrets for the mistakes she had made. Swamping her with a pain that was as great and as terrible as she had feared and then greater yet, a pain that shook her from head to foot, that gripped her heart and mind, that took every emotion and twisted it until she wanted to scream, to beat at it with her fists, to kick and fight against it. But it was too strong to fight, too powerful to resist. It battered her again and again, like waves on a storm-driven shore, until she lay helpless and spent, and let it wash her to and fro like a piece of jetsam on the stony beach.

This, surely, was as bad as pain could be. This, surely, was as low as she could go. No human being could suffer more than this and live. This must be the end, the bottom, the depth of despair.

And in her last agony, like a prisoner almost welcoming the execution he has dreaded, she opened her heart to the anguish and suffered it without resistance. It was all she had left.

But those who reach the bottom know that there is now only one direction in which they can go; and that is, back up again. And to Rebecca, lying before the dying embers on that bitter night, came the knowledge that her tears had brought about a change. That there was something else in her heart, besides the torment of her loss. And she touched it wonderingly, as if with a gentle finger, afraid that it would burst and disappear like a bubble of soapy water, and recognised it for what it was.

Gratitude.

And it did not burst and disappear, as a bubble would have done. It stayed steady and bright under her hand. It grew, iridescent as the bubble would have been, and she watched its beauty, fascinated.

If I have nothing else, she thought, I have this. Gratitude that I knew Francis, that I loved him; gratitude that he loved me. That we had so many years together.

So many? Until this moment, she had only thought of them as being so few.

She sat up, brushing back the hair she had loosened at some time during her paroxysm of despair. The fire was completely out now, a heap of dull grey ashes with no spark of life that could be blown into flame. But I'm not dead, Rebecca thought. There's still life in me – and there are still people who need me. William, Daniel, Tom and Nancy. Vivian's daughters. Maybe even Vivian himself. Our lives are all intertwined and we all have our part to play.

And if there is anything left to me, can it not be this? The knowledge that I have played my part; the satisfaction of seeing my sons grow into the fine men they must become? Isn't that more than many people have in these sad days?

The house was silent; the servants had had their own celebration below stairs and gone to bed hours ago. Even Polly had been sent away, for Rebecca had known that she would want to spend this last evening of the year undisturbed. And now she realised that the bells had stopped their pealing and the noise from the streets had stopped, as folk finally went to their beds.

She got up and went to the window, drawing back the heavy curtain. A brilliant moon shone down upon the tumbled roofs of the town, lighting their frosted tiles with gleaming silver. The sky was pale, the stars eclipsed by the splendour of the moon. Away in the distance, the rolling hills made a voluptuous, curving horizon, edged with the stark shapes of leafless trees.

From here, she could look down to the cottages where she had grown up, her ears filled with the clatter of her father's loom. She could look down at the dark, high buildings of the carpet shops. And she could look across to the little hill where

Matthew Farrell had built his house and lived until the terrible night of the riot.

Matthew . . . Did this same moon beam down on him, as he lay under the Australian sky? How was he faring, so far away at the other end of the world?

Would he ever return?

Once more, Daniel had escaped from the loomshop and his Uncle Tom's surveillance and was taking refuge in his cousin's schoolroom.

'Won't your uncle notice you've gone, and tell your mamma?' Lucy inquired as she stretched before the fire, toasting bread on a long fork. 'This piece is done now. Spread the butter on it, will you?'

Daniel obediently did as he was told. Outside, the clear frosty weather that had ushered in the new year had changed, and snow was falling heavily. A fierce wind howled around the walls and it was already growing dark. Inside, the fire's glow made the room a warm and secure shelter, and the smell of toast hung enticingly in the air.

Daniel passed Lucy the buttered toast and took the next piece from the fork.

'Yes, he'll notice I'm not there. But I don't suppose he'll say anything. He knows I'm not much use around the loomshop – not like Will. *He* already knows more than I ever will about making carpets.'

Lucy gave him a shrewd glance. 'That's because he's interested, and you're not.'

Daniel sighed. 'I know. But what can I do? I'm going to have to learn, someday. And I don't understand why I can't. I can learn Latin and Greek and mathematics – why can't I learn about carpets? But it's like a closed book, one I can't open.'

'It's because you're not interested,' Lucy said again. 'I'm the same with my needle. Do you know, it makes me feel actually *sick* to try to thread a needle. And sitting over a piece of work for hours and hours gives me the most terrible headache. Thank goodness your mamma understands that and has never made me work at samplers and things like other girls. If my Aunt Sarah had been in charge of me . . .' She shuddered. 'I'd have gone mad long ago.'

'We're misfits,' Daniel said gloomily. 'Good at the wrong things. What are we going to do, Lucy?'

'Eat buttered toast,' she said practically, 'and try to stave off the moment when we have to grow up at last and do the things that don't interest us. And it can't be so very far off now. I'm seventeen, you're fifteen. Aunt Sarah is already trying to persuade Papa to start holding balls for me. As if we were aristocracy! And she'll be wanting to take me about with her, visiting people.' Lucy's tone showed quite clearly what she thought of these plans. 'And I suppose Papa will want me to start to keep house for him, interview servants and all that kind of thing, and be a hostess at dull dinner parties.'

She stabbed viciously at another slice of bread. They sat in silence for a few minutes, watching the snowflakes whirl past the window, large as guinea pieces. A particularly fierce gust of wind rattled the panes. Lucy sighed.

'What will you do, Daniel? Oh, I know – go into the co-operative with your uncle. But what do you *want* to do?'

Daniel grimaced. 'Not that! That's if there's even a co-operative left when I'm old enough, anyway. Your father thinks it will fail long before then – I've heard him say so. But even if there is . . . no, it's not how I want to spend my life, with the looms clattering in my ears and the stink of wet wool in my nostrils. I don't really know what I want to do, Lucy. Study, I know – learn all I can at school and, if I could, at Oxford. Perhaps then I'd know what to do with all that I'd learned. There must be something – some use for knowledge. More than just passing it on to other people, I mean.'

'Perhaps there isn't anything else,' Lucy said. 'Perhaps that's what knowledge and learning are for, to pass on until somebody finds out what to do with them. That's what school-masters do, after all. Your Great-Uncle Geoffrey did that.'

'Yes,' Daniel said thoughtfully, 'so he did. And I never heard anyone say that his was a wasted life.'

There was one slice of bread left, but neither wanted it. Daniel put some more coals on the fire and they sat together on the hearthrug, watching the flames. Outside, darkness had fallen. The world seemed to have contracted to be only this warm glowing circle of companionship and contentment. Hardly thinking what he was doing, Daniel put his arm around Lucy's shoulders and she leaned against him.

'I wish life could always be like this,' he murmured drowsily. 'Just the two of us, and nobody else to interfere. We seem to understand each other so well. Why can't other people see how simple life could be if they just didn't try so hard to make everyone fit their own pattern?'

'And how impossible such a task is, when there are so many different patterns to fit,' Lucy agreed. 'Young ladies must behave with decorum and stay at home all the time and know nothing, just as if they were all exactly like each other, out of the same mould. While young men can go everywhere and know everything –'

'But are still expected to do what their parents decide with their lives,' Daniel continued. 'Well, I suppose that isn't really fair. Mamma would never force me to do anything I didn't want to. But I know she *hopes* I'll go into the business – and that's why I have to try, for her sake. I can never let her know how I really feel. She'd be so upset.'

'So you're being forced just the same,' Lucy said. 'Just as I'll be forced to do what Papa wants, but in my case it's because I'll have no other choice anyway. I have no education and nothing to do with it if I had. I have "accomplishments". I can play the pianoforte – a little. I can sing – a little. I can sew – as little as possible. And what use will any of those things be to me? Absolutely none! Do you know what they are supposed to do for me, Daniel? They're supposed to catch me a husband. A husband! What man worth having would marry me for my ability to pick out a few tunes on the piano or sew a sampler?'

'I wouldn't,' Daniel said with a grin. 'If that was what I wanted in a wife, I wouldn't even look at you! I've seen your attempts at sewing samplers. Though you aren't too bad on the piano – so long as you keep to the nursery tunes. So it's just as well, isn't it, that I don't want that kind of wife.'

There was a tiny pause. Then Lucy said in a careful voice, 'What do you mean, Daniel?'

'Why,' he said as if they had been discussing it for years, 'you *are* going marry me, aren't you? Later on?'

'Am I?'

'Well, of course,' he said. 'I thought that was understood.'

'Yes,' Lucy said after a moment, and in her voice was a hint of the surprise of someone who has opened a box to find some long-lost treasure has been hidden in it all the time. 'Yes, I suppose it was. I've just never really thought about it. Everything's been so pleasant as it has been – you and William coming here with your mamma, me and the others coming to your house. We've been like one family since – well, since my mamma died and yours began to take care of us. Perhaps I thought it would always go on like that.'

'But it wouldn't, would it?' Daniel said. 'Not if you married someone else. He would take you away and we'd never see each other. And even if you stayed in Kidderminster, you wouldn't be allowed to do whatever you wanted. You'd have to play at being wife to him. You'd probably have to have children. We wouldn't be allowed to sit like this on the floor and make toast, or go walking together.' He was silent for a moment, then added in a low tone, 'I couldn't bear to see you married to someone else, Lucy.'

'Nor could I bear being married,' she whispered, and turned in his arms.

Their lips met, softly and tremblingly. Daniel touched her cheek with his fingertips, stroked a few wisps of hair back from the fire-warmed skin. It was like silk under his caress, and he felt his heart shiver and his skin tingle. A warmth that had nothing to do with the fire began to spread through his body, and he drew her a little closer.

'You will marry me, won't you, Lucy,' he whispered against her ear, and felt the tremor of her body in his embrace.

'Daniel . . .' she breathed. And then drew sharply away as they both heard the tread of heavy footsteps on the stairs outside. With a swift, instinctive movement, she picked up the toasting fork again and jabbed the last slice of bread on its prongs. It shook as she held it to the flames, and then the door was open and Vivian's heavy body was silhouetted against the candlelight on the stairs.

'Sitting in the dark? What are you about?' He peered in and came forward, carrying a sconce, and used it to light the candles that stood on the mantelpiece. 'What mischief is this?'

'No mischief, Papa,' Lucy said. 'We're just making toast. Look, there's one piece left, would you like it?'

'No, thank you. I'm not a child, to sit before the schoolroom fire as if I had nothing better to do.' His eyes moved over them narrowly, taking in Lucy's flushed face and tumbled hair. 'And neither are you two. You're looking hot, miss. Should you not be with your sisters?'

'They play such childish games. I wanted to be quiet.'

'And your games are not childish?' His voice was sharp. 'And Daniel, why are you not with your brother and uncle in the loomshop? Do they know you're playing truant?'

'They were busy enough,' Daniel muttered. 'There was nothing for me to do.'

'Then you should have found something. At the very least, you could have been at your studies. Your mother tells me you want to go to Oxford University. Do you think that will come from sitting dreaming by the fire?'

'I don't think it will come at all,' Daniel answered gloomily. 'If all my Uncle Tom says is true, there will be no money for University and I shall have to work in the loomshop soon enough – that's if there's a place for me.'

'A place for you? What do you mean?'

'Why, only that William will soon know all that there is to know about the carpets we make there, and how to sell them and buy materials and everything. And he and Uncle Tom seem to understand each other more than I could ever

76

do. And he's liked by the weavers. I don't know how to talk to them.'

Vivian sat down in the old chair by the fire and looked at him consideringly. Daniel, still on the hearthrug, sat with his arms folded about his knees, looking more like a sullen little boy than a youth on the brink of manhood. Lucy had got up quietly and now sat in a chair on the other side of the hearth, her face in shadows.

'So,' Vivian said at length, 'you aren't altogether happy about taking over your father's business.'

'I'm not at all happy about it. But that doesn't matter, because I don't think it will happen. William means to do that.'

'And you? What do you mean to do?'

Daniel shrugged, looking suddenly lost. 'I don't know. I know what Mamma wants me to do – what you think I should do, too. But how can I, when William and my uncle are there before me? And I know the business is going through a difficult time – we've lost several orders recently, from customers we thought reliable. There isn't really room for both me and William. And I know Will's younger than me, but it doesn't seem to make any difference.' He lifted his shoulders again. 'But I don't know what else there is for me.'

'Don't you?' Again, Vivian watched him in thoughtful silence for a while. Then he said, 'There might be something else for you. Something better – and something that would allow you your studies at Oxford too.'

Daniel looked up. His forehead was creased, his brows low over the dark eyes. He turned his head slightly, almost suspiciously.

'Something better? What could that be?'

'Wouldn't working with me be better?' Vivian asked, and Daniel looked at him in surprise. 'Learning the kind of business I control? It's bigger, Daniel, and more suited to your capabilities. That co-operative of your father's – it's all very well in its way, but it will never grow any bigger. And that will be its downfall.' He leaned forward. 'The time is coming when industry must expand to succeed. Small enterprises like

Pagnel & Himley may struggle on, making a living of sorts for those involved with them – but they'll never really achieve anything notable. Oh, yes, they may make you a carpet that no one else has, but of what use is that if an order is lost when the carpet's half-made? I've seen it happen, Daniel – good carpet, splendid carpet, rolled up and stacked in a corner of the warehouse and left to rot. Carpet designed specially to match a certain ceiling – and then the lady of the house changes her mind about the decorations and demands different colours, a different pattern. And who wants her cast-off?' He shook his head. 'No, it's too risky, that business. The only way to succeed is my way – making good quality carpet that will find a ready market. Special orders, yes, but nothing exclusive. Nothing that can't be sold to Lord B if Lord A changes his mind. Not that many of my customers do change their minds,' he added with complacency. 'Indeed, they recommend me to their friends. You would not be coming into a failing business if you came in with me.'

Daniel looked at him. In the flickering light, Vivian looked big and bulky, his shadow looming behind him. Always intimidating, there was a hint of menace in that rearing dark shape, and Daniel shivered a little.

Immediately, he chided himself for his imagination. Behind him, he was aware of Lucy, as delicate and ethereal as her father was solid. And what menace could there be about her father, the man he'd always looked on as an uncle? Overbearing though he could be, he was still one of the family, familiar to Daniel for as long as he could remember.

'I'd have to discuss it with my mother,' he said hesitantly. 'I don't want to fail her . . .'

'And how would you be failing her?' Vivian's tone was robust. 'Your father had his part in Pagnel Carpets too. You would be doing no more than take over that part – if that was all you wished.'

'All I wished?'

Vivian leaned forwards. 'There could be more for you, should you wish to take it, Daniel. You know that as yet I have no son – no heir. Nor any likelihood of one, as far as I can see. There's been no woman for me since my dear wife died.' He paused, as if still coming to terms with his sorrow. 'I need an heir,' he said quietly. 'And I've been watching you, Daniel. You seem to me to be a promising young man. Good at your books, eager to study further, anxious to do whatever is right by your mother – all commendable traits. And how much more you could do for your mother, were you to allow me to take the worries of your education and future off her shoulders.'

Daniel stared at him. 'I don't understand.'

'I am offering to take over all the expenses of your education – now, at school, and later when you go to Oxford. As go you assuredly will, if you and your mother agree. In return, you will come into the business with me later on – when you're ready, not before – and in the event of my still having no son of my own, you will formally become my heir.' He sat back in his chair, his eyes fixed on Daniel's face. 'Now, isn't that a fair enough offer? Would it not take the crease from your mother's brow, the shadow of anxiety that I see there so often? And there need be no rivalry between you and your brother, either. You would each have a future.'

Daniel sat very still. He looked from his uncle's face to the fire. The flames had died down now and the red glow heated his skin. The slice of toast Lucy had begun to make when her father had come into the schoolroom lay untouched on the hearth. Outside, the storm still raged and he could hear the wind howling in the chimney.

'And you want nothing in exchange for all this?' he asked at last in a low voice. 'I am to have all that I want – I am to go to Oxford and study for as long as I wish – and you ask for nothing?'

'Nothing,' Vivian said. 'I simply want to repay your mother for all that she's done for me, and I want to make sure that you enjoy the life and prospects you deserve. That your father would have wanted for you.' He paused, then added with a small laugh, 'Oh, I suppose you might say I do want something. I want an heir, after all – I've admitted that.

And while considering that aspect, it might be as well to make some formal arrangements about that. For instance, it would probably be best if I were to adopt you.'

'Adopt me? As – as your son, you mean?'

'Why, of course.' Vivian moved his hands in an outward, almost dismissive gesture. 'Merely as a formality, of course, to make the matter tidy. It need make no difference to your relations with your own family, naturally.'

'But you would look on me as your own son? You would expect me to think of you as – as my father.'

'Well, yes, I suppose so, if you put it that way.' Vivian sounded as if he had hardly considered the matter. 'You may not wish to do that, of course. And I would not want to force you. You have your memories of your own father, after all. But ... well, I think we would understand each other, wouldn't we? And it seems a small enough price to pay, when you consider the gains you'll make.' He rose to his feet. 'However, I must go now. I have things to attend to.' He stood over Daniel on the hearthrug, looking down at him. With his shadow thrown on the wall by the firelight, he looked immense. 'And may I give you one word of advice, Daniel? As a young man with what many would consider a very rosy future before him, you might think perhaps that schoolroom teas should be part of your past. Something that should be put away, with other childish things.' He turned to his daughter. 'And you too, Lucy. You're a young woman now. I hope I don't have to find you sprawling on the floor again in that rather hoydenish manner. It's not at all becoming.'

He left the room. There was another silence.

'I think,' Lucy said in a tight little voice, 'that I have been reprimanded.'

'I think we both have,' Daniel said. He reached for her hand. 'I'm sorry, Lucy.'

'Sorry!' she exclaimed. 'I'm *angry*! That he should speak to us so – as if we were *children*!'

'He meant to point out that we were behaving like children.'

'By sitting on the floor making toast on a snowy afternoon? How is that childish? It may be the kind of thing that children *do* – but that's because children have more sense than adults. Children understand the important things of life – like being together, doing simple things, enjoying the pleasures that come so easily and don't cost a lot of money. People like Papa think that nothing is worth having unless it's been paid for with vast sums, so that everyone can see that only a few people could even afford it.'

She slipped down to the floor beside Daniel and put her arms around him. 'You won't become like that, will you? Promise me you'll never become like that.'

He smiled and hugged her. 'I'll never be like that. But I do have to think about what your father has offered me, Lucy. And not just because I want to go to Oxford and come into his business – indeed, that part is the least attractive. But to be able to help Mamma, that I do want. Because I'm afraid he's right about the co-operative. It may not fail, but it will never truly succeed either. And there is no room in it for all of us.'

Lucy drew back a little. She searched his face. Her eyes glimmered in the ebbing light, but although the glow was still red on her cheeks, he had the impression that her own colour had left her.

'You want to do it, don't you?' she said in a whisper. 'You want to take his offer and go to Oxford and work with him. You want to be his heir – his *son*. Daniel, don't you see what this means? Don't you understand what it means for *us*?'

'For us?' He shook his head. 'Why, Lucy, what difference can it make to us?'

'He wants you to be his *son*,' she repeated. 'Daniel, if you're his son and I'm his daughter . . . how can we ever be married?'

On the first Monday of the new year, Tom came into the loomshop early. But he was not the first to arrive. There in the little office, sitting at his desk, he found Rebecca.

'Becky! What are you doing here?'

She glanced up at him over the big ledger she was studying. 'I've come to work, Tom.'

'To work!' He dropped into a chair, staring at her as if she had suddenly run mad. 'But why? What sort o' work do you mean to do?'

Rebecca closed the ledger, keeping her finger in it, and looked at him gravely.

'I did tell you, some time ago, that I meant to take my part in the business,' she said. 'Until now I've been feeling so sad and wretched that I couldn't summon the energy. But with a new year coming, I've decided that the past must be put into the past. We have a future, Tom, you and me and the others. And it's my job to make sure that future is a good one – if only for my sons' sake.'

Tom scratched his head. 'Well, yes, I can see that, Becky. But you know you don't hev to worry about that. I'll see to everything. And young Will's doing well too, he's taking a real interest now and got his head screwed on right too. You don't hev to come in here and worry yourself over the business.'

'I'm sorry, Tom, but I think I do,' she said quietly. 'I've been looking at this order book. We've lost a good deal of business lately. Why do you suppose that is?'

'Business is bad all over the shop. You knows that, we've talked about it often enough. Even the big manufacturers hev problems.'

'But they can stand it better than we can. They have larger resources. They can ride out a difficult period. We can't, Tom. We've very little behind us and we need all the business we can get.' She tapped the ledger with her fingernails. 'We can't afford to lose custom as we're doing now. And it isn't just that we're not getting so many orders. We're losing orders we thought were secure. Why? What's happening?'

Tom shook his head unhappily. 'I don't know, Becky. It's as if they've lost trust in us – yet we haven't let anyone down, we're doing just as good work as ever and we deliver on time. I don't understand it and that's the truth.'

'Well, it's clear that something has to be done.' Rebecca

opened the ledger again. There was a new ring of determination in her voice. 'And I intend to do it. I shall visit every one of our customers, taking samples of new designs, and ask them for new orders. If they've cancelled orders I shall ask why, and I won't be fobbed off with evasions. I shall want to know the real reason. We're going to beat this, Tom, and build the co-operative up again to the dream Francis once had for its future.' She lifted her eyes and Tom saw the glitter of tears on her lashes. 'He didn't work himself into his grave just so that it could all fall away to nothing,' she said. 'Our co-operative was supposed to be the first of many – he saw it as the way to the future. I mean to make it so.'

Tom could find nothing to say. He looked at his sister, so small yet so indomitable behind the high desk. At thirty-two years old, her tawny hair was still as richly glowing as a beech in autumn. Her skin, pale as ivory, was as clear as a girl's and her waist as small as it had ever been, in spite of the births of three children. She could have been half her age.

Yet there was a sense of power there, a hidden strength that no young girl could ever project. Rebecca's life had given her the durability of steel, an unswerving determination to win over all odds. She might be left shaken for a while by a blow such as the death of her husband or child, but she would always return, stronger than ever, ready to fight again.

But could even Rebecca surmount the difficulties that faced them now? Even the big carpet manufacturers were feeling the draught. Broom himself, one of the greatest of them all, the man who had first installed Jacquard looms, was threatened with bankruptcy because he had lost his American orders. And who was going to return their custom to Pagnel & Himley just because Rebecca had big brown eyes and a tiny waist? They probably wouldn't even see her. Women just didn't do that sort of thing. She'd be lucky not to find every door in Kidderminster closed against her for such temerity.

'I shall start at once,' she was saying. 'I want a list of every customer we've lost in the past six months, Tom, and details of the order cancelled. I shall call on each one and ask for an honest reason to be given. And I expect to come back with at least half those orders reinstated. Most people are reasonable, after all. I can understand with Francis dying, they might have lost confidence in us. But when they see that we mean to carry on, giving as good or even better service – well, I think we'll find our problems are at an end.'

She stood up, closing the ledger with a slap. 'Get the clerk to make that list out for me, Tom, while I write a letter that can be sent to each one letting them know I'll be coming. I'll have to make arrangements for travel to some of them. I'll start with the local ones.'

Tom found his tongue at last.

'Becky, d'you think this is a good idea? I mean, what are they going to say – you, arriving on their doorsteps dragging a load of samples like some salesman? It don't seem right. I don't reckon they'll see you, half of them.'

'Then I'll see the other half,' Rebecca said. 'And if I regain only a half of those orders, it'll be worth my while. Tom, we're going to be in serious trouble if we don't do something drastic. And as for all that nonsense about my being a woman – have I ever allowed that to stop me before? Have I ever sat at home doing my needlepoint and receiving calls? Can you *imagine* me doing such a thing?'

Tom sighed and admitted that he could not. All the same, he was uneasy. It was good to see Rebecca her old self again, determined and invincible, but he didn't think she was going to find it as easy as she thought to win back these old customers. And how would she be feeling in another six months, when she was faced once again with the proof that they just couldn't keep the co-operative going any longer? Because that was how Tom saw things going. And he didn't think it would have been much different even if Francis had lived.

People just didn't want manufacturers and workers living side by side and sharing their profits. It was a threat to the whole system – the system of master and man, the way industry had developed. As long as manufacturers – not just of carpets, but of any of the goods that people wanted to buy –

could stay on top, with the workers kept firmly in their place, there would be plenty for those who had the money to buy, and enough cheap labour to make it for them.

But once the workers began to earn more money and to demand the things that went with it – education, better homes, good clothing to keep them warm, good food to fill their bellies – then anarchy would result. Why, next thing they'd be wanting the vote – there were already murmurings about that, growing daily. And then they'd be wanting to go into Parliament themselves, have a say in how things were run. And then what would happen?

Tom had heard it all. And dimly he knew that there was a connection between these fears and the orders that the co-operative had lost. And understood that nothing Rebecca could do would halt their losses. It was almost as if there were a conspiracy to see them fail.

And you wouldn't need to look far, he thought grimly, to find out just who was behind it.

Chapter Five

Rebecca began immediately to organise her new life. Polly, already in charge of the house, was given the extra authority that would be needed while Rebecca was away. The boys considering themselves too old for a nursemaid, a young tutor was appointed who would oversee their evenings after school, make sure they did their preparation and give them any extra coaching that might be needed. During the day, he taught the sons of one of the women who had helped Rebecca with the Wives' Group during the Great Strike of 1828, and the arrangement suited them both.

'Do you really mean to go about, seeing people and asking for custom?' Daniel asked dubiously. 'Won't they think it strange?'

'Probably,' Rebecca answered. 'But someone has to do it. And there's no one else at present, until you or William are old enough. We can't wait that long, Daniel.'

He sighed. 'I wish I were older. I wish I could help you now. It doesn't seem right.'

'There's nothing to worry about,' she told him. 'People have always thought my situation strange anyway – they'll soon become accustomed to the new idea. And you mustn't let it interfere with your own plans, Daniel. I know you want to go to Oxford and I mean you to go, somehow. But that makes it all the more important to make the co-operative a success. We need the money, all of us, to live.'

Daniel hesitated, wondering if he should tell his mother about his uncle's suggestion. But he didn't want to tell her yet. He was still thinking about it, lying awake at night while Vivian's words circled endlessly in his mind, his voice persuasive as he pointed out the advantages. And there were advantages, Daniel could not deny. But always, when he had thought of everything, always weighing against them, always tipping the balance, came Lucy's warning.

'If Papa adopts you as his son, you'll be my brother . . . and we shall never ever be able to marry.'

He moved restlessly, torn by the conflicts within himself. If there had been no one else to think of, how easy it would have been! He would have gone to Oxford, given himself up to a life of study and teaching, content to live simply, unconcerned by material trappings. But that was impossible. His life was not just a thing of the intellect, he was driven by his love for his mother, his brother, for Lucy; he was beset by their needs, the demands they made upon him without even being aware that they did so.

He wished he could suddenly be five years older. He would be old enough then to take on this task his mother had set herself, to win back their old customers, find new ones. He would be old enough to marry Lucy, or at least become betrothed to her, and he wouldn't have to be beholden to his Uncle Vivian.

But none of it would be possible without Vivian. Without his uncle's financial help, he wouldn't be able to go to Oxford at all. In five years' time there would probably be no co-operative left, and Vivian would certainly never countenance any engagement between himself and Lucy.

He sighed again. How impossible life was! How did anyone ever decide what was right, when there were so many conflicts to weigh up?

Rebecca gave him an anxious glance. Daniel had seemed restless lately, she thought, as if beset by worries. She had been talking about him to Nancy only that morning, saying how pale and silent he'd been lately. 'He was just the same after Geoffrey died,' she'd said. 'As if he blamed himself, though everyone knows it was no fault of his. And he can't possibly blame himself for his father's death.'

'Course not,' Nancy said stoutly. 'All the same, it might be sort of bringing it back to him, in his mind. Trouble with Danny is, he don't talk enough. Keeps it all inside. Still, I 'spect he'll sort it out for hisself, one way or another.'

'I hope so.' Rebecca frowned a little. 'I wish he would talk to me. I feel so close to him sometimes – and at others we might as well be a world apart. There are things happening to him, Nancy, that I know nothing of, and it worries me.'

'What sort o' things?'

'I don't know. Things he's worrying about – as you say, he keeps it all inside. If only he'd talk, I might be able to help him – but if I ask, he just looks at me and smiles and says there's nothing. And I know it's not true. If only he'd trust me.'

'I don't reckon it's anything to do with trust,' Nancy said. 'I reckon he just don't know how to say it – whatever it is. But I'll bet it's nothing much. We all has these worries when we're young, and they don't never amount to much, you knows that.'

'Perhaps.' Rebecca thought of her own youth. At Daniel's age she had been working as a housemaid in Pagnel Court – the very house where she was mistress now. Her life had been a series of fears: that she might not do her job properly, that one of the Family might see her carrying out some mundane task, that she would break something and be dismissed. And there were other fears too. That her father and mother, worn down by poverty, would sicken and die. That her brother and sister, fled to London after the death of a weaver, would be found and arrested for murder.

Had there been any room for worries that 'didn't amount to much'?

'Thank heavens William is easier to understand,' she said. 'He may throw a tantrum and he may sulk when things don't suit him, but you always know just what is the matter. He makes sure of that!'

'Tom says he's going to be a good worker,' Nancy remarked. 'Already got the weaving at his fingertips, as you might say, and getting a grasp of the business side too. He'll be a real help when he's older.'

'I know.' Rebecca was silent for a moment. 'And to tell you the truth, Nancy, that's another worry. Unless the business expands greatly in the next three or four years, there simply isn't going to be room for both William and Daniel. What am I going to do then? Daniel's the elder son – but William's the one who shows most interest. And even if I can afford to let Daniel go to Oxford, that only postpones the problem. The day is going to come when he needs a place – and by then William will be an experienced man. I simply don't know how it's to be managed.'

'And if I was you,' Nancy said shrewdly, 'I wouldn't even worry about it. A lot o' water's going to flow under the bridge before that day comes. Get on with the life you got now, Becky, that's my advice, and stop worrying your head about things that ain't going to happen for years yet. It'll all be different then, one way or another, so why waste your strength now?'

Rebecca looked at her sister-in-law. Then she smiled and gave her an impulsive hug.

'You're right, Nancy, of course. I've got quite enough to do now, getting the business back on its feet. Perhaps something will happen to show me what to do about the boys.' She hesitated, wondering whether to tell Nancy how Vivian had offered to adopt Daniel as his own son and make him his heir. So far, she had mentioned the idea to no one. Perhaps she ought to talk it over.

The truth was, she had put Vivian's offer out of her mind as much as possible. Every instinct she possessed had rejected it. It seemed such a betrayal of Francis, to give his son away, and to his most bitter rival – for there had always been a rivalry between the two, with Vivian so jealous of Francis even though materially he had possessed so much more. Yet in Vivian's offer there seemed to be no motive other than a wish to help and, by so helping, a desire to attain the son he had always so much desired.

Was it not a fair bargain?

But Daniel is Francis's son, she argued. Not a possession to be bartered and exchanged. And yet again, he was his own self, with his own desires and needs – needs and desires that Vivian could fulfil. Was Rebecca to refuse him these, simply because of her own instincts?

If only there were someone she could talk to, someone who could advise her. She looked again at Nancy, respecting her robust commonsense and almost tempted to confide in her. But Nancy and Tom had no conception of what Oxford meant to Daniel. Barely schooled at all themselves, the amount of education Daniel had already enjoyed was outside their experience.

The only person Rebecca felt she could have talked to about her dilemma was Matthew. And he was far away.

'And these are our newest designs,' Rebecca said, displaying the drawings she had been making over the previous few weeks. She flipped up sheet after sheet of paper, each covered with the coloured whorls and scrolls that she had taken from the ancient Persian and Chinese designs and adapted for English drawing rooms. 'These are becoming very fashionable now, and of course each design can be changed to suit your own wishes. And with the improvements in dyes now, we can be much more sure of matching the colours so that even a large carpet will be quite even.'

Percy Talbot, one of Kidderminster's leading bankers, glanced towards his wife and looked a trifle embarrassed. Both had shown surprise when Rebecca had come in and she knew quite well that they had expected a man to bring the designs he had asked for. However, neither had made any comment and she had quickly begun the small speech she had prepared, giving them no time to object.

Rebecca laid down her portfolio. She looked at the two well-dressed, well-fed people in their elaborately furnished drawing room. They were the fourth customers she had visited, and she was beginning to recognise the signs. Her heart sank and she prepared herself for the platitudes she was becoming accustomed to.

'My brother and I were disappointed that you should have

cancelled your order,' she said quietly. 'We had hoped to go on making carpets for you for many years.'

Mr Talbot's face grew a little redder. He was a bulky, highly coloured man, seen as often on the hunting field as in his bank, and his fleshy jowls betrayed his liking for hearty food and drink after the day's sport. He glanced away from Rebecca and stroked his whiskers.

'Well . . . hrrrmph!' He cleared his throat noisily. 'It seemed to me that you might have more on your hands than you could cope with. After – well –'

'After my husband's death?' Rebecca had grown tired of the evasions and euphemisms people employed to avoid having to mention what was an irrefutable fact. Francis had died, and left her with a pain worse than she had dreamed of, but it didn't help to pretend it hadn't happened. To pretend he had never even lived . . . 'But I still need to earn a living,' she pointed out.

Mrs Talbot's cheeks were scarlet now, as if Rebecca had used coarse language and drawn attention to some unmentionable bodily function. She brushed at her skirt and avoided Rebecca's eyes, but Rebecca kept hers fixed on the powdered face, well aware of what troubled her but determined to give her no help.

'Is something the matter, Mrs Talbot? You seem a little distressed. Mr Talbot, have I said anything to offend? I came with the best intentions, to show you what we are making now so that you can reconsider if you want to.'

He struggled for words. 'Indeed, Mrs Pagnel, you must know . . . it's not at all usual . . .' He stumbled and stuttered, perspiring now in his discomfort, and Rebecca felt almost sorry for him. But her irritation overcame any compassion she might have felt. Once again, she was faced with what was 'fitting' – and what could it matter, beside her and her sons' need to live? Were they supposed to sink into genteel poverty – whatever that might mean, for Rebecca knew only one kind of poverty – and then disappear quietly without trace, simply that people like the Talbots need not have their sensibilities disturbed?

Mrs Talbot had recovered herself. In a voice of ice, she said, 'What my husband is trying to say, Mrs Pagnel, is that even though we understand that with your origins you are not to be blamed for your ignorance, in our circles it is not done for a lady to go canvassing amongst her friends for trade. Such things are best left to the gentlemen whose business it is, and kept out of the drawing room. I'm surprised that even you don't seem to be aware of this. I would have thought that poor Jeremiah Pagnel would have seen to it that you were educated when he was forced to accept you into his family.'

Rebecca felt the knot of irritation swell into anger. How dared this woman speak to her like that! Wasn't she pleased enough to sit in this over-furnished room, with her feet on carpets that Rebecca's own father might have woven? Wasn't she thankful that some people were 'in trade' so that they might provide her with all the material goods she craved for her comfortable life? And so that her husband could make the money to pay for it all in his way?

Was his way so much better, simply because he did not come home with soiled hands?

'I'm sorry if I've offended you,' she said, keeping her temper. 'But I have a family to rear and this is the only way I know of doing it. A housemaid's wages are not enough, unfortunately, to raise two growing sons on.' She gave the other woman a direct look, so that she should understand that, humble though Rebecca's origins might have been, she considered them no matter for shame. 'I've noticed certain orders given to us before my husband's death have been cancelled,' she went on, now addressing Mr Talbot. 'It seems sensible to try to discover why. If it's simply because you felt we wouldn't be able to fulfil your order, please let me assure you that we can and will. And if you want to change your mind about the design . . .' She touched the portfolio by her side. 'If there's nothing here that you like, I can probably make up a design that would suit you – exclusive to you, of course, just as we've always done.'

Percy Talbot's small blue eyes flickered over her and then at his wife. He seemed to hesitate.

'Well, mayhap we could have a look at your drawings. What do you say, my love? If Mrs Pagnel could leave them with us, perhaps? We do need that new carpeting for the dining room, after all. And there's your boudoir . . .'

'I am happy with the carpet we've already chosen for that,' Mrs Talbot said austerely. 'I see no reason to begin again. As for the dining room, Mr Vivian Pagnel has that in hand. He seems altogether more reliable, and understands the social niceties of these things.' Her glance swept coldly over Rebecca. 'You would not find him bringing his work into a lady's drawing room on pretext of calling for tea.'

Rebecca bit her lip. It had been the only way she could think of to get into this house at all, but she could see now that it had been the wrong thing to do. Perhaps she should have approached Mr Talbot in the bank.

'I think I had better go,' she said, getting up and gathering her drawings together. 'I'm sorry you don't wish to return your order to us, but so long as you're happy . . .' She bowed slightly to Mrs Talbot, who looked down her nose, and then walked to the door. 'I'm sorry to have wasted your time.'

Mr Talbot followed her into the hall. As the maid came to open the front door, he helped Rebecca with her cape. His hands lingered on her shoulders.

'Hrrrmph . . . I might have some custom for you at the bank,' he said in a low voice, glancing towards the drawing room door as if afraid his wife might hear. 'I need some new carpeting for my own office. Why don't you call in sometime, my dear? Bring your samples with you, of course.' He gave her a smile, his lips thin and damp between his whiskers. 'There may be some other way in which I can help you, too.'

Rebecca stared at him. Then she turned and walked quickly out of the door, her heart hammering in her throat.

When she reached the loomshop, she went straight to the office, took down the ledger and made two bold, black strokes through the name of Talbot.

'I don't like to think of you travelling about the country touting for business, Mamma.' Daniel kept his hand under Rebecca's elbow as they walked through the snowy streets on their way to Vivian's house. 'Especially at this time of year. Won't you at least wait until the spring? I could even come with you, during the Easter holidays.'

Rebecca shook her head. 'I can't wait, Daniel. We've lost too many commissions. If we don't regain some of them we shall have to close down. It's as bad as that.'

'Then let me leave school now and go with you at once. It isn't right that you should travel about alone.'

Rebecca smiled wryly. To have her own son telling her now what was 'right' and 'fitting'! And yet who had worried about the young maidservant, pregnant and penniless, who had set out to travel alone to London, with little hope of finding her brother and sister when she got there? Who had thought about 'right' and 'fitting' then?

'I'm perfectly capable of looking after myself,' she said. 'And I've learned lately how to talk with men who see me as some kind of freak simply because I set out to earn a living for myself and my sons.' She stopped in the snow and faced Daniel. 'Is it something to be ashamed of?' she demanded passionately. 'Is it so repellent, to want to continue the task that your father and I began together? Is it so dreadful to want to lead a useful life rather than sit about in drawing rooms sewing things nobody will ever want?'

She looked around her, at the narrow, twisting streets, the crooked roofs. 'It looks clean and pretty in the snow, doesn't it. But I know what lies beneath that white coverlet, Daniel. I know what's hidden behind those crumbling walls. Poverty – the poverty I grew up with and that your father and I fought by forming the co-operative and forming a Wives' Group to try to feed the weavers when they seemed like to starve. And that poverty is still there. The battle still needs to be fought.' She turned her dark eyes upon him. 'Who will fight it, if we don't?'

Daniel shook his head. 'But what does this have to do with your going about, trying to get business for the co-operative?'

'It has *everything* to do with it! The co-operative is work, Daniel. It means food for the weavers, homes and clothing for their families. It means a proper wage for them, a fair share in what's been earned, not a few pence or a shilling a yard set by manufacturers with more concern for their own bellies than for their workers'. And it ought to mean the future – the way all industry should go.' She paused again. 'If we fail now, we shall never be able to start again. The men will have lost confidence in us. That's why I must get these orders back, Daniel. That's why I can't wait for you to grow.'

'It isn't just for us then.'

'No. We have a share in Pagnel Carpets, as you know, and I am sure Vivian will be meticulous in seeing that we are properly paid that share. He should do,' she added a trifle bitterly, 'since it seems that most of our reneging customers are turning to him. That would be just enough to keep us – though not enough to send you to Oxford, I'm afraid. But it wouldn't keep Tom and Nancy, of course, and it wouldn't be enough to keep the co-operative going. And those are the things I feel obliged to do.' She was silent for a moment, then added, 'I want to do them, Daniel. I want it very much.'

They walked on. Although Vivian's daughters were growing now, with Ann married and Susan betrothed, Rebecca went to Vivian's house most mornings to see that all was well with the younger girls and to talk with his housekeeper. And Daniel accompanied her whenever he was free to do so, for there were now few occasions when he could see Lucy. Vivian seemed to have come to a sudden realisation that his daughter was fast growing to womanhood, and was strict about her being alone with any young man. Solitary walks in the fields and cosy teas by the fire had been forbidden.

'I can understand it,' Rebecca said when Daniel protested to her about the new rules. 'Lucy isn't a child any more. And it's not healthy for her to want to go on behaving like one.'

'Not healthy? What do you mean?' Daniel, aware that Lucy didn't at all want to behave like a child, was diverted.

Rebecca hesitated. It was difficult to explain to Daniel what she believed must be in Vivian's mind – the memory of his young half-sister, Isabel, who had grown up with Francis and dreamt herself in love with him. Isabel's dream of love had been a fantasy, in which she saw them living forever as children, playing with treehouses in the garden and fishing for frogs in the stream. When her dream had crashed about her head, she had taken refuge in an eternal childhood, starving her body in an attempt to halt its growth, until she had faded away from life altogether.

'Young girls must grow into women,' she said at last, 'and boys into men. That's natural and right. And as our bodies change, so do our minds and our feelings. If we try to prevent them we do ourselves a kind of damage.'

Daniel said nothing. He knew that Lucy's only objection to growing up was to the restrictions that it would impose. That was why she clung to her childhood, still wearing her hair flowing loose down her back, still keeping a pinafore over her dress. But beneath the pinafore and the flying hair was a woman, determined on her own way and ready, when the time came, to fight for it.

And he, although two years younger than Lucy, was already a man. But nobody else seemed ready to recognise it.

'I don't know what to do,' he confessed to her later that morning, as they sat apart from the others in the window of the schoolroom. 'Mamma seems set on working like a man, going about selling carpets. Uncle Tom says the business is going to fail anyway, no matter what she does. William is far better at the business than I am, but it'll be much longer before he can be of any real use. And I'm just –'

'You're going to go to Oxford,' Lucy interrupted, 'to learn as much as you can and be a brilliant headmaster with your own school. Or stay at the University and be a Don. And everyone will say how clever you are.'

'And wonder why I do nothing to support my family.' Daniel shook his head. 'It's no good, Lucy. I can't do that. Even if Mamma could afford it.' He shook his head.

'But you want it, don't you?' Lucy said softly. 'You want it more than anything.' She took his hand in hers and stroked it.

'Not more than anything,' Daniel answered as quietly, and turned his hand so that their palms met.

There was a whoop from the younger girls, playing a new game that their eldest sister had brought them. Ann, who now lived in Cheshire, was on a visit and Lucy admitted that she'd been driven almost mad by the constant reminders of her own still single state. 'Anyone would think eighteen was completely on the shelf,' she said bitterly. 'And Susan's just as bad – she acts as though to be engaged were only one step away from heaven. Well, perhaps it is,' she added with a smile, 'when it's the right person you're engaged to. But have you *seen* her fiancé? Twenty years older than she, with whiskers as stiff as a scrubbing brush. Ugh! Thank goodness she's on a long visit to his home in Stafford at present and I don't have to see him every day.'

They sat silent for a while, then she said, 'Have you been thinking about Papa's proposals, Daniel?'

'I've thought about little else.' He sighed and ran his fingers through his dark chestnut hair. 'It would answer so many problems, Lucy. Mamma's worries would be at an end, with my education provided for and William's future assured with the co-operative. All I have to do is agree to let your father adopt me, and become his son.'

'And my brother,' she said in a low voice, and fixed her eyes upon his.

'I know,' he said helplessly. 'Lucy, what am I to do?'

But she had no answer for him. And when Rebecca came back to the schoolroom she found the two of them sitting in silence, staring down into the garden almost as if they had quarrelled. And on the way home, Daniel was just as silent, until she was driven to ask what was the matter.

There was nothing, he said. But Rebecca, watching him through that evening as he sat with a book he was clearly not reading, knew that there was something very wrong.

He was worrying about her, she thought. About the need

for her to take on Francis's role in providing for the family. About the future of the business, about his own future and the education he so badly wanted. About Oxford.

And she turned her own mind to Vivian's suggestion that she should give her son up to him.

Was he right? Was she being unutterably selfish in not agreeing? Wouldn't it solve all their problems – and what harm could it do, really?

They both went to bed at last, each longing for someone to talk to; neither knowing that they had only to turn to each other.

Rebecca and Daniel were not the only people to be concerned with the future of Pagnel Carpets, or Pagnel & Himley. Vivian too was absorbed with the problem as he paced a few mornings later by the Stour. He paused on the bridge, watching the dyed wools being washed on long poles in the river so that the colours flooded into the water and flowed away in a swirl of muddied variegation. It was a sight so familiar to him that he barely noticed it, and only glanced up when Ben Messinger came along the footpath towards him.

'So here you are,' Ben greeted him. 'Still wondering how to win the lovely Rebecca? I saw her a day or two since – a fine young woman. How long is it she's been a widow now? You'd better be ready to snap her up when the time comes, or some other young whippersnapper will be ahead of you.'

'I haven't been thinking of marrying again,' Vivian growled. 'Too much bother, having a wife about the place, always whining for this and that. New gowns, new furnishings . . . it's bad enough with daughters, but at least they grow up and leave you, save the one you need at home to keep house.'

'And which one will that be?' Ben leant over the bridge with him, watching the dyes flow beneath. 'Lucy's next eldest, isn't she? Turning into a fine young woman, too. I might make a bid for her myself. Who comes next?'

'Mary, Jane and Margaret, with no more than four years between the three of them. A fine quiverful! Why I had to choose a woman who could bear children so easily and yet bear only daughters . . .' He shook his head. 'Can you wonder that I'd rather take on a ready-made son, and one already bearing my name, than risk marriage again? It's a lottery, Ben. At least if you're breeding cattle you take account of the animal's past performance before paying your money – with a wife, it's a game of chance and a damned expensive one at that.'

'But surely with Rebecca you've got just the proof you need,' Ben said slyly. 'Two sons already – no, three, there was the one who died. And still in her prime. I don't know why you're waiting, Vivian.'

'I told you – because there's a boy there, nearing manhood, who'll suit me just as well as taking a chance and then having to go through another eighteen or twenty years' waiting for him to come to manhood. No, I'll not marry again, much though I'd like a son of my own.'

'Of course,' Ben said, 'if you wed Rebecca you'd have the one and very likely the other too. And if they won't agree to your adopting Daniel and then some other suitor takes her fancy . . .'

There was a long silence.

'You're right,' Vivian said slowly at last. 'Ben, you're right. I've been dragging my feet, thinking I had all the time in the world. They must come to a decision, those two. If I can adopt Daniel, I will. If not . . .'

'As I said before,' Ben said, 'it's time to go courting again.'

Vivian lost no time. Daniel was at school again, but at home in the evening. He sent a message inviting the boy to supper with himself and Lucy, intending to speak to him privately immediately afterwards.

Daniel arrived, wearing a new waistcoat which Nancy had embroidered for him, and looking rather shy. It was the first time he had been formally invited to Vivian's house and he felt nervous. He had a very good idea why he had been invited and was still undecided about what he should answer if his uncle should ask him again to agree to adoption. On the one side, his concern for his mother as well as his own desires for education weighed heavily; on the other, Lucy stood alone but held the balance in her slim hands. What was he to do?

He looked across the table at her, dressed tonight in a gown he had not seen before. It made her look more grown up and he remembered that her Aunt Sarah had been visiting recently and had brought her dressmaker with her. Lucy had grumbled about the tedious fittings she had been forced to endure for the new dresses her aunt had decreed should be made for her. This must be one of them.

It was made of fine challis of natural cream with a satin stripe of shimmering green, so pale as to be almost translucent, woven into it. The style was all curving lines, leading gently over Lucy's still budding breasts to the downward point of her small waistline and then billowing over slim hips to a hemline that was like a bell around her feet. Her hair, shining like a pale yellow sun, was up – the first time Daniel had seen it so – and the low neckline of the dress showed off her slender neck and shoulders. Looking at her, he was aware of a stirring deep within him, a warm hunger that spread through his loins and created an ache in his heart.

She met his gaze. Her eyes looked darker tonight, like sapphires against the creaminess of her skin. There was a message in them, an appeal he could not deny, and he knew that there would never be any possibility of his looking upon Lucy as his sister.

'Do you not agree, Daniel?' Vivian said with a touch of impatience in his voice, and Daniel realised with a start that his uncle had been speaking to him.

'Yes – oh, yes,' he stammered, without the least idea of what he was agreeing to, hoping too late that he hadn't committed himself to anything. He glanced at Lucy again and was relieved to see a slight twitching of her mouth. Well, at least he hadn't made any drastic decision with his thoughtless reply. But he made up his mind that he must try not to think about Lucy, and concentrate on her father instead. It would be all too easy to make a fool of himself this evening, where he was the focus of attention.

However, Vivian spoke only of general subjects for the rest of the meal. When inclined, he could be good company, with a fund of anecdotes which he was skilled at tailoring to his audience. There was no sign this evening of the Vivian who would reduce his labourers' wage almost to nothing rather than go without his own meat, no hint of the contempt he had so frequently expressed for the co-operative. Instead, he was all concerned interest when such things were mentioned, but for the greater part kept to a more entertaining turn of conversation.

'Let's not talk about business tonight,' he declared, raising his glass. 'This is a celebration. Lucy has finally decided to admit to being a young lady. I shall hold a dance for her later, of course, but she begged me to let tonight be a private occasion, to mark her very first day with her hair up. How do you like it, Daniel?'

'Very much,' he said, looking across the table. He felt unaccountably shy. Was this really the tomboy who had run with him in the garden, climbed trees and played at hide-and-seek? Was this suddenly beautiful woman really the girl who had sat by the fire with him, making toast and talking dreamily about marriage?

But when he met the sapphire eyes again and saw the gleam of the old mischief still there, he knew that Lucy hadn't changed at all. It would take more than a gown that showed off her maturing figure or hair that turned her into a woman, to alter the essential Lucy who lived behind that smooth brow.

'So let's drink to my daughter.' Vivian poured more wine and indicated a toast. 'To Lucy.'

Daniel lifted his glass. His gaze was fixed upon Lucy's face and as she lowered her eyelids and then slowly raised them again he felt a thrill that ran through his body like a shock. The message in them was quite unmistakable and the thought of being considered her brother – even her cousin, for there was no blood relationship between them – was suddenly obscene.

'And now,' Vivian said when the meal was over, 'Daniel and I will go and sit in the library. I have something I wish to discuss with him. Lucy, your sisters will be in the playroom now. You had better go and join them for an hour before bed.'

She turned to him. Her eyes flashed a little but her voice was demure as she said, 'But I thought I was to be considered grown up now, Papa? Wouldn't it be more suitable if I were to go and wait for you in the drawing room?'

'Wait for us? I've told you, we're going to the library. There's no point in your going to the drawing room. You'll be alone there.'

'Then perhaps you should join me,' she said. 'I can't be a young lady at one moment and a child, relegated to the playroom, at the next. If I am to be grown up, I must be grown up all the time.'

Vivian's face darkened a little. He glowered for a moment at his daughter, but she met his gaze steadily and without fear. After a moment, with a brief glance at Daniel, he grunted.

'Very well, miss. Since you wanted this to be a celebration, I'll let you have your way. Daniel and I will sit here and drink our port together and then we'll come to the drawing room. But I'll remember those words of yours next time I see you romping about the grounds like a schoolgirl. Remember, being grown up lasts a very long time.'

Lucy bowed her head, but not before Daniel had caught the quick flash of triumph in her eyes. And as she got up and passed his chair, seeing that her father was engaged at the sideboard, she bent and whispered in his ear.

'I couldn't go to bed without seeing you again! He wants to talk to you about – you know what. Try to tell me what he says, won't you?'

Daniel had no time to answer, for Vivian was already turning back towards the table, the decanter in his hand. With a little laugh, as if Daniel had made her some compliment,

Lucy straightened up and glided to the door. She opened it and paused, looking back at them over her creamy bare shoulder.

'Don't sit too long, Papa,' she said with the demure note back in her voice. 'I shall be waiting for you.'

Vivian set the decanter on the table and sat down. His expression was a mixture of exasperation and unwilling pride.

'That girl's a minx. She's always been the same – too saucy for her own good yet somehow she always manages to get her own way. I don't know where she gets it from – her mother was never like that. A meek, submissive woman, ideal qualities in a wife.' He shook his head. 'The sooner I find a husband for her, the better. She's eighteen, quite old enough – I hadn't realised how grown she was until recently. My sister tells me I've been remiss in not allowing her to come out of the schoolroom earlier, but with two older girls to get off my hands . . . Still, it shouldn't be too difficult to find a suitable man. Someone older, I think, and well settled – more interested in owning a pretty young wife than getting a fortune.'

Daniel listened in horror. Did Lucy know that her father was making these plans for her? And should he tell Vivian now about his hopes regarding his future and Lucy's? Wouldn't his uncle merely laugh at a boy barely sixteen years of age, talking about marriage?

'Suppose a younger man asked for her hand?' he ventured, but Vivian laughed.

'You think she'll make a love match? No, I'd not consent to that, Daniel. Not unless he was very well heeled. It's an expensive business, having daughters, and I'm determined that they all make good marriages. A solid middle-aged ironmaster or something of that sort, that's what young Lucy needs. He'll be able to discipline her too – a young man would simply let her twist him round his little finger, and what recipe is that for marriage? No, I'll not look at anyone under thirty-five unless he has a sizeable income, and if Lucy doesn't like the idea now she'll come to thank me for it later.'

Daniel was silent. He knew his uncle well enough to understand that Vivian did not speak in jest. It would be of no use to tell him now that he and Lucy were in love and wanted to marry in a few years. All he could do was hope that no suitable man would be found. He had no doubt that Lucy would refuse any suitors her father offered. But could she actually be forced to marry against her will?

Vivian was speaking again.

'You'll be needing this kind of advice yourself, before very long, Daniel – what to look for in a woman, how to choose your future wife. And how to enjoy a full life as well. You'll come to me for that, of course. Your Uncle Tom would be quite unable to give you the proper kind of guidance.'

Daniel took some port. He had never been spoken to quite like this, as a boy on the verge of manhood. All the same, he was aware that Vivian didn't expect him to reply in kind. He was still expected to accept the advice he was given.

Vivian filled his own glass and lit a cigar. He leant back in his chair and regarded Daniel through narrowed eyes.

'So tell me, Dan. How are you getting along at your studies now? Are you still doing well? Are your masters pleased with you?'

'I think so, sir, yes.' Daniel was a little startled by the shortening of his name. William often did it, and Tom and Nancy too, but so far no one else had used the diminutive. But Vivian had always been a man for using his own names for people. Daniel remembered him calling his father 'Frank' instead of Francis. It implied a certain familiarity.

'And are they still keen for you to go to Oxford?'

Daniel shrugged. 'I haven't discussed it with them lately. It seems rather useless when I know it can never happen.'

'Never happen? Why do you say that?' Vivian's tone was sharp.

'I've talked about it with my mother. The co-operative has lost more orders. She's having to go about trying to regain the customers we've lost and find new ones.' Daniel raised his eyes to Vivian's face. 'I can't spend the next five years or more studying while she does that. I know I must finish my

105

schooling – but I'll have to leave as soon as possible so that I can help her.'

'And what about Will? I thought he was anxious to go into the business.'

'He is, but –'

'More anxious than you, in fact.'

'Yes, but –'

'So why must the responsibility rest only on your shoulders?' Vivian leaned forward suddenly. 'Very well, I know he's younger than you are and not ready to leave school. He needs to learn a good deal more before he can take on such responsibility – he's far too hot-headed at present anyway. But when he's older, he'll do very well with your Uncle Tom. They'll be happy to trudge along, the pair of them, in their own little world of ideals and sharing their profits with the man next door, swimming when he swims and sinking when he sinks. As sink they will, eventually. But you –' he jabbed a finger towards Daniel '– you're destined for better things. You've got a head on your shoulders and a good brain inside it, and I don't want to see it wasted. You're too good for the co-operative but you're not too good for Pagnel Carpets. You're exactly what I need – a young man, ready to learn, ready to work, ready to take the business into the second half of the century. And that's not so far away now! We're standing at the beginning of a new era, Daniel. We've got a new monarch, slip of a girl though she may be – she'll marry before long and it's to be hoped she'll marry someone strong enough to lift the monarchy out of the mire it's slipped into over the past few decades. And then the country will march forward as it's never marched before.'

Daniel shook his head, overwhelmed by the torrent of words. 'But I don't see how I –'

'Have you forgotten my suggestion to you? My proposal? All you have to do, Daniel, is agree to become legally my son. You'll enjoy all the benefits, including your studies at Oxford. And I'll look after your mother and brother.' Vivian drained his glass and poured a second. 'Now, what is your hesitation? What doubts can you possibly have?'

Daniel shifted uncomfortably in his seat. How could he tell Vivian the truth? It was more likely to antagonise him. He remembered his uncle's reaction when he had come upon Daniel with Lucy in the schoolroom. It was only since then that they had been prevented from being alone together. Clearly, he would disapprove strongly of any close relationship between them.

And that could affect his mother too. If Daniel were to turn Vivian against him, might he not withdraw all his support from her and from William? Daniel knew that Vivian had been a source of a good deal of help and advice to Rebecca, that he seemed to care about her welfare. How could he risk her losing that?

'I'm sorry, Uncle,' he said at last. 'I have thought about your suggestion – and I feel proud that you should have made it. That you think me fit to become your – your son. But ... I think it's too soon after Father.' He struggled to find the words. 'He's not been dead a year, Uncle Vivian, and Mamma still grieves for him, I know. How can I tell her I want to be another man's son simply for the sake of my own education, or even the business? She would see it as a betrayal.'

Vivian stared at him. 'A betrayal? When it could be the salvation of your family? Daniel, you're not thinking. For God's sake, you wouldn't even have to change your name. How could there be any betrayal?'

'If we could just wait for a while,' Daniel said helplessly.

'While your mother tramps the country like a vagabond? Are you happy to see her doing so?'

'No, of course I'm not, but –'

'Well, that's what it'll come to!' Vivian's face was dark with anger. He stood up suddenly, jerking his chair away from the table. 'And you'll be responsible, Daniel, when the business fails even after all her efforts and the three of you are reduced to the workhouse. As you will be – mark my words, as you will be.' He stood for a moment breathing heavily, glaring at Daniel. Then he threw down his cigar and stamped towards the door. Just before opening it, he paused and looked back, very much as his daughter had done, but in his face there was only rage and in his voice fury.

'You may go, Daniel,' he said in a voice that shook with wrath.

'You may return when you've thought better of your foolishness. Meanwhile, ask yourself whether your father would really have wanted to see his wife travelling dangerous roads in an uncomfortable coach, making a spectacle of herself by trying to do the work of a man and failing ignominiously in the process. Ask yourself if he wouldn't rather have seen you completing your studies while your mother and brother go on living as he saw them do before his death. As he wanted. And ask yourself whether it is for you, with all the wisdom of sixteen years in your head, to determine the future of your entire family, yes, and that of the weavers you're all so fond of too. Are they too to find themselves in the new workhouse, simply through your obstinacy?'

He disappeared. Daniel heard his footsteps loud on the stairs. He sat silent and miserable, unsure what to do next. And then heard the door open again and softly close, and a moment later felt Lucy's soft arms about his neck.

'I heard it all,' she whispered in his ear. 'Oh, Daniel, what are we going to do? He'll never let us marry, I know it. Nobody defies Papa and wins. Out of spite, he'll never allow it now.'

'I don't know what we're going to do,' he said, catching her hand in his and holding it against his cheek. 'But I know this, Lucy – I shall never, *never* agree to be his son.'

Rebecca was in her own drawing room, absorbed in Matthew's latest letter, when Vivian was announced.

She looked up rather absently, still lost in the world of which Matthew spoke so eloquently. Such a strange, outlandish world it seemed, where men worked in gangs chained together yet could, by earning a free pardon, become respected members of the community. Where convicts were landed from ships after a voyage it seemed impossible that anyone could survive, and sent immediately to walk alone for hundreds of miles into virtual jungle, to reach the farms where they were assigned to labour out their sentences. Why didn't they abscond? she had asked Matthew in one of her letters, and he had replied: 'For, the simple reason that there is nowhere else to go. The bush, as they call it here, is as hostile a place as you could imagine, with nothing fit to eat unless you can catch one of the jumping animals they call kangaroos, and a sun so merciless it would flay the skin from a man's back like the cat o'nine tails that is used so readily to maintain discipline . . .'

Today's letter was a cheerful one, telling her of the work he had been doing on the farm where he had been assigned. After his first assignment, which had ended in such disaster, he had soon been taken from the ranks of the common labourers and made overseer on a large sheep farm. His experience with the wide open spaces of America had been invaluable; being accustomed to timber felling and driving cattle on the prairies had made it easier for him than for most men to settle into his new life, sometimes overseeing the clearing of acres of gum and mahogany trees, sometimes riding for days across the vast empty pastures to guard and care for the roaming sheep. 'Sleeping at night under the stars is nothing new for me,' he had written, 'and the wide open spaces hold no terrors, as they do for many of the men who have lived all their lives in mean little streets. I feel sorry for them, for they're often too afraid to close their eyes in case some spectre should come to haunt them, or a wild animal devour them. But for me, it's almost as good as being free.'

Like other convicts – or 'government men' as they were more usually called these days – he was allowed to 'sell' his overtime after the statutory hours of six in the morning until three in the afternoon and work for whom he liked, for pay that was his.

'It amuses me to tell you how much this pleases me. To be able to earn a few shillings of my own, when in England I am a rich man! But I tell you, I have never been so proud of any of the fortune left me by my parents as I am of those few shillings. Perhaps I needed this experience, to humble me a little. I must have been a very arrogant man, back in Kidderminster . . .'

I never thought of you as arrogant, Rebecca thought sadly. Just as Matthew, so full of life and gaiety, who made the very air sparkle ...

As the door opened, she turned her head, half expecting to see Matthew himself and it was only slowly, as if a blurring of vision needed to clear, that she realised it was Vivian. With regret, she laid down the letter and saw Vivian's eyes follow the movement.

'From your antipodean murderer?'

'Matthew was not a murderer,' she answered quietly. 'He killed Bill Bucknell by accident, as you well know. As everyone knows.'

'He went out with a gun.'

'To help the magistrates! Vivian, you are the last man to criticise him – you would have executed every man on the Strike Committee. Matthew was on their side – why would he kill one of them?'

'A shot that went astray, I think they claimed,' Vivian murmured. 'Who knows who he was really aiming at? But I didn't come here to discuss Matthew Farrell. I know we'll never agree on him. I came on a friendlier errand.'

'Did you?' She looked at him doubtfully. She had been half expecting this visit for several days – ever since Daniel had been bidden to supper and come home looking unhappy and withdrawn. He had refused to tell her what was wrong, and she had been afraid that he had quarrelled with Vivian. Since then, he had declined to go to the house at all and had shut himself away in the schoolroom with his books.

She knew, too, that Vivian disapproved strongly of her intention to start travelling as soon as the weather improved. He had already complained about her visits to customers in and around Kidderminster, though refusing to accept that she had any legitimate complaint about the fact that many of them had transferred their orders to him. 'Of course they're likely to do that,' he had said. 'They see Pagnel carpets as the parent company, God help us all, and think it more loyal to do so. It isn't my fault that you and Francis decided to use the family name – indeed, I never really understood why Father allowed it.'

His announcement that he had come on a friendly errand struck her, therefore, as unlikely. But he was smiling and apparently at ease; perhaps he had really come to bury any hatchets he might feel needed burying.

'Sit down, Vivian. It's good to see you. Will you take a drink – a brandy, perhaps?'

'That would be very acceptable.' He waited while she went to the sideboard and brought the decanter and glass, and she knew that he was concealing his irritation. He had never grown accustomed to her habit of doing for herself small tasks like this, rather than ring for a butler or maid. But this was a matter on which Rebecca was determined not to give in. She had lived long enough below stairs to understand the weariness that came from having constantly to answer a summons from the Family, especially in the evening when the servants might be enjoying their only brief rest of the day.

Vivian poured his brandy. He sipped it while they talked of small, ordinary things and Rebecca wondered why he had come. To try again to persuade her to give up her plans to continue with the business? To ask her again to give him her son?

In both cases, she knew the answer must be 'no'.

At last, Vivian finished his brandy. He leaned forward and laid his hand over hers. His fingers were large and warm, and there was a certain comfort in them. She looked down at their entwined hands, then up into his intent, dark eyes.

'Rebecca,' he said very seriously, 'I've been wanting to talk to you about this for a long time. At least, it seems a long time to me . . . But long though it's been I knew it was too soon. Now . . .' he paused. 'Now, I feel that the time is coming when you may be able to give some thought to what I am about to ask you. And, I hope, to agree.'

'Vivian, if it's about Daniel –'

He shook his head. 'It isn't about Daniel. Oh, he'll be affected, of course, but only in the best of ways. And so will we all. What I'm about to ask you, Rebecca, is something that can only benefit the whole family – and all those who depend on us.'

She stared at him. Her heart began to thump suddenly, as if it knew what he was about to say. But the knowledge was still hidden from her mind. What could it be? What could he possibly have come to say?

She was suddenly afraid and didn't want to hear it. But there was no escape.

'Rebecca,' he said, and his hands tightened on hers. 'I'm not asking for an answer immediately, Rebecca – I know you'll want time to think it over. But don't keep me waiting too long, I beg you.' He paused again and she could hear the steady, deep ticking of the tall clock that stood in the corner of the room. She could remember Francis coming home with that clock, not long after they had been married. 'I've come to ask you – when you're ready, when you feel you've mourned long enough for Francis – I've come to ask you to marry me. To be my wife.' There was a silence. Was it brief or was it long? Even the clock seemed to hold its breath. 'I want you to be my wife,' Vivian said again, his voice low. 'I want it very much indeed.'

To be his wife. To take the place of poor, dead Maria. To be Mrs Pagnel still . . . but no longer Mrs Francis Pagnel.

To be Vivian's wife.

Chapter Six

The silence stretched around them. Rebecca sought for something to say, some reply that might be made, but could find none. She looked up at last and found Vivian's dark eyes upon her.

'You ... ask me to marry you?' she whispered through trembling lips. 'Vivian, do you mean this?'

He shifted impatiently in his chair. 'Would I make such a suggestion if I did not mean it? I'm not in the habit of making jokes, Rebecca. I may tell you, I've given the matter very careful thought. It's no sudden whim.'

'Of course not,' she murmured. She knew as well as anyone that Vivian rarely acted without careful thought or good reason. Such a proposal would indeed be no whim.

'But why? Is it because Daniel —'

Vivian moved again, abruptly, flinging out a hand in denial. 'It's nothing to do with Daniel! The boy's young and foolish yet but he'll do well enough when he grows. No, this is between you and me, Rebecca.' He stared at her, his brows drawn together. 'Good God, do I have to give any reason other than the usual one? I want you for my wife, Rebecca — because I think we suit each other well and because I think we need each other.'

'*Need* each other?'

'We're both widowed,' he said bluntly. 'I for too long — you, admittedly, not for long enough as yet. But the time's fast approaching when any man might ask you for your hand, and I don't intend to be lagging in the queue.' He reached out and took her hand again. 'Rebecca, I've waited long enough.

113

Maria's been dead these seven years and more, and it's time I found myself another helpmeet. And you need protection. You need help with those boys of yours – and who better to give it than I, who have known them all their lives? That's why I say we need each other.' He paused then added, 'You'll need me for other reasons too, before long. The co-operative cannot continue much longer in the state it is now.'

Immediately, she felt the fire flicker within her. 'I'm managing the business quite well enough. I'm seeing people already, gaining new orders –'

'And losing old ones. Do you think the whole of Kidderminster doesn't know what's happening, Rebecca? Don't you think they watch your pitiful tramping from customer to customer, begging for orders like a vagabond scrounging for pence? How many new customers have you gained – and how long do you think you'll keep them?'

Rebecca flinched at his words but, cruel though they were, knew she must heed them. As far as the carpet business went, Vivian was no fool and his ear must necessarily be closer to the ground than hers could be.

'Listen to me,' he said, and she could hear him trying hard to soften the roughness of his tones, 'you know as well as I do that the failure of the co-operative is inevitable. More than that, all the new customers you gain by making a spectacle of yourself now, will end up coming to me or to one of the other big manufacturers. You're doing our work for us, my dear. And while we flourish, you and your precious brother will go to the wall. Aye, and your sons with you.' He paused, then went on gravely, 'I don't want to see that happen, Rebecca. You're part of my family, I'm fond of you and your boys. I was fond of Francis, even though we didn't always see eye to eye. I can't stand by and watch you founder.'

'I don't mean to founder,' she said steadily. 'I mean to go on as Francis and I always planned. And I can do it, Vivian – I know I can. Only this week I gained two new orders, valuable ones, and the looms will be busy for the next three months while I find further ones. Why, Tom is even talking of expansion.'

'*Expansion!*'

'Yes, expansion. A new loom, perhaps even a new shed with room for more than one. We have new designs to offer – the kind of special designs we've always offered, the kind of carpet that the big manufacturers can't or won't make.' She met his eye. 'You forget that I know this business too. I know that even if our customers do go to you, they won't get what they really want – a carpet that's designed and woven especially for them. You make carpet on the grand scale, Vivian, huge widths and lengths on your big looms, and we can't compete with that. But we can give the Mayor's wife a carpet that no one else will have in their drawing room. We can give her something exclusive.'

There was a darkness in Vivian's face that brought a tremor to her heart. But she stilled it firmly and after a moment he spoke, his voice quiet.

'We seem to have strayed from the subject, Rebecca. I was offering you marriage, not a business partnership. And speaking of the Mayor's wife – perhaps it's a good moment to remind you that that is exactly what you might be yourself before long, if you accept my offer.'

She stared at him. Was he offering her prestige, as an enticement? Did he really believe that the possibility of such status would be enough to make her agree to be his wife?

Looking at it from his point of view, she supposed that it was quite reasonable. To Vivian, social and political prestige were important. His wife Maria too would have revelled in being the Mayoress. It was not surprising that he should think Rebecca equally impressed, particularly coming as she did from a weaver's hovel.

Except that if he truly knew her, he would not have thought such a thing for one minute.

'Are you sure I would be acceptable?' she asked coolly. 'I would not wish to stand in your way at all, Vivian.'

He glanced at her, letting his eyes move slowly over her

widow's weeds. Her black gown was fitted closely to her slender figure, outlining her breasts, drawn closely about her narrow waist. She saw his glance linger and felt a warm self-consciousness. The full meaning of what it would be to accept his proposal struck suddenly at her mind, and she felt the breath escape from her body in a small gasp.

'I think any woman on whom my choice fell would be acceptable to Kidderminster,' he answered at last, equally coolly. 'I have a certain standing in the town now, Rebecca. It might be as well for you to remember that.'

She bowed her head, knowing that he was right. Since old Jeremiah's death Vivian had grown in stature, and even more since Francis was no longer there to remind people of his true position. The fact that the old man had been no more than Vivian's stepfather, that there was no Pagnel blood in his veins, could well be soon forgotten. The more concrete evidence that he now owned and managed the whole of the carpet business which led Kidderminster and kept the town ahead of such places as Wilton was enough to satisfy his rivals and fellow manufacturers.

There was a silence between them. Then Vivian rose and took his leave.

'I won't press you for a decision now. I know you need time to think this over, and I'm sure you'll decide wisely.' He took her hand in his and she looked up into his eyes. 'Your willingness to try to carry on the co-operative alone does you much credit, my dear,' he said softly. 'But you know in your heart, don't you, that it can be only a matter of time . . . And you know that I'm here, waiting. But don't make me wait too long, Rebecca. I'm a patient man, but there may be a limit even to my patience.'

He went then and left her alone. Restlessly, she moved to the fireplace and stood gazing down at the flames, disturbed more by what she had seen in his face and heard in his voice than by the actual words he had spoken.

Vivian had never been good at accepting rejection. And she had rejected him before – once long ago, when she was a maid in his mother's household, and again when he had offered to adopt Daniel as his son.

She had known when she had come here as Francis's wife that the first rejection had not been forgotten, but Vivian seemed to have put it out of his mind. Now, she was not so sure.

He had said he was a patient man and his patience had lasted for many years. But what if she should reject him for the third time?

Vivian was a good man to have as a friend. But he would make a bad enemy.

'So froggie went a-wooing, did he? And the little lady wouldn't have any of it.' Ben Messinger shook his head sorrowfully. 'You must be lacking in your touch, Vivian.'

He scowled, unamused. 'She'll come round. Once she finds life treating her a little more harshly. The reins have been used lightly so far, Ben, but they can be drawn in sharply enough when the time comes. Or maybe a little touch with the whip . . .'

Ben glanced at him. 'You're enjoying this, aren't you? In an odd sort of way. She's made you angry, yet you're enjoying it.'

'Enjoying it.' Vivian rolled the phrase around his tongue. 'Yes, perhaps I am. There's something about that woman, Ben. She's always had the power to rouse this anger in me – and, yes, I do enjoy it. Or maybe what I enjoy is the thought of taming it – taming *her* – some day.' He smiled and his teeth gleamed. 'Now that, I *am* going to enjoy,' he said softly. 'And it wouldn't be nearly so well worthwhile if she hadn't roused my temper to begin with.'

Ben shifted a little, and his voice was uneasy. 'You're a queer sort of cove, Vivian. I always said so. But you'd not hurt her? She's a brave little thing and maybe wrong-headed but there's a softness about her. I wouldn't want to see her harmed.'

Vivian laughed. 'So she's got you ensnared too! By God, I wonder what it is about her. Nothing but a weaver's daughter, dragged up in a hovel to the clatter of a loom, and yet wherever she looks with those big brown eyes of hers, the men fall like ninepins. Soft – Rebecca? Don't be deluded, Ben. If that woman's soft, I'm the next King of England! As long as she's a free woman, she'll do as she wills, and be a thorn in my side like her damned husband was.' His face darkened. 'Francis Pagnel! He was a blight on my life from the day he was born, and has gone on being so since he died. But I'll be free of him yet, you see if I'm not – and if the only way to lay his ghost is to marry his widow, then marry her I will, and take what pleasures I can from it. There are hidden fires there, Ben, and not so far below the surface either. That woman is a volcano waiting to erupt.'

'Then take care you don't get burned in the fire,' Ben said, but Vivian snorted.

'I think I know how to take care of myself, Ben, thank 'ee. And I know how to take care of her too. Francis Pagnel!' He spat the name contemptuously as if it were a taste he despised. 'She may have been wed to him for fifteen years, aye and borne his sons as well, but I'll wager she's never known what it is to have a *man* in her bed. But she'll find out.' A slow smile curved his fleshy lips. 'Aye, she'll find out . . .'

As soon as the February snows melted away and the March winds dried the miry roads, Rebecca set out on her travels. She took her maid Betsy and, after some pressure, the footman Robert.

'I don't need two servants,' she protested when discussing her plans with her disapproving family. 'Betsy and I will manage very well.'

'And who will carry your luggage?' Tom demanded. 'You mean to hump boxes and trunks about all by yourself, do you? A fine picture that will give your prospective customers!'

'And it's no use saying you won't take much,' Nancy added. 'You know very well that each dress you wear will need a box to itself. Besides, Tom's right – people take a lot of account of appearances and if they think you're too poor to employ a manservant to see you about the roads –'

'Oh, very well.' Rebecca gave in. 'I'll take the boot-boy.'

'The *boot-boy*?' Polly, also present at this conference, was outraged. 'Why, he'd be worse than no one at all. And don't say you'll take Billy either – he's all very well for an odd-job, but he'd be worse than a child out on the roads. No, you need someone who's travelled a bit himself and knows what's what. Robert will do. He comes from Yorkshire.'

Rebecca smiled faintly but agreed that Robert, who had at least some experience of the world outside Kidderminster, would be the best person to go with her. And the household would manage better without a footman than without an odd-job man, for Billy was always busy mending this and repairing that, doing all the small tasks essential in any household.

The next few weeks were taken up with preparations, but at last everything was ready. On the day before she was due to leave, Daniel came into the room where Rebecca sat going over her lists for the last time.

'Mother, are you sure you don't want me to come with you?'

Rebecca looked up and smiled.

'Daniel, we've talked about this so many times. Your place is here, looking after things and getting on with your studies. Jaunting around the countryside with me isn't going to get you to Oxford.'

Daniel sat down, leaning back in his chair, and stretched his legs out to the hearth. A beam of pale April sunlight shone through the window, lighting up a bowl of daffodils. It touched his head in passing, bringing the warmth of auburn to his dark hair. He frowned at his boots.

'I'm not sure I want to go to Oxford after all.'

Rebecca laid down her pen and stared at him.

'Not want to go to Oxford! Daniel, you're joking.'

'I'm not.' He turned his dark eyes on her. 'What's the use of it, Mother? Spending my life in study, while you work like a slave to keep me in comfort. And what will I do with what

I learn? Simply pass it on to others, who may in turn do the same. The same knowledge, being handed down through the generations, and nobody actually *doing* anything with it.'

'But it must be handed down,' Rebecca said. 'We can't let learning die. It must be used.'

'*Used*, yes. Someone, sometime, will be able to take that knowledge and make use of it in some real, practical way. And I agree, that to be used it has to be passed on. But that's all I'll be – just one in the line, passing it on like a bucket of water in a chain of firefighters. I won't be using it. And I feel I should.' He lifted his feet from the hearth and tucked them beneath his chair, leaning forward to gaze at her. 'Mother, I know I have a good brain. That's no credit to me – I was born with it. It's more credit to you, that you've encouraged me to use it and given me the opportunities to improve it. But is it right to use it just to amass knowledge – and not even new knowledge, but simply learning what other, wiser men have acquired? Isn't that just treating it like a basket – something to be filled? Shouldn't I be doing something with it – something *new*?'

Rebecca felt helpless, and a little angry. As if she had not enough to be thinking of at this moment! But she controlled her irritation. Daniel had a right to be thinking of his own life, after all.

'Don't you think that you'll be able to consider that better when you've been to Oxford?' she asked gently. 'By all means, use your brain, Daniel – it's why it was given you. But learn as much as you can first. When you've done that, you'll know better how to use what you've learned.'

'Will I?' he asked. 'Or will I simply know what a lot of old men want me to know? Perhaps by then I'll have forgotten the things I know today – perhaps I'll have lost more than I gain.'

Rebecca gazed at him, at a loss to know how to answer. What was in his mind? she wondered. What was it that put that troubled look on his face?

For some time now she had been uneasily aware that all was not well with Daniel. Several times, she had caught him with a strange, yearning expression on his face, yet when she had questioned him he had answered that nothing was wrong. And, knowing that he had even as a little boy preferred to keep his troubles private, she had not pressed.

Perhaps I should have, she thought now, watching his brooding face. Perhaps I should not have respected his privacy. But he's always seemed to need it – ever since Geoffrey died, he's been over-quiet, thinking his own thoughts, and I've allowed him to do so. And now . . . Now, he's in trouble and I can't get near him.

'Daniel,' she said gently, 'you know that I've always believed you capable of thinking for yourself. But don't forget that you're young yet. You know you haven't learned everything there is to learn. Don't be afraid to ask for help when you need it.'

He looked at her. 'Do you think I need help now?'

'I think you may do,' she said and for the first time felt a deep regret that she was going away, leaving her sons. And for a moment, she wondered whether she should indeed let Daniel come with her.

But before she could say more, the door opened and they both turned to see Vivian enter the room. He glanced at Daniel, frowning, and the boy got hastily to his feet.

'Vivian.' Rebecca held out her hand, hiding her disappointment. Just when she and Daniel might have been on the brink of a confidence . . . But the moment was gone. A quick look at her son's face showed her that he had retreated into himself again. Sighing a little, she summoned up a smile for Vivian, though since his proposal she always felt a little uneasy in his presence.

He bowed briefly over her hand. 'I thought I'd come to see if there were any last-minute tasks I could undertake. I imagine there is no chance that you'll have a change of heart and abandon this foolish scheme.' She shook her head, smiling. 'No, I thought not. Well, at least I can see to affairs here for you. You'll want your household looked after as well as your business.'

'It's all in hand, Vivian. Daniel is a sensible boy, he'll see that William doesn't get into mischief, and Polly will look after the house. As for the business, Tom will naturally be in charge there.'

Vivian looked exasperated. 'Daniel! Polly! A sixteen-year-old boy and a housekeeper. Forgive me, Rebecca, if I say that to me your arrangements seem remarkably lax. As for the business –'

'Tom's perfectly competent. And I trust Polly as I would trust a sister. I don't expect any problems while I'm away, Vivian.' She looked at his darkened face and relented a little. After all, he had offered help and it was churlish of her to refuse it. 'But I would be glad to know that they could come to you for any help that might be needed,' she added, and gave him a smile.

Vivian grunted. He sat down in the chair Daniel had just vacated, shooting a look at her from under his brows. 'You'd better let them know that then.' He glanced at Daniel, standing uneasily between them. 'I'd like a private word with your mother, if you don't mind.'

Daniel turned towards her and she nodded, though not entirely happy to be left alone with Vivian. She had never given him any real answer to his proposal and had avoided any discussion with him of her future, beyond making it clear that she intended to make this journey. But he could not be avoided for ever, and she supposed that it was inevitable he should insist on a confrontation tonight.

'Go to bed now, Daniel,' she said quietly. 'I've an early start in the morning and I should like you to see me off. Perhaps your uncle has brought Lucy with him? You could go and talk with her a while.'

'I didn't bring Lucy,' Vivian said abruptly, and Rebecca saw the hot colour flood into Daniel's face. It was something to do with his uncle, this trouble that nagged at him, she thought anxiously, and once again wondered if she were being wise in leaving Daniel here. He was growing so fast, almost a man – who knew what might be going on in that head of his?

Daniel took his leave and the door closed behind him.

Rebecca turned back to the fire, still uneasy, and Vivian took out his pipe and began to fill it.

'You don't object if I smoke?' He tamped the tobacco down and made a light. 'I don't have to tell you, Rebecca, that I disapprove most strongly of this hare-brained scheme of yours. Jaunting off around the country, making a spectacle of yourself . . . But I haven't come to talk to you about that. It's quite useless. No, I want to talk to you about something different.'

Here it was. She braced herself then said quietly, 'You're waiting for an answer to your proposal.'

'And is it surprising?' he demanded. 'I made that offer weeks ago. In common courtesy, I might have expected an answer by now.'

'You told me you didn't wish an instant answer. You know I'm only just out of mourning. You said I could have time –'

'And by God, you've had it. Time enough to plan this ludicrous journey. If you've time for that, you've had time to consider whether you're to be my wife or not.' She watched as the muscles of his face tautened. 'How long does a man have to wait, Rebecca? Do you have any idea what it's like to be in my position?'

She stared at him. No, I don't, she thought in surprise. I don't know at all what it's like to be in your position. Because I don't know what you're really thinking, feeling.

'Why do you want to marry me, Vivian?' she asked curiously. 'Is it because you love me – or is it something else? Can you tell me?'

'Love?' He gave a short bark of laughter. 'That's the stuff of romantic stories, Rebecca, the kind of thing your housemaids read in their beds. But you've been married – you know it isn't like that, all gallant knights and ladies in distress.'

'Francis and I loved each other,' she said quietly. 'I couldn't offer you that kind of love, Vivian.'

'And I don't ask for it,' he answered at once. 'I know nothing of that kind of love, as you call it. Being dependent on another person for happiness – no, that's not my way. I'd not look to

123

you to make me happy, nor would I expect you to look to me. A wife is what I want, and you're the best person to be my wife, Rebecca. Haven't you been as good as a mother to my daughters all these years? Haven't you been in and out of my house until you know it as well as I do? Don't we see each other most days of the week as it is?'

'All those things are true,' she said thoughtfully. 'But seeing each other daily and being free of each other's homes isn't the same as living together, Vivian. We're both free now, able to make our own decisions – how will we feel when we have to consult the other before deciding anything? How if we don't agree?'

Vivian stared at her. 'It's an odd idea you have of marriage,' he said at last. 'Or an odd sort of marriage you had with Frank. Consultation? On what matters would we need to consult? The affairs of the household would be yours to decide, naturally – and all others, mine.' He smiled at her. 'You look surprised, my dear, but you surely know that this is the way all normal marriages are conducted. And once that's understood, what need is there for disagreement?'

Rebecca felt a coldness around her heart. She knew that Vivian's views were those of most men, and the basis of most marriages – and she had to admit that, as far as one could tell, such marriages could be content. But – for her? After loving Francis, after living with him, working with him, planning their future together, striving together to bring the co-operative into being?

Marriage with Vivian, or with any man who would see her as a normal, subservient wife would be like living in a cage.

'Well?' he said with a touch of impatience in his voice. 'Do you have an answer for me, Rebecca? Can you give me any hint of what I might hope for when you return from this escapade?'

She looked at him, wondering what he would do if she said yes. Presumably he would consider himself already to have rights over her, rights which he would begin to exercise at once – by forbidding her to go on her journey. The cage would close around her before she had finished speaking. There would be no more freedom – no more visiting the carpet shops at will, no more consulting with Tom, talking to the weavers; no more decisions to be made. Everything she possessed and loved would become Vivian's, to do with as he wished. And she knew exactly what he would do.

'I'm sorry, Vivian,' she said in a low voice. 'I can't give you any hope at all. You see, for me to marry anyone I *must* feel love – the sort of love you say yourself you don't understand.' She looked at him with appeal. 'I wish you could understand it, Vivian – I wish you could feel it. It must be so cold and lonely if you've never experienced real love.'

She saw his face darken and wondered if she had gone too far. Perhaps her words had struck him somewhere very deep. He had, after all, been married and widowed – and who was to say what his feelings for Maria had been?

Then he spoke, harshly. 'You're a fool, Rebecca. One would think that after all that's happened to you, you'd take a more sensible view of matters – but no, you still fill your head with romantic nonsense. Well, you'll learn eventually – perhaps this ridiculous journey of yours will teach you. And when you do, maybe you'll be glad enough to turn to me.'

He rose from his chair and looked down at her, and she looked back into his hard, angry eyes and realised the baffled disappointment that lay behind them. Poor Vivian! she thought. He could never accustom himself to not getting what he wanted. And yet, how many times has he been given what he wanted? No son, no wife . . . She felt a sudden warm need to allay his disappointment, and got up to stand with him, laying her hand on his arm.

'Vivian, I'm sorry. Please don't be angry with me. And – yes, if you would be good enough to oversee things here while I'm gone, I'll be very glad of it. I'll feel happier, knowing that Daniel had you to turn to.' He glanced down at her, his dark eyes unreadable, and she went on quickly, before she could change her mind. 'And at the carpet-shop too – I'm sure Tom would be glad to have your advice. There are bound to be problems he'll need help with. Just an eye cast over the ledgers – that sort of thing. Will you do that for me, Vivian? And we'll talk again when I come back.'

She regretted the last sentence immediately. Would Vivian interpret that as a sign that he might after all have hope? But it was too late to take it back, and at least he was looking less angry now.

'You'd better let Daniel and Tom know that you want me to do that,' he said. 'Or they'll not let me in. Your brother doesn't trust me in the carpet-shop office as it is.'

'Oh, he doesn't mistrust you. He's just jealous of his position there and a little afraid that I might give him another clerk – he's always been proud of his learning.' She laughed a little. 'He's suspicious of anyone who sits at his desk, but he won't be afraid you're after his job. But I'll tell him. And I shan't be away so very long, after all – only a few weeks.'

'And you really expect to gain enough orders in that time? Enough to save your business?'

Rebecca looked into the fire. 'I have to,' she said quietly, and knew that it was true. Every carpet manufacturer in the country was facing a difficult time, and the co-operative more than most. If she could not pull it to its feet with this one last great effort, she might as well close down the looms and turn the weavers into the street.

And that, she thought passionately, she would never do. She had seen too much poverty, too much distress, ever to turn a single weaver away from her looms.

The co-operative would go on, whatever the personal cost to herself.

'So she's gone.' Lucy stooped to pick a daffodil and caressed its yellow trumpet absently. She glanced at Daniel. 'I thought she might take you or William with her.'

He shook his head. 'I wanted to go, but she'd have none of it. And Will would certainly have been more use to her, young though he is. I believe he knows as much about carpet-making now as any of the weavers – almost as much as my Uncle Tom. Which I shall never do.'

They walked slowly along the garden path. It was a rare opportunity to be together, afforded by Vivian's visit to the co-operative. Lucy, so closely guarded now by her governess, had slipped out on the pretext of going with him and time was short, for she must be back before her father returned for dinner.

'Don't you think you'll ever go into the business?' she asked. 'I know my father thinks you've a future with him, if you'd only agree to it.'

'Agree to become his, you mean, body and soul! No, I won't ever go willingly into carpets, Lucy – though I can see I might have to, if Mother needs me. But even that doesn't seem likely. William's all the help she'll need. No, I must find my own path.'

'Oxford,' she said, but he shook his head.

'I don't know. I feel less sure about that, these days. Oh, to study, yes – I want to *know* more. But to become a don or a teacher of any kind – no, there must be more than that for me. Just passing on knowledge . . .' He stopped and looked earnestly into her face. 'It's not enough. I want to *do* something – something useful. I don't want to live and die amongst my books.'

'What sort of thing?' she asked thoughtfully, but he shook his head again.

'That's just the trouble – I don't know. Not the usual things – the Army or the Church. Something other than that – something more real, in a way.' He sighed and paced on along the narrow path, towards the little wood that lay at the end of the garden. 'I wish Matthew were here. He could advise me – he's done so much, been to so many places.'

'Matthew Farrell? But he's in Australia now. He murdered a man.'

'He killed a man by accident,' Daniel corrected her. 'And he was my father's best friend, and I know my mother misses him sorely. He would have been so much help all this time. He knows the world – not just this narrow corner of it.'

Lucy was silent for a moment. Then she said, 'Are you tired of Kidderminster, Daniel? Is that what it is? Do you want to strike out – go to London, perhaps?'

'London? No, I've heard enough of that place never to want to see it again. But the idea of leaving Kidderminster . . .' They came within the shelter of the trees and he stopped and put his hands on her arms, looking gravely down into her eyes. 'Lucy, do you think you could make a life with me in America?'

'*America*?'

Astonished, she stared back at him. Then her blue eyes took fire and her face lit with excitement.

'Do you really mean it, Daniel? America? Us? But – what would we do there?'

'I don't know yet. But the more I think about it, the more I feel that a new country is what I am looking for. A whole new way of life – opportunities that can't be dreamed of here, in Kidderminster, or even in England. That's another reason why I wish Matthew were here. He's been to America, lived there – he knows the country. He's told so many stories of it . . .' Daniel's eyes took on a faraway look. 'I've kept my eyes on my books for long enough, Lucy. It's nearly time I began to look at other things.' And then he looked back at her and added, 'But only if you'll be there with me.'

'America,' she said softly, and then gave a little laugh of excitement. 'Oh, Daniel, it sounds wonderful.'

'So you'd come? If I finish my schooling and then decide to go? You'd come with me?'

'Come with you?' she said, and flung herself into his arms. 'Just try going without me, Daniel!'

He hugged her and they clung together for a while. Then she withdrew slightly and whispered, 'I shall have to go soon. Papa will be back and asking questions if I'm not there.'

'When shall I see you again?' he asked and she shook her head.

'I don't know – I'll get away at the first chance, you may be sure. But he keeps such a close eye on me now – he hates me to be out of his sight. And he talks of bringing home suitors. I ask you, *suitors*! As if I were some fairytale princess. He wants me married and off his hands, but I won't even look at any of the horrible old men he brings home. He can't force me to marry them, can he?'

'I hope not,' Daniel said gravely, though he knew that fathers could and did force their daughters to marry. He thought of Lucy, paraded before the kind of 'suitor' that Vivian would think suitable – rich, middle-aged or even elderly – and shuddered. 'Darling, if you ever need me, for whatever reason, you will let me know, won't you? I'd not let anything happen to you. I'd do anything . . .'

'It's all right.' She pressed herself softly against him. 'Papa's not that bad. He wouldn't make me do anything I don't want to do, I'm sure of it.' She looked up at him, her eyes shining. 'We only have to wait, Daniel. And we have time.'

'Yes.' He held her close, feeling an age older than his seventeen years. 'We have plenty of time.'

It became Vivian's habit to call in at the co-operative each morning and visit Tom in his office. His visits were no more welcome to Tom than they had been before, but Rebecca had told her brother before she went away that Vivian had offered his help and she wanted Tom to accept it. 'He means well by us, and he's the biggest manufacturer in Kidderminster now,' she had said. 'It would be very foolish to refuse any help he can give.'

Tom had pushed out his lip but said nothing. It was his opinion, given freely and often to Nancy, that Rebecca had never seen the truth of Vivian, but he knew better than to say so now. But he was careful about what he let Vivian see in the small, noisy office, and there were a good many new orders which were not entered in the big ledgers during those weeks.

'It doesn't look as if Rebecca's journey is achieving much,' Vivian remarked one morning. 'No new customers gained and several older ones lost. It's time she admitted the truth and came home.'

'And what do you reckon's the truth, then?' Tom said as little as possible to Vivian when they were together, but he couldn't let this challenge go by.

'Why, that the co-operative is facing ruin, of course.' Vivian glanced up and looked through the small window at the looms, working steadily in the main shop. 'Oh, I know you've work on at present, orders that were given some months ago – out of pity as much as anything, I imagine – but what will you be doing in six months' time? Nothing, by all appearances. No.' He slammed the big book shut. 'Time's running out for Rebecca and for you, and if you can't face it soon you'll get a very big shock. And it'll be no use running to me for help then, I've offered it long enough.' He met Tom's eyes. 'I'm willing to give you both one more chance – and only one.'

'And what's that?' Tom demanded truculently. He didn't want to ask at all, but even with the orders he'd kept hidden from Vivian he knew that the co-operative's future was uncertain. It was all too true that more old customers had left them, and he had a very good idea where they had taken their custom. Once again, he wished that Vivian had never been allowed into this office. It was only after that first visit of his that they'd begun to lose customers, and Tom had never rid himself of the suspicion that the other man had deliberately stolen them. There was nothing to stop him doing so again.

Vivian gave him a lazy smile, and Tom had difficulty in restraining himself from knocking it from his face.

'Hand everything over to me now,' he said. 'We'll come to a suitable financial arrangement when I've looked at the books – *all* of them,' he added with a look that told Tom that he hadn't been fooled in the least by the apparent lack of new orders. 'I'll combine your manufacturing with mine – the best elements of both, your designs and my looms. We'll keep these shops for making exclusive designs as they do now, and you can have a job as overseer. Far better suited to your talents, I think. You don't really feel happy working in the office amongst all these books, do you?'

Tom stared at him. What Vivian was suggesting was nothing less than a complete taking over of the entire business. The co-operative broken up, the weavers kept on or dismissed according to Vivian's whim, himself reduced to the position of overseer. And Rebecca?

Tom knew well enough that there would be no place for Rebecca. So what would happen to her?

'Well?' Vivian said softly.

'You call that a chance?' Tom said, his voice rough. 'It's no chance at all. You'll tek over everything and leave nothing. And what about Becky? What's she to do?'

'Rebecca would be well provided for. I'm not proposing to steal your business, Himley. A proper price would be paid.'

'At the lowest valuation you can get,' Tom growled. 'What's the worth of an ailing business?'

'So you admit it's ailing!' Vivian cut in quickly, and Tom cursed himself.

'Whether 'tis or not, you'd do your best to prove it so. And would that price be enough to keep Becky for the rest of her days? Bring up her boys and start them off? They ent like me, brought up to the weaver's loom – they're bred for summat different now. Would you see to it that they got their proper chances?'

'That would be between Rebecca and myself,' Vivian said coldly. 'William's already a useful young man and Daniel has a good head on his shoulders if he cares to use it. Provided they behave themselves, there would be nothing to worry about.'

Tom stared at him. Then he said, 'Well, we can't do anything about it till Becky gets back. I don't even know why you're talking to me about it now.'

'Because there's no reason at all to wait.' Vivian smiled at him. 'This is a co-operative, isn't it? Everyone has his say – or do I understand wrongly? Rebecca has no casting vote, nor any voice stronger than that of any man here.' He leaned forward, speaking persuasively, confidentially. 'You and I are men of the world, Tom. We know the truth and we can face it. Rebecca's a woman – oh, she's done wonderfully in her way, I won't deny that, but she's like all women, too emotional. She sees this business almost as if it's a child – her child. She'll fight for it even when everyone around her can see it's dying. She's doing that now. And you and I both know what the result of that will be – disaster. For you, for her, for the boys – and for every man working those looms out there.' He glanced through the little window. 'Do you think they'll thank you for waiting, when the looms stop and the doors close and they're all out in the street looking for new jobs – jobs which may not be there? Do you think they'll be grateful to you then?'

Tom shifted uneasily in his chair. 'But why should a few weeks make any difference? If you'll tek it over now, you'll tek it over then. Why not let Becky –'

'Two reasons.' Vivian held up his hands and laid one forefinger against the other. 'First, Rebecca won't see reason. You know that and I know that. She'll bring emotion into it, just as I've been saying. It's better that it should be done and over with before she returns. Second, you're losing time now, and with time you lose customers. Several have already left you.' He tapped the ledger. 'Oh, I know that I've gained some of your losses – how can I deny that? But they won't all come to me, Tom, some of them will go to other manufacturers. Those orders will be lost to both of us and we may never regain them. And who is to say how many orders Rebecca will lose by her tramping, to set against those few she may gain? Many people find the spectacle of a woman setting out to do a man's work distasteful – even offensive. I've heard of several men whose wives have shown very clearly that they don't want their husbands dealing with Pagnel & Himley. Not, at least, while it's being run by a woman.'

Tom was silent. Vivian's words were difficult to refute, yet he felt sure there was a flaw in them somewhere. He looked out of the window into the big carpet shop, saw the looms that Francis had put in so proudly, the men who had worked so willingly for them. He saw the Dream that Francis and Rebecca had talked of so often vanishing like a wisp of smoke. He shook his head, unable to make sense of it. Why had it had to happen like this? Was it just because Francis had died or was there some other reason? Would it have failed anyway – or were there other forces involved, undercurrents he didn't fully understand working to undermine all that he and his sister had built up?

'True enough, I never wanted Becky to go away,' he said at last. 'But she would do it and she was never one to give up easy. I think she ought to be let to have this chance – we ought to wait till she comes back and see what happens then.'

'I can tell you what will happen then,' Vivian said. 'The customers you still have will dwindle away. The new orders – if any – that Rebecca brings back will be cancelled. People will lose faith in Pagnel & Himley and when that happens you'll go down very quickly indeed. And you'll be glad of any offer to buy the shop and machinery then. Any offer at all.'

Tom pulled at his lip. Then shook his head again.

'I'm sorry, Mr Vivian, I can't do it. I can't go against our Becky behind her back. You'll have to wait 'til she's home again – and that's my last word on it.'

Chapter Seven

Rebecca came home on a day when bluebells were beginning to spread a misty carpet in the woods around Kidderminster. Unheralded, she alighted from the coach in the main square and looked around her at the familiar buildings.

It was good to be home again. Already she could see faces she knew, and she summoned a carter to take her luggage to the house on Mount Pleasant and sent Betsy and Robert with him, despite their protests.

'I've walked that short distance alone many a time,' she said firmly, 'and I'd like to do it now. And you can warn the household I'm coming – I know Mrs Barlow will be cross that she's not had time to make preparations. Not that she needs to – she'll have kept the house like a new pin, and all I shall want is a hot drink and a rest in my own favourite chair before I start work.'

'Start work!' Betsy commented as she and the footman rattled away in the cart, surrounded by boxes and trunks. 'As if she'd bin away on holiday. You'd think she'd want a few days to settle back in, wouldn't you?'

'Not her.' Robert settled himself as comfortably as possible on the narrow bench that ran round the inside of the cart. 'She could give a few of the masters I've had tips on how to get a day's work done. Comes from having bin a servant, I reckon – had her training in the right school.'

'Aye.' Betsy gazed around her. 'Well, I'm not sorry to be back, I'll say that. Never thought I would be, mind – some of the places we seen up north are right pretty. But there's nowhere like good old Kidder.'

'No, home's best,' Robert agreed. He looked at her and grinned. 'Still, it's bin a good trip for us, haven't it? Almost like a honeymoon ...' His grin widened as Betsy blushed and glanced quickly at the carter, sitting above them. Then he reached over, took her hand and dropped his voice to a whisper. 'Well, how about it, Bet? You know – what I asked you the other day? Now we've had the honeymoon, in a manner o' speaking, how about having the wedding?'

Rebecca watched the cart disappear up the hill and smiled to herself. She was well aware of what had been going on between her two servants and, apart from a quiet warning to both to be discreet and take care, had turned a blind eye. Most mistresses would, she knew, have dismissed the pair out of hand, but Rebecca had had her own experience of being sent away penniless after committing the crime of falling in love, and she would not inflict that despair on anyone. But she would be glad if, now they were home, the two were to ask permission to wed.

There was nothing to compare with the loving bond of wedlock, she thought sadly. Even though no marriage could run smoothly all the time – even she and Francis had had their misunderstandings, though born largely from their love. But to know that there was someone who loved you above all others, who put your welfare even above their own – and to return those feelings in full measure ... no, there could be nothing better than that. And no real marriage without it.

Her thoughts turned to Vivian and his proposal and once again her instincts made rebellion. There was not that foundation of love between them that was so necessary for a happy marriage. Oh, she knew that he admired her, that his hand would linger under her elbow, that he would make opportunities to brush against her as they passed. And she could not deny that she had sometimes felt a touch of excitement herself when catching his dark eyes on her. It had been so long since she and Francis had been able to love each other fully, even before his death, and her body was restless for a man's touch. But that – no, that was not love, and to lie with a man just to soothe that restlessness would be a betrayal of the expression which had given her and Francis such joy.

Perhaps Vivian would have decided not to renew his proposal. He must have seen that she meant her refusal and that it would be useless to press her. By now, he might even have found someone else to take Maria's place and be wife to him and mother to his daughters.

But Rebecca knew that this was unlikely. In the years since Maria's death, Vivian had shown no sign of wanting to marry again. And Rebecca was uncomfortably aware that she possessed certain advantages that no other woman could give him. Her son, who already bore the Pagnel name and would inherit the Pagnel house. Her business, with a name for fine quality carpets and original designs. Those loyal customers who had stayed with her and who, because of their names and status, Vivian would so much like to have on his own list.

She reached the gates of Pagnel House and stood looking down over the red roofs of the town. She had come here first as a trembling ten year old, brought by her mother to ask for a job as scullerymaid. They had stood here together for a moment, each aware that from now on life would never be the same. For a brief second, Rebecca could feel her small hand once more held within her mother's, and tears stung her eyes. Poor Fanny, whose life had been so hard and whose death so cruel. Would she have been able to believe it if she had been told that her daughter would stand here, years later, as mistress of the house? It would have seemed as likely as that Rebecca might become queen.

Yet here she was, and about to walk up the wide drive, not going round the narrower path to the kitchen door as she had then. For a moment, she hesitated – why not go straight to the kitchen which had been her home for so long, and surprise Polly who had befriended her on that first day? And then she knew she could not. Friend she might be, but mistress she was, and there were certain rules that even she must obey. And to go unannounced into the servants' quarters when she was still thought to be away from home, would be breaking those rules.

For the first time, Rebecca felt the width of the gulf between

137

herself and her servants. And a shadow of loneliness fell upon her heart.

'Mother! Why didn't you let us know you were coming?'

Rebecca swung round and a smile broke upon her face as she saw her elder son coming up the hill behind her. She held out her arms and he came and hugged her, and she felt the warmth of his body and smelt the good, male smell of him. Then she withdrew from him slightly and gazed at him, and it was as if she saw him for the first time.

And perhaps she did. Because this Daniel was not the Daniel she had left behind, a lanky and uncertain boy. This Daniel was a boy no longer but a man, tall and strong. And there was a new maturity in his face, a new sense of purpose about his bearing. She looked at him, suddenly shy – shy of her own son! – and he smiled the old grave smile that had always been his, and she laughed with relief.

'Danny! For a moment you seemed quite a stranger. You've grown so much – have I really only been gone a few weeks?'

'It seems longer to us all,' he said. 'I'm glad you're back. But you should have sent word.'

Rebecca shrugged. 'It would have taken almost as long to reach you as I did myself. And once I'd decided to come, I couldn't wait – I wanted so badly to be home.' She linked her arm in his. 'I've missed you all so much, Daniel.'

'No more than we've missed you. The house has seemed empty.' They began to walk up the drive together. 'Has your journey been successful, Mother? Was it worth making?'

'Tell me first about things here. How are all the family? Is William behaving himself? Tom and Nancy, are they well? And Lucy and the other girls, how are they? Have you seen much of them?'

'A little.' Daniel hesitated and she glanced at him, aware of some conflict going on within him. Fear gripped her heart. Was someone ill? And she remembered that other time when she had returned from a journey and been told that her second son, Geoffrey, had been drowned.

She clutched his arm. 'Is something wrong, Daniel? Is

anyone ill or – or . . . Tell me quickly, for God's sake, if anything's happened.'

He looked down at her, surprised, and she relaxed. 'Of course no one's ill. Everyone is as healthy as when you went – and William is fast making himself completely indispensable in the factory. I shan't be surprised if he asks you again to let him leave school. Uncle Tom and Aunt Nancy are just the same as ever and have looked after us well. Uncle Vivian has been into the house most days, and the factory as well, though I'm not sure Uncle Tom welcomed his help there.' He hesitated then went on rather quickly, 'And the girls are as pretty as ever, of course. Susan's looking forward to her wedding and making plans all the time, and the little ones have a new game . . .'

He rattled on, telling her of all the small doings she wanted to hear, and Rebecca watched his face and listened to his tone as he did so. It was unlike Daniel to talk so freely that it was almost chatter, and she wondered again if something had happened that he wasn't telling her. Yet what could it be?

She remembered that moment just before she'd left Kidder-minster – the sense that Daniel was in some kind of trouble. Yet what possible troubles could he have? Surely nothing serious, nothing more than the troubles any half-grown child would have, looming so large yet really so little.

They were at the door now, and as they approached Rebecca saw it swing wide open and William come tumbling out. As he fell into her arms she saw that all the servants were in the hall, caps hastily straightened, fresh aprons quickly put on, with Polly at their head. And as, laughing, she caught her son and looked past him to the men and women who were also a part of her family, she felt the warmth of homecoming spread through her heart and body.

Her worries over Daniel faded. Pains he might have, but they were growing pains, nothing more.

'Now that you're back,' Tom said, 'mebbe there'll be no more need for Vivian Pagnel to be in and out of here like he owned the place.'

139

Rebecca looked at him. They were sitting in his small, dusty office, with the clatter of the looms filling the big carpet-making shop and the three clerks working industriously at their ledgers in the outer office.

'He hasn't bothered you, has he, Tom? He knew you were in charge – he only offered to give an eye to things and help if he were needed.'

'Aye, and so he might, but it weren't needed, were it?' Tom sounded sulky and Rebecca sighed a little. Her brother had grown more morose lately, seeing the dark side of every issue, and she had known that he would resent Vivian's presence.

'Well, I'm glad it wasn't needed,' she said calmly. 'And I never thought it would be. I trust you completely, Tom. But when Vivian offered, I could hardly say no. I didn't want to offend him.'

'No, rather offend your own flesh and blood,' Tom said, and then coloured. 'I'm sorry, Becky, I shouldn't have said that. But why should you be so heedful of his feelings? He's never been friend to us after all.'

'Now, that's not true. He's been good to me, Tom. And he did help you and Bessie get away to London.'

'Aye, because he thought to have us there to serve his own purposes. You know what he had in mind for our Bess.' Tom spoke angrily, and Rebecca was silent. 'I'm sorry, Becky, I don't trust him. And I'm surprised you do. Last time you let him in here we lost half a dozen of our best customers – now, that weren't no coincidence. I just wonder how many we'll lose this time.'

'None, I'm sure.' Rebecca spoke strongly. 'Vivian wishes us well, Tom, I'm sure of it. It must have been a coincidence. Anyway, I see we still have all the new orders I gained on my journey, so he clearly isn't stealing them, as you suspect.'

'No, because I kept all them orders separate. He never knew where they came from. But if you keeps on telling him all our business –'

'I don't do that!'

'Don't you?' Tom gave her a level look from beneath shaggy brows and reminded her suddenly of their father, Will Himley. 'So what were you talking about so quiet-like when I come into your drawing room last Sunday evening and found you with your heads together? Not that game of cribbage you were supposed to be playing, I'll warrant.'

Rebecca felt herself blush. 'We were just discussing all the things that have happened since I went away. Tom, I don't know why you're so suspicious.'

'Don't you? Well, mebbe I'll tell you.' Again, Tom shot her that disturbing look. 'Mebbe it'd surprise you to know that your precious Vivian came in here not three weeks since and tried to persuade me to hand over the business to him – lock, stock and barrel. Aye, and wouldn't even offer a price until he'd been through all the books and made his own valuation on it – and we can all guess what sort of valuation *that* would be.' He watched Rebecca's face as he spoke, taking a grim sort of satisfaction from the shock in her eyes. 'And to top it all, he offered me a job as overseer. *Overseer!*'

There was a moment's silence. Then Rebecca said in a faint voice, 'You must have misunderstood him, Tom.'

'Oh, yes – *I* must have misunderstood him! It couldn't be *you* who misunderstood him, could it? It couldn't be you as wears blinkers where that man's concerned.' Tom leaned forwards over his desk and jabbed his fingers towards her face. 'I tell you, Becky, Vivian Pagnel means no good by us and if 'twas left to me he'd never be let over the threshold again.'

Rebecca pulled herself together and spoke more firmly. 'Tom, you're letting your own emotions run away with you. You've never liked Vivian and I understand you have good reasons for that. But what he was in the past and what he is now are two different things. And I'm sure he –'

'You think he's changed?' Tom cut in. 'You think he's different now – thinks different, acts different? Tell me this, Becky, do *you* feel any different now from when you were a young girl? Do you think *you're* a different person?'

Rebecca hesitated. Did she feel differently from the young

Rebecca who had set out for London, alone and afraid? Was she a different person from the girl who had become Francis's wife, who had borne his children, helped him set up the co-operative? Reluctantly, she shook her head.

'No, I don't.'

'No,' Tom said. 'Neither do I. Nor does anyone, I don't suppose – and *nor does Vivian Pagnel*. He's the same man he's allus been, Becky, and don't you forget it.'

Rebecca sighed. There was clearly going to be no shifting Tom from his stance, and no point in further argument. But she must know more about this offer he had made – whether Tom had got it wrong or not, she still needed to know.

'Tom, are you sure you understood aright about Vivian's wanting to buy the co-operative? It sounds so unlikely. And why should he make such an offer with me away? Why not wait until I came back?'

'Because he knew you'd never agree, of course. He told me that himself – said you'd bring emotion into it, that you'd treat the business like a child and fight for it even when it was dying.' He stopped suddenly and gave her a glance of apology. 'I'm sorry, Becky, it was him said those things, not me. He sees things different.'

'Of course he does.' Rebecca strove to keep her voice brisk. To let her emotion show through now would only prove Vivian's words. 'But even if he had persuaded you, Tom, he would still have had to wait for me to return.'

'No,' Tom said flatly, 'he wouldn't. I said that too. I told him I couldn't discuss it without you – and you know what he said? He told me you weren't necessary. You didn't have a casting vote. The business is a co-operative and if enough of us agreed to his taking over, we could fix it all up there and then, while you were still away. And that's what he wanted to do, Becky.'

Rebecca stared at him. Her heart was cold, a piece of ice beating jaggedly in her breast. She shook her head unbelievingly.

'It's not true, Tom. You must have got it wrong. You've misunderstood him.' But she knew, as she looked at his face, that she had not. Tom might be uneducated but he was not a fool. And he would not have misunderstood plain speaking.

But Vivian's words were not always plain. He spoke often in metaphor, or with hidden meanings. Sentences that came smoothly from his lips turned out afterwards to be obscure, so that although you felt at the time that you understood him you were confused later. His mind worked in devious ways, pursuing a labyrinthine path of its own.

'I'll talk to him,' Rebecca said at last. 'I'll ask him just what he had in mind, and why he couldn't wait for me to come back. And meanwhile –'

She hesitated, but Tom supplied the words. 'Meanwhile, you'll tell him he's not welcome in here any more?' He looked at her face and then said, more gently, 'All right, Becky, I can see you don't want to say it in so many words. I'll tell him myself, if he comes nosing round here again. Unless you says different – but if you do, we'll have some plain talking to do, you and me.'

'Yes.' Rebecca looked at her brother and knew that whatever had happened between him and Vivian, it had left him deeply angered. It must be sorted out and brought into the open. She could not have Tom upset. Yet neither did she want to lose the friendship between herself and Vivian which, uneasy though it might at times be, she still valued.

Vivian was the only man she could turn to, now that Francis was dead. If Matthew hadn't been transported, it might have been different – Matthew, the wanderer, laughing and merry, had nevertheless had a serious and dependable side to him that both she and Francis had recognised. And there had been something else, something private between herself and Matthew, never acknowledged but known to them both, that might now have developed into something stronger. Something she desperately needed.

But Matthew was far away in Australia and might never return. And meanwhile she was here alone, with the burdens of sons and a business upon her shoulders, and no one to help her but Vivian Pagnel.

But could she really depend upon him, if all that Tom had said were true? And if not – what then?

'Well, of course I won't go into the office if it upsets your brother so much.' Vivian stretched his legs out to the fire and spoke lazily, as if it couldn't matter less. 'I'd no idea he had any objection – he never said a word to me about it. In fact, we had some quite productive talks. I thought he was beginning to trust me after all these years.' He gave Rebecca a slow, confidential smile. 'But he's always been a little – well, unpredictable, hasn't he?'

'Unpredictable? What do you mean?' Rebecca felt a small twinge of discomfort. 'What are you hinting at, Vivian?'

'Hinting at? Why, nothing. What is there to hint at? Really, Rebecca, don't you start being touchy too. Tom's a fine man, I've always thought so – why else would I have helped him, all those years ago? But that's just a case in point. He took my money and my help and simply disappeared. He –'

'He was robbed. You know that.'

'Oh, I know that's what he told us. But we've never *really* known what happened, have we?'

'Bess –'

'Your sister knew no more than anyone else,' Vivian stated firmly. 'They were separated when he lost the money and only Tom knows the truth. Oh, I've no doubt it's true enough – there's many a gullible country bumpkin rooked of his money in London. But there was nothing to prevent him from sending me a message, was there? I'd already helped him once. Why should he just disappear like that and go into hiding for six years? Unless he had a guilty conscience,' he added thoughtfully.

Rebecca stared at him. Her heart was beating fast with anger, but through her anger ran a thread of discomfort. Suppose Vivian was right? It was true that nobody but Tom knew exactly what had happened in London. And now that she came to think of it, it *was* odd that he hadn't applied again to Vivian for help. Or at least left a message for

144

him at the address he'd been given. What had he to fear, after all?

'He was very young then,' she said after a minute or two. 'And he'd had a dreadful shock – Jabez dying like that, the fear that he'd be accused of murder . . .'

'Certainly, certainly. It must have been very unpleasant for him.' Vivian paused. 'Enough to turn any man's brain, wouldn't you say?'

Rebecca felt her anger flare again. 'Tom isn't mad, if that's what you're saying! He's as sane as you or I and one of the most dependable men I've ever known. And I don't say that just because he's my brother.'

'Of course you don't,' Vivian said soothingly. 'Rebecca, I'm sorry if I've said anything to upset you. You know I'd never want to do that. But I'm sorry to say that poor Tom does seem to have been behaving a little – well, let's say irrationally, lately. The things you say he told you, for instance. I suppose I could have expressed myself very badly, so that he misunderstood, but – well, can you really believe that I would have tried to take your business over as soon as you were out of the way? Does it sound likely? Obviously neither Tom nor the other men would have agreed to such a suggestion, so why should I have made it?' He shook his head. 'No, your brother has got that completely wrong. I'm only thankful that you've had the good sense to come to me and lay your cards on the table. Why, such a misunderstanding could have ruined our friendship – not to mention any future relationship we might have.'

'So what did you say? What suggestions did you make?'

Vivian shifted in his chair, then leaned forwards to the fire, still needed even though it was now May. He took the poker and altered the position of a lump of coal, turning the smouldering embers into a sputtering flame.

'Why, I simply offered to help a little more in the office, that's all. It seemed to me that the ledgers weren't showing all the business you were doing. If they were, then you were certainly in trouble – but any new orders you were gaining weren't shown at all, and I was afraid they'd got lost or overlooked.'

145

Rebecca opened her mouth, then closed it again. Tom had told her that he hadn't entered the orders in the ledgers for fear that Vivian might poach the new customers. She had been concerned by these worries of his, wondering then if he were being over-cautious. Was this what Vivian meant?

'Whichever it was,' Vivian went on pleasantly, 'it seemed to me that you needed a more careful eye kept on the business. I had your interests completely at heart, Rebecca, believe me. I admit it was a mistake to discuss possible changes with Tom, but you've always looked on him as an equal partner and –'

'Possible changes? What possible changes?'

'Why, a merging of our two businesses. It's a sensible thing to consider, after all. If you really are in serious trouble, which it was beginning to seem you must be, you won't be able to continue. Something will have to be done – and you know I'd do everything I could. I didn't discuss this fully with your brother, of course, that would have been most improper. But I did mention it – more to allay his own obvious fears than for any other reason. And I'm afraid that's what he's misunderstood.' Vivian looked at her, his eyes wide and frank. 'I'm sorry if I've caused any trouble between you.'

'There's been no trouble between me and Tom,' Rebecca said shortly. She sat thinking for a while, then said, 'And you really didn't suggest buying the business out before I came back? You didn't suggest to Tom that it wasn't necessary to wait for me to come back – that I had no casting vote, that I'd be too emotional? You didn't say I thought of the co-operative as a child?'

'As a *child*?' Vivian gave an incredulous laugh, then sobered. 'Rebecca, I'm sorry to say it but it seems that Tom has let this whole affair get completely out of proportion. Oh, I don't blame him – he's had a difficult life and we don't really know what happened to him all those years ago in London. Look at your sister and how she ended. No, if you'll take my advice you'll watch him rather carefully in the future. Let him have responsibility, by all means – but be very sure that it isn't sole responsibility.' He shook his head, then smiled at her. 'Don't look so anxious, Rebecca. Remember that you can always call on me for help. Though of course I'll stay away altogether if that's what you'd prefer.'

She made a gesture, then let her hand fall back on to her lap. How could she answer him? Vivian was so plausible – but he always had been, hadn't he? Yet she had known her own doubts when she'd talked with Tom. What he had told her had sounded so incredible. What *was* the truth?

And if Tom were really beginning to lose his mind – no, she could not, she *would* not countenance such a terrible thought. But ... if he were beginning to misunderstand in such a way – how could she manage? How, without asking for Vivian's help?

He reached across and took the hands that had somehow twisted themselves together on her lap. He unpicked her fingers and held them warmly between his palms.

'I didn't want to trouble you with this as soon as you came home,' he said gently. 'But if you really are in difficulties, Rebecca, don't you think we should talk them over? After all, who else is there for you to turn to? None of the other manufacturers in the town would agree to discuss business with you – and certainly none of them would be willing to help you recover. They'd stab you in the back the moment you turned away. But you and I – well, we've known each other a long time. We're family. Who better to help you?' He paused, then went on even more quietly, 'Who better to go into business with?'

Rebecca looked up at him quickly, but his face told her nothing. 'As I said a few minutes ago,' he went on, 'it's the sensible answer. And even more sensible if –' He hesitated.

'If what?' Rebecca asked, already knowing the answer, and he answered slowly, deliberately.

'It would be even more sensible if you married me. No, don't pull away. Rebecca, you know how I feel, you've known a long time – don't pretend you've not been aware of my regard for you. Even before Frank – well, we won't talk about that.' He spoke hastily, sensing her instinctive withdrawal. 'But I've always been very fond of you, Rebecca. And I've admired you, too – your beauty, your courage, the way you've never let circumstances defeat you. The way you've taken so well to a life which is so different from that you were brought up to.'

'And how would you know what I was brought up to?' Rebecca cut in, with sudden anger. 'The way a weaver lives has always been a mystery to you, Vivian, and one which you were glad to let remain so.'

He smiled. 'I like your temper too,' he said softly. 'Flaring like an ember suddenly blown into life. It reminds me of the times when you were a maid and fought me for your honour.'

Rebecca felt her cheeks burn, and could almost feel too the blaze of her eyes. 'How dare you, Vivian! How dare you talk of that! I'm amazed that you aren't too ashamed to speak of such behaviour.'

'Why should I be? It's no more than the behaviour of any young man towards the maids in his mother's house. No more –' He caught her eye and stopped, and she knew what he had been about to say. *No more than the way Frank behaved.* And if he had dared to mention that, he would have been ordered from Pagnel House forthwith and never allowed over the threshold again. But the words remained unsaid. And Rebecca, meeting his glance and holding it until at last he let it drop, almost wished that he had spoken them after all. For then this duel between them would have been at an end, and the tension given a focus, a resolution.

It would have to come sometime, she realised then. A climax of some kind to this strange spark that seemed to take fire whenever they were together. And she felt a shiver of curious excitement, almost as if she were doomed, and both feared and welcomed that doom. Like someone walking to her execution and wondering just what it was going to be like . . .

What a morbid thought! She chided herself silently for over-dramatising the situation. And realised that Vivian was still speaking.

'. . . a long time ago,' he was saying. 'I was a young man

then, spoiled I daresay, and more than a little headstrong. But we all have youthful follies to remember.' He seemed to realise that he was once more upon dangerous ground and looked down again at her hands, so small within his. 'Have you had time to consider my proposal?' he asked in a low voice.

Rebecca hesitated. She knew that a great deal of what Vivian said was true. The co-operative was in difficulties, even with the new customers she had gained – and of whom Vivian knew nothing. But he knew about those who had been lost, and it would have been easy for a man with his knowledge of the business to make an accurate guess as to the true state of affairs now. There was little use in her denying it.

And a merging of their two businesses would certainly be an answer. *An* answer, yes – but *the* answer? She shook her head. It would be the end of the Dream she and Francis had worked for, the end of their vision. For Vivian would have no traffic with a co-operative; the men who had shared in the business would become once again no more than common weavers, hired or dismissed on their employer's whim. And Vivian would be that employer; she had no illusion that he would allow her or Tom to remain in charge.

And even less if she should marry him. For then the business would be his, as would all her property – including the house in which they sat now. As she would be herself.

She shook her head again. 'I'm sorry, Vivian. I know you mean it well, but – I have to go on, I have to try my hardest to make the co-operative the success that Francis dreamed of. It's his trust to me, you see. I can't betray it.'

Vivian's face darkened. 'And will you not be betraying it when you watch its looms close down and its doors shut for the last time?' he demanded. 'Will you not be betraying every man there when you see them walk into the street to seek new jobs? Will you not be betraying it when your sons – *his* sons – have to come to me, cap in hand, asking for work? When you come yourself, looking for a roof over your head?'

Again, Rebecca felt her anger flare, but this time it was tinged with a fear that lent ragged edge to her voice.

'I'll never do that, Vivian! Never. I'll never need to – the co-operative *will* succeed, and you'll have to eat your words.' She faced him proudly. 'You may have seen the ledgers, you may have seen the orders we've lost – but you don't know how many I've gained. Good orders, Vivian, large ones, from customers you'll envy when you know them. Except that you never will know them all – for I think it's a good idea, after all, that you do stay away from the office from now on. I don't know what went on while I was away, but you've upset Tom and upset him badly. And I don't want him upset any more. He's been my right hand ever since Francis died. He deserves proper consideration.'

Vivian gave her a long, hard look. She met his eyes steadily, though their darkness seemed to penetrate to her very soul, filling her with unease. Then his shoulders moved in a shrug and he let go of her hands and rose to his feet.

'So be it, Rebecca. You make yourself very clear – and I've never been a man to beg any woman. I've never had need.' He strolled to the door, then turned back. 'Let us hope,' he said, 'that you never have need either.' And then he opened the door and went out.

Rebecca sat quite still then she turned back to the fire. The coals Vivian had rearranged were now almost burnt away. Only ashes remained, with a dull red glow somewhere beneath them. She felt a sudden chill and shivered.

Yes, she thought, I too hope I never have need to beg for Vivian's help. And she was aware that somehow their relationship had changed. The unspoken duel that had gone on between them for so long, buried under the guise of friendship, had surfaced again. And would at some time have to be fought to the end.

Vivian strode away from Pagnel House, his brows drawn together in an angry black bar across his forehead. Once again she had eluded him, the sly vixen! Once again, he saw his own desires swamped by a woman's obstinacy. And there was nothing, *nothing,* he could do about it.

Or was there? He came to the bridge across the Stour and stopped, leaning on the parapet to stare down into the muddy waters. Surely he wasn't going to allow himself to be beaten? He, Vivian Pagnel, one of the most powerful men in Kidderminster, a magistrate like his father, soon to be Mayor, defeated by a chit who had been a skivvy in his own mother's kitchen? Never! It was unthinkable.

But, angry though he was, he did not underestimate Rebecca. His words of admiration for her courage and determination had been sincere – unwomanly though he might think them, those qualities had to be acknowledged. And he knew that she would never give in for reasons of her own comfort. The only way to win her, and her business, was to make it impossible for her to continue it.

Vivian straightened up. He stared unseeingly at the river bank, at the racks where the dyed wool was hung to dry after being swilled in the water. Here it was that Rebecca had come as a small girl with her mother, on the way to the winding sheds. And further down this same river her son Geoffrey had tumbled to his death.

There was no help to be had here. No answer in the waters that swirled sluggishly beneath him.

He walked on, sunk in thought. His hidden battle with Rebecca was now occupying his thoughts more and more. He wanted her business – and he wanted Rebecca herself. He no longer wondered why – reasons had ceased to be a part of his thinking. But he knew, with savage insight, that it was to do with Francis. Francis, true son of Jeremiah, true Pagnel where Vivian was no more than adopted. Francis who had been cherished and loved as Vivian had never been, who had married the woman Vivian had lusted after, who had been left the family house Vivian had believed would be his. Francis, who had sired sons.

He had everything, God rot his soul! Vivian thought passionately. But I'll have the last laugh. I'll have it all before I'm through. His wife, his house, his business, his sons . . . all of it. I'll win in the end. And he'll never stop me now. Because he's dead and I'm alive. I can take it all!

It was dark when Tom left the tavern. A little unsteadily, for he had taken more ale than was his custom, he walked slowly through the streets towards the house where he and Nancy lived. The air struck cool on his cheeks and he felt suddenly dizzy. The ale must have been stronger than he'd thought.

Better take a bit of a walk before going home, or Nancy would be after his blood for coming home tipsy. She didn't mind his going to the tavern but she didn't like him to come home the worse for it. And tonight he hadn't intended going at all – he'd told her he'd be home straight after work. Wouldn't put it past her to be making her way to the carpet-shop this very minute, to find out just where he'd got to.

Well, mebbe he'd better walk round that way, just in case. It would clear his head and if she were on her way he could save her legs and make it up to her a bit, with a faggot or two and some peas from the shop. She was always partial to faggot and peas, and it saved her getting a meal ready.

The kidney stones were hard under his feet as he walked through the darkened streets. Some were lit, but as he drew closer to the co-operative buildings he found it difficult to make out anything. Not much of a moon tonight, he thought, glancing up between the roofs. Just a fitful gleam, peering between the scudding clouds. It was there now, lighting up a scampering cat; a moment later gone, leaving the alleyway in pitch darkness.

It was quiet, too, down this way. Only his footsteps echoing between the walls. Or was it an echo? Was it someone else, walking ahead of him – or behind?

He stopped, glanced round, but there was nothing to see, nor anything to hear. Must have been an echo.

Tom walked on. Mebbe he was getting fanciful, just like Becky said. She'd had a real go at him that day, telling him off for the things he'd said about Mr Vivian, things that were true as he'd stood in her drawing room while she went on at him. Telling him he must have misunderstood, that Vivian had never suggested buying the business out while her back was turned, telling him he was imagining it all . . . But he hadn't imagined it. It had happened just as he'd said, only once again that slimy bastard had got her wrapped around his little finger and managed to convince her. And Tom had never been that handy with words. He'd stood dumb as a sheep while she tore strips off him, and not been able to think of a word to say that would make her believe the truth.

He was near the workshop now. He could see the bulk of the big building, blotting out the dim-lit clouds above. And then the moon came out again, suddenly bright for a moment, illuminating the scene almost as if it were day.

Tom gasped. There *was* someone. Slipping out of the door, surely, there in front of him? Someone he could almost recognise – but before he could form the picture accurately in his mind, his attention was caught by something else. Another light. A sound. A sound that should never be heard anywhere near a carpet-shop.

The crackle of fire – of flames, catching at wood, and not wood that was safely confined to a fireplace. Flames that spread wildly, joyfully, amongst wood that was never meant for burning. Flames with a feast to devour and nobody to stop them.

The carpet-shop was on fire! And the figure he'd seen slipping away, out of sight now, was forgotten in the terrible urgency that caught at Tom's breast now. Already he could see the flickering glow in the windows, knew that the flames had got a hold, were probably consuming the looms at this very moment. And not just the looms – the carpets that were half-made too, the rolls that were stacked in a corner, the wools that were ready for weaving. All being caught up in a dreadful inferno.

Tom ran towards the building, then turned and ran away. There was no hope of his fighting the fire by himself – he must get help. The firemen. Rebecca had been adamant that they subscribe to one of the firefighting services that had been set up in the town. He must call them out, get them here quickly. Whether they could get their horses and their carts through the dark, narrow streets in time to save anything, he did not know. But he must try.

He ran away, through the ill-lit streets, and behind him the fire crackled and consumed and grew. And he never saw the other figure that had gone through the streets just ahead of him. He never saw the outline of a plump body, silhouetted against the searing light of the flames. He never saw Nancy's horror as she stared at the burning building.

He never saw her rush for the door and force it open, convinced that Tom himself must still be inside.

Chapter Eight

'*Fire*? In the carpet-shop?'

Rebecca was on her feet, already reaching one hand towards Daniel as the news was panted out to her. The shock was like a blow striking her in the stomach and she felt a sickness in her throat. The room swayed about her, but she thrust the sensations impatiently aside. This was no time to give way to the vapours.

She stared at the small boy who had come flying up to Mount Pleasant, and her head shook in denial. 'It can't be true. Who sent you to frighten us like this?'

The boy shook his head in turn. 'It's right, missus. I seen it meself, great big flames. Look, you can see it from here.' He turned back to the front door, left open in the flurry, and Rebecca saw the leaping light that burnished the roofs. 'The fire engines are down there already, but they don't reckon they can save much.'

Rebecca was no longer listening. She whirled round on Daniel, who was at her side, aghast, as he too gazed down on the light that glowed red as an angry sore in the streets below. 'Daniel! We must go down at once.'

'I'll go, Mother. There's nothing you can do.'

'Nothing I can do? And you, I suppose, can put it out with your bare hands!' She turned and began to snap out orders to the servants. 'Betsy, my cloak and outdoor shoes. Robert, you'll come with me. Polly, send someone – the boot-boy will do – to tell Mr Vivian. Daniel, fetch your brother. He will at least know whether any of the weavers would have been there. Oh, if anyone is lost through this . . .'

She thrust her feet into the boots Betsy brought her and was shrugging her cloak around her shoulders when she found William at her side. 'William! Do you see what's happening? A fire –'

'I can see, Mother.' His voice was grim. 'And how did that start, I'd like to know?'

'Never mind how it started, it's ending it we must think about. The boy said the fire engines were there already – that means someone must have called them out.' She was out of the door and running down the drive, her sons beside her. 'Is anyone there at night, William? We're not working twelve and twelve, surely?'

'There should be no one there at all. Perhaps the watchman or the constable?'

'It must have been. Well, at least we won't have lost any men. I'd never forgive myself if anyone died. Oh, what a blaze!' She paused at a street corner and stared in horror at the glow that now filled the sky. 'We'll lose everything!'

The streets were filled with people now, running, walking, hobbling in their anxiety to see what was happening. Amongst them, Rebecca caught sight of familiar faces – weavers from the co-operative itself, people she remembered from her childhood in the narrow streets. Their faces were harrowed with fear, already recognising the disaster, and when they saw Rebecca they drew near, their eyes questioning, looking to her already for answers.

'It's past saving,' one man told her gravely. 'Your Tom saw it start and got the engines out straightaway, but there weren't no saving it. Must hev gone up like a torch. Thank God there weren't no one inside.'

They came to the corner of the street and stopped, unable to go any further.

'Oh, God,' Rebecca breathed, and caught at Daniel's hand. The entire building was in flames. Long fingers of fire curled from the windows, reaching blazing talons up the walls. Inside, fused together, was a mass of shifting incandescent colour, as red and gold as a sunset. Swords of light darted through the roof and sliced through the thick black smoke that rose into the sky to blot out the stars, and through it all was the pervasive, acrid smell of burning wool.

The crowd moved and shifted at the corner, making little surges as if to go nearer, then drawing back defeated by the intensity of the blaze. The heat seared their eyes, scorched their nostrils, caught at the backs of their throats. They felt it on their faces, raddled by the orange glow, yet shivered with the dread of what it meant.

Rebecca stared numbly at the sight that met her eyes, and then turned away. Blindly, she reached out her hands and Daniel took them in his. She buried her face against his shoulder.

'Oh, Mother.' He folded his arms around her, and she heard the despondency in his voice, even though he tried to sound hopeful as he said, 'The firefighters are there. They're getting it under control . . .' But his voice cracked and faltered and she knew it was hopeless. It had probably been hopeless from the beginning. Hard though the firefighters might work to save the factory, it must have been well alight before they came on the scene and they could do little more than prevent it spreading.

She felt a touch on her shoulder and raised her head. Tom was there, looking down at her, his face grimed with soot and heavy with despair. As they gazed at each other, his face worked as if he were about to cry, and then he said in a voice that was blurred with tears, 'It's all gone, Becky. Everything. Everything we worked for, you and me and Francis. All gone.'

She shook her head. 'It can't be, Tom.' But she knew it could not be denied. 'How did it start? Does anyone know?'

He shook his head. 'I was just coming down the streets when I saw it. I went for help straightaway, but . . . I dunno what it was, Becky. A candle left burning, summat like that. Summat stupid that should never hev happened. There was nobody in there, I know that – nobody that should hev bin, anyway.'

She stared at him. 'You don't think – you don't mean it was deliberate?'

Tom wiped a weary hand across his face. 'I don't know, Becky. Don't take no notice – I dunno what I'm saying, hardly. Mebbe we'll see in the morning when we get a bit of light on it.' He glanced over his shoulder. 'Looks like it's nearly out now, anyway. At least it won't spread.'

Rebecca gazed along the street. The flames had died down and the acrid smell of wet burned wood and ash hung heavy in the air. People were moving closer to the ruin and she looked around for her sons.

'William! Where's William?' Suddenly panic-stricken, she clutched Daniel's arm.' 'Where's your brother? He was here with us.'

'I know. I was talking to him – he wanted to go and fight the fire. I told him it was useless.' Daniel stepped forward, searching the faces. 'I can't see him, Mother.'

'*William!*' Fear tore at her throat. Had he rushed into that inferno, that wild son of hers? And if he had . . . was she to lose another of her boys, one by water, the other by fire? 'William! Oh God, if anything's happened to him –'

'Hold still, Rebecca.' Another pair of arms held her now and a stronger voice spoke calmly in her ear. 'It's useless for you to go rushing to save him. Not that he needs to be saved.' She turned and looked up into Vivian's face, lit to a ruddy glow by the dying flames. 'He's a hasty young fool but he's no idiot. He'll not have come to any harm.'

'How can you know?' she gasped. 'The fire – nobody could have survived it.'

'And nobody could have got past the firefighters.' His arms held her fast, quietening her struggles. 'Daniel, Tom, go and ask after him but don't get in their way. The fire could break out again.' Rebecca watched them go, then looked up at him again. He met her look gravely and she felt an odd movement deep inside her.

How did it happen that Vivian was always close to her at moments of crisis? When Geoffrey had drowned . . . when

Francis had died . . . whenever she faced a challenge, Vivian was always there.

'Vivian –' she began uncertainly, and he put his finger over her lips.

'Not now, Rebecca. We'll have time for talking later.' He glanced at the smouldering wreck of her hopes, of Francis's dreams. 'I need hardly say how sorry I am about this.'

She nodded dully. The full import of it had hardly begun to register with her. Her eyes searched the crowd constantly, looking for William. What had happened to him? Could he have got past the firefighters, gone into the hell that had blazed before them? Where was he?

Something was happening. Some commotion, at the gaping hole where the main door had once been. A crowd of people surging forwards, gathering round. She could see Tom silhouetted against the light, briefly, then Daniel. Her heart in her throat, she broke free from Vivian's arms.

'They've found something! William!'

Vivian was following her, still denying that William could have been inside, but she took no notice. Something had happened, something bad, something worse than the burning down of a factory. Someone had been killed . . .

William.

She could see more clearly now. Something was being carried out. People were pushing forwards. Tom . . . Daniel . . . And she knew by their stance, by their movements, that whatever was being brought out was a body. And she could see the horror in every line of their bodies.

William . . .

She must have been screaming, for she could hear it, a thin, keening sound that rose above the murmurs of the crowd. They turned and saw her and parted to let her through. And so it was that she came to her brother and her son and looked at what they were looking at, saw what they saw. And felt their horror.

William was there, certainly. But not dead, not burned. Only dirty, covered with ash and soot, and with a little blood seeping slowly from a cut on his forehead.

And in his arms a body that hung as limp as a dead pheasant. Somebody, as Tom had said, who should never have been inside.

Rebecca looked down at the dead, blackened face. It was scarcely recognisable, but she knew at once who it was, and the bile rose in her throat and the world swam about her.

Nancy ...

Simultaneous with her own dawning horror came the sound of Tom's shouting.

At first his words were unrecognisable, but whether this was the effect of Rebecca's own protesting mind she never knew. She could hear them like hammerblows on the surface of her mind, but could at first make no sense of them. Then, slowly, they became clear.

'Nancy – my Nancy! No, it can't be. Why should she hev bin in there? She should've bin at home, getting my supper ready, that's where she should've bin. Aye, and would hev bin too, hadn't I stayed overlong in the tavern. But she didn't never need come looking for me down here.' His voice was thick with tears, with a grief too powerful to be restrained. 'So 'tis all my fault. All my fault she's dead – but she *can't* be dead!' His voice rose with the anguish of his denial.

'Not my Nancy – she can't, she can't.'

'Tom.' Rebecca dragged her wits together and laid both hands on his arm, pulling him round to face her. 'Tom, don't. Come away, come home with me. And don't blame yourself – it wasn't your fault she came here. It was a terrible accident. Nobody's fault, nobody's at all.'

Tom stared at her and she saw the madness in his eyes and understood it. The madness of grief, the refusal to accept a dreadful truth, the blame that must be laid at someone's door. But not yours, Tom, she said silently, never yours. Nobody cared more for his wife than you. Nobody except ...

But she would not think of Francis now, would not let this tragedy remind her of what she had lost. This was Tom's time of need and she must answer it.

160

'Nobody's fault?' he repeated. 'Nobody's fault? Don't talk so far back, Becky – of course it were someone's fault. Someone started that fire.'

'Yes,' she agreed eagerly, anxious only to prevent the torment of his own remorse, 'yes, of course, someone must have started it and so it's their fault. But it was still an accident, Tom, nobody ever meant to –'

'An accident?' he interrupted, and his eyes focused suddenly on hers. There was an intensity in them that struck fear into her heart and she caught her breath, but before she could say a word he was speaking again. 'You think it were an accident? You don't think it were . . . deliberate?'

'*Deliberate*? Tom, what –'

'Aye, deliberate,' he broke in again, and his voice rose once more as his gaze shifted past Rebecca and she saw his eyes widen. 'And we don't need to look far to see who did it either, do we?' he shouted. He lifted one hand and pointed a shaking finger past his sister's head. She turned slowly, scarcely knowing who or what she expected to see. Who could Tom mean? Did he even know himself what accusation he made?

Behind her, she met Vivian's eyes, saw the expression in them and, frozen with shock, heard Tom's voice, almost unintelligible again now, with only a few words coherent through the pain that blurred his tones.

'Him – it were him – killed my Nancy, my Nance that never did no one no harm . . . Saw him, I did, creeping away . . . burned to death, burned away, my poor Nance . . . killed – murdered . . . oh, Nancy, what did he do to you, what did he do, my Nance, my Nance . . .'

His words were broken, torn with anguish. For a few minutes he ranted at them all, then as if his pain had become too much he lunged towards Vivian, his hands outstretched, and Rebecca saw murder plain in his eyes. With a gasp she flung herself at him, catching at his arms, intent on preventing further tragedy. But William was there before her, dragging his uncle away, and Daniel left her side to go to his brother's

161

assistance. Together, the two boys held the older man in restraint, but it seemed that nothing could stop his distraught accusations.

'He killed her, I tell you. He did it, he started the fire that killed my Nancy. Get the constable to him! He oughter be locked up – he's a murderer, a bloody murderer. He killed my Nancy sure as if he'd cut her throat with a carpet wire!'

'As you did Jabez Gast.'

Vivian's voice cut through the babbling incoherencies, and Tom's voice stopped as if he in turn had been sliced across the throat. There was a moment's utter silence then Rebecca, sick with horror, turned upon Vivian. But before she could speak, he took her by the arm and shook his head.

'I'm sorry, Rebecca. I had to stop him somehow.' He looked at the two boys, still holding their uncle between them, and at Tom who almost hung from their arms now, his head drooping as if he had been dealt a mortal blow. 'It was the only way – either that or strike him, and you wouldn't have wanted that.'

No, Rebecca thought, she wouldn't have wanted that. And yet – was this way any the better? She looked at Tom, cringing now like a whipped puppy, and thought of the shock he must have suffered in his mind. Was that really better than a physical blow which might have been quickly forgotten?

'Take him away quickly, while he's quiet,' Vivian ordered. 'And some of you men, find something to carry this poor woman's body on. We must get her away from here. The rest of you, if you're not helping the firefighters, clear the street. There's work to be done here and no spectators are needed. Best leave it to those whose workplace this was. The rest get away home.'

There was a general movement, a shuffle and a murmuring as the crowd began to disperse. Rebecca saw several of her own weavers among the throng and felt a warmth in her heart, mixed with pity, as she watched them go forward to the firefighters who had now put out the flames and were picking their way through the steaming rubble. There could be little left there now, but they would salvage what they could. And then what? They had seen their livelihood go up in flames. What would be their future now?

A heavy depression settled itself about her, like a dark, weighty cloud, and she turned away, unable to bear the pitiful sight any longer. Ahead of her, she could see a silent group of men, a hastily formed cortège bearing Nancy's body away from the blackened wreck that had been her funeral pyre. Behind it, quiet now, his head bent in mourning, Tom followed, supported on either side by his sobered nephews. She felt a sudden rush of grief for him and for the woman who had been her companion ever since those long-gone days in London.

'Don't give way now, Rebecca,' a quiet voice said in her ear. 'Be strong until you are home, at least.'

She looked up into Vivian's face and saw the gravity there and was grateful for it. At least he did not offer false comfort, at least he recognised the situation for what it was – a tragedy not only for her and Tom, but for every weaver who had been part of the co-operative.

And once again, he had been there when she faced crisis. Once again, he had offered his arm, his shoulder; once again, he had been at hand.

'Poor Tom,' Polly said sadly, setting down the tray beside Rebecca's elbow. 'He's been knocked all of a piece by it. Seems he can't hardly live without his Nancy, and don't much want to try neither.'

'I know.' Rebecca lifted the teapot and looked at the single cup and saucer on the tray. 'Polly, why don't you bring one for yourself? I don't want to sit alone and it seems as if you're the only real friend I have left.'

Polly looked gravely down at her and rang the bell. When Betsy came with the second cup she filled it and then sat down in the other chair.

'It's not so easy being well off,' she remarked shrewdly. 'Back in the cottages, you'd hev had folk running in and out and all the company you wanted, time like this. But as you are –'

'As I am, there are rules to follow and be obeyed,' Rebecca said with the ghost of a smile. 'Mourning, the funeral, all the trappings of what is *fitting* – oh, how that word has followed me through my life! When all I want is to forget the rest of the world and be a comfort to my brother. What has it to do with anyone else, anyway? Only Nancy's friends and family have a say in how her memory should be kept.' She sipped her tea. 'If only I could be more help to Tom,' she said at last. 'But he won't let me do anything. He's refused all my efforts to get him to come and stay here for a while, he insists on staying in Unicorn Street, and I know he spends all his time brooding by himself. It can't be good for him, Polly.'

'Nothing's good for him just now,' the housekeeper said. 'There's no way of comforting a man when he's hit that hard. He just don't want to be comforted, that's the truth of it. He'd feel guilty if he started to feel better about it – think he was betraying her in some way.'

'I know.' Rebecca thought of her own despair when she had lost Francis. But she had had the boys to live for. Tom and Nancy had never had children and the comfort and the burden of them were denied him. 'I feel so worried about him,' she said in a low voice. 'You say he doesn't seem to want to live without Nancy. And I'm afraid that one night, when he's there all alone –'

'He won't do that,' Polly said positively. 'You see, he's got to stay alive just so he can go on suffering. It's as if the only way he can keep faith is by being miserable enough to die himself – but if he did, it'd be a sort of release. And that'd make him even more guilty!'

Rebecca stared at her, then smiled unwillingly. 'It sounds very strange, but I believe you're right,' she said slowly. 'I've thought once or twice that Tom seemed almost to be wallowing in his grief. But perhaps that's the answer – he needs it. And as long as he needs it, we must allow him it.' She frowned a little. 'What's more worrying is this conviction he has that Vivian had something to do with the fire.'

'He's certain he saw someone skulking around that night,'

Polly agreed. 'And just as certain it was Mr Vivian. But I don't see how he can be so sure. It was dark, there weren't even much of a moon, and there's no street lamps down that way.'

'He says he saw this person, whoever it was, in the light of the fire itself. And he could tell it was Vivian by the way he moved, by his shape.' Rebecca sighed. 'It *is* possible to recognise someone by their walk, I know. But – it's also possible to believe you've seen something you really didn't. Especially when you've had as terrible a shock as Tom had.'

'You reckon it's turned his brain,' Polly observed, and her tone was such that Rebecca could not tell whether it were a statement or a question.

'Polly, I can't believe that. He's still stunned by it – as you said, he's been knocked sideways by it all. Losing Nancy and in such a dreadful way. He still blames himself that she was there at all, you know. If he'd gone straight home that evening . . . But there's no help in telling himself that over and over again, it just makes everything more unbearable.'

'So if he can blame someone else, it helps a bit. And if it's someone he never liked or trusted anyway –'

'And who he's been trusting less and less just lately.' Rebecca shook her head slowly. 'Polly, I just don't know. Tom's never felt happy about Vivian. It was a long time before he would agree to come back to Kidderminster, for fear of what Vivian would do. And then poor Bessie – he never forgave Vivian for his part in that. This hostility of his has been growing over the years. Perhaps his mind is playing tricks now, perhaps he never saw anyone at all that night, but if so he's never going to admit it. He believes it himself, absolutely.'

'And so what you're saying,' Polly said quietly, 'is that his brain *has* been turned.'

Rebecca felt the tears prick at her eyes and knew a sudden anger against this life that seemed to bring nothing but tragedy. It seemed that no sooner had the family begun to look forward to good times than everything was kicked away again. Death, sickness, poverty – each seemed to circle around like a ring of menace, each leering its threat as if to warn against complacency. So you think you're all right? these menacing Fates seemed to ask. Well, look at what we're going to do to you now . . .

What was it all about? Why did babies have to be born into poverty and disease? Why did people have to struggle against such odds only to fail through no fault of their own? Or was it, in some obscure way, their fault after all? If Tom had never mistrusted Vivian, would things have been different? Would he have come back sooner from London? Would he have disappeared there in the first place? Would he have stayed so long in the tavern that night and if he had, would he have imagined that he saw Vivian lurking near the factory just as the fire burst into life?

These were questions that had no answer. Life had to be accepted as it was, with all the troubles it brought with it, and there was nothing that anyone could do but live on in the best way possible.

With Tom buried in his grief, Rebecca was compelled to take on her shoulders all the burden of responsibility for the destroyed factory. She was offered help on all sides but accepted none other than that of her sons. Even Vivian was refused, with a regretful shake of the head. As long as Tom still suffered from his own painful beliefs, delusions though they might be, she could not betray him by accepting the help of the man he believed to be their enemy.

'The boys and I will manage,' she told Vivian when he came to see her soon after Nancy's sad funeral. 'There's a good deal to be done, I know, but what else is there to occupy us now? I'm more concerned for my weavers. They've lost everything too, and they need their work. If you could take some of them on . . . ?'

Vivian shook his head. 'Not without extra work as well. I've enough weavers of my own. If I could work on the orders you had . . . Rebecca, you must see it's the only way. Those customers won't wait for ever. They'll stay with you a while, perhaps, out of loyalty and sympathy for what's happened. But how patient must they be? Some of those carpets were almost finished – they'd have been delivered within the month. Do Mrs This and Lady That have to wait another six months while you rebuild the factory and install new looms? *Will* they wait that long?'

'Enough will,' Rebecca said, but again he shook his head.

'*Some* may. Not enough. And what of the new orders, the ones you hadn't even begun yet? They'll be put back even longer – a year or more. And those customers have no loyalty towards you. Why should they wait?'

Rebecca sighed and thrust her fingers through her hair. She was wearing it loose this morning and it hung past her shoulders, thick and dark as it had been when she was a girl. If only she could go back in time – to those early days of her marriage, when she and Francis had been in London together, building up their business with Tom and Nancy. Bessie had been alive then, with her own milliner's shop, and it had seemed for a while as if they had found the direction their lives needed, living modestly but in comfort and with none of these worries and responsibilities that oppressed her now.

Perhaps Bessie and Tom had been right to be reluctant to come back to Kidderminster. Perhaps their feelings of doom had been a prophecy she and Francis ought to have taken proper notice of. Looking back now, it seemed true that nothing had gone right for any of them since they had moved back. Bessie dead, Geoffrey lost in the river, Francis and now Nancy. And the business destroyed beyond rescue.

Beyond rescue? No! With a sudden angry movement, she slammed her hands down on the table and thrust herself to her feet. Her eyes flashed as she turned them on Vivian and it was with satisfaction that she noted the startled look on his face. Yes, she could surprise him yet, she could surprise them all – and would, too. If anyone thought she was beaten . . .

'None of my customers will have to wait,' she declared. 'The carpets they ordered will be supplied – a little late, perhaps, but not the six months or a year that you talk of. I'll rebuild the factory and buy new looms.' She faced him proudly. 'You've forgotten one thing, Vivian. This was no ordinary factory. This was a *co-operative*. And it will still function as one.'

Vivian stared at her. Then he gave an abrupt bark of laughter.

'And you think your weavers will rally round you in your hour of need? You think they'll rebuild your factory and contribute money to buy those new looms? Rebecca, you're living in a land of fantasy – but then you always did, didn't you, you and your husband? And now he's out of it and you're alone – and you've nothing but that fantasy to keep hold of.' He laughed again, then shook his head and regarded her gravely. 'I'm sorry for you, Rebecca. You've a great disappointment coming to you. But if you're determined on this course . . .'

'I am.'

He rose to his feet. 'Then I'll leave you to it. There's clearly nothing more I can do to help. But remember –' he stretched out his hand and his smile illuminated his dark face '– when you realise at last that you can't manage alone, remember who helped you before, remember who has always been at hand. Come to me then, Rebecca.'

She felt his fingers close around hers, warm and strong, and for a moment her heart moved within her breast. Why did she struggle on so when Vivian could so easily come to her aid? Why did she so consistently turn him away?

She looked up into his face, as if to search there for her answer. And perhaps she found it there, for she knew that she could not give way now, that she had to make this one last effort, for Francis's sake if for no other reason. She had to make this one last act of faith.

'I'll remember,' she said quietly and he gave her a searching look then nodded, as if satisfied, and left her.

Rebecca sank down on a chair and gazed out of the window. What had she promised? What did Vivian believe she had promised?

She had only said she would remember. And there were so many things to remember . . .

Her eyes moved to the small table in front of her and

she reached out for the sheets of paper that lay upon it. A letter from Matthew, far away in Australia. Another man she remembered.

What would I feel now if you were here, Matthew? she thought and was suddenly shaken by a longing that gripped her so hard, so unexpectedly, that she gasped. If only he were here, in this room with her now, his laughing face sobered by the problems that surrounded her, his strong hands holding hers, his eyes looking into her face as Vivian had done a few moments ago, yet with understanding and love . . .

Love?

Was it love that she had seen so many times in Matthew's eyes? That darkness, that light, those changing shades? Were they love?

She remembered the last time she had seen him. She and Francis had been permitted to go to Portsmouth to say goodbye to him, just before he had sailed for Australia. He had been aboard the hulks in the harbour then for several months, chained to the lower deck with a motley of 'criminals' – some murderers, some thieves, many other unfortunates who had done no more than steal a loaf of bread to keep their families alive.

During the days, he had told her and Francis, he and the others had been rowed ashore to work on the dockyards. Still chained, dressed only in prison rags, they had been forced to parade through the streets, a spectacle to the people of the town and to others who came to watch and to jeer.

Rebecca remembered the way he had looked at her as they said their last goodbye. He had grown a beard by then and she could imagine him as a Viking warrior with his waving red-gold hair and beard. But he did not look like a warrior then, clad in his rough, ill-fitting prison clothes, his hair and beard unkempt, his hands rough and dirty.

Their meeting had been brief and heartbreaking. And afterwards she and Francis had mounted the steps of the Sallyport, at the entrance to the harbour, and watched as the ship sailed out through the narrow neck of sea and into the reaches of the

Solent. But although she had waved her hand, she had known that Matthew could not see her, for he was below again, in his chains, with no hope of seeing daylight until the ship was well away from England's shores.

Had he lain there then, in the dark, noisome hold, thinking of her with love?

She stared out of the window at the fading bluebells that misted the grass. It was all so long ago. Yet there had been so many times when she had turned to Matthew for company, for laughter, for understanding. And were these not the ingredients of love? Had it been there all the time, without her knowing it?

But I loved Francis then, she thought sadly. And so Matthew, if he loved me, had to keep his love hidden. And now – now, when I might turn to him, when I might find I loved him too – he's gone. And will never return.

Instead, there was Vivian.

'What is your mother going to do?' Lucy asked. 'What are *you* going to do?'

Daniel shook his head. He kicked moodily at a stone and it bounced down the riverbank and into the water. He watched as it entered the water with a 'plop' and sent ripples spreading on the surface.

'I don't know what's going to happen. Oxford is forgotten, of course – well, not forgotten, she's full of apologies over it and won't believe me when I say I didn't want to go after all. It's been my dream for so long – hers too, I suppose. But I really don't feel sorry about that. I already knew it wouldn't be right for me. Having enough brain doesn't automatically make studying the right way to spend your life.'

'So,' Lucy repeated, 'what do you mean to do?'

'Anything I can, I suppose. Help Mother in whatever way I can though heaven knows what way that is. Just what can she do now, Lucy? She talks of rebuilding the factory and starting again, but how can we do that? All the money we had was invested there, in the looms, in new wools, in paying the men.'

'*Paying* them? But surely the carpets –'

'The carpets didn't pay their way,' Daniel told her. 'They would have done, eventually – at least, that's what we all hoped, of course. But meanwhile Mother was so anxious to pay each man fairly after Father died and things began to be difficult, that she put her own money – the money that Father left her – into it. She never told anyone, just struggled on. And now all that money's gone – up in flames with the rest of it,' he concluded gloomily.

Lucy stared at him. 'So there's nothing left? No money at all?'

'None. Oh, just enough for us to live on for a while. We won't starve yet. But the weavers –'

'They've got no jobs,' Lucy said in a low voice. 'And nothing else. But, Daniel, she was wrong to do that. A co-operative should be what it says. *Everyone* profits – or everyone loses. Isn't that what it's for?'

'Of course. But you know Mother. She lived as a weaver's daughter herself, she knows what it's like to be poor. And we were never as poor as that, nor likely to be.'

'Until now.' Lucy's eyes rested on his face. 'Daniel, how far does this go? Does your mother have any debts?'

He met her gaze and then looked away. Beyond the town, the fields stretched away to woods and low, rolling hills. The red earth was freckled green with the shoots of growing corn.

'She won't say,' he answered at last. 'But I shall be very surprised if she doesn't.' His mouth twisted a little. 'We may find ourselves back in a weaver's cottage yet, Lucy. And if that happens there'll be no hope, ever, for you and me.'

She stared at him. Then, with a sudden violent movement, she caught him by the shoulders and twisted him to face her.

'Don't you dare say such a thing, Daniel Pagnel,' she hissed. 'Don't you *dare*. There's *always* hope. There's always a dream – and dreams can come true. You can *make* them come true – and so we will.' Her eyes blazed as she shook him. 'You're a man now, and William almost so. You don't have to rely on your mother to see you through life – you can do it for yourself. Let her rely on you for a change. Doesn't she have a right to? Isn't it time she could turn to you? What are you, Daniel, a man or a –'

'All right, Lucy, you don't have to say it.' He pulled her against him, into his arms. 'You're right, of course. It's time I stopped behaving like a schoolboy and took some responsibility of my own. I should stop playing about with lessons and look for work, find some way of supporting myself and my mother.' He held her close for a moment, frowning, then said, 'But what can I do? William will have no problems in finding work – he knows as much about carpet-making as any manufacturer, even though he's so young, and anyone would be eager to take him on in some capacity. But I –'

'You know about carpets too. You've grown up with them.'

'But they're not in my blood,' he said. 'I've never had the interest that William has. What I know, I've absorbed through growing up with them – but most of the time I've been more concerned with my books. And I haven't learned enough from them yet, not enough to be of any use to anyone.'

'There must be things you could do. A schoolmaster – you could find work in a school. Or as a clerk.'

'Neither of which,' he said, 'is going to help support my mother and run Pagnel House.'

They looked soberly at each other. The reality of the situation was only just beginning to sink home.

Neither of them expressed the thought that was in both their minds: that Daniel might after all be forced to accept Vivian's offer of adoption.

Vivian approached Pagnel House slowly. It was not his habit to be circumspect – he liked to stride through the town, enjoying the sense that everyone he passed recognised and respected him. One of the major manufacturers of Kidderminster, a magistrate, about to become Mayor – yes, he was a figure in the town now, a figure to be looked up to.

There was only one person in the borough whose feelings he was unsure of, and that was the one person whose respect he wanted most. And even while he acknowledged this, he felt irritation that it should be so. Rebecca – what was it about her, after all? A girl from the weavers' hovels, a slut from his own mother's scullery, a sly chit who had somehow wheedled his cousin into marrying her when she found herself carrying his child – why should he, who could have any woman in town, care about Rebecca?

Yet he did. She was a thorn in his side and always had been. A vixen he couldn't tame, a she-cat who would purr in his arms one minute and scratch his eyes out the next. She irritated him and aggravated him; yet he admired her and lusted after her. And until he had her submissive, he would never feel completely satisfied.

Any other woman, he thought, would have seen sense and accepted his offer of marriage – jumped at it. Any other woman would have been only too glad to give up her business, let him merge it with his, and settle back into a comfortable matronhood. Any other woman would have borne him a son or two gladly, in payment for that comfort.

But Rebecca – no, obstinate as ever, she had still eluded him. Insisting on running the co-operative, cavorting about the countryside like a gipsy, bringing scorn upon herself by her hoydenish actions. Or should have done – but he was uncomfortably aware that there had been less scorn than he would have liked, that she had in fact come back with a fair degree of success, having gained a good many new orders. Too many. Even though that damned brother of hers had never let him see the books, he knew that there had been too many.

Well, they were lost now and so was everything else, and she would have to listen to him. And maybe this time that obstinacy of hers would be quelled, the wildness tamed. Maybe now she'd be ready to see reason.

The door was opened by a neat enough little maid, but Vivian took scant notice of her. His days of seducing maidservants were long past. He handed her his hat and walked into the drawing room.

'*Rebecca*! What on earth are you doing?'

Rebecca looked up. She was sitting on the floor, surrounded by scraps of wool. Several large sheets of paper lay strewn around, covered with coloured patterns. On a low table were a palette and paints, with a pot of water and a jar of brushes.

'Oh, hello, Vivian. I didn't expect you.'

'No, so I see.' He stared down at the disarray and unconsciously continued with his earlier thoughts. 'Any other woman would be having tea at this hour. What *are* you doing, Rebecca?'

'Tea?' She looked about vaguely. 'There is some somewhere about, I believe. Betsy brought it – oh yes, there it is, on the table in the window. Do pour yourself a cup, Vivian. I just want to finish this . . .' She picked up a brush and dipped it into a pool of dark red paint. 'As for what I'm doing, I should have thought that was obvious. I'm making some new designs, of course.'

'New designs? But you haven't got a –'

'A factory?' She put a finishing touch to a whorl of colour and looked up at him calmly. 'I know that, Vivian. But it won't be long before I do. And meanwhile we shall need new designs so that we can be ready as soon as the looms are in. I can remember the old ones, of course, and there are carpets made that we could use as patterns . . . but somehow I don't want to do that. We have to make a fresh start, so it seems a good time to try some entirely fresh designs. Something a little different.'

'Different?' He came across and stared down at the turbulent colours that blazed from the papers. 'Rebecca, have you gone mad? No one will buy these – they're outlandish, like something from a pagan temple. Or a Red Indian wigwam.'

'Yes, they are, aren't they?' She sat back on her heels, gazing down with some pride. 'Quite different from the patterns that have been in favour for so long. And I think people *will* buy them, Vivian. People are ready for something different.'

'Some people, perhaps. Others have more taste.'

'Then they can buy from you,' she said cheerfully. 'I don't need hundreds of customers. Just enough to keep my weavers in work and a roof over my head. Did you pour yourself some tea?'

'No, I did not,' he said crossly. 'I'm not accustomed to waiting on myself. Nor do I feel comfortable with you scrambling about on the floor like a schoolgirl. Get up, Rebecca, for goodness' sake, and talk to me like a human being. I came for a serious purpose.'

'Oh dear, did you?' Rebecca pulled a face but got to her feet and went over to the tea-tray. She poured two cups and brought them across to the armchairs where she and Vivian sat facing one another. 'Do you know, I feel quite tired of being serious all the time. So many terrible things have happened, it seems to me it's time to rise above them. That's why I want to make these designs, I suppose. They seem so full of life, so exciting. Like a promise of better things.'

'And I hope you will have better things,' he said. 'But not like this. Rebecca, don't you think it's time you stopped trying so hard? Don't you think it's time you accepted the reality of it all?'

'Reality? What do you mean by reality?' He saw her stiffen. 'I think I know what reality is,' she said quietly. 'I've seen enough suffering, enough pain, to know what is real and what is not.'

'Yes, yes, of course.' He cursed himself mentally. This was no way to win her over. 'And you've shown more courage, more strength, than many men would have done. But –'

'But I'm still only a woman. That's what you mean, isn't it? And the *reality* is that no woman can hope to keep going alone. Not in this world – this *man's* world.' She lifted her chin and he saw the glitter of her eyes. 'What you're telling me is that I should give up now and hand everything over to you. My factory, my weavers, my home, my sons even – and I won't!' The glitter was not of tears, but of defiance. 'I won't betray it all. I took on a trust when Francis died and I'll see it through to the end. The very end – no matter what.'

'But you've come to the end!' Vivian felt his temper slipping away from him and made an effort to keep it within his grasp.

175

'Rebecca, try to understand. You have no factory, no weavers – all that has gone. And if you don't do something about it, your home will go too. How will you afford to maintain it, this great house? How will you continue to educate your sons? How will you even feed yourselves?' He shook his head. 'You're living in a dream world, Rebecca. Making designs! Who is ever going to weave these into carpets?'

'Perhaps I've always lived in a dream world,' she answered, gazing down at her designs. 'Francis and I had a Dream – and we were making it come true. It can happen again. It can become a Glory. But only if I go on believing in it.' She lifted her face and now there were tears in her eyes and on her cheeks. 'I must go on believing in it,' she whispered. 'Or there's nothing left.'

Vivian hesitated. Once again, Rebecca had placed him at a disadvantage. The firebrand he could have fought with, the grieving widow he could have comforted, the purring kitten he could have stroked – but this Rebecca was one he had never known how to handle. This Rebecca went beyond his earthly experience into a realm where he could not follow. Dreams, glories – what did they mean? In his terms, nothing. Yet if he scorned them, dismissed them, he would lose her more certainly than if he threw her to the floor and ravished her. She might even enjoy that . . . But she would never forgive him if he violated her dreams.

'Rebecca,' he said gently, 'listen to me. I don't want you to stop believing in your dreams. They're a part of you. But how can you make them come true now? Where are your weavers going to work? How can you rebuild the factory? Where will the money come from to do all this, to buy new looms, new materials? You must have lost thousands of pounds' worth of wool in that fire, as well as all the machinery. How can you hope to build it all up again?'

'I can't, all at once. It will have to be done gradually. But the men will help. They'll help build.'

'As well as weave? And how will you pay them?'

'The bank,' she said. 'They helped me before.'

'And are still waiting for repayment.' He shook his head. 'I'm sorry, Rebecca, but we have to face the truth. You haven't any money, have you?'

'The house. I can raise money on the house. I can sell it.'

'Sell Pagnel House? You'll never do that.'

'I will,' she said, 'if I have to.' She met his eyes. 'You might buy it from me, Vivian.'

For a moment he struggled with the temptation. To buy Pagnel House from Rebecca ... to make it his at last. And then he shook his head. No. Never. Buy what should rightfully have been his by inheritance – and by so doing, enable Rebecca to rebuild her business and become once again his rival? When he could gain everything he wanted through other means?

'No,' he said. 'I won't buy Pagnel House from you, Rebecca. But neither will I see you lose it.' He reached out and took her hands in his, looking deeply into her eyes. 'Rebecca, I've asked you before this to marry me. Now I'm asking you again. Before you do anything hasty – before you do anything at all – at least think about it. Think of the difference it can make to us both.'

'Both?' she said. 'Both? What differences will it make, Vivian?'

He gripped her fingers. 'What differences? There are so many! For you, it will mean an end to all worry. You'll have your home, safe and secure – either in my house or here, whichever is your will. You'll have your factory – I'll rebuild it for you, Rebecca, exactly as you want it, aye and take on your own weavers too. Your sons' futures will be assured – Daniel can go to Oxford, William come into the business with me. You can even go on designing if you wish.'

'And Tom?'

Vivian swore silently. He had forgotten Tom, the one member of the family for whom he had no use. But he couldn't dismiss him – he was Rebecca's brother, and just one of the burdens she would bring with her.

'Tom will have his place,' he said steadily, and hoped she would not ask what that place was.

Rebecca gazed at him for a long moment, and he met her eyes. Then she said quietly, 'And what benefit will this be to you, Vivian?'

'What indeed?' he said lightly. 'You can't imagine now that I want to marry you for your carpet factory! No, Rebecca –' his tone deepened '– there will be only one benefit for me, and one I've long desired. I will have you for my wife. Do I need to ask for more?'

Chapter Nine

Dense fog shrouded the streets of Kidderminster. After a summer of heat, with all its epidemics, and an autumn of mists and golden colour, winter had come abruptly, reminding everyone of hardships to face. And Rebecca, walking slowly through the streets towards Mount Pleasant, came at last to realise that the choices she had thought were hers had been taken away from her. She too had hardships to face.

Unless . . .

Desperately, her mind twisted and turned through all the familiar paths. If she did this . . . or that . . . But she had been through all the arguments before, all the reasoning, all the seeking for some new answer. She had tried and tested them all, and now there were no answers left. None but the one she had so consistently avoided.

Today, she had made her final bid for independence. She had been yet again to the weavers' cottages, gathering around her all the men who had worked for her and Francis so faithfully – who had worked *with* them, she amended. The weavers who had been part of the co-operative, working side by side and sharing the profits. Except that there had been no profits to share – their payment had come from Rebecca's own pocket, and now they had no factory to work in and that pocket was empty.

'You mean we never really made any money at all?' one of the men had asked her. 'It was all fancy?'

'No, it wasn't fancy. We would have begun to make a profit soon – with the new orders gained.'

'But we didn't mek any, did we?' he had persisted, and

the others had joined in. 'It all come from you – you and Mr Francis. You carried it.'

'That's normal when a new business starts up,' she said a little desperately. 'You know we had money from Mr Farrell as well. But that stopped when – when he –'

'Got transported for a murderer,' Ned Lidgett said bluntly. 'So then we was on our own. Mebbe you should hev closed us down then.'

'Of course not! We were determined to carry on. And it would have been all right, if only . . . If only my husband had not died,' she said, taking a deep breath. If only, indeed, Francis had not died! 'And even then, things were improving. We lost some of our customers but I had new orders. It was the fire that made it all hopeless.'

'Aye, it were one thing after another.' Ned shook his head slowly. 'As if someone were working against us. Had a spite for us, like.' He glowered into the fire that burned in the small grate. They had gathered together in this small cottage for what they all knew was to be their last meeting. The spark of hope that each had carried through all the last few weary months was too small now to survive. Each one knew they were here to watch its extinguishing.

'And us wouldn't need to look far to know who 'twas,' someone else said from the shadows, and there was a murmur of agreement.

Rebecca spoke quickly.

'No, I won't hear you say that. Nobody has been against us, only fate. We all know that bad luck comes in runs – we've had ours, and that's all there is to it. Even now, if we could only keep going a bit longer . . .'

'Keep going? What with? What do we feed our childer with – and with winter coming on and all?' The men spoke together, one voice overlaying another, but all edged with the same discontent. 'What do you want us to do, missus? Weave carpets or turn ourselves into builders? Because we can't weave until we got a shed to weave in and wool for our looms.'

'I know.' Rebecca heard the depression in her own voice,

but try as she might she could not lift it. Not now, with her dreams like the ashes in the grate. 'And you've tried all these months, I know that. Clearing the site, carrying away all the burned wood, saving the bricks . . . it's been a hard task. But now –'

'Now we got to face that we just aren't going to be able to do it,' Ned said bluntly. 'It's no use hiding from it any longer. You can't go on paying us from your own pocket, and you got no money left anyway. That's the top and bottom of it, ent it?'

'Yes,' Rebecca acknowledged, 'I'm afraid it is.' She looked around the circle of faces. These men had been part of her lives for so long now. Some were men she had known as a child, had played with in the cobbled street outside. They had come to her when she and Francis had set up the co-operative, had worked willingly on the new designs, remained loyal and hardworking during all the difficulties, and had spent the last few months in endless endeavour to bring her dream rising like a phoenix from the ashes. And now, like her, they were having to admit defeat – and none of them liked it.

If there had been any chance at all, she knew, they would have gone on. But hungry children must be fed, and shivering bodies kept warm.

'Will you find jobs?' she asked, and they glanced at each other and nodded. There was something shamefaced in their manner and she gazed at them wondering why, and then knew. 'Mr Vivian – he'll take you on?'

'He's said he'll think on it,' Ned Lidgett said awkwardly. 'But it depends . . .' His voice trailed away and he stared down at his boots.

'Depends on what?' But none of them would answer. And after a while, when it seemed there was no more to be said, Rebecca rose to her feet. She looked gravely around at them all.

'You've been good friends to me,' she said quietly. 'And I'll be a good friend to you. Whatever it depends upon, I'll do my utmost to see that you all have work to go to. I'll never forget your loyalty to me.'

181

Now, walking slowly through the damp, chilly streets, she knew just what it was she must do. She knew, though no one had told her, what it was that Vivian's offer of work depended on. She knew the price that must be paid for her weavers to find employment, and herself and her family to be able to live.

There was, Rebecca's mother had sometimes said, no time like the present. The past was done with, the future still a mystery. All you had was the present, so if anything needed to be done it was best done at once. She might, Rebecca thought, have said that there was no time *but* the present.

Vivian's house was well lit and warm, a haven of comfort from the cold, foggy November evening. The maid showed Rebecca into a drawing room where a fire burned brightly in the hearth and comfortable chairs were spaced about.

Indeed, the room's atmosphere owed much to Rebecca herself, for Vivian had consulted her regularly over the years on furnishings, and she had enjoyed searching pattern books for wallpapers and upholstery fabrics to create the effects she saw now. It was almost, she thought wryly, as much her home as it was Vivian's . . .

As she stood before the fire, warming her hands at the blaze, the door opened and she turned to see Lucy coming into the room.

'Aunt Rebecca, the maid told me you were here. Can I offer you anything – tea or a sherry perhaps? It's so horrid outside.'

'Thank you, a glass of sherry would be welcome.' Rebecca shivered. 'The damp gets right into my bones – I must be getting old.'

'Old? Not you.' Lucy rang for the maid and ordered the sherry to be brought. 'Did you come to see Papa? He's out, I'm afraid, but he won't be long. Do you mind waiting?'

'Of course not. I'm glad to have the chance to talk to you. It seems a long time since we spent any time together.'

Lucy said nothing, and Rebecca wondered a little guiltily

whether the girl felt neglected. Ever since Maria had died, Rebecca had taken over a good deal of responsibility for the girls and had been at the house most days, overseeing their upbringing. But of late she had let her own problems take precedence. There had been all the months after Francis had died, when she had retired into mourning and then emerged only to throw all her energy into the business. The weeks when she had been away. And now, after the fire, her efforts to rebuild the factory and start again from nothing. No, she had not had much time to spare for Lucy and her sisters.

The parlourmaid came in with some decanters and glasses on a tray. Lucy poured sherry for Rebecca and then for herself. She did this quite casually, as if it were something she was accustomed to do, and it was this, more than the fact that she drank wine at all, which brought home to Rebecca the fact that the child had gone, the awkward schoolgirl disappeared, that Lucy had become a woman.

She took a more careful look. Yes, they were all there, the trappings of womanhood. The hair so competently arranged on her head leaving bare a neck almost fragile in its slenderness. The low-cut neckline revealing the smooth, pearly skin, the lace that covered the tender swelling of young breasts, the close-fitting bodice that followed their curves to the tiny waist. Youth shining in the translucent complexion, the sparkling eyes; maturity in the composure of expression, the assurance of her bearing.

Lucy was in the full flower of her womanhood. It was time she was married.

But Rebecca knew that Lucy was in no hurry to wed. Vivian had produced many eligible men as possible husbands, and each had been turned away. And, as he had told Rebecca, his patience was wearing thin.

'The chit seems to think she can decide who she'll marry – as if she has any understanding of what it's all about! Got some romantic nonsense in her head about love – seems to be all they think about these days. As if love had anything to do with a good working marriage!'

'I found it had quite a lot to do with it,' Rebecca had answered with some spirit. 'Do you think Francis and I would have married if we hadn't loved each other?'

'And look what it did for you,' he returned. 'Oh, I'm not saying you didn't have a good marriage – you had sons, you built a business. But all that went before – your dismissal, that time in London when anything could have happened to you –'

'It was worth it all,' she declared, but still he shook his head.

'Would you be saying that if Francis hadn't found you? Would you be *able* to say it?'

Rebecca looked at Lucy now and wondered, as she had wondered before, about her and Daniel. They had seemed so fond of each other as they grew up, and she had worried more than once that their fondness might be turning to something more serious. But they had been together less of late, so perhaps it had been no more than a childhood affection after all. Perhaps Lucy had some other lover to occupy her attention – someone who not even Vivian knew about.

But she hadn't come here today to worry about Lucy. There were more immediate matters to attend to, and she wished that Vivian would come home soon so that she could say what she had come to say and have it over with.

Lucy, who had gone to peer through the heavy curtains at the darkness outside, turned suddenly and came to sit on a footstool near Rebecca. She frowned into her glass of sherry and then looked up.

'Are you going to marry my papa, Aunt Rebecca?'

Rebecca stared at her, taken aback by the girl's directness. Too startled to dissemble, giving herself no time to think, she answered as directly and found the answer surprising even to herself.

'I don't know.'

'You don't *know*?' Lucy repeated, and for a full minute gazed at her without speaking. Her eyes searched Rebecca's face and then she looked back into her glass, raised it to her lips and sipped slowly. 'I think,' she said at last, 'that you mean you are.'

'Why do you say that?'

Lucy shrugged. 'Because until now, you've always said no. Now, you're not sure – or maybe you are. But you're not saying no any more. You're changing, and you'll go on changing until you say yes. Well, that's what I think, anyway.'

'And you, of course,' Rebecca said, conscious of a sudden anger, 'are an expert on such matters.'

'Such matters as marriage?' Lucy shook her head. 'I know nothing about it. I've had no experience of it, you see. My mother died years ago and even before then – I am not sure that what she and Papa had was *marriage*. Not as I'd like to experience it, anyway.'

Rebecca felt herself soften towards the girl. No, what Vivian and Maria had had was certainly not marriage as she understood it. And she had seen only a part of it. What it must have been like for Lucy, living with them . . . She leaned forward and reached for Lucy's hand.

'But you saw the marriage I had. And that was good.'

'I saw some of it,' Lucy said. 'But that was only the part you showed the world, just as Papa and Mamma showed only a part of their marriage to the world. How do I know what it was really like?'

Rebecca was stilled. She leaned back again and said, 'So in what matters are you an expert, that you talk to me like this?'

'I know you,' Lucy said, 'and I know Papa. And I think you've come here to say yes to him. Or if not today, you will very soon.'

'And would that be so terrible? We know each other well, we've been almost one family for years now. Why, I furnished this room – almost the whole house. I know it all as well as you do. And your papa has helped me. Doesn't it seem sensible?'

'Sensible?' Lucy echoed, and her voice was suddenly shrill. '*Sensible*? Is *that* all it means to you? You play with your life, with other people's lives, without a thought for what really matters, and you say it's *sensible*?' She jumped to her feet, suddenly transformed. The assurance was gone, the composure vanished, and in their place was a passion that shook her from head to toe. A fire blazed in her eyes.

'All you're interested in is your precious factory,' she exclaimed. 'Making carpets, that's all you care about – bigger, better, more expensive carpets, and never a thought for the people whose lives you ruin in the process. Don't you realise what it means if you and Papa marry? Don't you realise what it means to *me* – to me and to –'

Her words were cut short by a sudden movement and Rebecca, shaken and stunned by her outburst, realised that Vivian was in the room. How much he had heard she had no idea, but his face was almost black with fury as he gripped his daughter by the shoulders and began to shake her to and fro. Lucy's voice rattled in her throat and turned into passionate sobbing as her head jerked on her shoulders. Frantically, she struggled to free herself, lifting her hands to claw at Vivian's fingers, but his bulky strength was too much for her and she hung powerless in his arms, weeping.

'Vivian!' Rebecca recovered herself and leapt to her feet, pulling at his arms. 'Vivian, don't! You'll hurt her. Let her go, for pity's sake. She doesn't know what she's saying, she's upset –'

'Upset? I'll upset her,' he growled, but he released his hold on Lucy's shoulders and she dropped like a rag doll on to the sofa. 'Yes, miss, you may well sob – if you'd been a few years younger I'd have had you over my knee and spanked you. Get up now, and go to your room – and don't come out until I say you may. And prepare an apology for your aunt while you're there!'

'Really, there's no need,' Rebecca began, but he brushed her aside.

'I'll say whether there's need or not. A daughter of mine behaving in such a way – haranguing her elders and betters as if she knew more of the ways of the world than they do – I've never heard of such a thing. And I'll not countenance it, not for a minute!' He turned his furious face upon his daughter again. 'Get up, I told you! Or do you want me to lift you to your feet? I warn you, I'll not be gentle.' He waited for a moment, then made a movement towards her. Rebecca gave a little cry and reached to stop him, but Lucy was scrambling to her feet. She faced her father and though her face was stained with tears defiance still glittered in her eyes.

'Yes, that's right!' she cried. 'Hit me, push me, pull me – do whatever you like to me. It's only brute strength and you're a brute, Papa, you always were – to me, to Mamma, to anyone who dared go against you. Well, if Aunt Rebecca came here to say she'd marry you she knows now what you're like – and if she *still* wants to marry you, it's her choice. All right, you don't have to force me – I'll go to my room. But I'll never apologise – never! Because you're ruining my life – the two of you – *ruining* it!'

She turned and fled from the room. They heard her footsteps flying up the stairs, the slam of a door somewhere above. And then there was silence.

'And what,' Vivian said heavily, 'do you suppose that was all about?'

Rebecca felt a sudden deep embarrassment. Slowly, she sat down again and reached a shaking hand for the glass of sherry that she had put on the little table nearby. Lucy's was there too, set down when she began her tirade. The liquid quivered in the glass as she raised it to her lips, but the act of swallowing it steadied her a little.

'How much did you hear?' she asked in a low voice.

'Enough, I think. Enough to realise that my daughter's had far too much freedom, far too much say in the affairs of this household.' He poured himself a glass of brandy. 'I've spoiled that girl, Rebecca. Letting her have her head, say no to this suitor and that. I should have married her off months ago, to someone who would have kept her under control. Instead, she's grown so wilful she thinks herself fit now to control *my* life as well as her own!' He came across to the chair where Rebecca sat staring at the fire, and sat down close to her. 'I heard her talking about us,' he said quietly. 'A marriage between you and me. Why should you discuss such a matter with her, Rebecca?'

'I didn't. I didn't come here for that purpose. I came to – to –' She faltered, then gathered her courage and determination together. 'I came to discuss it with you.'

There was a very short silence. The fire hissed and spluttered. Vivian set down his glass and reached out to take Rebecca's from her fingers.

'You came to discuss our marriage?' His voice was very quiet.

She nodded, still keeping her eyes on the fire.

'You came to tell me that you'd marry me after all?'

'What else?' she whispered, and then turned her eyes upon him, knowing that even now she could only be honest with him. There must be no illusions about her acceptance. 'What else can I do, Vivian?'

He looked deep into her eyes. She searched his, wondering what really lay in their depths, what feeling he really had for her. But what right had she to ask? Did she even know what her own feelings were? Did she know the real reason why she was entering upon this bond?

'You're marrying me to save your business,' he said. 'That's true, isn't it, Rebecca? To save your business and your sons.'

'I don't –'

'Rebecca,' he said, 'do you love me?'

Before she could answer, he drew her close against him. She felt his arms hard and strong about her body, his hands on her head, in her hair. She felt his palm cup her cheek as he turned her face up to his, and as she closed her eyes she felt his lips on hers.

For a moment, she made instinctive resistance, quivering like a bird in his arms. Then she felt the power of his kiss, the strength of his mouth as it shaped hers. She felt its insistent vibrations pulse through her body, plucking at the strings of her heart, waking sensations she had forgotten, bringing to life a hunger she had refused to acknowledge. She felt her body tremble and wake, as if from a long sleep, as if her instincts had died with her husband and followed him into his grave. But they were not dead. They had never died.

Vivian withdrew and she opened her eyes to find him watching her. Immediately she was conscious of a deep warmth flooding her cheeks and knew that her skin must be suffused with scarlet. She saw Vivian smile. There was no hiding such a response from him, and no escape now that he knew it.

'So,' he murmured, touching her face with one finger, 'the tigress is still there. You keep her well controlled, Rebecca.'

'Vivian –'

'It's all right,' he said, taking her into his arms again. 'I understand. We understand each other, I think.' He looked down into her face. 'If you marry me, Rebecca, your weavers will have work, your business will be saved – as part of mine. Your customers will become our customers. Your sons will be educated as you wish and there will be a business for them to inherit. All you need and want will be yours, as I've always promised – and a fine long time it's taken you to see it!'

'And in return?' she whispered.

'In return,' he said, 'you will be wife to me for the rest of our lives together. You'll be mother to my daughters as I'll be father to your sons. You'll be wife in every way.' He gave her a slow smile and she felt again that dark movement somewhere inside. 'And I can't believe that I am altogether repugnant to you, Rebecca. I think we shall do very well together. I always have thought that – ever since you were a chit in a housemaid's apron, clearing out the hearth.'

He kissed her again. And Rebecca responded to his kiss and despised her response. And knew, as the hunger stirred again deep within her, that even while he satisfied that hunger, so her aversion would grow. And with it, yet, her need.

And told herself that this was the payment she must make.

'They're going to do it,' Lucy said. Her face was pale, her eyes swollen and her voice husky, as if her tears had drained her of all emotion. She came close to Daniel and laid her hands on his arms, gazing up into his face with a despair that shook her body. 'They're going to get married. Daniel. You know what this means.'

'It means we'll never be able to marry.' His tone was as hopeless as hers. 'Lucy, what are we going to do? We can't let this happen.'

'And how can we prevent it? Do we kidnap her on the wedding day? Keep her locked up somewhere until she comes to her senses – as Papa would like to do with me?' She shook her head. 'What *can* we do? We've no rights at all – we're just children to them, even though Papa calls me "young woman" when it suits him. They'll do just as they plan, and never give a moment's thought to what it means to us.'

'But they don't know what it means,' Daniel pointed out. 'We've been careful to keep our feelings hidden. Why should they know? Why should they consider us?'

Lucy stared at him. 'And do you think it would make one scrap of difference if they did? They're not marrying for love – it's as plain as a doorstep. Your mother is marrying my father simply for what he can do for her business. And he –' She stopped. 'I don't know why he is marrying her,' she said slowly. 'Sometimes, when I look at him, I think it's for some twisted kind of revenge.'

'*Revenge*? Revenge for what?'

Lucy shrugged and held out her hands. 'How do I know? What did she ever do to him? I tell myself it's a strange idea, but then I see that look in his eyes and . . . Daniel, even if it were not for us, I would dislike this marriage.'

Daniel's dark brows came together. 'You don't think he'll ill-treat her? If I believed that –'

'I don't know what he'll do,' Lucy said. 'I'm not even sure that the revenge is against her. Perhaps it's your father he's avenging – he was always jealous of him, you know. Perhaps in a way he's wiping him out. If he possesses all that was his – his business, his wife, his sons – he can pretend that Uncle Francis never existed. Oh!' She turned away, shaking her head. 'I'm talking nonsense. Don't take any notice of me, Daniel. And what does it matter *why*, anyway? The real question is, what are *we* going to do?'

'I'll talk to Mother. I'll try to make her see what she's doing. If you're right – and I have to take notice, Lucy, she's my mother and I can't let her make such a mistake – if you're right, she's got to understand that it would be a mistake. A terrible one. And if not . . .'

'If not,' Lucy said, 'what will you do? If she says she loves him?'

Daniel moved restlessly about the room. Then he came to her and took her in his arms. His face was grave, his mouth set. In that moment he could have been a man of forty rather than a boy of seventeen.

'I'll tell her the truth,' he said. 'It's time we had a chance, Lucy. We love each other too. Why should we never have the chance to share our love, as my mother and father shared theirs?' He shook his head. 'I don't believe she has this feeling for your father, nor he for her. And I believe she'll understand that.'

'*Marry* him?' Tom lifted his head and stared at her. 'You're going to *marry* Vivian Pagnel?'

Rebecca sat down on the chair nearest the fireplace and looked around the room. It was shabby and not as clean as it could be. The little touches Nancy had added – a pot of flowers here, a bright cushion there – were missing and everything seemed overlaid by a patina of dust. Did the housemaid never come in here to clean?

'I can't be bothered,' Tom said when she asked him. 'Girls fussing round me with dusters and such – we never had that sort of thing at home and we lived all right.' She looked at him in surprise. Did he really not remember the weaver's cottage where they had grown up? 'Anyway, never mind that now. Tell me you're joking, Becky – not that it's much of a joke. And not one my Nance would have laughed at either, seeing what he done to her.'

'Oh, Tom.' Rebecca reached a hand towards him. 'Tom, you

must stop brooding on that. I know it was a terrible thing to happen –'

'*Terrible?* It was murder, that's what it was. And why's he never bin brought to justice, tell me that? Why's nobody ever arrested him or sent him for trial? 'Tis easy to see why – 'cause he's a Pagnel, that's why, a big manufacturer and a magistrate as well. Standing to be Mayor of Kidderminster. Stands to reason nobody's going to go against him, 'specially when it's only my word.'

'That's nonsense, Tom. Justice would be served if there really was a case against him – but there's not. There's only your word, that you think you saw him – *think* you did, no more than that. There's no evidence at all. And who have you told, after all? Only your friends and family. You've made no complaint to the authorities.'

'Wouldn't be no use, would it?' Tom muttered, but he avoided his sister's eye and she sighed, feeling a great compassion for him but knowing that he must, for his own sake, be made to face the truth.

'No, Tom, it wouldn't be any use. But that's not the real reason, is it? The real reason is that you're afraid. You're afraid that if you do –'

'All right!' he shouted suddenly, leaping to his feet. 'All right, so I'm afraid. I got reason to be, haven't I? If I say one word against your precious Vivian, he'll drag up all that business of Jabez Gast that's dogged me through my life and stopped me ever getting anywhere. And if it comes to a fight between me and him about who done murder, I know who'll win and who'll lose. It'll be me that swings, not Vivian Pagnel. Me – that never willingly hurt a fly. Me!' He stopped and turned his head and she shrank back at the venom in his eyes. 'I tell you this, Becky, if ever I swing, it'll be for *him*. Aye, and gladly. It'd be a job well done, I reckon.'

Rebecca felt the chill of ice on her skin. She shuddered, distressed more by the force of his hatred than by his words. Did this bitterness eat at her brother all the time? Did it gnaw constantly at his brain, day and night?

'Tom –'

'And you come here and tell me you mean to wed him?' He swung round on her, glaring down with eyes that bulged in a face distorted by hate. 'Do that, Becky, and you're no more sister of mine. I'll not be brother to the man who murdered my wife. Never!'

'Tom, *please* – listen to me. I'm marrying Vivian for the sake of the business – for the weavers. For you and the boys. It's the only thing to –'

'For the *weavers*?' He almost spat his contempt. 'How's that, then? So that they can get work with him? Is that what he's promised? And don't you think he'd give 'em work anyway – aye, and lay 'em off the minute it suited him, too? He don't care about your weavers, Becky, they're just labour to him, so many hands on a loom, that's all. He's just playing on you – he knows how you feel about 'em.'

'Tom, I'm sure that's not true! He's promised to rebuild the co-operative and run it the way Francis and I wanted it run. He wants you to go on managing it, just as you've always done.'

'Then want must be his master,' Tom said grimly, 'for once that man teks over I'll not set foot across the doorstep again. If doorstep there ever is – I'll believe in his rebuilding when I see the walls go up, and not before. He's taking you for a fool, Becky, and you're letting him.'

'And what else can I do?' she demanded, suddenly losing patience. 'You know the position I'm in. Debts piling up about my ears for materials we no longer have, orders for carpets we can't make. The boys to educate and feed and clothe, the house to run – I have to do *something*, Tom. Can *you* tell me what other course I can take? And that's not to mention my trust with the weavers, which I cannot break.' She looked at him with eyes that flashed. 'Very well. Refuse Vivian's offer if you must – go on with this insane bitterness, which is destroying your life far more surely than any other man could do. And cut me out of your life, too, if that's how you feel. But don't tell me what I must and mustn't do, not when you can't offer any other choice. *I* have to live my life, Tom – not you. Just as you have to live yours. And I wish you joy of it.'

She rose to her feet and walked out of the room. Her head was held high but she could feel the heat of tears in her eyes and throat. If Tom had touched her then, she would have turned into his arms and wept. But he did not. He stood aside and let her pass, and so she went out of his house.

The air was crisp and cold against her cheeks, and the tears that lay on them felt like drops of ice. And the ice was inside her, a frozen, jagged pain that tore at her breast as her heart beat raggedly against its walls. It was a cold, heavy lump that lay in her stomach and weighed her down. It was a chill that numbed her legs and made walking a burden.

Almost blindly, she went down Unicorn Street but instead of turning at the end to go through the square and up to Mount Pleasant, she took the opposite way, through the newer part and out towards the fields where the biggest houses of all had recently been built.

It was there that Daniel found her, gazing at the house that Matthew Farrell had built only a few years ago. The house she had helped him to plan, had helped to furnish as she had helped Vivian – but with how much greater pleasure! – and had seen her own sister Bessie come to be housekeeper and enjoy the only happy time of her life. Until that terrible night when Matthew had gone out with a gun, and Bill Bucknell had fallen dead . . .

Matthew, she thought, Matthew. If only you were here to help me now.

But Matthew was far away, labouring out his sentence in New South Wales. He could not return for years yet – might never return. Except for the letters they exchanged, letters that had become increasingly important to her, Matthew was lost.

She turned as footsteps approached, and saw her elder son coming along the road. But there was little pleasure in the sight. For she was as much at odds with Daniel as she was with Tom, and for the same reason.

She watched him gravely as he came near. He had never looked so much a man as he did now. Always a serious child, always mature for his years, he was no longer a boy and could not be treated as one. Nor could his feelings be dismissed as mere calf-love, something that would pass, a mere part of growing up.

'Daniel, were you looking for me?'

He came to stand beside her, looking up at the façade of Matthew's house.

'Is there any reason why I should seek you here?'

Startled, she turned her head. 'None. None at all. I was simply wandering – I hadn't intended coming this way.' Why did she sound defensive, as if justifying her behaviour? Was there any reason why she shouldn't come this way, as easily as any other?

'It's not a pleasant morning for wandering,' he said, but she shook her head.

'I like it. I like this cold, crisp weather.' She hesitated. 'I've just been to see your Uncle Tom.'

She could feel Daniel's eyes upon her. 'And have you told him your plans?'

'Yes.'

'And does he like them?'

Rebecca felt a sudden impatience. 'No, of course he doesn't like them! Nobody likes them, it seems, except for Vivian and me. In spite of the fact that everyone will benefit.'

'Benefit? In what way will we benefit?' There was anger in Daniel's voice too. 'What will this marriage do for anyone except you and Uncle Vivian?'

'Daniel, I've told you why I'm doing this.' She turned away from Matthew's house and began to walk swiftly along the street, anxious now only to be behind her own doors, where she and Daniel could argue – if argue they must – in private. 'No, I won't say another word until we're home. And don't run away from me, saying you've other things to attend to, this must be sorted out between us. I can't have any more resentments around me.'

'I've no intention of running away,' Daniel said grimly as he kept pace with her. 'This is as important to me as it is to you. But I'll tell you this – you can't simply dismiss other people's "resentments" as you call them. Uncle Tom and I have right on our side, and you know it – and that right won't go away. If you persist in this madness –'

'*Daniel!*' They were climbing towards Mount Pleasant now. 'I've told you, I won't listen to such talk. And I *will not* argue with you in public. There are too many ears about. Wait until we're indoors and then you can say whatever you like.'

Daniel closed his mouth firmly and said no more. They came to the big wrought-iron gates and passed through them. At the front door, they stopped and Rebecca looked down over the town.

'See how it's growing,' she said quietly. 'See the new factories, see their chimneys sending smoke into the sky. That smoke means food, Daniel, food and warm clothes and a roof to every man who works there. It isn't pretty – not as the fields and woods are pretty. But neither is starvation pretty.' She turned and looked into his eyes. 'I've seen starvation. I've lived with it and the threat of it. I saw both my parents – your grandparents, Daniel – die of it. It's happening still, I know, and will go on happening. But as long as I can prevent even a small part of it, as long as I can save one man, one woman, one child, from dying of it, I swear I will do so. No matter what it costs.'

'No matter what it costs you?' Daniel asked. 'Or no matter what it costs others?' The door was opened by Betsy and he followed her inside. Barely pausing to speak to the maid, they went into the drawing room and there Rebecca closed the door and turned again to face him.

'No matter what it costs me,' she said, and the quiet note in her voice was threaded through with steel. 'Others must make their own decisions.'

There was a silence. Then Daniel moved away. He stood by the hearth, one hand on the high mantelpiece, staring down into the fire. When he spoke again, his voice was shaking.

'And what decisions can we make? One decision of yours decides so many lives and there's nothing we can do about it. *You* decide to marry Uncle Vivian – *you* decide to hand over the business to him – and what can the rest of us do? Look at Uncle Tom. He's been destroyed by what happened to Aunt Nancy, you know he believes Uncle Vivian responsible – what is it going to do to him? Can you really believe he'll work for you once you're married? And the weavers – it's easy enough for Uncle Vivian to say he'll employ them. He'll need more men anyway so all they'll have to do is ask for work. But do you *know* that he'll take them on, rather than others? And why should you be so concerned anyway?'

'Why?' Rebecca stared at him. 'Of course I must concern myself with them. They worked with your father and me, we set up the co-operative together.'

'The co-operative! Exactly. That's what it was supposed to be – with every man taking his own share of the responsibility. So why do you have to take it all now? Why is it suddenly all your burden?'

'Because I'm in a position to help them,' Rebecca retorted. 'And help them I will.'

'No matter what it costs,' he repeated grimly. 'No matter what it costs Uncle Tom – or me.'

'It need cost you nothing,' she began, but he cut in with a roughness that was uncharacteristic of him.

'Nothing? Do you call it *nothing*, when I see all my future happiness disappearing in a puff of smoke? When I know I'll never be able to marry the woman I love? Is that *nothing*?'

'Daniel, you exaggerate.'

'I do not,' he said flatly. 'I do not exaggerate. If you marry Uncle Vivian, I shall never be able to marry Lucy. She'll be my stepsister, and even though there's no blood between us –'

'Daniel –'

'If you marry him,' he said, 'you will kill Uncle Tom. And you might as well kill Lucy and me.'

Chapter Ten

Rebecca folded the pages and held them against her heart. She had a strange feeling, as if she were closing a door, a door that had been left slightly open for many years in case someone – someone half expected, wholly welcome – should come in.

As if in echo of her thoughts, she heard a tap on the door of her bedroom, and turned as it opened and Polly entered. She gave Rebecca the glance of an old friend who means to be blunt.

'It's time you took yourself out and got some fresh air,' she said. 'You've been moping in here for too long. What are you writing about now?'

Rebecca smiled faintly. 'I've been writing to Matthew. It's time I told him what's been happening here. I haven't written since before the fire – I hadn't the heart. Now he must know.'

Polly came over and laid a hand on Rebecca's shoulder. 'Are you telling him about Mr Vivian?'

'Yes.' Rebecca looked at the folded pages. 'I am.'

'Well,' Polly said after a moment, 'I daresay he'll be glad to know you're getting settled.'

Rebecca looked up at her. 'Do you think I'm doing the right thing, Polly?'

'The right thing? How does anyone know what's the right thing? Depends what you mean by "right", don't it?' Seems to me it's the *sensible* thing, if that's any use.'

'Do you really think so, Polly?'

'Well, of course I do. Stands to reason, don't it? Here's you all by yourself in this great house with those two boys to feed and no money coming in to do it with – and there's Mr Vivian in his house, with all those girls and all the money he could want. All he lacks is a wife, and all you need is a husband – so what better? And you could fare a lot worse than Mr Vivian. Still a fine figure of a man. You could end up with some old crab of a bachelor, just to get a roof over your head!'

Rebecca laughed, then said ruefully, 'You make it sound very easy. I wish I could be as sure . . . I keep having doubts, Polly. And everyone else seems so against it. Tom – Daniel –'

'They're not the ones who have to decide,' Polly said definitely. 'It's your life, Becky, and you've got to live it, best you can. Tom – he's still upset over Nancy, and no wonder, but he don't see things straight. You can't let him rule you. And Danny – well, he's still a boy for all he's got so tall, and he's just jealous. He's thought hisself the man of the family since his father died and he don't want to see no one else taking over. That's all that's wrong with that young man.'

'It isn't,' Rebecca said. She hesitated, then said, 'No one else knows this, Polly, but Daniel has other reasons for opposing my marriage. You see, he and Lucy think themselves in love. They want to marry.'

Polly stared at her. 'Those children! In *love*? They don't know the meaning of the word.'

'They believe they do. And, remember, I was younger than Daniel when I fell in love with Francis. I can't tell them they're too young. I can understand it all too well.'

'But Dan and Lucy! They've had no experience – not met anyone else. They grew up together. How can they know?'

'In just the same way as we did,' Rebecca said. 'By their feelings. Polly, I can't dismiss this as calf-love. Perhaps it is, perhaps they will grow out of it, but it's very real to them just now and I can't tell them to stop feeling it.'

'No, maybe not. But there's nothing they can do about it for years yet. Daniel's barely eighteen, he'll not be able to marry for years. And Lucy – well, I've heard Mr Vivian's got other plans for her. He won't want her on the shelf for the next five or six years, waiting for Danny to grow up.' Polly frowned. 'Anyway, I don't see why it should set 'em against your marriage. I'd have thought they'd want you on their side, thinking the way you do.'

'It's nothing to do with that.' Rebecca sighed. 'I don't suppose Daniel would ever have thought of this. But Lucy's a sharp-witted girl and she saw the difficulties immediately. You see, Polly, if Vivian and I marry, Daniel and Lucy will be stepbrother and sister. And Lucy says they won't be allowed to marry. Even though –'

'Here, but could they anyway?' Polly interrupted. 'I mean, they're cousins and I know there ent no law against cousins marrying, but still a lot of folks are set against it. And it's up to the vicar.'

'I was going to say,' Rebecca said, '"even though there is no blood relationship". You've forgotten – and I daresay a lot of other people have too – that Francis and Vivian were never true cousins. They shared no blood tie at all. And in any case, Lucy and Daniel would only have been second cousins. But as stepbrother and sister –' she moved her hands, spreading them palm upwards '– I simply don't know. Again, I think it might be up to the vicar. Perhaps even the bishop. In any case, it would be bound to be difficult.' She paused for a moment. 'Even if Vivian himself were to agree to it.'

'And you think he won't?'

'Can *you* see it, Polly? Lucy being allowed to remain unmarried for another seven years or so until Vivian decides that Daniel is old enough to marry her? Even then, will he be able to support a wife? And Vivian wants a wealthy husband for each of his daughters – which Daniel will never be now. Unless –'

'Unless you marry Mr Vivian,' Polly supplied. 'And there we are back at the beginning again.'

'Exactly. So – you see my dilemma.'

'Aye, I do. But I still don't see as you have to let other people rule what *you* want to do,' Polly said stoutly. 'Look, Becky, your life's the only one you can live. You can't live other people's lives for 'em, now can you? So why should you let them live yours? Dan and Lucy's problems are *their* problems, not yours

– and who's to say they're going to go on feeling like this for another five, six, seven years? Even another five or six months – you know how young folk change. All right, I know *you* never did – but that don't mean Dan and Lucy can't alter their minds. And very likely will.'

'But if Lucy's right – and even if the law isn't against it, Vivian will never allow it.'

'Then he'll never allow it anyway,' Polly declared. 'You and him being married isn't going to make one scrap of difference to that. And he won't look on Danny with any more favour because he's a pauper. Which is what he's going to be, if you don't take this chance now, mark my words.'

'Polly, it's not that bad. I can still find a way –'

'What way? You've tried starting again, rebuilding the factory, and you know it won't work. The weavers hev done their best, but they can't work for naught, they've got families to feed as you know all too well. And if they'd managed to get the building standing again, where were you going to find money for looms? Who was going to let you have wool and dyes and bobbins on credit?' Polly shook her head. 'I'm sorry to be so blunt, Becky, but you got to see sense. You know the only way to keep going is to wed Mr Vivian and you ought to think yourself lucky you got the chance.'

'Yes, I suppose so,' Rebecca said after a pause. She looked up and gave Polly a wry smile. 'So instead of selling carpets, I have to sell myself.'

'And what does any woman do when she gets wed?' Polly demanded. 'Why does a man marry unless he wants summat from his wife – money, a name or her body? And what's she doing but giving – *selling* – it for whatever he's got that *she* wants? That's what marriage *is*, Becky, not some fairytale romance. And if you'd stop seeing your life with Mr Francis through rosy spectacles, you'd know it. It weren't always easy, even for you.'

'No, it wasn't.' Rebecca thought of the time when she and Francis had seemed to become estranged, when everything they did or said seemed to drive them further apart. 'But I don't think I *sold* –'

'No, you didn't.' Polly spoke more softly. 'But it was different for you then. You were just a housemaid, and him a son of the house. There had to be summat special to keep you two together. But most women of the class you're in now – well, their marriages are like what it'll be between you and Mr Vivian. Advantages on both sides, see. That's what you got to look at. And you just hev to make the best of it. Not that I can see you'll hev any cause to complain. He's a fine man, Mr Vivian, and there'll be many a Kidderminster widow envious of you.'

'Yes, I daresay.' Rebecca smiled faintly. 'But Polly, when you've known love –'.

'You've been luckier than many. And now you got to do what the rest of us hev to do and take what life hands out.' Polly bit her lip. 'I'm sorry, Becky, I've been speaking out of turn. There's nobody knows better than you about taking what life hands you. And I don't blame you for not wanting to lay yourself open to more trouble. But what choice do you hev? It's trouble if you don't take him – and if you do, will it be so bad? He's mellowed a lot over the years.'

'I know. And he's been a good friend to me. No, it's just Daniel and Lucy that worry me.'

'Then don't let 'em,' Polly advised. 'Take my word for it, Becky, they might make a fuss now but in a few months' time they'll hev found summat else to think about. Lucy'll hev her head turned by some other young man – someone her Pa will approve of, I wouldn't wonder – and Danny'll hev *his* head stuck in a book, same as always. And you'll be the Mayor's wife and queening it over all of us.'

Rebecca laughed. 'I'll never do that, Polly – and if I did, you'd soon cut me down to size!' She gazed with affection at the housekeeper. 'You've been a good friend to me over the years,' she said quietly. 'There are times when I don't know what I'd have done without you.'

'Aye, and times when you might hev been better off,' Polly

said shortly, and Rebecca knew that she was thinking about the day when Geoffrey had fallen into the river. 'Well, none of us can alter the past and what's gone is gone. It's the future you wants to be thinking of now, Becky, and you know I'll be your friend whatever you makes up your mind to do. And now I'd better get back to the kitchen. It's Cook's afternoon out and there's no knowing what them girls will get up to with my back turned as well. They're not like they were when we were maids, Becky – seem to think they can do what they like, no discipline at all.'

She got heavily to her feet and lumbered from the room, leaving Rebecca looking after her with an affectionate smile on her lips. Dear Polly. It was strange to look at her now, a stout, almost majestic figure in her black bombazine, and remember the skinny little kitchenmaid who had dumped a load of dirty dishes in front of the timid new scullerymaid. But I don't suppose I look much like that scullerymaid, either, she thought. What a lot had happened since those days.

And how much was still to come? Still only midway into her thirties, she wasn't even half through her adult life. What more lay in store, during the years ahead? Marriage with Vivian – and then what? Was she really to settle down into matronly middle age, as everyone must expect? Or was there more upheaval, more turmoil to toss her about like a boat in a storm?

Rebecca looked again at the letter she had finished just before Polly had come into the room. By the time it reached Matthew, she might be already married. And if she waited . . . ?

With a shake of her head, she sat down again and picked up her pen to write his address.

'So they really do intend to do it.' Lucy withdrew herself from Daniel's arms and looked up into his face. 'You've talked to your mother?'

'Yes. And I can see her tearing herself apart over it all. She really does feel for us, Lucy, but at the same time she –'

'She doesn't believe it will last. She doesn't believe it's *real*.'

Lucy spoke bitterly. 'We're too young, we don't know what we're talking about. Yet for her, at sixteen, it was real enough. She was just lucky enough to be a housemaid, with no one to forbid her –'

'She wasn't exactly encouraged,' Daniel pointed out quickly. 'Dismissed without a character, with only enough money to go to London to find her brother and sister. It wasn't easy, Lucy.'

'No, but she was able to marry your father in the end. She did have what she wanted. Whereas we . . . What does she think we should do, Daniel? Forget each other – when we'll be living in the same house? Wait for years and years, not even knowing whether we'll be allowed to marry in the end?'

'I suppose that's all we can do,' he said miserably. 'What other course is there, after all?'

'There would be no need for either if *they* didn't get married,' Lucy said savagely. 'Oh, we'd have to wait a while, I know that. But we'd know we *could* get married at the end of it. We could be engaged. But this way – don't they realise, Daniel, it's our *lives*?'

'It's their lives too,' he said. 'And Mother is in a difficult position. If she doesn't marry, she'll have to leave the house – sell it, just to live. And who else is she to marry? Would you have her sell herself to the highest bidder? At least she and your father know each other well and are friends.'

Lucy gave him a glance of contempt. 'I see you've been persuaded. There's no more to be said, then. We're to be brother and sister, no more.' She held out her hand and spoke coolly, as if to someone she had met only briefly at a soirée. 'I wish you well, Daniel. Will you still be going to America, do you think?'

Daniel stared at her. 'Lucy, don't speak to me like that, so coldly. Don't look at me like – like a stranger. I can't bear it.'

'And how else am I to look at you and speak to you?' she demanded. She turned away from him and paced to the window, staring down into the wintry garden. 'Won't it be best if we think of each other as strangers from now on?' She turned back and gave him a long, deliberate gaze. 'Won't it be best if we forget everything that's happened? Everything we ever wanted to happen?'

He took a step towards her. 'No! It wouldn't be best – it would be torment. You know we can't forget, Lucy. And if we have to live in the same house, seeing each other every day, pretending all the time ... I won't be able to bear it, Lucy. I won't!'

'Then *do something about it!*' she exclaimed. 'Daniel, don't you see it's no use just *accepting* things like this? We can't let our parents rule our lives in this way. They've had their chance – we haven't even begun yet. It's our turn to make our lives. If theirs haven't turned out as they wish, it's not our fault. And they'll do what they want to do anyway. So why shouldn't we?' Her eyes blazed at him. 'Why don't we just *do* it, Daniel? Why do we have to *ask* all the time, especially when we know we'll be refused.'

'Just do it?' he repeated, and then more strongly, 'Just *do* it? Lucy, you're right. We *will* just do it. We'll run away. We'll elope. We'll get married – and then let them do their worst. Let them marry or not, as they will. We'll be far away and beyond their reach – beyond caring.' He came forward and his face was alight as he gripped her by the waist. 'Lucy, we'll go to Scotland. We can marry there without consent. And then we'll go to America. I'll find work there. We'll start a new life, and *no one* will tell us what to do!'

He pulled her into his arms and began to kiss her. And Lucy clung to him, returning kiss for kiss, laughing with excitement as her hair came loose and flowed like a shimmer of sunlight over her shoulders and over his burning face.

Scotland. America. A new life for both of them.

And no one to tell them how it should be lived.

Christmas came with a whirl of preparation. Vivian had decided to give a large party, at which he and Rebecca would announce their engagement. Every large manufacturer in the town would be there, together with several other men of importance and those whom Vivian thought it wise to cultivate. The house was brightly lit with candles and Chinese lanterns and decorated with holly; there was a tree in one corner, hung with bunches of sweetmeats and almonds wrapped in coloured paper, and in the centre of the hall hung a huge ball of mistletoe.

'For the happy couple to kiss beneath,' Vivian explained as Rebecca came in and gazed about her. She had been forbidden to visit the house until everything was done, and only now, the day before the party itself, was she allowed to come and inspect his preparations. 'Well? Do you approve?'

'It all looks beautiful,' Rebecca said. In fact, she was surprised at the colour and gaiety that Vivian had produced; the house, built for him when he had married Maria, had always seemed gloomily cavernous to her. 'Did Lucy help you with it? I've hardly seen her lately.'

Vivian scowled. 'That young lady help me! I wish I could say yes, but she's been even more difficult these past few days. Still sulking over our marriage, saying we're ruining her life – I really have difficulty in keeping my hands off her at times. A good whipping is what that girl needs and if she were a few years younger I'd give it myself, gladly.'

Rebecca sighed. 'I know. Daniel's been the same, though he doesn't say much now. But I'd begun to think they were getting over it – Dan's seemed better lately, more cheerful, as if he'd accepted the situation. I'd hoped Lucy might have done so, too.'

'Well, she's stopped her tantrums,' Vivian admitted. 'But you know Lucy – she's a headstrong, wilful girl and never gives up when she really wants something. And she certainly hasn't helped with all these preparations!'

'I hope they won't be troublesome at the party,' Rebecca said anxiously. 'It would be dreadful to have a scene just as we make the announcement.'

Vivian smiled at her. 'That won't happen, my dear. Lucy won't even be here. No, she hasn't refused to come – though I'd not have been surprised if she had. I've decided to send her away for Christmas. She'll be spending it with my relatives in Wiltshire. My mother's sister has been asking to have one of the girls for a long time now, and Lucy will do well there. She might even find some young man to take her mind off Daniel.'

'Sending her away?' Rebecca stared at him. 'But – do you think that's wise? It'll look so odd.'

'Not at all. Why should it? Young girls often spend the festive season with relatives. The fact that we're announcing our engagement at the same time has nothing to do with it. And she'll be back for our wedding, naturally. You'll want her to be a maid of honour.'

'Yes, of course. But Vivian, if she and Daniel still –'

'They won't,' he said with confidence. 'And now, my dear, let's forget those foolish children. Come and give me a kiss under the mistletoe, just to make sure that it's adequate.'

Rebecca laughed, feeling a nervous quiver touch her heart. 'Adequate, indeed! Vivian, you –'

But her words were lost beneath his lips as he pulled her close against him and laid his mouth on hers. She felt his arms, like iron bands around her, his body hard against hers, and knew that he was aroused. A flash of excitement surged through her and she shuddered against him and knew that he felt it and knew it for what it was. His hands moved over her body and with the excitement she felt an instant repulsion, and shivered again.

Vivian let her go. He looked down at her, his eyes dark, and she stared back at him, knowing that if there had been no risk of discovery he would have taken her there and then. But they were in the big hall, where at any moment a servant might pass through or someone knock at the front door. For the time being, she was safe.

Safe? Was this how a bride should think when kissing her husband-to-be? Particularly a bride who had already been married and knew all that it involved. And how was it that she could feel this thrill of fear, alongside an equally strong quiver of excitement?

Rebecca remembered the excitement she had never failed to feel when she and Francis had lain together in love. She had felt no fear then. But this sensation was different. This excitement did not burn with a clear, light flame like the fire she had kindled with Francis. There was a darkness in this blaze, a physical need that had nothing to do with love, as she had known it. Her body would respond to Vivian's touch and take pleasure in it while she in her turn pleasured him. But this flame would burn darkly, as if clouded with smoke. As if it were in some way contaminated.

Nonsense! she told herself angrily. You're thinking nonsense. You can't expect it to be the same as it was with Francis. As for love – Vivian and I have been friends for many years, I'm fond of him, isn't that enough? And if I can find pleasure in our marriage and give it to him as well, what is wrong with that?

So why did she feel this tremor of fear? Why this shadow, cold upon her heart?

The next day was busy in both houses with preparations for the party. Rebecca was caught up with last-minute fittings for her new gown. She had chosen a brocaded silk, richly patterned with flowers of deep red and gold, which echoed the tawny colours of her hair and the dark topaz of her eyes. The neck was low, revealing her creamy shoulders and dropping to the swell of her breasts, and the waist was drawn in small, belling out to a hemline nearly four yards wide. The sleeves were fashionably tight and as she gazed at herself in the mirror she knew that Vivian could have no complaints about the picture she presented. It was difficult to believe that she had once been a housemaid.

'It's perfect,' she said to the seamstress. 'You've worked very hard on it, Mrs Welling. Thank you.'

The dressmaker got to her feet with some difficulty. Her knees were swollen with arthritis and she didn't know how long she would be able to go on doing this, crawling round the floor with a mouthful of pins and sewing far into the night so that some fashionable lady would be able to queen it at a swell party. But when it was someone like Mrs Pagnel, you didn't mind so much. Always gave a thought to those who worked for her, and always remembered to say thank you, too.

'Well, it do look lovely on you,' she declared. 'Be the belle of the ball, you will. They say the whole town will be there at Mr Pagnel's house, and the place lit up like a fairy palace.'

'He certainly hasn't spared any expense.' Rebecca thought ruefully of what the money spent on decorations could have done for her weavers. Rebuilt half the factory – set them up with new looms – paid them for the next six months . . . But it was no use thinking on those lines. Vivian would have laughed outright at any suggestion that he might spend the money in that way instead. And he had been as good as his word, after all. He had taken on almost all her weavers in his own carpet shops, and had begun the rebuilding as well.

It was almost time to leave. Her maid had spent an hour or more dressing her hair, and she was now ready. She looked again into the mirror and wondered just how it had come about that little Becky Himley from the weavers' hovels had turned into this glittering creature. I don't feel like myself at all, she thought, staring at her reflection. I shall be glad when all this is over and I can be my real self again.

'Where are the boys?' she asked as Polly came in to admire her, and then caught sight of them just behind the housekeeper. 'Come here, both of you.' She caught her breath, suddenly unable to speak.

'Aren't they fine young men?' Polly said. 'Look at William, he's grown so much lately he's almost out of this suit afore he's worn it! And Dan – pass for a man of thirty, he could, any day of the week.'

'Yes. He could.' Rebecca stared at her sons and felt a lump in her throat. If only their father could have been here to see them now, so tall and grown up. Neither of them fair like him – Geoffrey had been the most like Francis – but Daniel, although dark like Rebecca herself, had the same air of quietness and reserve, the same sense of integrity. She would always be able to trust Daniel to do what he believed to be right.

William, beginning to fill out now, was going to be big and broad like both grandfathers, but he had Jeremiah's features, his heavy brows and straight glance. And would be as positive, she knew, for William had never been a child to suffer either fools or discomfort gladly. It was difficult to remember that he had ever given her any worry as a baby, yet he had had a poor start and sometimes she had doubted whether he would grow at all.

'Well, Mother?' he said now, parading in front of her in his new mulberry tail-coat, its long lapels revealing a silk waistcoat as richly embroidered as any lady's evening gown. 'Are you proud of your sons? Don't we look fine?'

'Very fine indeed,' she said, holding them in turn by the shoulders to inspect them. 'You're quite the dandy, William.' She turned her eyes on Daniel, more discreetly dressed in dark grey, with a waistcoat in silver figured silk. 'And Daniel will be sought by every mother with a marriageable daughter.'

As soon as she had said it, she regretted the words. Daniel's face darkened and he turned away from her. But when he spoke, his voice was as calm as ever.

'I'll come to you for protection, then. And now there are one or two things I must attend to before we go. The carriage is ready, Mother.'

'I've brought your cloak.' Polly came forward and draped it about Rebecca's shoulders, taking care not to disarrange her hair. 'I hope everything goes well,' she said softly, and Rebecca felt the sudden sting of tears in her eyes. This was the end of something, she thought as she squeezed Polly's hand. The end of an era. When she came back into the house later tonight, she would no longer be Rebecca Pagnel, widow of Francis. She would be engaged to Vivian, with different responsibilities and different matters on her mind.

The house was filled with guests, as glittering in their newly fashionable clothes as the decorations Vivian had caused to be hung around the walls, shimmering like the lights in the chandeliers that hung from the ceilings. Rebecca moved amongst them, feeling as if she had wandered into some strange fantasy world. In all her life, she had never known a ball like this one; even Jeremiah's wife, Isabella, had never given anything so grand, and Vivian had rarely entertained on any scale.

She felt the now familiar quiver of excitement and apprehension whenever she caught sight of him. On the stroke of midnight, he would draw her to his side and announce their engagement, and from that moment she would be committed to him. His, for the rest of their lives. And everything she owned his, likewise.

But how much did she own anyway? Without Vivian's help, she would have been forced to sell Pagnel House and move into something much smaller. She would have had to use the bulk of the money to pay her debts; there would have been little left for her living expenses and those of her sons. No, Vivian was gaining little enough of material value from their marriage.

The ballroom had been cleared for dancing, with the musicians on the stage at the far end, and the dining room laid for supper. In the throng, it was easy to lose sight of people and by the time Vivian led Rebecca into supper she had barely seen her sons. She caught sight of William laughing with a throng of young women who clustered about him like flowers, and sent a message across the room to him, by way of raised eyebrows and parted lips. Where was Daniel? But William nodded reassuringly and grinned in his old, schoolboyish way so that she felt at ease again. It was disconcerting, seeing her sons grow up so abruptly, but William at least was still his old self and more likely to slip a spoonful of jelly down his cousin Margaret's back than to cause any more serious mischief.

Before she could look around again for Daniel, Vivian was offering her a plate of glazed ox tongue, cut from the great arched tongues which, decorated with truffles, hard-boiled eggs and parsley, formed one of the centrepieces of the supper table. Alongside were ranged several cold roast goose and other fowl, and a side of beef; great bowls of vegetables and silver *attelettes* threaded with aspic shapes, cocks' combs and mushrooms.

'Your kitchen servants must have been busy for days,' Rebecca said, accepting the plate and following Vivian to a small table. She sat down, looking at the gleaming, colourful food and thinking of the commotion each dish must have caused, to create such perfection. 'I hope you give them a generous Christmas box for their trouble.'

Vivian looked exasperated. 'Trust you, Rebecca, to be thinking of the lower orders! It's their *job*, my dear, and very well paid they are for doing it. Not that I shan't be generous, of course,' he added a little hastily as she raised her eyes. 'I think I know how to treat my staff. But they enjoy using their skills, and now let us enjoy the fruits of them.' He touched her hand and smiled at her. 'This is a happy occasion, my dear.'

'Yes, of course.' Rebecca smiled back, but there was reserve in her smile. Once again, she was conscious of the fact that tonight would change everything. And a feeling too that there might be more change than they had accounted for.

She ate slowly, absently, her thoughts far away. What was Matthew doing, so far away, on the other side of the world? It must be the height of summer now. Was he too preparing for Christmas? Were the women of the household busy cooking, making pastry, baking cakes? Did they have suppers like this or was their fare simpler?

She wondered, as she had wondered several times lately, if Matthew had ever found a woman to love. Convicts did, she knew, and even married sometimes, and it seemed that Matthew's master now was a kindly man who treated his assigned men well. And was it reasonable to suppose that a man like Matthew, so strong, so virile, so attractive, would remain long without a woman? The thought brought her a sharp pain, and she tried to thrust it away as she had done so many times. But each time it returned, nagging her like an uneasy tooth.

Had Matthew received her letter yet? Did he know about

the fire – about her marriage to Vivian? And if so, what was his reaction?

Suppose he were to come striding through the door now, his face tanned from sun and open air, his body lean and hard with toil, his eyes and hair bright, his presence like a gale of fresh air amongst all these padded, pampered town-dwellers. What would she do?

'. . . another glass of champagne?' Startled, she realised that Vivian was still speaking, and refilling her glass. She felt her skin warm with a blush as she realised how far her thoughts had taken her – and into what dangerous realms. Never before had she allowed herself to think of Matthew in that way, never had there been any hint that she should do so. When he had left, Francis had still been alive, and there had been nothing but friendship between herself and Matthew. A warm friendship, admittedly, but that warmth no more than it should be. So why were her thoughts taking her in this direction now?

I'm behaving like a foolish girl, she told herself firmly. I'm making romance in my head because I don't have it in my life. All this – these glittering lights and dresses – they don't make the kind of romance that Francis and I knew or the love we shared. And perhaps I expect too much in thinking it might come again. Polly's right. What Vivian offers me is the kind of life any woman would envy, and I must do my best to give him whatever it is he wants from me. I must be a good wife to him, in every way.

She smiled across the table and lifted her glass. 'Yes,' she said, 'it is a happy occasion.'

Supper had been served early especially so that Vivian could make his announcement at midnight. The hour was fast approaching and once again Rebecca looked about for her sons. But neither was visible now, and when it wanted only five minutes to the hour and Vivian led her to the stage, she was trembling with anxious irritation. Where were they, when they should surely have been by her side?

The musicians gave a flourish, a fanfare of music and a roll of drums. As the dancers stopped and looked up and others crowded in from the supper room, Vivian held up his hands and the ballroom fell silent.

'Ladies and gentlemen,' he began, and his voice resonated through the great room. 'Friends. I have gathered you all here tonight, not simply to celebrate Christmas but to join me in a special occasion of my own. After more than eight years of widowhood, I have decided to marry again. And my waiting has proved to be more than worthwhile – for I have been fortunate enough to secure the hand of the beautiful woman you see by my side, and whom you all know. Rebecca Pagnel has promised to be my wife and I know you'll all congratulate me on my good fortune.'

There was an astonished silence – though why they should all be so surprised, Rebecca didn't know, since Vivian had been so emphatic that it was the obvious thing to do – and then the guests broke into applause. The musicians struck up with a sentimental ballad, and Vivian led Rebecca down to the floor to begin the dancing. As they swirled about the floor, others joined in and they were thronged by people wanting to offer their congratulations.

They seem really pleased, Rebecca thought, dazed. Except for those other widows and spinsters and mothers of young, unmarried girls who are jealous underneath their smiles. And the fathers who see Vivian's wealth escaping their own daughters. And the married women who would have liked to become his mistress – those who have not already done so.

And those others, her own friends, who looked at her with concern and even pity. And from them all, she turned away. She knew why she had taken this step, and she knew she had had no choice. Let those who had choice think of their own good fortune, and let no one envy hers, for who knew how lives would turn out?

By four o'clock the tables had been cleared of the debris of supper and laid again with breakfast. Scrambled eggs, devilled kidneys, bacon and mushrooms appeared on large, covered platters, and the guests declared themselves famished and began to pile their plates again. Rebecca, still thinking of those below stairs, declined any more to eat.

'I'm so tired, Vivian – I'll have to go home.' She glanced about her. 'Where *are* those boys? I've scarcely set eyes on William, except to see him surrounded by girls, and Daniel might never have been here at all. Find them please, Vivian, and tell them I want to go home now.'

He laid a hand on her shoulder and went off. He had been very kind, she thought, watching his broad shoulders make a path through the crowd. He had looked after her well, knowing she wasn't accustomed to functions like this one, and had behaved in every way like the solicitous suitor he was. Nobody, observing him tonight, would have any doubts about his being a good husband to her.

She leant back her head and closed her eyes. It would be good to get home and sink into her own bed. She hoped that Betsy would have gone to hers, as instructed. Rebecca knew what it was like to wait up into the small hours for the family to come home, and had no intention of making her own maid wait for her.

'*Rebecca!*'

Startled, she opened her eyes. Vivian was standing before her, his face like thunder. Beside him was William, looking half defiant, half scared. Bewildered, she looked from one to the other.

'What is it? What's happened?' Suddenly afraid, she began to rise to her feet. 'Is it Daniel? Has something happened to him?' She reached out and caught at Vivian's sleeve. 'Is he hurt?'

'Hurt?' Vivian snarled. 'He will be by the time I've finished with him – once I've caught up with him, the young scoundrel! Do you know what they've done, the pair of them? Do you know what ridiculous folly they're perpetrated now – what downright lunacy –'

'Vivian, stop it! Tell me what's happened. Where *is* Daniel? I haven't seen him all evening.' She stared at him and a terrible fear dawned on her. 'Vivian, what has he done?'

'He's run away with my daughter, that's what he's done.' Vivian's voice was hoarse with fury. 'A message came a few minutes ago, from Wiltshire. The minx never turned up there. And when I find William and ask him where his brother is, he first tries to fob me off with lies and then eventually comes out with the truth. It was all arranged, apparently. They've run away together.'

'*Run away?* Daniel and Lucy?' Rebecca stared at him, then turned her eyes upon her son. 'William? Is this true? Did you know about it?'

He nodded, shamefaced but meeting her eye. 'Yes, Mother. It's true enough.' He paused, then said with a tinge of triumph he could not quite conceal, 'Dan and Lucy have eloped.'

MATTHEW

Chapter Eleven

The last stand of timber for the day had been felled and the sweating, exhausted convicts were shambling back to the Barracks. Matthew watched them go. It had been as hard a day as he could recall since the morning six years ago when he had landed in this strange, beautiful, terrible place they called New South Wales.

He followed the last and slowest of the line, the men in irons whose ankles were shackled together so that they could walk and do the work set them, but never move with freedom, never run or jump. Not that many of them were fit to do either, he thought bitterly. The toil of their days and the vicious punishment they suffered at the slightest offence used all the poor strength they possessed.

Around them as they shuffled along the rough road, deep in mud from the day's rains, lay the fallen trees. Trees such as never grew in England – eucalypts, with peeling white bark and tough leaves that shivered in the breeze. Homes for the odd little bears that lived in their branches, too sleepy to move, stretching out a weary paw now and then for another fistful of leaves to chew and, like so many of the other animals inhabiting this topsy-turvy land, carrying their young in pouches in their stomachs, or on their backs; as amiably attractive as a child's toy until you disturbed one, when it could lacerate you with claws of poison.

A kookaburra chortled raucously from the trees as if someone had just told a dubious joke, and Matthew permitted himself a small, wry smile. It was the only laughter heard in these parts, a mockery that came from the country itself and heightened by the fact that the mocker was a bird. You heard it in the morning, as you trudged in line to begin the day's labours, and again in the evening as you crawled back to the meagre comforts of the huts. And at times during the day, amidst the cacophony of screeches and warbles from the other birds who flocked above your head.

White cockatoos with brilliant yellow crests, grey, pink-breasted parrots, tiny green parakeets; animals that bounced rather than walked or ran – it was like working in a zoo. Correction: it was like being the inmate of a zoo, while the birds and animals roamed free around your cage.

He was conscious of someone walking beside him – Jake, his fellow overseer, another convict promoted because of his experience in farming. The kind of ruffian Matthew most despised, mealy-mouthed and obsequious with authority, vicious towards the men who had been his comrades only a short while before. He carried a whip and used it as he walked, flicking the buttocks of the men at the end of the line as if by so doing he could make the whole platoon go faster.

'Why bother?' Matthew said. 'It doesn't hurt the ones at the front and men in irons can't go any quicker than that anyway – not at the end of the day.'

'Then it's time they could. And a little ticklin' does 'em no harm.' He flicked a little harder. 'I'd like to make 'em squeak. Stone men, they call themselves! They wouldn't be stone for long if I had the floggin' of 'em, I can tell you. This tickler's no use for man nor beast.' He glanced with disgust at the whip. 'A proper cat, that's what we need here, and not one of those government jobs either, unravelling after fifty lashes. I'd make my own, good and hard and stiff, with a bit o' iron whipped into the ends.'

Matthew kept his repugnance from showing on his face. Jake was as capable of denouncing him to the military as he was of 'tickling' the convicts' backsides with his whip. And it would benefit nobody if Matthew were to be back there amongst them, shuffling in irons at the end of the line to be tickled in his turn. At least as an overseer he could lessen their sufferings

222

a little, and he was no more anxious to return to the line than any other man might be. The miserable life of a convict – or 'government man' as they were coming to be called – was one that no sane person would wish to continue, and Matthew's main ambition now was to gain his ticket-of-leave and live as a relatively free man.

But he wasn't prepared to achieve this freedom at the expense of his fellow sufferers. Crawling to the soldiers, fawning and kow-towing to them, catching animals or birds to add to their rations, accusing the convicts of idleness or insolence so that they might be flogged – Matthew turned his face away from all of this. It didn't make him popular with the soldiers, nor with overseers like Jake Withers, but that didn't matter so long as he did nothing they could actually complain of. But neither did it bring his 'freedom' any closer.

Freedom! he thought ruefully. So this was what he had come to – shackled by his principles as surely as these poor villains were shackled by their leg irons. And yet reluctant to lose even the few small advantages he had – the privileges accorded to one who had 'special' knowledge. And Matthew's knowledge was more 'special' than most. His years in America, riding the prairies, felling timber, driving cattle and fighting the Indians, were almost unique amongst the crowds of felons who had lived all their lives in England or Ireland, many of them scraping a living from the crowded streets of the cities.

Even those who came themselves from farming stock knew little of living under the stars, making camp and hunting their food. Poachers and gipsies came off best in this country, he found; they at least were used to slipping through the trees at night, snaring animals and throwing them in the pot. But convicts were rarely allowed such freedom, and these skills were called into being mostly by men who tried to escape. And even then they were often beaten by the country, whose harshness they had underestimated.

The rain was falling again as they reached the collection of huts where the convicts lived. It was a strange kind of prison, this, with men living together almost as in a village, cooking their own rations, looking after themselves. A few in each hut, and as close as brothers – mates, they called each other, and they stuck together like limpets. A rough kind of brotherhood but all the human feeling they were allowed and perhaps all the more intense because of it.

Matthew and Jake parted to go to their own quarters. They lived with the settlers to whom they had been assigned – men who had left England in an attempt to find here some trace of the prosperity that had eluded them at home. There were many of them. Army officers, returned from the Napoleonic Wars to find themselves no longer wanted, turned away with a pension that would have kept them only in poverty and given a parcel of land in a continent so far away, the home country could conveniently forget them. Farmers whose crops had failed during the famines of the past few dry summers. Younger sons and 'black sheep' who had been sent here with some money to start them off in the hope that they would be no more embarrassment to their families.

You could be as badly off with your master as you were in convict quarters, but Matthew was lucky. Simeon Cooper, a blunt Yorkshireman who had arrived with the intention of farming sheep here, was a hard enough man but not a cruel one. As a wool man, he knew something of the carpet trade and the difficulties it had faced and, although in England he would have stood with the manufacturers rather than the weavers, he had some sympathy with their cause.

He treated Matthew more as a member of the family than as a convict, and the two men would sit of an evening deep in discussion while Simeon's wife Rose sewed in her chair. He had asked Matthew once how he had come to be transported and listened gravely while Matthew spoke of the Great Strike, the riots a few years later and the terrible night when it seemed that the whole of Kidderminster was in anarchy and he had been asked to go and help quiet the weavers, taking the pistol he had brought back from America because it was feared there would be real trouble.

'It was never intended for use,' he told Simeon, not long after he'd arrived. 'I'd loaded it only in order to fire a few shots into the air. You see, it wasn't just the weavers who were rioting – there were other factions, set on making trouble for the honest men who only wanted a fair wage for the work they did. Those were the men we feared, and that's why even the Committee who had organised the strike wanted the trouble stopped. But I never thought to kill anyone, and certainly not a man who had been my friend.'

'And they didn't accept this at your trial?' Simeon asked.

Matthew shook his head. 'There was never any chance of that. They wanted a scapegoat, you see, and my lawyer had already got justice for eleven weavers. He might have got it for me too, but for the fact that he was taken ill and his junior had to argue my case.' He shrugged. 'Perhaps I malign him. Even Godson might not have got me free. They saw me as a traitor to my class, you see, and that was my greatest crime. Murder they might have forgiven – but the fact that I stood with the weavers, never!'

'Aye, I can understand that.' Simeon was silent for a moment. 'So you got fourteen years. It must have seemed like the end of your life.'

'The end of that life, certainly.' Matthew thought of his years in Kidderminster. His schooldays at the Grammar School, where he had met Francis. His adventures abroad, travelling across the perilous plains of America, where he had met pioneers, explorers, even Indians. And his return to Kidderminster, where he had grown to know and love Rebecca.

Rebecca . . . His best friend's wife and therefore out of reach, but the only woman he had ever felt he could have spent his life with.

And now, lost to him for ever, for the sake of a moment's madness; for the sake of a pistol, held carelessly, a jogged elbow and the death of a man he had called his friend.

'But it could be the beginning of a new one,' Simeon said. 'You're doing well here – a Special, assigned to me as overseer. You could get your ticket-of-leave soon and work for yourself.

225

Then a conditional pardon – good as being a free man. You'd not be able to go back to England, but what'd be there for you by then? You'll know New South Wales as well as any man by then – you'll be as well off here, getting your own farm and settling down. Getting wed, maybe. Aye, you could do a lot worse – many do.'

'Yes, I could.' He was right, Matthew thought. By the time he finished his sentence, he would be almost fifty years old. Men aged quickly in this country, and even if he could go home, how many changes would he find? Would there be anyone there, save for Rebecca and Francis, who would know him?

No. The sentence passed on him that day in Worcester had changed his life irrevocably. There could be no going back. Only – when he had finished this interminable standing still that was a prisoner's lot – a going forward. And that was something which nobody but he could achieve.

And there were compensations. To a convict, New South Wales was a hostile place, a hell of searing heat in summer and dreary chill in winter. A place of constant toil and struggle against both environment and elements, where trees grew as fast as weeds, where the ground was either as hard as iron or as treacherously soft as quicksand. Where a bite from a spider could kill and a snake meant instant death, where the waters were guarded by sharks that could tear a man in two with one bite and the bush by savages who would spear him without a thought. There was no need for bars in this great open-air prison, for the land itself made as effective a barrier.

But even so, a man could – if he were lucky – rise above the misfortune that had brought him here. He could, as Simeon had said, gain his pardon, start up in his own business. He could make a good living – he might even make a fortune. It had been done, was being done all the time.

A man with Matthew's advantages – education, experience, wealth – could find contentment here, despite all the difficulties.

And, he thought as he came into the yard on that rainy evening towards the end of July, 1837, there was Cathy.

She came to meet him as he approached the door. Pale as always – she had never acquired the sunburnt looks of most convict women – and frail, in spite of Simeon Cooper's good feeding, she aroused in him at once the same protective compassion as he had felt when he had first seen her on the ship. She still had that timid look about her, as if the entire world were about to turn on her, red in tooth and claw. And who could blame her? For hadn't it done just that?

'Go inside. You'll get soaked,' he said as he paused in the doorway to take off his boots. The kitchen was warm with cooking and the smells good. She came close and he bent and gave her a swift kiss. It was seldom enough they could exchange any token of affection, and the nights they could spend together were rare. Simeon was strict about his male and female convicts mixing. But there were few days when Matthew could not give her at least a glance or even a touch, to remind her that she could still depend upon him.

He wondered at times how he had come to let this waif attach herself to him so firmly. That she was also attached permanently was never in any doubt.

Another reason for not going back to England. For how could he abandon her? She was his for life, like it or not.

He went in, shrugging off his wet jacket, and stood steaming by the stove. At this time of year, its heat was welcoming – he had been long enough in Australia to find a July day, at almost the same temperature as a cool summer's day in England, uncomfortably cold.

At the same time, he gave a thought to the convicts in their huts, with only the meagre fire they lit to cook their rations, and no clothes other than the ones already wet upon their backs. Simeon was not cruelly harsh, but he wasn't soft either. The men were here to be punished, he said, and their living conditions were part of their punishment. What was the point of making them too comfortable? They'd have a flood of miscreants coming out from England, eager to join in the fun, once word got back.

Matthew became aware that Cathy was holding something

out to him. He stared at it for a moment, then reached out and took it quickly. A letter! A letter from England. A ship must have come in. Bringing more of Simeon's 'flood'. Bringing news.

Rebecca's handwriting stared up at him from the packet. That was unusual. Rebecca had learned to read and write only after she and Francis had married, and she was self-conscious about her writing. She always wrote him a letter when Francis did, but the address was always in Francis's handwriting. Matthew felt a quick stab of apprehension.

He tore the package open. It was thinner than usual, and the pages too were in Rebecca's writing – nothing from Francis. With mounting fear, Matthew began to read.

'My dear friend Matthew, I have sad news for you. My husband Francis passed out of this life a week ago. His consumption, which had seemed so much better, suddenly grew worse and he suffered a fatal haemorrhage last Wednesday. It was very quick. There was nothing anyone could do to save him . . .'

Unable to read any further, he laid the letter on the kitchen table. He stared before him, his eyes blank, seeing nothing of his surroundings. Instead, he was back in that cold prison cell in Worcester Gaol, bidding goodbye to his friends Francis and Rebecca and wondering if he would ever see them again . . .

From Worcester, Matthew had been taken with other prisoners to the hulks that lay in Portsmouth Harbour, awaiting the sailing of the fleet for Australia. The journey had been long and uncomfortable; the worst he could ever remember. For whatever hardships he had suffered during any of his previous travels, he had suffered them as a free man. He had not been shackled with irons and bound to the next man.

At last they arrived at Portsmouth, where the dreaded hulks lay in serried ranks upon the water. Matthew and the rest of the prisoners stood on the wharf, shivering in a raw breeze that blew straight through the harbour mouth and up towards the green downs that lay at the head. He looked across the water at the little town of Gosport that had grown on the opposite shore. God's Port, they said it was, a haven to some holy man driven in by a storm. But no haven to him, nor to any of the miserable wrecks of humanity who waited with him.

The longboats were arriving and the convicts, men and women, hustled roughly aboard. Matthew found himself near the bow, facing forwards. He stared across the choppy grey water, watching the rotting warships, no longer fit to put to sea, where he was to spend the next few weeks, or even months. They carried an air of hopeless decay that fitted well with the mood of many of his fellows, who saw transportation as nothing more than a slow execution.

These ships, like the prisoners who were being carried towards them, had no future, only a past. For some it was a past of glory and honour but all that had been forgotten; they lay here now, wallowing on the swelling waters of the harbour, places of dread and derision where the manners of the world counted for nothing and men and women were lower than hungry dogs that slunk about an alley.

They had even stopped looking like ships, he thought as the longboat drew nearer. Their gunports, where once had breathed the menacing fire of cannon, were barred like the prison windows they now were. Their sides, battered and holed in conflict, were roughly patched; at the waterline it could be seen that they must be leaking. And there were strange, unwieldy edifices clinging to them; sheds and plat-forms and rickety stairways that looked as if they had been blown there by a gale and left to hang until the next strong wind blew them away again.

The boat came alongside one of these ungainly craft and the prisoners scrambled awkwardly up the rope ladders. With shouts and curses they were then herded along the heaving decks to the quarterdeck, where the captain stood above them on the poop, surveying them with hard eyes.

'Ruffians and villains, the lot of you,' he declared. 'Expect no mercy from me or my men on this ship. I'll brook no disobedience, no insolence and no idleness. Flogging's the order of the day here and we've some fine new cats and some powerful men to swing 'em. And if there's not room to swing 'em below decks, there's plenty above, and you'll all be mustered to enjoy the sight, so 'ware.'

He paused and his small, cruel eyes moved slowly over them. A bitter, disappointed man, Matthew thought, reduced to command of a ship that would never sail again, a ship with its honour stripped away. And ready to take vengeance for his disappointment on the prisoners who formed the cargo he would never deliver.

'You'll hand over any money you might have brought aboard with you,' the captain continued. 'I'll look after it for you. And you'll declare any other property to my officers.' The officers, a gang as villainous-looking as any of the prisoners, moved forward a little. 'These are the items you'll be allowed to keep: Combs for your hair. Braces. Needles and threads for mending your clothes. Spare buttons . . .'

The list was short but even so, Matthew doubted if many of the prisoners still had such possessions. 'Next you'll all be given a bath – I'll have no lice on my ship. Long hair harbours such vermin, so you'll be barbered. And you'll all be issued with prison uniform – any clothes fit for wear can be sold to the dealer who comes aboard for the purpose. After that, you'll be ironed and shown your quarters, and then you'll be ready for work.'

'Work!' muttered the young Irishman beside Matthew. 'And what sort of work does he think we'll be fit for, at all, treated like animals as we've been these past months?'

'*Silence!*' the captain roared. 'I told you, I'll have no insolence – the next man to speak will be flogged.' He continued to read out his orders, so many and so detailed that Matthew knew there was no chance of anyone remembering and obeying them all. It looked as if the captain would soon be bringing his floggers into action. But at last the harangue ended and the officers came shoving amongst them snatching at the money that was held out to them. Little enough it was too, but no note was made of who had handed it over, or how much, and it was clear that none was likely to be returned. And what use would it be to them anyway, in Australia?

The long day dragged on. At the end of it, having been soaked in icy sea-water, their hair shaved close, their clothes taken away – and they might as well have been stolen outright, Matthew thought wryly as he handed over the shilling or two the old Jewish dealer had paid for his own jacket, shirt and trousers – and an iron weighing a good stone riveted around each man's right ankle, they were led at last to a hatchway which opened to reveal a steep, narrow gangway into a hollow and evil-smelling darkness.

Accustomed as they were to the foul smells of prison, the first of the prisoners retched and drew back. But their guards, furnished with rope-ends, flourished their weapons and drove them on like cattle into sheds. Slowly, feeling their way, they began their descent.

'Holy Mary and all her angels,' the young Irishman muttered, hesitating on the steep gangway, 'what the devil do we have here?'

'Get along down, there!' bellowed the officer who was driving them. 'What are ye waiting for, damn your eyes?'

'And do I still have eyes, will ye tell me that?' the boy demanded, still keeping his voice low. 'Begod, it's as black as a dog's belly down here and smells worse, and nothing to show me where to put me feet.'

'Just as long as yer don't put 'em on me, mate,' growled a voice from the darkness, and Matthew realised that the hold was filled already with people. As he stumbled on, pushed by the pressure of the men behind, he could feel them around him – hands, reaching out to claw at his legs, skeletal fingers exploring, catching at the rough material of the canvas trousers he had been given, making his skin crawl. Now and then he would trip on an outstretched leg and hear its owner curse. A flailing fist might catch him on the knee, or he might feel only the draught of its movement. And still, pressed by those behind, he must lurch along the narrow and invisible gangway, wondering how far he must go and whether he would ever find a place to rest himself.

But now his eyes were becoming accustomed to the blackness, and he saw that there was some light filtering in, through cracks in the deck above or through the rotting sides of the ship. The glimmer of rheumy eyes peered up at him from all sides and slowly he began to make out the pallor of faces, the shadowy, half-recumbent shapes. The hold was surely full, with no room for the new arrivals – but before he could think any further, the inhabitants of this noisome hell had risen up in a body and made a rush to surround them. And the hands that had grabbed at his legs were now all over his body, searching his clothes and dragging out the few poor possessions he had been able to keep.

'This un's well furnished, mates,' a rough voice rasped in his ear, and he knew that he had seen the last of his comb, the sailor's 'hussif' of sewing equipment that had accompanied him across two continents, and the other trifles that had become so precious. Unless he was willing to barter his bread and meat for their return, and even then they would probably be stolen again while he slept.

All around him he could hear the curses of other men being similarly robbed, and the murky darkness was filled with the shadows of struggling figures. But the 'new chums' had little chance against the old hands, some of whom had been aboard these hulks for months now, and soon quiet was restored and the new arrivals found places to sit or lie amongst the ragged horde already there.

'Well, there's one thing to be thankful for,' the young Irishman observed. 'We can't be robbed again. There's nothin' left to steal unless they rip the teeth from me mouth, and I wouldn't put that past these scum. What would me poor old mother say if she could see me now? And where's me poor darlin' sweetheart Cathy, that did nothin' to deserve it at all? D'ye think I'll ever see her again?'

Matthew looked at him and saw the anguish in his eyes. 'Your sweetheart? Is she being transported too?'

'She is that. And her only seventeen years auld and pure as the Virgin herself. Or was, before she fell foul of the peelers.' The boy ran shaking fingers through his hair. 'It was all a great big muddle that night. Oh, I know I was doin' wrong to rob the auld man – but what would you have done, eh, if you'd been starving and seen him with that fine big goose under his arm, and him as fat as a pig's grandmother? And if he'd wanted it that bad, he'd never have left it on the windowsill, now would he?' Matthew caught the glint of his eyes and heard, with surprise, a hint of mischief in the voice. But it was soon gone again as the young convict went on soberly, 'And Cathy, all she did was help me pluck it. But that was enough for them. The auld man was a magistrate and the peelers caught us fair and square. So that was Olly Connor and Cathy Brady for the hulks, and never mind asking why we'd had nothing to eat for four days before we found that goose.'

'Have you seen her since then? Have you had news of her?'

Oliver shrugged. 'I saw her at the trial and I caught a sight of her once on the road down, when the women's coach stopped at the same place as ours. So I know she was heading for Pompey, same as us. But where she is today . . .' There were tears in his voice now and he stopped for a moment. 'Well, maybe we'll see each other again when we get to Australia. Maybe we could even get married. They say you can, out there, if you get with a good master.'

Matthew was silent for a moment, picturing these young lives, so brutally wrenched apart and all for a platterful of goose meat. 'How long have you been in England?' he asked. 'How did you come to be there?'

Oliver shrugged. 'A lot of us came over from Ireland together. The men worked as navvies, ye know, digging the cuts – and the women came with us. Me feyther and Cathy's was mates so we grew up together, more or less. We've been sweethearts since we were babes, almost, so we have.'

'Your fathers were navigators?'

'Aye, came to dig the canals and the railways with the rest

233

of 'em. I did it too, and so did me brothers. Me mother and sisters looked after us and Cathy did for her dad, but 'twasn't the life for her, poor flower. She's always been different, ye see – sort of gentle and soft, not like the rest of the floozies. So one night, we just slipped away and went to London – to seek our fortunes.' He gave a short, bitter laugh. 'Fortunes, by all the saints! It's death in two easy lessons there – starve or freeze.' He turned tormented eyes on Matthew. 'I had to do something, didn't I? I had to find something to put in her poor belly. And that man didn't have need of it, I'll swear he didn't. And now she's fetched up on a prison hulk for doin' nothin' at all, and God only knows if she'll even live to see Australia.'

Matthew reached out and touched the young man's arm. He felt an overwhelming pity for the boy and his girl, just two more victims of a society that cared nothing for those that slipped through its wide-meshed net and fell into the writhing heap of destitution below. He thought of Rebecca, penniless and pregnant in London before Francis had found her; of her sister Bessie and brother Tom, living on their wits for years in the teeming, narrow streets. This could so easily have been their fate too.

They were woken early next morning by the yells and curses of the guards. Scrambling clumsily to their feet, hampered by the still unfamiliar weight of the basils that chafed at their ankles, they were given a hunk of bread before being loaded once more on to the longboats and rowed ashore. Here, chained together, they shuffled through the streets to the naval dockyard where they were to work.

'And make a sight for children to jeer at,' Oliver muttered as they shambled along, ungainly as bears in their irons. 'Look at 'em, will ye, all got up in their best clothes to see the sight. Ah well, I suppose we're a lesson to 'em and it ain't their fault. I'm just thankful me poor mother's not amongst them to see her son's shame, at all.'

Matthew said nothing. He too felt a burning humiliation at being forced to scuffle along the streets in the coarse clothes of a branded felon, open to the mocking gaze of any free man who might be passing. And Oliver was right – some of them had come especially for the spectacle, and brought their children with them as if in dreadful warning. Mortification crept through his body, dragging at his limbs and weighing on his heart. To be brought to this! To find himself chained to a gang of other ill-clothed men and forced to go through the streets as the butt of a jeering mob. And this only the beginning of his punishment.

The days and weeks dragged by, each following the other with a cruel tedium that seemed like to destroy the souls as well as the bodies of the convicts. And then, at last, as they rowed the longboats ashore one pearly autumn morning, a shout went up from the men in the bow.

'The ships! The ships – look there, they're sailing in, see!'

All eyes strained at once towards the harbour mouth. There indeed, like ghosts in the mist, were the sails of the great ships that had transported the last quota of convicts to New South Wales.

They filled the narrow entrance, blocking off the shadowy view of the Isle of Wight as they sailed slowly, majestically, up the harbour.

'Bin to China to pick up tea and such,' a man near Matthew said, picking his teeth. 'Now they'll unload it and we'll be put on as cargo. It's a hundred days at sea for us now, brave boys, and no quarter given.'

Matthew stared at the ships. As they came closer he could see that their majesty had been a trick of the light, an illusion lent by distance. They looked smaller now, as if the misty droplets had magnified them, and meaner too. Never used in war, these had always been merchant ships with deep holds for cargo, and few portholes other than those needed in the sailors' accommodation. He imagined the depths of darkness that he and his fellows must live in for the next four months, and shuddered. And he thought of the tales he had heard about the transportation ships – the weeks without light, with insufficient food and water, the cruel floggings and the numbers who died before they reached

Australia and were considered by their mates to be the lucky ones.

But those were old tales. Conditions were better now, so they said. And although the voyage was no holiday and there was inevitably suffering, far fewer died. And if you were fortunate enough to have a good captain, you might even arrive in good health, fit to begin the next stage of this gruelling revenge.

For it was more than punishment, this soul-wrenching destruction of unfortunates. This was a revenge by society on the people whose very presence reminded it of its own shortcomings. What else could explain a sentence of fourteen years on a pair of sweethearts who, starving, had done no more than steal a goose? How else could you understand the savage tearing of a suckling child from its mother's breast, the disposal of the infant who knew where, so that she could be sent unencumbered (though half mad) to the hulks? And what other reason could there be for a young girl, slant-eyed, moon-faced and barely able to talk intelligibly, being sent away for seven years for stealing a yard of linen?

No, these were not punishments. They were the shamed reaction of people who preferred not to know about the poverty and degradation on their doorsteps, and struck out at the cowering wretches who through their own need to eat and clothe their shivering bodies brought their condition to public attention. And in an effort to thrust away the shame and the guilt, so the paupers, the petty thieves, the felons and the thugs were treated alike as a 'criminal class', and sent away, to a hostile land where they could be forgotten, leaving Britain a cleaner, better place.

Except that it didn't do that, Matthew thought. He remembered the poverty of the weavers and the strike that had ensued. A strike that was echoed by other trades – by brickmakers, glassblowers, all those who were becoming aware that they were not paid fairly for work they did. And he thought of the men he had met and talked with during the months he had spent on the hulk. Rogues and villains they had seemed at first sight, and so some of them were. But most of them were no more than the victims of a society that was riddled with greed, clawing to itself riches that were beyond its needs and seeing no cause to share its goods. Most of them had been driven to commit the crimes that had brought them to the hulks.

Over the next few weeks, the ships were unloaded and went through the repairs and refitting necessary after any long voyage. The convicts were loaded aboard, and the fleet set sail again. But Matthew and his companions saw nothing of their almost stately exit from the harbour mouth or their progress down the Solent. As he had expected, they were confined below, chained in fours to the six-foot-square berths that would be their accommodation until they reached Australia.

'Bayside' they called it, as if it were some seaside resort. But there would be little ease to be found there. And Matthew, along with the other convicts, lay in his bunk in a darkness that was almost solid, breathing in a stench that was to grow daily until the hatches might be opened, and longed with all his heart to be back in Kidderminster.

Walking in the fields with Rebecca. Sitting before a glowing fire with Rebecca. Looking into her warm, dark eyes, yearning to touch her soft, creamy, forbidden skin.

And then that last sight of her as he stood shamed with the other convicts on the hard at Portsmouth; chained, ragged, unkempt, awaiting the longboat that would take them back to the prison hulk for the last few days before being crowded aboard the merchant ships for their long voyage to New South Wales.

Rebecca and Francis had come to wish him goodbye but he had been almost too ashamed to meet their eyes. He recalled how Francis had laid a hand on his shoulder, how he had felt the friendship still there in the firm, steady touch and had raised his eyes to look for the last time on the face he had known since boyhood.

And then Rebecca . . . but the expression in her darkened eyes had brought a pain too sharp to be borne, and he had been able to do no more than take her soft hand in his own, conscious of the roughness of his skin against hers, and then turn away. And when his ship had finally sailed, he had lain amongst the other convicts imagining his friends standing on the Sallyport to watch the sad departure, and in his heart had wished them goodbye for ever.

Oh, Rebecca, his heart cried, what must you be thinking of me now? Do you remember me at all? And have you any idea at all what life is like for me, or will ever be like when I know I can never see your dear, dear face again?

The convicts were kept below decks until the ship reached 'blue water' and then their irons were removed and they were allowed on deck, a group at a time. They emerged through the heavily guarded grilled hatchways, blinking in warm sunlight. Matthew and Oliver stood for a moment by the rail, gazing at the wide expanse, shielding their eyes against the brightness.

'We're lucky,' Matthew said at last. 'We've got a good captain and a good surgeon. Many fare worse than this.'

'Aye, I know.' The young Irishman stared around at the other ships still in view. 'I wonder if Cathy's aboard one of those. I'd dearly like to know how she is.'

'Perhaps you will, once we arrive. And if conditions are no worse than ours, she'll be all right.' Matthew spoke cheerfully, as if they were aboard a luxury passenger ship, but he knew his words could bring only the smallest comfort to the anxious boy by his side. For even the best ship could still be a hell-hole, especially in bad weather or in the heat of the doldrums, when they lay wallowing on a slow, heavy swell with no breeze to move them along or relieve the stifling heat. And although they were lucky enough to have a surgeon who cared well for them and seemed to take a pride in keeping disease at bay, not all the transports were so fortunate. In some, where the inmates were kept below decks for the entire voyage, fever could run riot, picking off the weaker victims as a man with a gun will pick off pigeons. From these ships, it was said, more corpses had been unloaded than living bodies when the hatches were finally opened.

But there was little to be gained from worrying about the other ships. Gradually, the winds dispersed them and although they knew – or hoped – that their companions were only just over the horizon, they found themselves alone on a vast blue disc of ocean with only the birds and the fish for company.

The days settled into a routine of work on deck – the most menial tasks such as swabbing, scrubbing or holystoning. As the weeks passed they were allowed to stay on deck longer and in larger numbers. They began to evolve pastimes. They fished for the shoals that swam alongside the ship, and ate the catch which added to their monotonous diet of 'salt horse', pork and rice. And from the bones that were left from their meat they carved scrimshaw – toothpicks, cigar-holders, ornaments that they hoped they might one day be able to sell, or perhaps even give to the loved ones left behind.

'We even managed to enjoy ourselves at times,' Matthew wrote later to Rebecca and Francis. 'You would have laughed, I think, to have seen us dance on the decks. The sailors taught some of the men the hornpipe and they were not half bad at it. And when we had our nightly issue of port wine – oh, yes, we lived well aboard the *Lady Jane*! – we were expected to dance for it, to amuse the crew and, I suppose, to make sure we had some exercise. Our surgeon was very anxious that we should remain strong and fit and not suffer from any disease he could prevent. So as well as port wine, we had lime juice to prevent scurvy, and to keep us sweet we were allowed a little sugar. And I'm sure it was very good for me not to have the rich diet I enjoyed at home in Kidderminster. Few of those poor wretches had ever seen such food, other than through a rich man's window, and I feel ashamed now of all the good meals I have wasted.'

Not that he need tell Rebecca about poverty or the waste of good food, he thought, she knew more about that than he had ever realised. And he thought of those like Vivian, who turned away from such knowledge and brushed it aside. A short holiday aboard a transport shop would do more good to society than any of the savage punishments meted out to the 'criminal class'. Let them just endure a taste of the sufferings these unfortunate victims endured, and compassion might enter even their iron souls. And with honest work to fill their days, with food to fill their bellies and money in their pockets, would there be a criminal class at all? Or would there be no more than a few hardened rogues, and the rest content to live in peace?

The ship ploughed on across the oceans. The doldrums were passed at last and then the storms began, terrible buffetings that tossed the craft from wave to wave like a child's toy. Once more the convicts were battened down below, the hatches fastened against them, and they lay in a torment of sea-sickness and foul air, clinging to their berths and to each other to avoid being tossed about the rocking hold. Above, they could hear the shouts and curses of the sailors and officers as they fought with sails that would rip from top to bottom in one powerful gust and leave them helpless. Again and again, the ship rolled so wildly that they were certain she must overturn, and the air was filled with sobs and cries, even prayers. Beside him, Matthew could hear Oliver calling on the Virgin Mary, on the Holy Ghost, on St Christopher, St Nicholas and every other saint he could think of. There was little rest for anyone and no way of knowing how time was passing. They could only lie there and wait – even pray – for the end.

But at last the turmoil stopped and the ship came through into more peaceful waters. It was hot again and their sojourns on deck little better than those below. The sun blazed down from an almost white-hot sky, and they crowded together under the shadow of the sails. There was little dancing now. They wanted only for this interminable voyage to be at an end and themselves on dry land once again; land that would stay still under their feet and a horizon that would remain steady to their aching eyes.

'We'll be making landfall soon,' a passing sailor told Matthew, and indeed it was only a day or two before they caught their first glimpse of the long, wooded coastline of Australia. They crowded the decks, staring hungrily at a sight that had been denied them for over four long, weary months. For a short time, it hardly mattered that more privations awaited them there. It was land, and that was all they could think about.

Slowly, the ship moved into the great harbour and came to rest at last beside the wharf. On shore, Matthew could see all the bustle of an ordinary port, with the buildings of the town rising beyond the dockside. It was a ramshackle place, unlike Portsmouth with its great cathedral and bluff sea walls; here, there seemed to be few stone buildings and those were of crude design and construction.

It looked what it was – a settlement hastily thrown together by inexperienced hands. Even those tasks that in England would be carried out by educated minds – the planning of streets and buildings, the organisation of a community – had to be left to convicts, for no architect, engineer or lawyer who enjoyed any kind of success in his home country would have dreamed of emigrating to Australia.

But there had been a few arrivals who were able to draw plans or interpret the law, and these were quickly given special responsibilities. And as the convicts went ashore, they were questioned as to their previous trades and abilities. Brickmakers, fishermen, farmers, all were quickly assigned to where they might be most use.

'A gentleman, eh?' The official looked Matthew up and down, a sneer in eyes and voice. 'Well, we don't have much call for your sort here.' He had been in the country a long time, Matthew thought, noticing the strange, nasal accent that he had already heard in several of the voices here. 'I suppose you never did a day's work in your life, that right? Maybe we'd better start you off on stone-breaking.'

'I've worked a good deal,' Matthew said, resisting the temptation to add 'more than you'. 'I've farmed and driven cattle in America and I've felled timber too.' He glanced out through the window of the shack at the hills that rose beyond the town, still thickly wooded. 'It looks as if there are plenty of trees here.'

The man laid down his quill and stared. His eyebrows drew together and he looked for a moment as if he would order Matthew to be flogged for insolence. Then he grunted and picked up his pen again.

'Hmph! So you think you can be of some use in the timber, do you? Well, we'll see. Maybe a few weeks in the bush'll cure you of yer big talk. It ain't like America here, y'know. We got snakes that can kill just by lookin' at yer, and spiders with teeth like a shark's. And if they don't get yer, the sunstroke will. So get up in the bush and see how you like it.'

He sounded as if he'd be glad to see Matthew bitten or stung to death, but already the line was moving on and Matthew found himself outside. He stood for a moment, trying to steady himself against dry land that seemed unwilling to stay still. The months at sea had left them all with an unsteady impression that everything was moving, and some of the men felt sicker than they had on the ship.

But they were out of their irons, free to move about, and it was more like a hiring fair here than a prison. To their astonished gaze, the scene was almost friendly – men who were clearly convicts, walking about freely, talking together, even laughing. Was this what they had dreaded so much? Was this the terrible punishment they'd been sent to endure?

Oliver stood nearby. He nudged Matthew sharply.

'Look! Women! They must have come off that ship next to ours. I wonder –' He started forwards. But even as he moved, there was a hastening in the steps of the men who were wandering about the quays. They gathered around the line of women, young and old, who had appeared on the quay and began to examine them, calling coarse remarks to each other and reaching out with grimy hands to touch their ragged clothes and greasy hair. The women spat back at them, screeching out worse abuse, and there was some laughter amongst the men who seemed to take this as a signal that their attentions were welcomed. They crowded

242

closer, grabbing and slobbering, their eyes red with the heat of rapacious desire.

'My God . . .' Matthew said, but his exclamation was interrupted as Oliver gripped his arm, the fingers biting into Matthew's flesh. He turned quickly and saw a light in the Irishman's eyes, a light that burned with both torment and joy.

'Cathy! It's me own darlin' Cathy, saints be praised, she's lived through the journey. Did ye ever see such a beautiful woman, now?'

Matthew stared in the direction pointed out by Oliver's shaking finger. At first glance, the line of women all looked alike – an unkempt crew with straggled rat's tail hair and tattered clothes. But after a moment he saw the one Oliver gazed at with such anguish, such relief – a pale wisp of a girl, fragile as a wraith, with hair that must, when clean, be almost white and a body slender enough to be blown away in the next ripple of breeze.

The marauding men were beaten back with whips and curses as the soldiers, wooden-faced, paraded the women convicts across the quay. Matthew felt Oliver start forward, as if to rush across the space between them and he reached out automatically and grasped the Irishman's arm. Already their own guards were shouting at them to get a move on, and the gap between them and the women was widening. He could feel the young man's despair and knew his own frustration at their helplessness.

'Cathy . . .' Oliver whispered, and as if she had heard, the girl turned and looked across at them. Matthew, gazing at her, saw the expression on her face, saw it change from numb hopelessness to an incredulous joy. For a moment her eyes, grey and limpid as sea pools left by the tide, widened and held; and Matthew, glancing at the boy by his side, saw that for just that brief space of time there was nobody in the world but the two of them, the recognition of survival, the testimony of their love.

And then the line was pushed roughly on. Cathy, jerked by a brutal hand on her shoulder, was forced towards the barges and disappeared in the crowd of shoving, swearing women. And Matthew realised that he too was being sworn at, cursed and told to move along if he didn't want a turn on the Triangle.

He had no time to wonder what the Triangle might be. With Oliver and the others he was thrust into a compound, as if they were cattle waiting to be auctioned. And Matthew felt the Irish boy's despair settle again like a cloud, and knew that it was a despair that was common to every man there.

Chapter Twelve

There was no time to talk. Within minutes the guards had shut them all into the pens where they were to be picked out by the settlers who had come in from their farms for fresh labour. Again, Matthew was reminded of a hiring fair. But there was none of the attendant fun here, no sideshows or stalls of gingerbread and candy. Here, the faces of the hirers were for the most part grim and contemptuous as they walked amongst the convicts, staring at them as if they were cattle and touching the shoulders of those they most fancied as servants or workmen.

'This un says he has experience in timber, Mr Harris,' the guard said, jerking his head towards Matthew, and the settler he addressed came closer and pushed his face close. He was a pig-faced man with small eyes and a snout of a nose, and he breathed with a whistling sound. He looked Matthew over and thrust out his thick lips.

'What sort of experience?'

'In America and Canada,' Matthew answered. 'I've worked as lumberjack in the forests there.'

'America, eh?' There was a sneer in the voice, but after some more examination, the man nodded and grunted. 'I'll take him, he looks healthy enough. And this red-haired cove next to him too –' he indicated Oliver '– he's big enough, I ought to get some work outa him.' He glanced across the quay to where the women waited in a ragged group. 'Put 'em by for a bit. I want a couple of cattle, too.'

He walked on down the line, passing some men with barely a glance but picking out one or two more who joined Matthew and Oliver to form a small, separate group. Then he strode across the quay to the women.

'So we're going outback to clear bush, are we?' one of the other convicts said. He stuffed a wad of tobacco into his cheek and began to chew. 'Well, it'll be all right if it don't kill us first. And if it does – well, the boss'll just come back and find a few more like us. It's like slaves used to be in America – plenty more where that one came from, so why worry? Don't seem no shortage of crooks in England. And they'll breed others once they're here, anyway.'

'Breed?' Oliver said. 'You mean they really do let the convicts marry?' There was a sudden eager hope in his voice and Matthew glanced at him with pity. Oliver was watching the women, and as Matthew followed his glance he saw their new master walk slowly down the line, staring each one up and down.

'If you like to call it that. There ain't no ceremony about it. But an old hand can get a woman if his master agrees – why not? Keeps the men happy.'

'And the women?' Matthew asked quietly. 'How do they feel about it?' He saw Harris reach out and with a rough movement jerk one of the female convicts out of the line. She stumbled against him and Matthew heard the settler's coarse laugh. Beside him, he felt Oliver stiffen with anxiety.

The second convict looked at Matthew with some astonishment. 'The bunters? They're lucky to be let live.' He drew in his breath and shook his head. 'Wish I could get ahold of one – I'd give her what for, that I would! A good thrashing Saturday nights, that's what they need to keep 'em in order.'

Matthew said nothing. He glanced at Oliver and saw that the boy's face was white. Harris was standing in front of Cathy now, staring at her. Oliver's tension was almost palpable and Matthew felt it stiffen in his own body. Could it be possible that the settler would pick Cathy to be one of his servants – that she should go to the same farm as Oliver?

He watched as Harris reached out and caught Cathy by her pale, straggled hair, lifting it away from her fragile neck. He stared for a moment more, pulling her towards him by the hank of hair; then he thrust her back into the line and moved on. Matthew saw Cathy raise her hand and rub her neck, as if his grasp had hurt her, and he was aware of Oliver moving beside him, trembling with frustrated rage.

The sun beat down upon their heads. How long were they going to be kept standing here?

He looked again at the man on his other side. He was staring morosely out across the quay, watching the few fishing boats that were coming in with their catch. For some convicts, surely, life wasn't so bad? Those lucky enough to have a trade could continue with it here, and find themselves valued too. Boat-building, fishing, farming – all these needed some special knowledge which must be useful. But for the ordinary man, the petty thief who had run the streets without ever having a real job, there was nothing but hard, repetitive toil. And for the women . . . ?

For little Cathy, so frail and timid?

'You know a lot about what goes on here,' he said. 'You've not just arrived, have you?'

'Me, a new chum? Not likely!' The first man spat over the side of the rails that fenced them in. 'Bin here three year. My old master just died and his place taken over by a feller got his own blokes. So I bin sent back to be assigned to someone else. Just my luck to cop Arthur Harris. One of the hardest men on the Bay, he is. There's not many men dares go agin him.' He nodded towards Oliver. 'Saw you lookin' at that bleached mott. If she's your girl, you be thankful she ain't bin took by Harris. Better off in the Female Factory, by a long chalk.'

'The Female Factory?' Oliver asked. 'Is that where they work?'

'Where they lives, if no one wants 'em. Up Parramatta. Fancy-lookin' place, it is, got a little tower and a clock and all, but they says it's no: so pretty inside. Mind, most of 'em don't stop there that long, not if they're merit – bin on good behaviour, that is. And even the generals get picked out by the old stringy-barks from outback who just want

247

a woman about the place and don't much care what she's like.'

'Generals? Stringy-barks?' Matthew was accustomed to cant, but these terms were new to him. 'What do you mean?'

'Why, generals is mostly girls sent back from their assignments 'cause they're in the family way. Some stays where they are and has their brats out in the bush but a bunter workin' as a house servant generally gets chucked out. Only 'tisn't like it is back at home, slung out on the streets – here, someone has to look after 'em. So they comes to the Factory, see, till the kid's shucked and they can get assigned again. Or get picked out, like I said.'

'Picked out for what?'

'Why, a wife, of course,' the second convict said. 'Some of these settlers, they never had a woman around – what woman would come out willing to this godforsaken country? So they don't mind takin' a Factory lass. Where else they goin' to find one, eh?'

'You mean they get married? Even though she's still under sentence?' Oliver's voice was trembling and again Matthew felt a stab of pity.

''S right. She gets her own clothes back, if she's lucky, Gov'ment gives her ticket-of-leave and off she goes.' He grinned. 'Mind, it don't often last. Poor old stringy-bark thinks he's got a bargain and after a month or two she's back in Sydney, all dressed up and flaunting herself around the dancing halls like the floozy she is. But that's cattle for you. Like I say, a good thrashing coupla times a week's what they need, and what most of 'em gets, too.'

Oliver groaned, laid his arms on the rail and rested his head upon them. Matthew touched his shoulder.

'Bear up. You don't know that Cathy'll get a bad master. Maybe she'll be lucky and be assigned as a house servant to someone kind.' He glanced at their informant. 'It looks as if we'll be working together then. My name's Matthew Farrell and this is Oliver Connor.'

'Ned Bright, at your service.' The man stuck out his hand.

'And this here's Joby Pierce. But you ain't the common sort o' sneaksman. You talk like a nob. What got you here, two pops and a galloper?'

Matthew smiled. 'No. I'm no highwayman – never robbed anyone in my life.' He hesitated, then decided he might as well begin with the truth. Someone would find out anyway. 'As a matter of fact, I killed someone.'

Ned Bright drew back, whistling. 'Whee-ew! What was it, a duel?'

'It was an accident.' Matthew spoke briefly, finding suddenly that he didn't want to discuss the night Bill Bucknell had died. Since leaving Worcester Gaol, he had never talked about it with any man; he didn't want to start with Ned.

Before they could say more, their new master had come up to their enclosure with the two women he had picked out, and was unlocking the gate. An odd precaution to lock it at all, Matthew thought, since they could easily have jumped the railings – but where was there to escape to anyway? The whole town was one big prison, with soldiers as plentiful as convicts about the streets. And prisoners seemed to move about with considerable freedom, though he had already caught a glimpse or two of chain-gangs shambling along the dusty roads.

'All right, you can stop your idling and gossiping.' The piggy eyes looked them over as they stood sweating in the heat. 'You ain't here on your holidays. You've had a nice long sea-voyage for the good of your health, now we'll see what you're made of.' Grabbing their shoulders, he shoved them before him across the big yard towards a cart which stood with a horse nuzzling at a nose-bag. Harris wrenched the bag off and jerked at the horse's harness. 'Greedy brute, you've near emptied it. Well, you'll take us back all the faster.' He pointed at a heap of sacks and boxes. 'Get them loaded.'

The four men began to pile the luggage on to the cart. Clearly, it was not for them to ride in. Matthew wondered how far away Harris's settlement was. He and Oliver were still badly affected by the swell of the voyage and felt more at risk of falling on land than they had aboard ship.

'You.' Harris was beside him. 'What were you about in America? You're too young to have been transported there. Logger, did you say?'

'That's right.' Matthew shrugged. 'I was just travelling – I wanted experience.'

The pig's eyes stared at him. 'Experience! You mean you didn't *have* to do it? You didn't need the money?'

Matthew said nothing. There was nothing in the regulations that said he had to tell this man his history. Harris stared at him and the small eyes grew smaller. He seemed to hesitate, as if debating whether to force Matthew to talk, then seemed to lose interest. He turned away and climbed up into the cart, taking the driver's seat. 'Well, little it matters anyway. And I've no time to stand idling here. Fall in beside the cart, you scum, men on the right, women on the left, and make sure you keep up with me. If you don't, I'll see if a bit of a tickle with the whip won't make you move, so no slouching, hear me?'

Ned, Oliver and Matthew took their places at the side of the cart. The heat was unrelenting but at least they were able to move freely. Matthew glanced across at the two women. Both looked about forty, raddled with poor living, their grimed faces sullen as they waited by the cart. What crimes had brought them here? he wondered. Murder and robbery – or some trifling offence like stealing a yard of calico or a few buttons to keep themselves clothed? He thought of Oliver and Cathy, here because of a goose, and shook his head. England had sent thousands of convicts here in the past forty-five years, hoping to reduce and even eliminate the 'criminal class'. Yet still, young men and old women, hardened criminals and bewildered children, were being shipped out like the cattle Harris so contemptuously called them, to spend probably the rest of their lives here, to be forgotten.

Had it made England a better place? Had it made the cities any safer, the lonely country roads any less dangerous? Or did the truth lie in the possibility that there was no such thing as a 'criminal class' – that crime came from some quite different cause?

'All right, get moving there!' Harris's voice broke roughly in on his thoughts. 'We ain't got all day. I want to get back by nightfall, so pick up your feet, you lazy sluggards, and trot.' He cracked his whip and the tip of it flicked close to Matthew's face. Startled, he flinched and Harris laughed. 'Not used to it, eh? Well, you'll soon know what a whip tastes like – aye, and a cat too if you don't toe the line. So get up, there!'

They moved off across the quay and along the untidy city streets. To Matthew, accustomed to the townships in America, it all looked familiar enough – streets wide enough to turn a horse and cart, ramshackle wooden buildings built on steps to keep out vermin, with tethering rails outside. But to eyes that had only seen the narrow streets of London or the clustered cottages of a village, the sight must be strange indeed.

He looked up towards the hills that ranged beyond the town. Past them, away in the distance, he could see a higher mass. Mountains, surely, blue with distance. Yet another barrier to escaping convicts.

So this was to be his life for the next fourteen years. Slave to a man whose threats did not ring hollow, forced by law to do his bidding whatever it might be.

As it so often did, his mind turned to his home in England. He thought of Kidderminster, narrow and riddled with poverty and greed as it was, yet still home. And he thought of the friends who lived there. Francis, Tom, Nancy.

Rebecca.

Cathy watched with numb despair as the cart clattered away from the quay and disappeared along the bustling street. Repelled though she had been by the pig's eyes and snout of the man who had twisted her hair in his fingers and pulled her towards him, she had still hoped that he would take her. At least she would have been near Oliver. She would have known where he was, what was happening to him, they might even have had opportunities to be together. But Harris had flung her back into the line as if she were worthless, and chosen a big-boned woman from the other end of the line, a woman Cathy had known on the ship and feared for her spiteful nature.

Most of the settlers who were being assigned convicts had now dispersed. The men who had not been assigned were being marched away towards the town. Cathy, feeling sick in the heat, wondered how long they were going to stand here and what would happen next.

'All right, get shifted.' Their guard had returned from the knot of soldiers who had been talking and smoking in the shade of one of the shacks that stood on the quay. His hard eyes surveyed them from a face burnt almost black by the sun, seamed and wrinkled like the bark of an old tree. He swaggered in front of them, a sneer on his face. 'A pretty lot you are, I don't think! Strumpets, the lot o'yer. Well, you won't find much chance to sell yer favours hereabouts, we takes 'em as read, see? Not that any bloke worth his salt'd want to get near enough to filth like you – still, there's no accountin' for tastes.' He flicked his whip and Cathy jumped, feeling the sting of it around her ankles. 'Makes yer jump, does it?' His eyes fastened on her, suddenly hot. 'Here, you ain't such a bad piece under all the muck. Not very old, I'd say – what, twenty, twenty-five?'

'Seventeen,' Cathy whispered, and a slow grin spread across his face.

'Seventeen, eh? Bet you've been around, all the same. Maybe you'd like to tell me about it sometime – teach me a few London tricks. Or maybe I could teach you a few Australian ones.' He came closer and, as Harris had done, twisted a hank of hair around his hand and pulled. Cathy gasped and felt the tears surge to her eyes. A whimper left her throat, and the soldier laughed.

'Not so tough, after all. Well, it might be worth my while to take you in hand, once you're cleaned up a bit.' He let go suddenly as a shout sounded across the quay and a senior officer strode towards them. 'All right, quit your staring,' he growled at the rest of the line. 'And get moving, like I said – over there, to the barges. Quick, now, we ain't got time to stand about enjoying ourselves. Got to get you lot up to Parramatta, sharp as can be.'

'And where might that be?' muttered the girl next to Cathy. Not much older than her, she had given birth to twins on the voyage. One had died only a few days old but the second had survived and lay in her arms now, wailing fitfully in the heat. The girl jiggled her baby about and parted her clothes to give it the breast, but the nuzzling lips were weak and after a few feeble tugs at the nipple the little face fell away and screwed up once more in miserable protest.

'Poor little toad. Her don't even want to feed no more. Not that there's anything there worth having. I don't reckon I got any milk left.' The young mother looked hopelessly down at her child. 'Better if her'd died too, same as her brother.'

'Oh, Milly, don't say that. She's just hot and tired, like we all are. She'll be all right once we get to – what did he call it?'

'God only knows. Some outlandish name, sounded like parrots or something – why they couldn't give places good Christian names we could all understand, I dunno.' Milly sighed. 'Seems we're like to be savages here anyway.'

They were being herded across the quay now to where a row of barges waited, moored to the wharf. With much shouting and cursing, they were shoved aboard where they settled as best they could on rough wooden seats and waited with the patience of total resignation for whatever was to happen to them next.

Cathy sat gazing down into the water. It was clear enough for her to see to the bottom, where fish darted amongst gently moving weeds. But she could also see a multitude of rubbish which had been flung into the water from the quay and from the ships that lay moored or at anchor in the great harbour. Rags, sodden and disintegrating paper, the bodies of cats and dogs, refuse of all kinds floated on the surface or had sunk to the rocks and sands which lay below. And fish that had lived for centuries in innocence of such litter, nosed amongst it, corrupted surely by the corruption on which they fed.

'Look at this place,' she said to Milly, as her eyes moved

253

slowly around. 'I've never seen anything like it, so I haven't. It's beautiful.'

The harbour was immense, far larger than Portsmouth from where they had sailed. The water reflected the intense blue of the sky; it lay calm as a mirror, with not the smallest ripple to crease its immaculate surface. It swept away into the curves and inlets of a thousand smaller harbours, tiny havens and coves fringed with trees and bushes and alive with the colour of birds such as Cathy had never seen or dreamed of. Out on the blue water lay ships at anchor and small boats plied between them, while above it all wheeled huge white birds with enormous bills, circling higher and higher until they were mere specks against the immensity of the indigo sky.

And around the harbour, sheltering its grandeur, were rolling hills and steep yellow cliffs, fading to the distant peaks of misty blue mountains. A barrier that no one could cross, she thought, and understood why this place had been seen as ideal for a prison colony when convicts could no longer be sent to America.

The barge was cast off from its moorings and began slowly to move away from the quay, hauled by horses already dripping with sweat that stained their dark bodies. Cathy watched, fascinated, as they followed the shoreline into a broad opening. A river, she thought, seeing the current flowing towards the sea. A river, like the Liffey at home, like the Thames in London. And she felt a sudden wave of longing and homesickness.

But there was little here to remind her of home. The banks of the river were unlike anything she had seen before and she stared wide-eyed at the twisted shapes of the white-barked trees with their shivering leaves, and gasped as clouds of tiny green birds swirled suddenly from their branches. Sometimes amongst the bushes she caught sight of movement, as if some strange creature lurked there, and she remembered tales of animals that bounced and fish that crept out of the water and crawled on the mud. Nervously, she moved a little nearer to Milly and the two girls sat close, unable to take their eyes from the strange, wild beauty that was so alien to them.

'I don't like it,' Milly whispered, shuddering. 'All those queer trees . . . they look like they've been there for hundreds of years, always the same. 'Tisn't natural.' She drew in her breath sharply as a flurry of white birds, the size of cockerels, flapped suddenly from a tree and wafted overhead, their heads afire with golden crests and unearthly shrieks issuing from their hooked yellow beaks. 'My stars! I thought it was ghosts come to get us.' She watched fearfully as the birds wheeled overhead and then returned to their tree to settle grumblingly on the distorted branches. 'Don't they have no nice Christian sparrows here? Does it all have to look so different?'

'We're the other side of the world,' Cathy said. 'I suppose 'tis all bound to be different. But I'd give a lot to see a nice green field, so I would, and to feel the good soft rain on me face.'

'Rain!' Milly said in disgust. 'I don't reckon as they know what rain is in these parts. Look how dry it all is, and brown, not a green shoot anywhere.' She sighed. 'Us used to have fresh clotted cream on the farm when I was a little maid. Proper stuff, that was. Us'll never see that in this place.'

'I never saw it much anyway.' Cathy gazed at the landscape that moved slowly past. She heard Milly's baby begin to cry again, weakly and fitfully, and turned to see Milly once again offering it the breast. 'Perhaps she'll feed now.'

'Reckon her would, if there was anything to feed her on.' Milly's face, thin, pinched, old before its time, was creased with worry. 'I've lost me milk, that's the truth of it. And no cow's milk or even goat's to be had here, that's for sure.'

Cathy stared at her. 'Ye mean she'll starve?'

'You got any better ideas?' Milly asked bitterly. 'I told you, better her'd pegged out when the other one did. This ain't no place for babbies.'

Cathy looked at the white little face at Milly's breast, searching now for the milk that would only ooze slowly from the sore, swollen nipples. The breast was patched with red and looked lumpy and painful, and she could see that Milly flinched whenever the baby's gums closed on the stretched skin.

'You're ill,' she said with sudden concern. 'That's why you've got no milk.' She touched the other girl's forehead. 'You're hot as fire, so ye are. Why didn't ye say?'

'And what would have been the use of that? Fetch a doctor to me, would they? You seen enough sicken and die this trip to know one more or less ain't going to make no difference. You heard what they call we – cattle. And twice as useless, can't even give milk.'

Milly laid her head back, looking suddenly weary, as if admitting that she was ill had made it all the more real. Cathy gazed at her, distressed and helpless. What could she do? Milly was right – the guards wouldn't care, their only task was to deliver the same number of women at the end of the trip as they had taken aboard at the beginning. Whether they were all alive or not probably didn't matter at all – no doubt a few were expected to die, just as they had on the long voyage from England. And of those few convict women with any nursing skills, most had been taken as assigned servants. There was little help to be had on board the barge.

The day wore on but at last the sun began to dip low in the sky and the barge arrived at a small settlement of shacks and shanties. Here their guards hustled them ashore and they stumbled, exhausted and hungry, along the dusty, trodden bank to a ramshackle building which appeared to be some kind of inn.

'Inn!' Milly muttered scornfully. 'Maybe they'll serve we with tankards of good old Devon cider. I don't think! And look at that old crab by the door – he ain't no jolly taverner.'

'No, he's not, at all.' Cathy gazed at the man who filled the doorway of the hut. His hard eyes, narrowed in a burnt, seamy face, watched their approach and she had a feeling of being summed up; a feeling that had been familiar ever since the day she and Oliver had been caught with the goose. Peelers, constables, the judge himself, sailors on the transport ship, the guards and soldiers assigned to watch over them – every one had looked at the women with that same assessing look. Cattle, she thought. It's a good name for us, for it's all we are now. Not human beings any longer. Just cattle.

They were pushed into the back room of the hut, a long, bare space with neither seating nor anywhere to lie other than the beaten earth floor, their bedding no more than a few piles of dirty straw. Here they were given a bowl of thin gruel each and some water to drink. When Milly asked for some milk, the innkeeper stared at her and laughed.

'Milk! What d'you think this is, a nursery? Give the kid some rum, do it more good. Plenty of that here for those with the money to pay.'

'Money,' Milly said in much the same tone, when he had gone, 'And where does he think I'll get that from? Anyway, if I wanted to poison the babe I could do it for nothing.' She tried again, painfully, to coax the baby to suck at her breast, but it was clearly empty and the infant's wailing, thin and weak as it was, pierced Cathy's ears.

One of the other women came across. Cathy recognised her as the one they called Moll, a blowsy girl who had somehow managed to maintain a certain plumpness throughout the voyage. Her own baby had been born soon after they had left Portsmouth and seemed to be thriving, a lusty infant now almost four months old.

'Here,' she said, holding out her arms, 'let me try. I reckon I got enough milk left to give her a drop. I heard someone say you lost yours.'

Milly lifted her face and looked at the other girl as if she had just been offered the Crown Jewels. Her flushed, fevered face twisted as, without a word, she handed the baby over.

'Poor little mite,' Moll said, pulling out a breast as big as a melon, and as round and full as a cow's udder. The baby fastened on to it and began to suck greedily. 'Reckon you got a touch of that mastitis,' she continued, giving Milly an expert glance. 'Well, there ain't much we can do 'bout that, except wait for it ter get better. But I'll give your babby a suck after mine all the while I can. Can't let the poor scrap starve, can we?'

'I'll be that grateful,' Milly whispered, and Cathy saw that there were tears on her cheeks. 'The man said to give her rum. Rum!'

'Well, I'm going to have some,' Moll declared, 'so she'll get a tasty brew tomorrow! But I reckon if anyone can turn rum into good milk, I can. Always bin a good cow, I have, known for it down our way.'

'You've had babies before?'

'Three of 'em. Had the first when I was fourteen.' Moll's face twisted slightly and she looked away. 'Bloke down our way got drunk one night and I happened to be around . . . Lost her in an accident in the street – fell under a horse she did, poor little tyke. The other two – well, I had to leave 'em behind, didn't I? Old Sal down the street said as she'd look after 'em but I reckon they'll be in the workhouse now, 'less summat worse has happened. I'll never know, anyway.' She looked down at Milly's baby, sucking fitfully now. 'Look at her, tired out already, ain't even got the strength to feed. Still, she's had a bit, see her through the night.'

Milly took the baby back and held her close. 'It's right good of you and it's done her good already. See, there's roses in her cheeks, she was white as wax before. Thanks, Moll.'

Moll shrugged and pulled her shawl around her. 'Don't hurt me none. I'll be by in the morning, give her another suck. Now I'm off to get some rum – ain't had a good booze in months, and they say it's as cheap as dirt here. Ain't you havin' none?'

Cathy and Milly shook their heads. Cathy had never been fond of spirits and had never even tasted rum, while Milly was interested only in her baby. They watched as Moll made her way across the crowded hut to where the innkeeper was doling out mugs of drink. Some of the women were already drunk and cackling.

'I hope she'll be fit to suckle in the morning,' Milly said. 'I don't reckon any of 'em's going to be up to much.'

Cathy gathered together a pile of straw. Exhaustion was overcoming her and she wanted nothing more than to lie down and sleep. Together, with the baby between them, the two girls made themselves as comfortable as possible and closed their eyes.

But there was little sleep to be had for a long while yet. The carousing of the other women, plied with liquor for the first time in months, grew more raucous as the hours crept by. And there were men too; men who came from somewhere out in the darkness, men who understood very well that these women had been starved of more than food or drink since before they had left England.

Cathy and Milly lay in the darkness of their corner, listening to the sounds that went on all around them, inside the hut and out. But eventually the shrieks and giggles of the women subsided, the hoarse cries of the men quietened and the silence of stupor fell on the heavy, foetid air.

There was only a stealthy shuffling to be heard between the snores. But by that time, nothing could keep the two weary girls awake.

They were woken in the morning by the shouts of the barge constable as he strode amongst the sprawling bodies, thrusting his truncheon between them, kicking them awake with his heavy boots. Groaning and cursing, the women slowly opened their eyes and sat up. They held their heads and moaned in pain; some vomited and this drew further curses from those close to them.

'Thought we'd had the last of that when we come off the ship,' one crone grumbled, wiping herself with a handful of straw. 'Oh my, that rum was strong! Maybe it's because we just ain't used to it no more.'

'Here,' someone else exclaimed, 'where's my comb? I had it here last night, done meself up for the party with it, I did.'

'And I've lost me mirror,' another woman discovered. 'Me little mirror what my Bill give me afore we sailed from Pompey. That bastard that took advantage of me last night, he musta took it.'

The other women began to search their bags and clothing. There was little enough that any of them possessed, and none of it of any value except to them, but it soon became clear that they had all been robbed as they lay stupefied by drink. And Cathy remembered the stealthy noises she had heard after the others had fallen asleep, the shuffling and scraping as cautious hands had felt amongst the recumbent bodies.

But there was no time to do anything about the robbery, nor anything to be done. The constable, when appealed to, did no more than laugh and advise them to be more careful next time. 'You oughter know there'd be thieves in a place like this,' he said and accepted another rum from the innkeeper. 'Why, even old Joe here come as a convict, didn't yer, Joe? Got his freedom and runs a tidy little business – shows what can be done if you keeps yer nose clean, eh? Right, now get along back on that barge, I wants to make Parramatta by dinner-time. And stop yer snivelling, you dirty cows. Combs! Mirrors! You ain't going to need none of that up in the Factory.'

Slowly and unsteadily, the women staggered back along the riverbank to the waiting barge. Around them, the collection of tumbledown shacks was empty, their occupants already out in the bush, felling trees or preparing ground for planting. Cathy wondered if they too were feeling the effects of last night's debauchery. But perhaps they were used to the innkeeper's rum. It seemed as if the convicts were allowed a certain amount of freedom within the area and not forced to stay in cells at night. Things certainly seemed very different in this strange, outdoor prison.

Milly walked beside her, carrying the baby. Moll had not appeared this morning and she was looking anxious. She had tried yet again to feed the child herself, but her breasts were clearly empty, their swelling caused by the mastitis rather than by milk. She looked poorly, Cathy thought, her face flushed and hot, her eyes over-bright. The baby lay in her arms, pale as wax once more.

'She'll die,' Milly said hopelessly. 'I know she'll die. My poor little babby. My poor, poor little babby.'

Cathy felt the ache of anguish in her throat as she stared at the tiny, white face. It seemed to be shrivelling before her eyes, the milky blue eyes sunk into dark hollows, the lips cracked and dry. Why did such a tiny scrap of innocence have to suffer so? Why had she been born at all, if only to die in the cramping agony of starvation?

The two girls found a corner on the barge and huddled there, gazing with unseeing eyes at the riverbank. Once away from the settlement, they were passing through thick bush – a tangle of shrubs and trees, their branches intertwined so that to walk between them must have been impossible without an axe to hack a way through. Now and then they caught sight of a road which followed the river's course, and saw a cloud of dust rising from horses' hooves or from a cart being driven along. They heard shouts from convicts working at clearing the bush, perhaps making new roads. But for the most part, the silence was broken only by the cackles and screeches of birds, most of all the raucous laughter of the kookaburra.

Halfway through the morning they were given a ration of water. Milly tried to fed her baby with some, wiping a wet finger across its cracked lips. The tiny mouth moved, trying feebly to take in some nourishment, but it was clear that it was now too weak to suck. Milly filled her own mouth with water and pressed her lips to the baby's, so that the water could flow in, but most of it ran out again and down into the creases of the thin neck.

'I wonder what happened to Moll?' she said again. 'She promised she'd come. And she had plenty of milk, more'n enough for my little one as well as hers. I reckon she got drunk and just forgot.'

Another woman, sitting nearby, turned. 'You talkin' about Moll Dawson, her with the yellow hair? She didn't get on this barge. She was put on the one behind – you'll see her again when we gets to whatever godforsaken hole they're takin' us to.'

'But that might be too late,' Milly said. 'My poor little babby needs a feed now – look, she's hardly strong enough to suck my finger. We don't know what time we're going to get there, it might be hours. Days.'

'The constable said he wanted to be there by dinner-time,' Cathy reminded her. 'And it can't be far off that. Look, the trees are thinning out – we're coming to a place now. Maybe this is it.'

They turned their heads to look over the side and Cathy's heart rose as a few buildings began to come into sight. Ramshackle buildings, like the one they had spent the night in, but soon it could be seen that this was a far more substantial settlement – a real township, in fact. Eagerly, they craned their necks and those in the middle of the barge surged to the side, pushing and shoving in their efforts to see whatever could be seen. Comments and remarks flew about Cathy's head as she stared at the place that was to become her new home.

'Here, it don't look too bad.' 'What – with all those trees? Ain't there no streets?' 'Well, it's country, innit? Fields and woods and such. What d'yer expect, St Paul's Cathedral?'

They laughed and cackled with excitement, almost as if they were coming home after a long holiday. And in a way, that was what it was like, thought Cathy who had never been on a holiday in her life. And if she had, would have known that it was nothing like the long voyage they had just undergone, with all its hardships and discomforts. But that had all been an interlude – it was here that their sentence really began. Here that they would live and labour for the long years of punishment meted out to them by an English judge many thousands of miles away.

The horses came to a halt and the barges were moored to the wharf. With the accompaniment of more shouts and curses, the women were disembarked and lined up. Then they were marched through the town to the Female Factory where most of them were to live.

'Here,' a voice said in Cathy's ear, 'where's yer friend? I got put on the other barge this morning – bin worrying ever since about that kid of hers. Still livin', is it?'

'Oh, Moll, 'tis you,' Cathy said in relief. 'Sure, it's alive but only just. She'll be that pleased to see ye. Milly! Milly, look, it's Moll come to find ye.'

Her face alight with thankfulness, Milly handed the baby over and Moll put her to her ripe breast. But the feeble mouth could not suck much and after a while the sunken eyes closed and the head fell back.

'Well, she had a drop,' Moll said, giving her back to her mother. 'And it's good rich milk. We'll try again in a bit. Here – is this it? Where we're going?' She stared across the stretch of open ground towards the long wall which ran round a cluster of large, three-storey buildings with a small clock-tower in the centre. 'Looks as if it don't know whether ter be a fact'ry or a prison. Suppose there ain't much to choose between them anyway. Wonder what we'll do there?'

They were led through a large, solid door in the wall and into the courtyard. Here, women in the grey flannel dresses issued to all female convicts were walking about, some sitting in the sunshine, others choosing the shade of the walls. They stopped and stared as the new arrivals entered and there were a few catcalls and coarse remarks. But for the most part, they were silent, merely staring as Cathy and her companions were taken across the yard and into the main building and handed over to a grim-faced matron.

'You needn't think it's always like this,' their new mentor said. 'This is the dinner-hour – they'll be back at work soon enough. And so will you, soon as you've got yourselves sorted out.' She jerked her head. 'Come with me.'

They followed her through the long hall and upstairs to an equally long dormitory. This was clearly where the women slept, but there were no beds; merely piles of reeking raw wool, stained with the dirt and grease of the sheeps' backs.

'If you've got your own bedstuff, you can use that,' the matron said. 'Otherwise there's a heap of wool leavings over there you can use. You don't get mattresses or blankets, so it's that or nothing and since it can get cold here at nights you'd better make sure you get your share. There's a space over that end left clear for you, fit in as best you can and then come down for your dinner. After that, you can start work.'

She clumped away down the bare wooden stairs and the

women stood still for a moment, gazing around. It was bleak enough, but no worse than many of them were used to. And they could smell something cooking downstairs. Broth of some sort, they thought.

Moll's baby began a lusty wailing and she sat down on a pile of rough wool and began to feed it. There was a thin, feeble cry from Milly's child.

Cathy moved over to the window and stared out through the bars. Somewhere out there, Oliver too was beginning his new life. Had he found a good master? Or was he already in trouble, unable to hold his tongue or his temper, already being punished even further just for being himself?

And will I ever see him again? she wondered. We're both here in Australia – but sure it's a big, empty place. We could live our whole lives out here and never meet.

She rested her forehead against the bars, and tears crept slowly down her face.

Arthur Harris's farm was one of the furthest out, past Parramatta on the very edge of wild bushland. Tall eucalyptus trees with peeling bark grew on the fringes and within the forest itself bigger trees with immense trunks and heavy foliage. They reminded Matthew of the giant redwood trees he had seen in America and he wondered if they were expected to fell these, and what sort of tools they would be given to work with.

Oliver gripped his arm.

'Look over there! Savages – dwarf savages!'

Matthew stared. Dusk was gathering rapidly and he could barely make out the shapes against the dark shadows of the forest. But there they were indeed, short squat creatures with a mop of black hair that hung past their ears. They stood unmoving, making no sound, apparently staring at the newcomers; there was something strange about them, something alien, as if they were beings from another world, and he felt his skin crawl. Beside him, he felt Oliver draw a little closer and then he heard Ned Bright's sudden caw of laughter.

'Them! They're not savages – they're trees.'

'*Trees?*'

'Aye, that's right. Little short trees with trunks like iron. Black Boys we calls 'em – everyone that sees 'em thinks they're savages to begin with. But you don't have to be skeered of Black Boys.'

Matthew relaxed and laughed ruefully. 'We must be getting mother-scared, to be frightened of a few little trees. But are there any savages around here? Aborigines?'

Ned spat. 'Oh, aye, plenty of 'em out in the bush. And they comes around here too, for what they can get. You got to be careful of 'em though. Don't go messing with their women or nothing like that. And if they catches you trying to escape, they're like to bring you back for the reward. Aye, they're on the milit'ry side all right.'

'Would they kill you?' Oliver asked.

'Might, if they felt like it. Who knows?' Ned shrugged. 'Plenty of men have tried to get away and died in the attempt – we'll find their skeletons if we're put on to clearing, bound to. Walking to China, most of 'em – never heard tell of anyone getting there, though.'

'Walking to *China*?' Matthew repeated, amazed. 'But you can't – there's an ocean between us.'

'Aye, well, most of us don't have the benefit of an education like you do,' Joby Pierce growled. He had been taciturn all the way, barely speaking, his eyes mostly on the two women. 'Anyway, I don't suppose you knows it all. People bin talking about China ever since I can remember, stands to reason it's got to be there somewhere. And how do we know some of 'em didn't make it, eh? Tell me that. I'd go, if my leg would stand it, so I would. And I wouldn't let no Abo cut me up for mincemeat neither.'

They had been unloading the cart as they talked and now Harris came back, having taken the two women to a hut on the far side of the compound. His own house, Matthew surmised to be the large building at the other side. There were various other small huts and what looked like storehouses, and by the edge of the clearing a large stack of felled trees.

Matthew paused for a moment. For a brief space, he was back in America, working in the loggers' camps. In a moment he would see the glow of the camp fire and hear the cheerful voices of the men as they gathered round for their evening meal – a stew made of the meat from whatever animals the hunters had been able to trap or shoot. Perhaps someone would produce a concertina or a mouth organ and start to play. Some of the others would join in, singing softly, and as the stars grew bright and the howl of the coyotes began to sound, they would drift away to their bedrolls and sleep until morning . . .

But this wasn't America. And although a camp fire might be lit and the men cook their supper on it, even though someone might begin a song and the others join in, it would never be the same. For here the stars were different, unfamiliar and unwelcoming constellations that looked down from an alien darkness. The sounds of the bush were different too as kangaroos thumped unseen like native drums that beat out a message of menace. And, unlike the rough, independent loggers, nobody here was free.

Fourteen years, he thought, staring across the compound as the dusk gathered its shadows into the heavy darkness of a moonless night. Fourteen years. I shall be almost fifty years old. An old man. Unless I get a pardon before then – unless I can work my way out of it, as others have done before me.

'All right,' his new master said, jerking his head towards the nearest hut. 'Get yourselves in there. There's food and ale and bedding – I don't want to hear anything more from any of you before morning, understand? Be out here at first light and I'll hand you over to your overseer. And don't forget, you're here to work, and work's what you'll do.'

The four men turned and went into the hut. As Harris had said, there was bread there, and a jug of weak ale. The bedding was no more than straw, but they were all glad to lie down on it and rest their bones, so unaccustomed to the exercise they had had that day.

Matthew fell asleep quickly. But at some time in the night

he woke to hear a muffled sobbing and realised that it was Oliver. He reached out a hand and the Irish boy gripped it, too distressed to be ashamed of his tears.

'What is it?' Matthew whispered. 'Cathy?'

'I can't help thinking of her, so I can't,' Oliver whispered back. 'Wondering what's happening to her and all . . . I tell ye, if I could go back to the day I saw that goose just lying there with no one wanting it, I'd cross the road to pass it by, that I would. I'd never have done it if I'd known it'd lead to this.'

Nor would any of us, probably, Matthew thought. Of all the men he had met during this long, weary journey, few had committed a crime of any seriousness. Yet here they all were, petty thieves and innocents lumped in with hardened felons and murderers – like me, he thought wryly – and sent far away from home and family, simply because nobody knew how to deal with their problems at home.

They're just pushing us under the carpet, he thought with sudden anger. They don't really know what they're sending us out to – and neither do they care. They just send us here to get us out of sight and out of mind.

He stared out through the open doorway at the unfamiliar stars, and felt a sudden surge of determination. We can beat 'em yet, he thought with unexpected exhilaration. We can do as some of the old convicts have done – get our pardons, be given a grant of land, turn this strange new continent into a place that's fit to live in. A place people will be pleased to come and settle in.

We can turn Australia into a nation.

Chapter Thirteen

'My dear friends,' Matthew wrote, 'It is now 1834 and here I am, beginning the third year of my sentence in New South Wales. Only two years passed, and it seems a lifetime that I have been here in this strange, wild, terrible yet beautiful country. And if I were here as a settler, free to farm my own land and have my own friends and family about me, I believe I could be happy enough. There is an excitement about a raw new continent that nobody has touched – for most of Australia is yet completely unexplored except by the native Aborigines who wander the land and seem to need so little, yet have so much.

'They are a strange race. Wholly uneducated, yet they have a vast knowledge of the ways of the creatures that live in the bush. They grow no crops but know every root and berry that is fit to eat – they even dig fat little grubs from the ground and eat these, with every appearance of enjoyment. And they seem to have other senses too, senses that we know nothing of. An Aborigine can track a man for miles in the bush or in the desert, though there is no sign visible to a white man's eye. And they seem to be able to send messages through the air to each other, so that news travels as if by some mysterious kind of telegraph. They even claim to be able to kill by this means!

'My life proceeds in much the same way as I have told you in my previous letters. At about five each morning, we rise and go out to begin work. Most of the clearing is completed now and the vines and fruit trees we planted near the farmhouse last year are thriving. My master intends soon to enlarge his flock, which will demand a shepherd capable of living alone with them out on the pastures. Because of the thin growth of the grass, a sheep needs much more area to range upon here than in England and the "freedom" of living alone in the wide spaces of the pasture appeals to me greatly, so as you may imagine I am hoping to be chosen for this task.

'My young friend Oliver goes on in much the same way. He still frets constantly about his young sweetheart Cathy, and asks for news from anyone who comes from Parramatta, but there has been no word for some time now. I sometimes fear that he will make some rash and desperate act – he is hotheaded enough, and has already been taken before the magistrates three times for misbehaviour. And Harris has always been strongly prejudiced against him because he is Irish. Like a good many settlers and magistrates too, he believes that every Irishman is a "political prisoner" and therefore worse than any thief.

'My dear, dear friends, Francis and Rebecca, I think of you so often and long with all my heart to be able to return to you one day. Think and talk of me occasionally, so that you will know who it is when I come knocking at your door! And don't let the little ones forget me, nor Tom or Nancy or Polly. I keep you in my heart always.'

Matthew read the letter through and sighed deeply. They seemed so far away, Francis and Rebecca, and letters took so long to reach them. Sometimes a letter might take only three months – others wandered for a year before arriving at their destination. A letter written in July might arrive before one written in March, referring to matters that would remain a mystery until the explanation arrived in the form of the earlier letter. There might be a death or a birth, not known of for many months.

A death . . . Always, in Matthew's heart, was the dread that one of his friends might die before he had the opportunity to see them again. Yet every time the thought entered his mind, he reminded himself that he had few prospects of ever returning to England anyway. It was far more likely that he was never going to see any of them again.

Far more likely that he was going to end his days here, in this land of searing white sunshine and tangled forests, of azure seas and red, endless deserts; with England, and Kidderminster, no more than a fading memory of greyness and chill.

But the memory of friendship would never fade, never grow cold.

He looked at the letter again. It told them so little of what his life was really like. The 'comforts' that the men could buy – would they understand that much of the overtime money went on procuring the services of the convict women who lived in the huts on the other side of the farm? Would they realise that this was the only way the women could earn any money at all, and that since they were all considered whores anyway, nobody saw anything amiss in this?

And Oliver's three visits to the magistrates in Parramatta – how could he tell them that each one had resulted in a flogging? How could he describe the journey he had once made with Oliver, the two of them alone on the dusty road, trusted to walk there because there was nowhere else they could go – and because even for convicts expecting a flogging at the end of it, the trudge was the nearest they were ever likely to get to a holiday.

That was the time when Oliver, maddened beyond endurance by his master's constant jibes and the spite with which he was being treated, had turned on Harris and twisted the whip from his hand, obviously intending to give him a beating with it. Horrified, Matthew had leapt forward and dragged the weapon from his hand, knowing that if Oliver had struck the man the punishment would have been terrible. Men had died on the Triangles for such rebellion. But his interference hadn't been enough to save the young Irishman. Harris, his pig's eyes red with fury, had sent them both to the magistrate – Oliver to be charged with mutiny and Matthew to act as witness against him.

'How can I do that?' Matthew had protested. 'Oliver is my friend – I can't testify against him.'

'Can't you?' Harris sneered. He had never liked Matthew either, but had been unable to find any fault with him, try as he might. All his spite, all his unfairness, had been ignored. Matthew, well aware of the consequences of reacting as Oliver had done, was too determined to earn his ticket-of-leave, the nearest thing to freedom that he dared hope for yet.

'You know what happened,' the settler went on craftily. 'You tried to prevent him. All you have to do is tell the truth. I thought you had a lot of regard for the truth – or don't it signify, when it means trouble for your mate?'

'But you could tell the magistrate what happened,' Matthew said. 'They don't need my evidence.'

'Oh, I shall.' Harris grinned, showing broken, stumpy teeth. 'I shall be there, don't you fret, and I'll tell 'em what happened. *And so will you.*'

Matthew looked at him. The man wasn't just spiteful or vicious, he realised suddenly – he was evil. That grin of his . . . he was taking pleasure in the thought of the pain and misery he was about to cause. Physical pain as Oliver was flogged, and the misery of Matthew's betrayal of his friend. I wish I had let him kill you, Matthew thought bitterly.

'Och, don't ye fret about that,' Oliver said when Matthew told him what was to happen. 'Sure, I know ye're as much a slave as I am, and don't have any choice. What would be the point of you takin' a flogging too? Anyway, if he's to ride and we're to walk we'll have a few days free of the auld ratbag, and time for a crack along the road. I might even get some news of my Cathy.'

'I believe that's why you did it,' Matthew said, laughing in spite of himself. 'Just to get a few days on the road and a chance of some news of Cathy. Don't you realise you could be half killed?'

'Oh, I'm a stone man,' Oliver said with a shrug. 'He'll not make me whimper. I've a back like an ox. And if I'm injured, sure it's him that'll lose me labour, and there's not many that can drag a tree the way I can.'

This was true, for Oliver was undoubtedly the strongest man on the farm, but Matthew doubted if his back was as leathery as that of an ox even if it were as muscular. And Harris was concerned more with revenge than with the work of the farm. If Oliver couldn't do his share, there were others who could be driven harder while needed. And who were not 'stone men' and feared the lash more.

They set off the next day, walking out of the compound to the cheers of the other convicts, many of whom had made this same journey and come back barely able to walk, their backs criss-crossed with fresh weals.

It was pleasant enough strolling along the road between the tall, shivering eucalypts. The scent of their resin filled the air, reminding Matthew of the chest-rub his nurse had made from herbs and goose-grease to use when he had suffered with childish coughs and colds. Birds fluttered amongst the branches – the rose-breasted galahs, white cockatoos and the brightly coloured parrots that were called 'twenty-eights' because of the call they made. Some of the men had caught and tamed them, teaching them to talk; one was patiently taking his through the numbers from one to twenty-seven, saying that he did it because he'd have no need to teach it the next in the sequence . . .

As they walked, Matthew and Oliver met other people on the road. Convicts who were trusted by their masters to go on errands to the town or to neighbouring farms; ticket-of-leave men, free to go about as they pleased provided they carried out their tasks and stayed within the district; Emancipists, freed by pardon or through having worked their sentences and now granted their own land or able to set up in business on their own account.

'They're good masters to work for,' Oliver remarked after they had left one such traveller and were walking on again. 'They know what it is to be a convict and treated like a dog. I wish we could get assigned to one, that's sure. And Cathy too. I'd want for nothin' else then.'

'Perhaps Cathy is already assigned to a good master,'

Matthew said. 'It seems certain she's not at the Factory any more.'

Oliver shook his head gloomily. 'No, she's been taken by some stringy-bark from outback. She'd have got word to me else. Bride to some old man now, she is, and slave to him too, I don't doubt.'

Matthew sighed. There was little he could say. Oliver's words were probably true and indeed it was a better fate than many.

'She may still have found kindness,' he said. 'Not all the old settlers are harsh to their Factory girls – they simply want a bit of company about them, a woman to make them comfortable and cook their meals.'

'Aye, you may be right.' But Oliver did not sound convinced. Only the sight of his beloved Cathy could reassure him, and he was unlikely to be granted that.

They were coming into view of Parramatta now and could see the cottages, the larger houses and the wall that surrounded the Female Factory. From this distance, with its green spaces and the tall eucalypts that had been left dotted about for shade, it had an air of serene elegance. They could see people moving about, carriages with good horses, women wearing clothes that had been fashionable in London when the latest papers had been despatched. By now, that fashion had probably changed but the women of New South Wales would not be concerned about that. It was sufficient that the change reached them at all, even though it might be six months or a year late.

'Well, there it is,' Oliver said with a touch of bravado in his voice. 'The courthouse. Better go and let them know their next victim's arrived. I suppose old Pigface will be here already, spinning the yarn. They'll not even want to hear you, after he's had his say.'

'If they do,' Matthew said, 'I'll tell them the truth. That he's taunted you and given you all the worst jobs and made you work harder and longer than anyone else, and that he's kept your rations short too.'

'And a great lot of good that'll do either of us. They'll just

274

take you for as big a liar as I am.' Oliver stopped for a moment, looking around him. 'Holy Mother, I'd dearly like to catch a glimpse of my Cathy the minute. Just to see she's keepin' well. It'd make it all worth while.'

'I know.' Matthew felt a helpless sympathy well up inside him. He knew just what yearnings surged in the boy's breast. But there was nothing he could do to help. Cathy had been moved from the Female Factory, that was all they knew, and the letters that Oliver had written her had never been answered. Perhaps never even received.

'There's Harris's cart,' he said, seeing their master's horse tethered to a rail outside the courthouse. 'We'd better go in, Oliver.'

'Aye.' For the first time, the Irish boy seemed to realise what lay before him. His eyes darkened and his jaw tightened. He seemed to hold himself still for a moment, as though gathering strength. Then he shrugged, lifted his chin and gave Matthew a defiant grin. 'Well, let's get it over, shall we?'

The scenes that followed were to stay with Matthew for the rest of his life. True, he had seen floggings before – nobody who had travelled on the transport ships and arrived in New South Wales could have avoided the sight – but he had never been forced to watch such a flogging as this. He had never been compelled to stand by while his own best friend – his 'mate'– was half killed by the savagery of the man who wielded the cat o'nine tails, egged on by the master who had brought him there.

'He attacked me like a madman,' Harris had told the magistrate. 'Turned on me like a lunatic, tore the whip from my hand and would have finished me there and then if the other men hadn't prevented him.' He nodded towards Matthew. 'He'll tell you. He got the whip off him. I tell you, I was afraid for my life – well, you can see the size of him.'

The magistrate, a bony, white-haired man, looked at Oliver, standing in the dock unable to conceal his size. With the labour of felling and hauling trees, his tall, broad body had grown hard and muscular. His dark red hair, witness to the temper Harris swore he gave vent to regularly, tumbled over his head, which he had ducked out of respect for the magistrate but which made him look more like a bull about to charge. It was easy to imagine this young man in a towering and frightening rage.

'You're a foolish fellow,' the magistrate said abruptly in a harsh, nasal voice. 'Abusing a good master, who treats you well. You deserve to be put into a chain gang.' He turned his pale eyes on Harris. 'Would this suit you? Do you think it safer that he should be chained?'

'I think a flogging would answer the ruffian better, sir,' Harris answered quickly. 'Chaining him would make him all the more insolent. I've seen it happen before. A good lashing would teach him a lesson and in a few days he'd be back at work.'

The magistrate nodded. 'Fifty lashes, then, slow time, and if I see you here again, it'll be the iron gang for you. Or Norfolk Island.' He picked up his quill and wrote in his ledger. 'Next case!'

Matthew started forward. As Oliver had foreseen, his testimony had not even been asked for. And Oliver himself had remained proudly mute throughout the whole proceedings, refusing to say a word in his own defence.

'Sir!' Matthew exclaimed. 'Sir, I was brought here to answer your questions.'

'Questions?' The magistrate looked down his long, thin nose. 'Questions on what? Who is this fellow?'

'Sir, I'm Matthew Farrell. I'm assigned to Mr Harris, along with Oliver Connolly here. I was there when the incident occurred and –'

'I've finished with that case. Are you deaf?' The magistrate waved a dismissive white hand. 'Take these fellows away.'

'But –'

'Any more interruptions,' the magistrate said, laying down his quill and fixing Matthew with a stare that was suddenly piercing, 'and you'll have a flogging of your own to think about. I told you, that case has been dealt with. I've no questions – Mr Harris's testimony is quite adequate.' He glanced around impatiently. 'Guards, take these two away and see that the sentence is carried out, at once.'

Seething with helpless fury, Matthew found himself led outside into the courtyard, where the wooden Triangles were erected ready for the prisoners who were to be flogged. He glanced at the large wooden constructions, feeling sickened. He had seen physical violence often enough before in his travels, but never anything quite so repellent as a flogging. Nor with any instrument as cruel as the infamous cat o'nine tails.

His master came to stand beside him. He was chewing a wad of tobacco and smelled of rum. His little eyes gleamed evilly in his reddened face.

'This'll teach the bastard,' he said with satisfaction. 'And you too, Farrell, you take note of all this. Put a foot wrong and it could be you. Don't think you fool me with your gentlemanly ways – I've seen the way you look at me. Insolent as a rat, you are, and one of these days I'll have evidence for the beak, same as I had for Connolly, and it won't be fifty lashes for you – no, I'll stick out for a hundred, two, three hundred. That's what flash coves like you need to put you in your place.'

Matthew said nothing, though he knew that this in itself could count as insolence if his master so wished it. It was inevitable that one day he would find himself here, his wrists and ankles tied to the wooden Triangle, awaiting that first slash. Masters like Harris seemed to get their pleasure from it, and a convict like Matthew, working hard and quietly towards his release seemed to be a challenge to them.

'Watch,' Harris said quietly and then, more loudly, '*watch*, damn your eyes!'

Reluctantly, Matthew turned his head towards the square. All was now ready. The guard who was to do the flogging approached, rolling up his sleeves. The cat hung from his hand, a short pole with the nine thin cords hanging from it, their ends whipped to keep them from unravelling. Fifty lashes, he thought. That meant in reality four hundred and fifty. How could any man survive such punishment?

But men did – and more. And 'stone men' like Oliver survived it without a scream or even a whimper to give satisfaction to their tormentors.

The magistrate had ordered the punishment to be given 'slow time', with a pause between each lash, so that the entire flogging took two or three times as long as it might have done. An especially sadistic touch, Matthew thought, and then all thought was driven from his head as the flagellator took up his position, lifted his arm in the air and waited for the count.

'One.'

The nine whips whistled through the air and landed on Oliver's back with a sickening crack. Oliver uttered no sound, but nothing could prevent his jerk of response. The lashes left nine red marks streaked across his back.

'Two.'

Again the whistle, the crack, the flinch of pain. But still Oliver made no sound.

'Three. Four. Five. Six . . .'

The blood was seeping now from weals that lay like scratches from a tiger's claws across the tanned skin. As the flogging continued, it flowed more freely. By the time the count reached thirty the skin was raw, flayed almost away, and muscle and sinew showed beneath.

'Are they stopping it?' Matthew muttered as the guard paused and examined his weapon. 'Can't they see he's had enough?'

'Enough?' Harris snorted. 'He's only half way through. No, it's the cat that's at fault – look at it, fraying already.' He watched as the guard shook out the blood-soaked cords. 'They're nothing but rubbish, these government cats – not made fit for the job they're to do. Ought to be made like the ones I've heard of in Van Diemen's Land – plenty of knots in the cords and then soaked in salt water and dried in the sun to harden. Like wire, they are, give a man a thousand lashes and still good for more. Not like this children's toy.'

Matthew turned and stared at him. There was no doubt that Harris was enjoying the sight. And it wasn't simply because he hated Oliver, either for himself or for being an Irishman. Quite simply, he enjoyed watching a man suffer.

The new cat had arrived and the flogging began again. And Matthew closed his eyes and waited until, at last, the terrible sound of whistle and slash had stopped and Oliver was released from his grim crucifixion and returned to Matthew's care.

Not that there was much Matthew could do, other than bathe his wounds and bind them, under the eye of the prison surgeon. But as he watched over his friend that night he felt a new and terrible bitterness towards the society that had sent them here.

He thought of Rebecca and Francis and the dream they were trying to realise. The dream of a society in which master and man lived in equality, with profits fairly shared amongst those who earned them, so that no man was too poor nor too rich.

Perhaps this is where it will finally come true, he thought. In this land, which is yet so harsh. For here, if you can survive the cruelty, the hard work and poor rations, if you can live through the heat and the lashes, you can eventually win your pardon and own your own land. You can become an Emancipist – a man as free as any settler. And you can be assigned your own convict labour.

It was well known that the Emancipists were in general better masters. Perhaps that was where, eventually, the dream would begin to come true.

Matthew folded the letter and sealed it. None of this could be told to his friends at home, though he knew that many of the convicts did write, railing against the conditions and the harshness of their punishments. But there was little use in telling Francis and Rebecca of Oliver's floggings or of the days when their meat ration crawled with maggots so that they had nothing but bread, or of the days when without apparent reason they were given no meat at all. What could

they do, besides worry? And what would be the purpose
of that?

No, it was best to be like Oliver, a 'stone man', enduring it
all doggedly without whimpering or whining; getting through
each day as best you could, taking what comfort was possible
from the thought that each one was a day nearer to the end of
your sentence. Looking forward to the day when you would, at
last, be free. An Emancipist, perhaps with some land of your
own, a chance at last to make something of your life. A chance
that many of his fellows would never have been given back in
England.

A chance for Oliver to marry his Cathy, if he could only find
her and if she were not already married to some stringy-bark or,
even worse, another convict. And there, at least, he was better
off than Matthew.

Matthew sat for a moment gazing at his folded letter; then,
with a swift, unaccustomed movement, he lifted it to his lips.
The only kiss, he thought sadly, that he would ever be able to
give to the woman he loved.

For a few days after their arrival at the Female Factory, Cathy,
Milly and Moll managed to stay together. Herded into the
spinning and carding rooms, they sat together to do their work.
The babies were laid on a heap of wool nearby where they slept
and kicked or cried between feeding-times, and whenever the
eye of the wardress wasn't on them, Moll would pick them
up for a quick, furtive suckle. Otherwise their mealtimes
were those of the adults and Milly fretted constantly that
her little one, its hold on life already frail, would find the
wait too long.

'She's doin' all right,' Moll said comfortingly. 'Like that good
clotted cream you're allus talkin' about, my milk is. Look at 'er
– content as a lamb now she's 'ad a good bellyful. At least she
knows when she's 'ad enough, not like my greedy little wench.'

'I don't reckon yours ever has enough,' Milly said with a rare
touch of humour. 'You could feed she all day and all her'd do
is grow. Wish my little 'un was like that.'

They had finished the day's work and were sitting outside the shed, keeping in the shadow of the wall. There was little for them to do now. Like the male convicts, their work finished in the afternoon and their time was now their own, to 'sell'. But how could a woman sell her time? they asked each other. Only by selling her body too.

'And everyone's on that game,' Moll observed. 'All got their own customers too, just like any bawdy-house back in London. I s'pose we'll 'ave to set up shop with the new chums. Still, a bit of a rest first won't do no 'arm. I ain't keen to start again straightaway, not in this 'eat.'

Cathy stared at her. 'Was that what you did before – in London? I mean, were you a – a –'

'A whore?' Moll laughed. 'Course I was! Weren't we all? Doin' all right, I was too, 'til I got above meself and gulled me best bloke. Went through his breeches, I did, while he was asleep. And bugger me if he didn't wake up and cop me at it. After that, it was the magistrate for me and no back-answers.' She grinned wryly. 'He got his own back, though. Didn't wear a cundum that last time and landed me with this little codger.'

'A cundum?'

Moll looked at Cathy as if she had suddenly grown another head. 'My, you are an innocent, ain't yer! Don't yer even know what a cundum is?' She looked at Milly. 'Here, you tell 'er. Or don't you know either and that's 'ow you got landed too?'

Milly grinned a little shamefacedly.

'I knows what it is,' she offered. 'I never had one meself, nor did my feller. My sis told me it all depended which way the wind was blowin' at the time, but I reckon her was wrong about that.'

'So what *is* it?' Cathy asked impatiently, and Moll laughed her raucous laugh.

'Why, you cully, it's a bit of old sheep's gut, what a feller wears over his cock-a-doodle-doo to stop him puttin' a kid in where it ain't wanted. They bin around for donkey's years, I reckon. Old woman down Half Moon Street used ter make 'em

281

years ago – made a fortune at it, so they say. And saved a lot of poor little beggars being born into misery, too.'

'Well, there ought to be plenty of sheep-gut around in New South Wales,' Milly remarked, jiggling her baby in her arms as it began to wail again. 'P'raps you could set up in business, Moll. Can't be many women here wants to get in pod.'

Moll's baby began to cry too and Moll bared her breasts. She had become adept now at feeding both babies together, and it seemed that her milk was as good as she claimed, for Milly's child was looking stronger every day. It was still small, though, and Milly was obviously consumed with anxiety over it, to the extent that she was constantly being reprimanded by the wardress and threatened with the treadmill if she didn't take better care to her spinning.

Dusk fell and the cooking pots began to boil. Each woman was given a daily ration of bread, with meat or cheese and some vegetables which they cooked for themselves. It was companionable enough, sitting round the fires and sharing their meal, but all were tired by the work and the heat. Most of the occupants of the Factory were either pregnant or were sick, the building being used largely as a hospital.

Cathy, who had been spurned by most of the settlers as being too weakly-looking, was thankful enough to remain in their company; all too soon, she knew, someone would declare her fit for outside work and she would either be assigned to a settler, probably as a house servant, or married off to a lonely farmer on some remote homestead. And although the other women assured her that this could be a better fate, she lay awake at night dreading it and trying to evolve ways of avoiding it.

'It's nowt to worry about,' one of the crones told her, a toothless old woman who had been transported for stealing a bonnet and had little hope of even seeing the end of her sentence. 'You gits a bit of a party, yer own clothes back *and* yer ticket-of-leave. Old stringy-bark takes yer off, yer gits as much as yer can orf 'im and then arter a coupla munfs, yer slips out one night and 'ikes down to Sydney and 'as the time of yer life. Plenty o' bawdy-houses there ter git lost in, and a good livin' ter be 'ad as well.'

'But, sure, I don't want to be married,' Cathy objected. 'I've got me own boy somewhere out in the bush and I want to wait for him, so I do. And –' she blushed '– I've niver been with any man before.'

'Cor, ain't we nice!' the old woman scoffed. 'What do it matter if another cove's been down yer alley, eh? Someone's goin' ter take a trip there someday, yer might's well be legal and git summat out of it. Anyhow, come you ever get back with yer feller, 'e ain't goin' ter let that worry 'im, is 'e?' She gave Cathy a sharp glance. 'Course, you're Irish, ain't yer? Don't believe in livin' in sin, that it?'

Cathy turned away and did not answer. She lay awake at night, thinking about it, imagining the parade with the women lined up like the cattle they were likened to, presented for inspection like so many prize cows. She thought of herself being picked out by a filthy old settler, one who had come out as a convict and stayed to work some meagre holding miles from the town. How could she possibly go to such a man as his bride, lie with him as his wife, when all the time her heart and body yearned for Oliver?

She slept at last, worn out by the fatigue of hard, tedious work and stifling heat. It seemed no more than a moment before she was woken in the morning. And then it was not by the clanging of the bell that normally woke them, sounding from the little tower above their heads, but by a screech of fear and panic from somewhere very close.

'What is it? What's happened?'

The women were all awake, leaning up on their elbows, peering about the half-dark dormitory. Cathy rubbed her eyes. Surely it was Moll who was shrieking. But why? What had happened to her?

'She's dead!' Moll screamed, and Cathy saw that she was bending over the little pile of raw wool beside her own bed. 'She's dead – *dead*! Me little babby, me own little Mag, cold as a bone. Someone's killed 'er, that's what, someone's done for 'er.' She had picked up the little body and was cradling it in her arms, hugging it to her as if her own warmth could bring back the life. 'Oh, me little Mag, me little babby, she was all I 'ad and now she's gone. She's gone – gone – gone . . .'

Her sobs became incoherent, a noisy, snorting grief that tore at Cathy's heart. Timidly, half afraid of such terrible distress, she edged across and touched Moll's arm. She could see Milly, already lifting her own child and staring in terror at its face, as if the scourge might have struck it too. Tears running down her own cheeks, she looked down at the ashen face that only a few hours ago had been so rosy. What could have made it die? There was no mark on it, no sign of illness; just this dreadful stillness, this certainty that life had fled far away and would never come back.

They took the baby away from Moll at last, though she clung to her as if she still could not believe that breath would not suddenly return. They took her away and, because she was so young, refused her any sort of funeral. What was done with the small body none of the women knew; they suspected it had been thrown on to a rubbish heap and burned.

Moll sat on her bed, deaf and unseeing. Silently, she mourned. Her screaming ended, she wept without tears, deep inside herself where the pain was too great to speak of. And when Milly, almost frantic about her own hungry child, timidly approached, she turned dull eyes on her and shook her head.

'Ain't you afeared I'll poison the poor brat, like I poisoned me own?' she asked in a voice as dry as dead leaves. 'Ain't you afeared she'll go the same way in the night?'

'But if her has nothing, her'll die anyway,' Milly said desperately. 'And it'd help you to feed she. 'T in't no good to let the milk clog up inside you. Please, Moll.'

But Moll shook her head again. She fumbled with her coarse prison smock and bared her breasts. They hung, hard and lumpy, and she squeezed them and flinched.

'It's all gone,' she said miserably. 'Me milk – it's all gone. There ain't nothing there now but cheese, I reckon. See, I can't

even squeeze none out and your poor little toad won't be able
to suck any stronger. I'm sorry, Milly, I'd do it if I could – but
there ain't nothing there. And maybe it's just as well anyway.
I ain't such a good cow as I thought.' And she sank once again
into her speechless, grinding agony of grief.

Milly turned away. Cathy, watching, felt the despair in her
own heart. Without Moll's milk, the baby must weaken again
and, this time, die. There was no one else to act as wet nurse,
no other way of feeding the doomed child.

This is a terrible place, she thought, going to the door to stare
across the wooded hills at the mountains beyond. A terrible
place to send people. And what for? Did any of us do anything
to deserve such as this?

'A clean, honest lass, that's all I ask,' the voice said, its clear
tones ringing through the building. 'Well – honest as far as can
be expected. One who will settle well into a good household
and behave herself. I don't want a girl who's going to be
slipping out every five minutes or entertaining followers.'

The three girls lifted their heads and stared at each other.
Several weeks had passed since the death of Moll's baby,
followed very soon by Milly's, and the strangeness of time
here had already made the deaths seem a long time ago.
The pain was still there, Cathy knew; but all women suffered through the deaths of their children, it was part of
their burden and must be shouldered and carried without
complaint.

She was thankful that she had been able to stay with her
friends for so long. Several girls had already been taken as
assigned house servants, or as wives by the gnarled men who
came in from the bush, burnt as black as savages. Each time
this had happened, Cathy had shrunk back in the line, hoping
to be unnoticed. Most of the men had indeed passed her by,
but one had come and stared at her for a long while before
passing on. Cathy had gazed back in terror, praying that he
would not take her. And he had finally shaken his head in
contempt and chosen a big woman with large breasts and

muscular arms, who would be strong enough to labour almost like a man.

But this woman, who was now walking slowly through the spinning shed, was something different. Tall, angular and dressed in clothes such as only the wealthier settlers could afford, she had large, dark blue eyes and a long, pale nose. Her hair was drawn tightly back with not a wave or a curl allowed to escape its severe style, and her skin was so fine that it looked as if it had been stretched.

'Here, she looks a nob,' Moll muttered. 'Wonder what she's doin'? Lookin' for a house servant, you think?'

'Could be, couldn't her?' Milly glanced up under her brows at the woman. 'D'you think the old cow'll tell she I bin a dairymaid back home? Turn my hand to anything round the kitchen, I can.'

'And so could any of us, if it meant a soft billet.' Moll glanced at Cathy. 'What're you lookin' so scared about? Don't you want to get assigned?'

'Sure, I don't know.' Cathy hardly understood herself. She had only just got used to the Female Factory, and dreaded the idea of being taken away, removed from her friends. Besides, while she was here in Parramatta there was always a chance she might see Oliver. Away on some remote farm in the bush, all hope would be gone.

The woman was coming closer, looking hard at each convict as she passed. Cathy tried to shrink behind the other girls, but it was of no use. The wardress stopped beside the three of them and waved a contemptuous hand.

'These three are my newest intake. Come off the latest ship, fresh from England, so got almost the whole of their sentences to serve. You'd get a good few years outa one of them. These two had brats when they arrived, but they kicked the bucket pretty soon, so you know they're clean – ain't going to spring no surprises when you've had 'em a few months. This little un looks as thin and pale as a yard of rainwater but she's strong enough, a steady worker and never bin insolent.'

'Yes, I see.' The woman looked them over thoughtfully,

her eyes taking in Moll's bold, brassy looks and the lines of misery still deeply etched in Milly's face. Her glance lingered on Cathy, who looked back fearfully, and she gave a sharp, sudden nod.

'I'll take that one. She looks trainable. Mind, I'll bring her back at once if there's any trouble.' She sounded as if she were back in England, interviewing servants, and perhaps that was how she saw herself. She gave Cathy another searching glance, then turned away and the wardress motioned to Cathy to come with her.

'But can't I have time to say goodbye to me friends?' She looked at Milly and Moll, suddenly terrified. 'I might never see ye again.'

'Get on with yer,' Moll said robustly. 'You've struck lucky, can't yer see that? Bin Milly or me, we'd have bin off like a shot, ain't that right, Mill?'

''Tis that. You'll be all right with she, Cathy. Got a handsome house in town, I reckon, and you'll live like a princess. A proper bed, good food, decent clothes. And we'll run into each other again – you could always put in a good word for us, couldn't you? She might want some other servants sometime.'

Cathy made no reply. Her eyes were filled with tears as she gave each of them a hasty kiss and then followed the impatient wardress. As she left the spinning room, she was conscious of the envious stares of the other women there, but she could only feel misery. Once again, she was being dragged away from all that was familiar, poor though it might be; once again she was having to start life afresh.

Chapter Fourteen

In the early morning, nothing moved. The kangaroos had bounced at last to their hiding-places amongst the tangled bushes, the kookaburras were yet to greet the dawn with their cackling, senseless laughter. A vast, impermeable silence hung over a landscape that seemed to stretch to the end of the world, a boundless space of iron-red earth and rock, of sparse patches of straggled grass, of eucalyptus trees that reached twisted, skeletal fingers towards a sky that was ever blue.

Matthew stood at the door of his hut and stared out at the inhospitable scene. Already he was hot, fresh perspiration mingling with the sweat that had dried on his body overnight. What wouldn't I give for a good shower of dirty, soot-laden Kidderminster rain, he thought with grim humour. For the sound of feet clattering over those hard 'kidney' paving-stones in the early mornings. The rattle of looms and the clash of machinery echoing through the narrow streets. The thought that at any moment I might see Rebecca's face . . .

Abruptly, he turned to go to the cookhouse for the day's rations. Since coming to Australia, he had missed Rebecca more each day, become hourly more conscious of his love for her. And what was the use of it? He would never see her again – and if he did, she was bound to his best friend by virtue not only of marriage, but of the love she bore him. She had never so much as looked at Matthew with more than friendship, nor had he ever given her any indication that his own feelings for her might be stronger.

So where was the sense in letting his thoughts dwell on her

so much, so often? Where was the purpose in conjuring up her face, to gaze upon it with his mind's eye?

Only that it brings some brightness into my day, he thought as he collected the bread and cheese and the bottle of water that was to last him the day out on the pasture. Only that if I don't have the memory of her face and her sweetness, I shall have nothing at all. And what harm does it do, after all? Doesn't every man here have his fantasy? Even a convict must have his dreams.

He made his way to the compound where the sheep were penned each night to keep them from the roaming dingoes. Today, he would take them in a different direction, for they had eaten all the grass they could find on the pastures they had been grazing during the past weeks. He would have to go further west, past the acres of box gum, to find some new grass. And that meant going near the boundaries of Harris's holding, which brought both risks and temptations.

Whistling to the dog Harris had reluctantly allowed him to help with the sheep, Matthew started to drive the flock out. Bleating, pushing and shoving each other, they massed in front of him, a sea of woolly backs. They had a long walk today, and it would have been better if they could have stayed at pasture, but Harris had never allowed any of his government men to stay out at night since two of his shepherds had gone bush and disappeared. On their way to China, presumably, Matthew thought wryly, and if Harris had ever bothered to find out what his present shepherd was like he would have realised that Matthew was never likely to follow their example. He knew enough about geography and too much about the perils of survival in such a hostile country to want to take such risks.

As he walked along the track already made by a thousand cloven hooves, Matthew noticed a small cluster of men standing by the gate that led out of the main compound. They looked up as he approached and parted to let his sheep through. To his surprise, he saw that Oliver Connolly's red flame of a head was amongst them.

'Olly, I thought you were still at the clearing.'

Oliver shrugged. 'Sent me out here, didn't he? Me and Ned here, we're to come along with you the day, see where ye've been pasturin' the mob, and then you an' me are both to go back to the homestead at the end of the week. Don't ask me why, the auld pigface doesn't take me into his confidence.'

'Oh, he's got his reasons,' Ned Bright remarked, spitting to the side of the track. 'Don't like none of his men out here too long, he don't, 'less they gets to like it. Man gets too confident like, he might go bush and that's another un lost. You're too sure of yourself out here, Matt, that's top an' bottom of it, so he wants you back under his eye. An' you an' Olly here, you're good timber men too – best he's got, though he'd never say so.'

Matthew grinned. 'Well, a day's a day's a day wherever it's spent, though you're right, I'll be sorry to go back. It's almost like being a free man, out here. Anyway, if you're to come with me we'd better be on our way, it's a long hike to the new pastures. And you can tell me what news there is as we go.'

The three men followed the sheep along the track, passing the thick mallee scrub where dingoes lurked and the box trees which sucked all the water from the ground and left it too dry for grass to grow. Beyond these, there was some pasture, but it was poor enough and Matthew often thought that the sheep must use as much energy reaching it as they gained in nourishment. 'If all the mallee and box could be cleared,' he said, 'we could grow grass nearer the station and not have to drive the beasts so far. And as Harris gets more stock – oxen and horses – he'll need more and more feed nearer to the compound. He'll have to let his shepherds stay out at nights, there'll be no way in which they'll be able to get back every night.'

Ned sniffed. 'And who's to clear it? All his men are back at the main farm, he ain't got no one else and he won't get assigned none either. He got his full quota now.'

Matthew pursed his lips. He looked at the eucalypts, their bark peeling and ragged, their branches twisted into shapes that had a strange, grotesque beauty. 'Ring-barking would do it,' he said. 'A circle of bark cut round each trunk. They'd die quickly and stop taking all the moisture, and grass would be able to grow. There's no need to fell them. And it would lessen the risk of bush fire.'

'How's that? They'd burn just as much dead as alive.'

'But they wouldn't *start* fires,' Matthew said. 'Oh, yes, I know men start fires as often as not – but sometimes it's the bush itself. The oil from the eucalypts seems to vaporise in the air. It forms a kind of mist, you can almost touch it, and then it just ignites. The sun, the heat – something sets it off as if it were tinder, and the whole bush is alight. It's almost as if it needs it in some way.'

'Needs it!' Ned said, and spat again. 'Well, *we* don't need it. I bin in a bush fire and I can tell you it ain't no joke. Well, you seen it for yourselves, musta done.'

'There was one near the farm once,' Oliver said. 'We went out and beat it down. And there was a swine of a one, a few miles away, took all the farm buildings, it did. Jesus, I wouldn't care to be caught up in the middle o' that.'

They walked on. Ned and Oliver gave Matthew all the news of the farm and he replied with what small events had happened out in the bush. Two skeletons had been found on a remote part of the holding and it was thought that they were those of convicts who had tried to escape several years earlier. One had clearly died after the other, and had tried to survive by wrenching off parts of his comrade – an arm, part of a leg – and eating them; there were traces of a fire and blackened bones. The men shuddered as he told the story. Cannibalism wasn't unheard of when men went bush, but it bore its own peculiar horror.

'I s'pose you'd do anything if you were starved enough,' Ned said. 'Mind, I don't reckon there'd be much meat on me – like string, I am, tough as an old hen.' He grimaced. 'What else happens round here?'

'Arnie Carroway at the next farm but one had all his sheep infected with scab,' Matthew said. 'Just about ruined him – he lost practically all the season's lambs and the wool too. That's why we're not allowed to go too near the boundaries – get the flocks mixed up and it runs like wildfire.'

Oliver grinned wickedly. 'Be a good way of getting back at auld pigface though, now wouldn't it! Sure, and we couldn't help the sheep mixing themselves together, they was only lonely like. And me an' the other feller just having a bit of a jaw, doin' nothin' wrong at all, at all.'

Matthew felt his own mouth tug into a reluctant smile. 'Well, don't do it while I'm around. I've no wish to find myself on a Triangle for the sake of a few sheep or a bit of revenge. And nor will you risk it, if you've got any sense.'

'Oh, he's a stone man,' Ned said. 'Don't feel right if he ain't had a few lashes for a month or two. Anyway, I hear old Harris is goin' off to Parramatta to pick up some new chums – maybe some cattle too. Give you summat to think about, a few different bunters about the place.' He glanced at Oliver. 'Look, Olly, you got to stop hankerin' for that bleached mott and start livin' nat'ral. No wonder you keeps gettin' into trouble. It's all the bad blood you're makin', holdin' yerself in all the time.'

Oliver reddened but said nothing. Matthew glanced at him and felt a pang of sympathy. He knew all too well what it was to yearn for one woman and know that no other could ever take her place. A night with another might relieve the gnawing pain momentarily – but that was all.

And when it returned, it returned all the stronger, and with the added bitterness of betrayal.

The three men spent the rest of the day pacing the pastures while Matthew pointed out the boundaries of Harris's holding. They ate their rations sitting in the shade of a rock, staring over the stretching landscape, their eyeballs aching in the searing sun. Only the sheep and a few birds moved in the heat, and the riverbeds that ran like torrents in the rainy season were dry and still. Why was this country ever considered suitable for sheep? Matthew wondered. They must be almost ready to expire in their woolly coats, and finding grass for them to eat grew more difficult each day. Yet somehow it seemed to work. They did produce fine wool, and as long as they could eat they could thrive. And the wool, when shorn, could be spun and woven into blankets, cloth, carpets.

Carpets . . .

Would Rebecca hold a piece of wool in her hands one day, and somehow know that he had handled it too? That he had tended the sheep from whose back it came, that he had sat here in a landscape she could never imagine, a convict in the company of other convicts, thinking of her and sending his thoughts across the world to reach her?

Would she be conscious of those thoughts? Was she even at this moment thinking of him?

They had to walk back to the farm, leaving Ned at the out-station with the flock that had been in Matthew's care for the past few months. Their rations in their pockets, they strode together along the dusty road, broad-brimmed hats shielding their heads from the sun, stopping to talk with other travellers, making the most of this brief holiday yet aware that if they lingered too long their master would have punishment ready and be only too pleased to administer it. And no man with any sense put himself in the way of punishment unnecessarily.

'D'ye think he's back from Parramatta yet?' Oliver wondered as they drew nearer to the clearing where they had worked together felling trees. The timber had been transformed now into paling fences and log huts, where convicts lived and horses and oxen were stabled. The farm had grown in the time that they had been here and, with the out-stations Harris had acquired, was growing larger. 'I don't see any new ch—'

His voice stopped abruptly. Matthew glanced at him in surprise and saw that Oliver's sunburnt face had turned almost white, so that the freckles stood out like a pox. His eyes were fixed in a wide stare and his mouth hung open as if in shock.

Matthew gripped his arm, concerned that Oliver had been taken with a stroke, that perhaps the heat had been too much for him. But the Irishman shook off his hand. Still wide-eyed, he moved forwards and Matthew realised that he was trying to speak. His mouth moved tautly, shaping a word that would not come and then, as Matthew began to turn his head to see what it was that had so shocked him, the name came out like a sigh.

'Cathy . . .'

Cathy! Matthew caught his breath and followed Oliver's gaze as the Irishman seemed to regain the use of his limbs and began to run. And there she was, Cathy, no longer the fragile waif he had seen on the wharf the day they had disembarked, but now a slender young woman with hair that shone like washed gold in the sun, very nearly beautiful. And wholly so, it was certain, in the eyes of the young Irishman who had yearned for her for so long.

'Oliver!'

The name jerked from her body as the big man caught her in his arms. She almost disappeared into his embrace, her pale, shimmering hair flowing over his arms as he wrapped them around her quivering body. Matthew watched as she lifted her face for Oliver's kiss, and he knew a moment of stabbing pain that this would never happen to him, that the woman he loved would never cry his name in that joyful, unbelieving way, never raise her lips to his with that tender abandon.

But the moment was brief. He felt a deep joy flood his heart, a thankfulness for the fate that had brought these two together at last. In the spaces of New South Wales, they might never have met again, yet here they were, assigned to the same farmstead, perhaps to stay for the rest of their sentences, perhaps even to marry as other convicts had done. And Oliver, surely, would find no need to court trouble any more, not now that he had his Cathy to court instead.

But even as these thoughts passed through Matthew's mind, a great roar of fury shook the air and everyone but the lovers stopped what they were doing and turned towards the farmhouse.

Harris was standing at the door. Even from this distance,

Matthew could see that his face was dark with rage, his small
eyes reddened, his mouth screwed into the snout it resembled
in his blackest moods. As Matthew watched, he reached out
and took the horsewhip that stood by the door, and then he
marched across the yard.

'Olly! *Olly* – take care.'

Matthew leapt across to the two who still stood entwined,
oblivious of everything but themselves, and tore them apart.
But even as Oliver turned on him, baffled and furious, the
first lash of the whip cracked across his shoulders, the tip
of it catching Matthew's hand and making him jump away,
startled by the sudden pain. He glanced at his fingers to see a
line of blood spring from the knuckles, but there was no time to
think of that now. Harris was slashing again and again with his
weapon, while Oliver staggered, blood pouring down his face
from a cut across his forehead, and Cathy screamed in terror.

'Take that, you Irish swine! And that, for daring to meddle
with my woman. And another, just to remind you when you
think I've forgot.' The whip whistled through the air and
Matthew recovered himself and caught at his master's arm,
forgetting his own danger in his efforts to stop the beating.
'And there's one for you, Farrell,' Harris snarled, twisting away
and turning the whip against him. 'Keep out of my road, you
bastard, or it'll be the Triangle for the pair of you. And you,
miss –' he jerked his head at the sobbing Cathy '– get back into
the house and stay there until you've permission to come out.
And don't let me ever catch you playing your whore's tricks
with the men again, or it'll be worse for you, understand?'

Cathy gave him a terrified look. She turned to flee, then
hesitated and looked back at Oliver, now half kneeling, barely
conscious and blinded by blood and dust. For a second, it
seemed as if she might go to him; then Harris made a threatening movement, flicked his whip and growled. With a last sob,
she scurried away, across the yard and through the door.

Harris stared after her. Then he grunted and turned back
to Oliver. He was just raising his whip again when Matthew
stepped forwards.

'Mr Harris – no more. The man's had enough, can't you see that? You'll have him disabled if you go on, and he's your strongest worker. Do you want to put him on his back, just when we need his muscle?' He saw Harris take in the words and consider them. 'They were sweethearts back in England,' Matthew went on. 'He'd thought never to see her again.' But even as he spoke, he knew that he might as well talk to a stone. Harris cared nothing for such matters and was more likely to use such knowledge as a means of hurting the pair. Too late, Matthew realised this and bit back further words. But perhaps his master hadn't heard them. He was grunting again now and folding his whip. He turned away, almost as if he'd lost interest, and there was a different gleam in his eyes as he looked towards the door where Cathy still cowered in the shadows.

'Get him cleaned up,' he said curtly. 'He's an offence to the eye. I'd not have him about if he weren't as useful as an ox. And then get to your hut, the pair of you, and don't let me see you again until morning. And be prepared to do a bit of work – you've had holiday enough, idling your way along the road.'

He strode away and Matthew saw Cathy back fearfully into the room beyond. He felt a surge of anger but controlled it, knowing there was nothing he could do. Instead, he bent and helped Oliver to his feet. The young Irishman was still dazed, his head swaying from side to side like that of a bull. He put a hand to his forehead and brought it away smeared with blood. Bewildered, he looked at Matthew.

'What happened? D'ye know, I thought for a moment I had me own sweet Cathy in me arms. What was it, a dream? A mirage? Am I running mad at last, Matt?'

'You're not mad,' Matthew said quietly as he led him to the hut they shared. 'Cathy was here – she *is* here. Harris must have brought her back from Parramatta. And you did hold her in your arms. But then Harris came out . . .'

'With his whip.' Oliver's eyes were clearing. He drew back from Matthew's grasp. 'Matt, what's going on? What

297

in the name of Mary and all the angels does he mean to do to her?'

'Olly, come into the hut. It's no use, you can't go rushing in there, you know that. He'd have you on the Triangle, and what good would that do Cathy or anybody?' Matthew finally managed to get his friend into the hut, where he sat him down on a pile of straw and sacking. Oliver sank down, clearly still dazed by the beating, and put his hand to his head again. He stared at Matthew.

'What does he mean to do to her?' he asked again in a whisper.

'Olly, you don't know that he means to do anything at all. He's got her just as a servant – a house servant. That's all there is to it.'

'All!' Oliver gave a short, unamused laugh and then flinched. 'Matt, we all know what he does with his servants. Look at that last one, Big Allie – work like a man, that one could, but he still wore her to a shadow with his filthy ways. And she was no innocent like my Cathy.' The lilting voice filled with horror and once again Oliver tried to struggle to his feet. 'Matt, I can't stand it, I can't at all. He's in there with her now and doing God knows what, and if she knows I'm out here and doin' nothing at all to help her –'

'There's nothing you *can* do, Olly.' Matthew exerted all his strength to hold Oliver back on the bedding. 'And you're not fit to stand, let alone go and commit murder – for that's what you'd do if you went over there now, it's in your eyes and don't tell me it's not in your heart as well. And it will do no good.' He knelt beside his friend and spoke earnestly. 'What comfort will it be to Cathy if she has to watch you go to the gallows? And we don't know that he'll misuse her. He doesn't like women like Cathy, small and slim. He likes them big and built like bolsters, you know that. So perhaps he does mean only to have her as a servant. At least let's wait until we can get some word from her.'

'And how will we do that?' Oliver said, but his voice had lost its edge of fury. 'She'll niver be allowed out of the door.

She'll be trapped in there and I'll niver see her or know how she is.' His voice began to rise again.

'Olly, *stop it*!' Desperate, Matthew went to the bucket in the corner and threw some of the water over Oliver's head. 'And you a stone man! I've never heard you so much as whimper at the Triangle and here you are –'

'Crying like a baby, I know.' Water, stained with blood, ran down Oliver's face and neck and on to his clothes. 'But it's not the whipping, Matt, ye know that. It's seeing her there, so sudden, and looking so grand. And the feel of her in me arms and the touch of her lips . . . And then that – that *bastard*!' Once again, his voice began to quiver and Matthew stood ready to hold him down again. But this time, Oliver caught himself up and did no more than beat on his head with clenched fists. 'Oh, ye're right, I know that. There's nothing I can do the night. But if ever I see he's ill treating her . . . Matt, I'll murder him so I will, aye and enjoy swinging for it if I have to. I swear if I go to the gallows, it will be for him and it will be for the best day's work I ever did in me life.'

Matthew looked at him. In the dim light from the doorway, the red hair flamed and the blue eyes glittered. And he believed the words his friend had spoken with such fervour. He knew that Oliver might well go to the gallows for killing his master. And go with defiance in his eyes.

Matthew closed his eyes and groaned softly. That moment of delight, of pure pleasure and happiness that had blazed so briefly in the yard, seemed now like a false diamond, sparkling with a promise it could not fulfil. It would have been better if Cathy had never been brought here, to Harris's farmstead. Better if the two of them had never met again.

Cathy moved uncertainly through the farmhouse door and into the large room beyond. It seemed to be used for everything, this room – for cooking, eating and sleeping. At the end by the door were the cooking range and a rough bench for food preparation. A few pots were littered on the bench, together with such utensils as were essential. There was a large table, with used dishes at one end and a miscellany of papers, tools, lengths of rope and other paraphernalia at the other. A few chairs stood about, mostly plain but including one large rocker with a cushion on it, and at the far end a bed was built against the wall, its bedding tossed and crumpled.

Was this where she was to live and work? It was all so different from Mrs Fraser's house in Parramatta. There, Cathy had found herself in a home such as she had dreamed of back in England, with gracious rooms and furniture that gave her pleasure to care for. Polished tables and sideboards, mahogany floors that could be made to shine like the peat-brown waters of an Irish lough, curtains that smelled fresh with washing and bedlinen that was soft to touch and cool against the Australian heat.

Not that Cathy had enjoyed such luxuries in her own quarters – as in England, she had shared a plain little room with other servants. But Mrs Fraser, wife of one of the most prosperous settlers in the colony, had been a kind mistress and had provided all that was needed to live decent, as Cathy put it to herself. And although the work had been hard enough and the hours long, it had been a good deal better than the prison life she had expected, or the horrors of being married off to some old settler in the outback who would have treated her worse than one of his own animals.

But good things never last, she had told Moll when she had found herself back in the Female Factory. She'd been lucky to have it at all for a while. And now Mrs Fraser was dead, taken with a sudden collapse one morning while she was entertaining some of the other ladies of Parramatta, and her husband had shut up the house and gone to live with his daughter in Sydney. And so here was Cathy, once more spinning with Moll and awaiting a new assignment.

'You've niver been taken by anyone then?' she enquired. 'Or are ye like me, sent back like a sheep goin' to market?'

Moll laughed. 'Must be me looks puts 'em off. They all think as I'll be off whoring the minute their back's turned – and so I would be, like as not. Any road, it's not so bad here. I can do a bit on the side after hours – got me clients, same's all the girls. It's tolerable. Better'n being out in the bush, anyway, with no one but a stringy-bark and a few sheep and oxen to talk to.'

'And what's happened to Milly? I hoped she'd be still here too.'

Moll's grin faded. 'Oh, Milly. Well, you know what she was, so took up with that kid of hers? Just went downhill after she died – didn't eat, didn't do her work properly, allus in trouble. But she didn't seem ter care any more. Turned her face to the wall in the end, and better off out of it, I reckon.' But her face twisted a little and Cathy caught the gleam of tears in her eyes. She reached out and touched Moll's arm, and the other girl looked down at her hand almost in surprise. There was a rough kind of comradeship in this place, but little tenderness. For a moment, the two of them were silent, then Moll spoke again, a little huskily.

'It's good to see yer again, Cathy. We was good friends, the three of us. But nothin' lasts, does it? You'll be off again directly. Now you bin a house servant in one of the best places, you'll be snapped up again before you can say Jack Robinson.'

'S'pose I will.' But Cathy spoke gloomily. She had been extraordinarily lucky, she knew, in being taken by Mrs Fraser. She could hardly expect the same good fortune again.

And it was barely a week before her foreboding was realised. The wardress came into the spinning room one morning and ordered all the women to stand. She was followed by a straggle of men and women, settlers who ranged from the 'society' that had slowly formed in Parramatta to the toughened farmers who lived on the most remote stations in the bush. Slowly, they paced down the line of women, looking them over with as much detachment as they might inspect oxen or sheep.

Cathy stood beside Moll, resigned this time to whatever fate might be hers. She hoped that Moll's predictions might be true and that she would get as good a place as she had had before, with a decent bed to sleep in, food to eat and honest work to fill her days. But just because a settler was rich and lived in luxury it didn't mean that he'd look after his servants. Cathy had known of several in her time with Mrs Fraser who had been ill used, starved and even sent to the Triangles and flogged for the smallest of misdemeanours. A girl would be better off on some outback farm with a master who was rough but kindly.

A large, hard-faced woman stopped and stared at her, taking in Cathy's fair hair, loose this morning instead of being twisted into the bun she normally wore. The eyes, brown and hard as pebbles, moved over her and then the woman turned and said loudly to her companion, 'This one's the right age, plenty of work in her, but look at that hair. Disgusting! Vain as a peacock, you can see that, and have all the male servants under her skirts the minute she walked in. You'd think they'd teach them modesty here, if nothing else.'

She moved on and the wardress followed, giving Cathy a look that boded ill for her later. Cathy felt her colour rise in humiliation. Didn't these people realise that the women were human beings, even if they had been sent across the world to pay for some felony back in England? Unaware that her grey eyes were stormy, she looked at the next settler, and felt her heart sink.

She had seen him before. Back on the wharf, where he had taken a hank of her hair and twisted it in his fist, jerking her towards him. And again here, in the Female Factory, before Mrs Fraser had taken her. She remembered his eyes, small as a pig's, his blunt snout of a nose, the cruel lines of his face.

He'd shown little interest in her before, tossing her aside in contempt. But now he was looking more closely. She met the narrow stare and watched in fearful fascination as his hand moved towards her neck and then, as she had known it would, gathered her flowing hair into a shining rope and pulled her closer.

'I've seen you before, ain't I?' he muttered. 'Miserable scrap of a thing you was then. But you've improved – aye, filled out a bit. And got a bit of fire in your eyes to go with it.'

He turned towards the matron. 'Reckon this one'll suit me. I'll take her now.'

The wardress shrugged. 'If that's what you want. The last mistress she had seemed pleased enough. But that was here in Parramatta. I don't know what she'll be like out where you live.'

'She'll settle in,' he said grimly, adding, 'if she knows what's good for her.' He glanced at Cathy. 'Get your duds together, girl, fast as you can. I ain't got time to hang about.'

Cathy gave him a quick glance of fear, then turned to Moll. The other girl was watching her with pity and Cathy gave a little sob and flung herself into Moll's arms. For a moment they clung together, and then she felt rough hands on her shoulders and was torn away. Half blind with tears, she stumbled up to the dormitory and gathered together her few possessions.

When she came down again the settlers had gone and the girls they had picked out were finishing their work before saying their goodbyes. Harris was waiting impatiently by the door and Cathy had no time to whisper more than a few hasty words before she was hustled away and forced to climb up into the cart that stood waiting outside. Within a few minutes they were rattling along the dusty road, out of Parramatta and into the bush.

Cathy huddled in her corner, her shawl held across her face to keep out the dust kicked up by the horse's hooves. Harris sat with the reins in his hands, taking little more notice of her than he took of the sacks of oatmeal and flour which surrounded her. Occasionally he would glance sideways, as if to reassure himself that she was still there, and each time she found his eyes on her she shuddered, as if touched by something creeping and slimy.

At last they came within view of the farmstead. Cathy sat up a little, interested in spite of her misery to see the place where she was to spend the next part of her sentence. She saw the long, low building which she guessed to be the farmhouse and the scattered huts where the convicts lived. Some of them were visible now, going about the chores of the farmyard, feeding stock and carrying water; others were gathered in small groups, talking. There was a large clearing around the compound itself, with sheep and pigs roaming free, and she could see trees being felled at the edge of the bush.

It all looked idyllically rural. But Cathy had been in the country long enough to know that the scene was less peaceful than it looked. Out there in the bush roamed the savages, the Aborigines, who might be friendly, but might spear you almost as casually as a white man would shake hands. In the undergrowth were snakes and spiders which could kill. And on the farm itself there would be fear; fear of this small-eyed, cruel-looking man who had mastery over everyone there, fear of one's fellows because denouncement could bring its own reward.

As the cart came nearer, she saw the groups break up and the men who weren't tending the stock disappear quickly into their huts. Harris grunted and flicked his whip, as if testing its flexibility. Then he stood up, cracking the whip loudly, and drove the cart straight at the gate.

Two men leapt to open it. The horse skidded through and came to a halt in front of the farmhouse. Harris jumped down and gave orders for the sacks and boxes he had brought to be unloaded, and then looked at Cathy, still crouching in the cart.

'Well, get down then, miss! You're not a lady's maid now, you know. You're here to work and work you will – and you're here to pleasure me as well. So get down and get into the house, and start making a meal ready. You'll find everything you need and water comes from the well over there.' Roughly, he pushed her towards the door. 'See that it's good food and plenty of it, or you'll be sorry for it later.'

He marched away across the yard and disappeared, and Cathy went into the house and gazed about her. She knew now what was expected of her, she understood what her life was to be. And as she looked about the long room and saw what was to be her home, her heart sank.

But there was no time for lingering. Harris had not said how long he would be, but he had made it clear he expected food to be ready for him when he did return. And the first requirement was water. Cathy found a bucket and went outside, intending to go to the well.

Outside, she hesitated for a moment. Harris had indicated the direction she must take, but the yard was still busy with men and oxen and she shrank at the thought of making her way through them, running the gauntlet of their stares and coarse remarks.

As she stood there, she was conscious of a sudden movement at the edge of the trees. Two men had emerged from their shelter, along a broad track which led between the tall, peeling gums. They were standing quite still now and as she stared she realised that one was tall and broad, a giant beside his fellows. A giant with hair that flamed against the sky like the cones that grew on the banksia trees. A giant who was even now breaking into a run, coming towards her, with her name upon his lips.

Oliver . . .

'So that's the kind of wench you are, miss.'

Harris stood in the doorway, his bulk darkening the room. His hands were at his waist, fumbling with his belt, and Cathy caught her breath. Surely he was not going to use that broad strap upon her? But she saw the look in his eyes and knew that he was quite capable of it. And of enjoying it too.

Holy Mary, she thought, what have I come to? And Oliver out there, whipped to his knees because of me, and me not here half an hour yet . . .

'A whore like all the rest of 'em,' Harris said, and licked his lips. 'I might've known it. Well, you might have had it easy up til now, my girl, but you're going to find it different here. Here you're *my* woman, understand? And I'll have no truck with you playing your filthy games with the men. You'll not set up shop here and sell your favours to any rogue who comes with a look in his eye and a wad of tobacco in his pocket, so remember.' He had his belt off now and Cathy watched in fearful fascination. But instead of taking the end in one hand and raising it to strike her, he tossed the leather aside and came closer, holding his breeches in place with one hand while with the other he caught again at the pale hair that had first attracted his attention. Roughly, he jerked her against him and she closed her eyes in terror, smelling the acrid odour of his body, feeling his heat.

'Let's get this clear right away,' he growled, and she felt the roughness of his beard against her cheek. 'Signed and sealed, as yer might say. You feel proud any time, it's me you looks to for your shagging, see, not some gov'nment man in the yard. Gaw! Hadn't bin here five minutes before you're at it! Well, I can fill a woman as well as any red-headed Irishman, and don't you forget it.'

'Please,' Cathy gasped, 'you don't understand – he was my sweetheart back in England. We haven't seen each other since we came here – I'm not a whore, I've niver been with any man, I swear on the Cross of Jesus. Please, Mr Harris, don't –'

'Sweethearts? Never bin with any man before?' Harris let out a shout of laughter, raucous as that of the kookaburra. 'Why, you must take me for a real cunningham. There's not a woman comes to this country but hasn't been with a man – most of 'em's lost count. Anyway, it don't signify. Another half-hour and you'll not be able to say it again, for every man with ears in this place will know the truth. Come here!'

Cathy screamed, but her cry was thin with terror and she knew that no help would come to her. The only man likely to care was Oliver, and he had been beaten almost senseless out in the yard. She felt Harris's arms close around her, and then one big, grimy hand began to fumble with her skirts. Sickened, almost paralysed with fear, there was nothing she could do. She could feel his rough fingers on her thigh now, the ragged nails scratching delicate skin. He pushed her ahead of him, forcing her back on to the tumbled bed, and she felt his weight upon her. His mouth fastened over hers, hot and wet, and as his tongue forced itself between her teeth she gagged, certain that she would either vomit or choke. And at the same time, his thick fingers were scrabbling at her thighs, groping and thrusting so that she twisted in both pain and fear, knowing that she was helpless yet still compelled to resist.

'Get off of her, you scum!'

The heavy weight was stilled for a moment. Opening her eyes, hardly able to believe her ears, Cathy looked up to see Oliver towering over the bed. His red hair stood on end like a cock's comb, his eyes were blue flames of fury and the muscles bulged in his bare arms as he jerked Harris off the bed and away from her body. She could see the weals left by the whip, still raw and bleeding, but Oliver seemed to feel nothing but the rage that shook him. He had Harris upright now, one great hand around his throat, the other raised ready to strike. As Cathy watched, he began to rain punches on the man's head, so that blood spurted from the snouty nose and his eyes swelled with the force and savagery of the blows.

'Olly! For heaven's sake –'

There was another man in the room now, tall and broad yet slight beside Oliver, who seemed to have swelled to twice his normal size. He caught at Oliver's arms, trying to drag him away from the farmer, but Oliver shook him off as if he were a fly and went on hitting. Regaining himself, Harris tried to fight back, but he was already staggering, hampered by the breeches that were still around his ankles. He began to swear and curse, lifting his arms to protect himself, but Oliver wrenched them aside and struck him again, and again.

'Olly, you'll kill him! Stop, for God's sake, before you do murder.'

'It's murder I'm after doing,' he panted. 'And that's too good for the swine. Did ye not see what he was doing, Matt? He was raping her – my Cathy, the sweetest, most innocent . . . Murder! I wish I could follow him into purgatory, so I do, and into Hell itself to stoke the fires hotter.'

With each word, he struck another blow to Harris's head and face. The man was barely able to stand now, but Oliver's powerful hand kept him from falling. Weak with horror, Cathy scrambled off the bed and retreated to a corner, where she stood unable to tear her eyes from the savage onslaught. Please,

Oliver, she begged silently, please stop it. He's right. You'll kill him.

At last the fury seemed to die away, as if spent, and Oliver let the body fall on to the bed. Harris lay there, eyes swollen and closed, blood still running from his nose, his face battered and bruised beyond recognition. He made no movement at all, and Matt knelt quickly by his side. He felt the dirty wrist, laid his hand on the hairy chest, listened for the beat of a heart. At last, his face grave, he stood up.

'You've almost done for him, Olly,' he said quietly, and glanced across at Cathy. 'He'll not touch your girl, nor anyone else's, for a long, long time.'

Oliver stared at him. Then he turned and walked across the room, his gait unsteady. He reached for Cathy and drew her against him, so that she could feel the jagged beating of his heart. Afraid, she pressed herself close.

'I'm not sorry,' Oliver said, and his voice came raggedly. 'Whatever they do to me, I'm not sorry. It's no more than he deserved. I only wish I'd sent him straight to his Maker to explain himself, except that I'd dearly like to be there to hear it, and see holy justice being done.'

'Well, he's still alive and I mean to keep him so.' Matthew bent again over the still figure. 'I don't want to see you on the gallows, Olly, and neither does Cathy. You'd better get someone off to Parramatta for the surgeon. And if I were you –' his blue eyes flicked over the two of them, standing so close '– I'd find somewhere quiet to be together for a while. Take her to our hut, Olly. You may not have many more chances.'

'Ye're right,' Oliver said slowly. He looked down into Cathy's face and she met his eyes, trying to convey to him all her love with that one look. 'All I can ask now is to have tonight with me sweetheart, for it may have to last us both the rest of our lives.' He glanced around the room and his lip curled in disgust. 'But not here, Cathy, me darlin'. I'll niver let ye come into this filthy pigsty again.'

They turned away, Cathy trembling in the circle of Oliver's

arm. At the door, Matthew came to them. He touched them both on the arm and looked seriously into their faces.

'I'm sorry this happened, Olly, even if you aren't. It's going to be bad for you once the authorities hear – and we'll have to let them know. But if it's any help, I'll promise you this. I'll look after Cathy for you, as well as I'm able. I'll do my best to see that no one misuses her – even if I have to marry her myself!'

Oliver stared at him. Then he said quietly, 'It may come to that, Matt. And if it does, I could want nothing better for her. I'll go to me fate in peace if I know that's what's going to happen.'

They turned away again and crossed the yard to the hut where Matthew and Oliver slept. Matthew watched them go. He felt almost as shaken as they, and not only by the violence of the afternoon. For a moment, he laid his head against the door jamb and wondered what he had done.

He had proposed protection – virtually marriage – to a girl he had seen only briefly once or twice in his entire life, a girl of whom he knew nothing other than the obsessive praises of her lover. A girl he did not love, could never love, for there was room for only one woman in his heart and that woman was Rebecca.

But he had made the promise and might well find himself having to fulfil it. And now there were more urgent things to be done. He saw Oliver stop and speak to one of the men, who came running immediately towards the house. Sighing, he went back through the door and moved across the room to look down again at Harris's body.

Still alive. And would stay so too, if Matthew had anything to do with it. For the idea of watching his friend swing for this bastard, he would *not* countenance.

Chapter Fifteen

'. . . to serve the remainder of your sentence upon Norfolk Island.'

The words struck like a knell upon Cathy's heart. She stared across the courtroom, desperately willing that Oliver should meet her eyes. In a little while, he would be taken from her and sent a thousand miles away to a lonely rock in the Pacific. And she knew he might never return. This could be their last chance to look at each other with love.

If only she had never been assigned to Harris. To have been married to some old stringy-bark miles away from Parramatta would have been a better fate than this. At least Oliver would still be on the mainland; at least they could have hoped to meet again and eventually marry.

Now there was little hope of either. Like everyone else, Cathy had heard horrific tales of life on Norfolk Island. All the worst offenders – the incorrigibles – were sent there, and many never returned unless it were to face the court yet again. And some committed crimes merely so that this could happen; though they might return to the gallows, they thought this better than living out the miserable existence that sentence to Norfolk Island meant.

As if he felt her thoughts reach him, Oliver raised his head and looked directly across the courtroom to Cathy, standing with Matthew in the witness box. Here they had been kept after having been forced to answer the judge's questions, so that they might witness also Oliver's final humiliation. But no one could prevent this last moment of communication, and Cathy stared hungrily across the crowded space between them, trying to reach out to him with her mind if she could not do so with her arms; trying to send all the love that was in her heart to his, so that he might carry it with him to the terrible place where he was bound.

She saw the understanding in his eyes, the softness in his face. And she knew that he was remembering, as she had done so often, that one night they had spent together in the hut on Harris's farm. A night when every man on the station had respected their privacy, a night of magic that had taken them beyond their troubles into touching distance of heaven.

Oliver, Oliver, her heart cried in silent anguish, is that to be all we'll ever know of each other? Is that all the loving we shall ever have?

Their glances held, became one gaze, deepened into total accord. And then the soldiers grasped Oliver's arms roughly and hustled him away. Her final glimpse of him was as he disappeared into the cells at the back of the courthouse, and she knew that this was the last time she would ever see him.

For a few seconds, she stood root-still, staring at that place where he had vanished. And then she felt Matthew's gentle touch on her shoulder, and turned to him with a sob and laid her head on his breast.

'Here, enough of that!' Their own guards were wrenching them apart, pushing them out of the box and through the crowd. Terrified, Cathy looked about for Matthew and saw his dark auburn head in front of her. She looked at his broad shoulders, muscled like Oliver's from strenuous work, and saw them as her only protection now in the dangerous and frightening world in which she found herself. Desperately, she struggled to reach him but her guard held her back.

'Not so fast, my lady. You're to go to the assignment office now. There'll be a new place for you, and 'ware you don't cause no trouble there. You're lucky they don't countenance women on Norfolk, or you'd be there too, along of your fancy man.'

And glad to be too, Cathy thought, as she was led to the office where new assignments were made. Normally this was where the men were taken, but it had evidently been decided that Cathy was not to be taken back to the Female Factory to await her chance there; she was to be assigned at once, rather than left to the choice of a settler.

But she had been in the room for only a few moments when the door opened and Matthew was hustled in. Surprised, she looked at him and felt an instant reassurance as he met her eyes and gave a small nod. As if he could have any say in what happened to her, she thought with unaccustomed cynicism, but it was a comfort to have him there all the same.

The assigment officer, a small, elderly man with crabbed features, looked bored. This was all in a day's work to him, and whatever troubles Cathy or Matthew had were no more than those of any other convict. He glanced down at the papers on his desk.

'A timberman, eh? Experience with sheep as well. Hmm . . . there don't seem to be any complaints against you, as far as your work goes. Friend of Connolly, were you?'

'I was,' Matthew answered steadily. 'And I'd like to say –'

The officer waved his hand. 'The trial's over and done with. You've come here to be reassigned, Mr Harris being unfit to run his farm now. And since you were a friend of the prisoner –'

He paused as the door opened and a second man came in and whispered in his ear. The assignment officer frowned and murmured a question, then shrugged.

'Well, it makes no odds to me.' He glanced at Matthew again. 'Seems you saved Mr Harris's life by giving him immediate attention. Well, it hasn't earned you a pardon, if that's what you were hoping for, but it might make a difference where you're assigned. And the woman too.' His glance flicked over Cathy. 'Is it true you've asked to be assigned to the same master if possible?'

'That's true,' Matthew answered, and Cathy gasped and looked at him with gratitude. Never would she have dared, or even dreamed, of making such a request. But Matthew had made a promise to Oliver and it seemed he meant to keep it.

She felt a surge of hope. At least she was not going to be totally abandoned.

'Well, it isn't usual. It isn't usual at all.' The officer shuffled his papers and stared down at them. 'Still, it's not my business to go against orders. If that's the way it's to be . . .' He moved one or two more sheets of paper, then seemed to make up his mind. 'Very well. You can both go to Simeon Ackroyd. He needs an overseer and a female house servant. And mind!' He glared at them both over his *pince-nez*. 'Ackroyd treats his government men and women well. Don't take advantage of him. I don't want to see either of you back here again.'

Cathy and Matthew were shepherded out and left to wait on a bench outside the office. Cathy sat down with a sigh, and then lifted her eyes to look up at Matthew.

'I'm real grateful to ye, sir. I thought when they took my Olly that I'd not a friend left in the world. But if I can stay with you –'

'Don't call me "sir",' he interrupted. 'My name's Matthew – Matt, most of them call me. And I've done nothing.' His face softened. 'But I'll be a friend to you, Cathy, as far as I'm able. You need never feel yourself alone while I live.'

Cathy felt the tears hot in her eyes, but before she could say any more a cart had rattled to a halt beside them and its driver was leaning down. She looked up at his whiskery face and felt a second flood of relief. The kindness in the eyes was unmistakable and she knew that life as this man's servant, while nothing like the life she had known in Mrs Fraser's household, would probably be hard but never harsh. And when she glanced at Matthew, she knew that he had recognised this too.

'Well, come on then, the two of you,' Simeon Ackroyd said, his voice rumbling somewhere deep in his beard. 'Climb aboard, we've a long way to go before nightfall, and work to be done when we get there. I doubt if young John will have managed to do all that I left for him.' He looked them over as they scrambled on the cart, and once again Cathy gained a strong impression of kindliness. She settled herself in a corner, and looked across at Matthew. He smiled a slow, reassuring smile.

I should feel happy, she thought. I should feel that at last everything's taken a turn for the better. A good master, a good friend – what more could any poor convict girl want?

But she could not forget Oliver, at this very moment being taken on the first part of his journey to Norfolk Island. She could not forget the stories she had heard, of men being flogged for such offences as singing a song, swearing or smoking at a forbidden time of day; lashed without mercy and left to moulder until maggots crawled in their festering wounds. Of rebellion and mutiny such as the one which had taken place only a year ago for which fourteen men, none over the age of thirty, had been hanged – and by all accounts, glad to be so relieved of their sufferings. For Norfolk Island was deliberately made a place of terror, a threat to be held over every convict in order to keep the peace on the mainland.

And this was the place where Oliver was now bound. And, with his Irish temper and his determination not to give in to injustice, she knew that he would not stay long out of trouble.

To Matthew, sitting in Simeon's kitchen two years later as he read Rebecca's letter, it seemed almost as if he had been always here in New South Wales and that any other life was no more than a dream. Yet as he read her words, the sounds and smell of Kidderminster came back to him so powerfully that he was almost transported there. Once again, he was walking the narrow streets, feeling the kidney stones under his feet, swinging his cane cheerfully and with no more thought in his head but the next enjoyment – a drink in the tavern with some friends, a game of cards, a meal with Francis and Rebecca.

Pleasures that would never now be repeated. A life that could never again be the same.

He raised his head and looked around the kitchen. With the rain lashing down outside, it had a homely feeling about it. Curtains were drawn over the windows, a lamp glowed on the table; there was a dresser with plates and bowls displayed upon it and a fireplace for the coldest evenings. And here, master and servants made one family as on an English farm, even though the servants were convicted felons and the master a free settler with the power to take a man before the magistrate and have him flogged.

It was a place where a man could be content, doing a good day's honest toil and returning to a meal that would nourish his body, yet with time for the thoughts that would nourish his soul.

He remembered how they had first settled down here, he and Cathy. From the first, Simeon and Rose and their son John, only a year or two older than Cathy, had been welcoming, listening to their stories with neither condemnation nor shock yet without being over-sympathetic. Wrong had been done and the law must be complied with. But as long as their assigned servants behaved as they should, neither Simeon nor Rose saw any reason to punish them further.

'There were plenty of lads and lasses in our village that could have been where you are now, happen they'd got wrong side of t'gamekeeper,' Simeon observed. 'Taking a rabbit or two for the pot was enough for some squires to send a man to prison, aye, and to the hulks as well. As for your bit o' trouble –' he glanced under bushy brows at Matthew '– well, murder's no light matter, but seems to me that was more like accident, and any one of us might have an accident. Mind, I think you were daft to take a gun out, but if 'twas like you say . . .'

'I was asked to,' Matthew said. 'The magistrates themselves sent word.'

'Aye, and then turned against you. That's if what you say is true.' Again, Simeon bent his sharp glance upon Matthew. 'And I reckon 'tis. You don't strike me as being a liar.'

'Thank you.' It was good, Matthew thought, to be believed, to be trusted. It made him want to give something back to this kindly man who had given him that trust.

There was nothing that he could give now but his work, to which Simeon was entitled anyway. But one day, he vowed, there would be more. One day, Simeon would ask for something more. And Matthew would give it gladly.

There was a good deal of bush to be cleared and Matthew's experience ensured that he was soon made overseer, a job which he shared with another government man working for a neighbouring settler. He would have preferred to be alone, finding Jake uncongenial company as they worked with the gangs, but there was no help for it; there were several farms here and the settlers had agreed to share labour.

Meanwhile, Cathy worked in the house with Rose. There were no other indoor servants and the two women spent their days together, cleaning, cooking, making and mending clothes. With work like this, there could be no set hours but Cathy seemed to be happy enough, working about the house or in the garden where they grew vegetables and fruit. And indeed, he thought, would have been completely happy had it not been for Oliver.

Reports came through regularly from Norfolk Island, for the harsh regime there was no secret; it was intended as a fearful deterrent to others, so the more that might be known about it the better. Stories came filtering through, of the new governor ordering a total of fifteen hundred lashes for five men before breakfast, of men spending years in heavy irons, of convicts desperate enough to poison themselves with berries, even to blind themselves in the hope of being left alone. And these tales were not denied by Oliver's letters, which came rarely enough and always had fresh atrocities to tell.

'He says he got a hundred lashes just for *smiling*,' Cathy told Matthew one day, her eyes filled with tears. 'Holy Mary, what does the man have to smile about, will ye tell me that? And then to be flogged so cruelly for it . . . They're barbarians out there, Matt, worse than Harris ever was. And I'm sure Oliver only tells me the half of it. They've been building a new gaol, he says, and it's cruel work, and most of them in irons too. And ye can't do a thing without being informed on. Every man is an enemy there.'

Matthew took the letter and shook his head over it. Punishment was one thing, but this was sadism of a degree that must sicken any decent man. Who were these lawmakers who could debase a human being in this way, treating him as no better than the lowliest of crawling animals? How could any man order such degradation, wiping out all acknowledgement of humanity so that in the end the miserable wretches in your control had nothing to lose by even the most evil of actions?

He thought of a man blinding himself, and tried to imagine the despair that must come before such an action. He thought of the suicide pacts – the groups of convicts, afraid to take their own lives because their God might exact an even greater retribution, planning for one of their number to kill the other and the rest to stand witness, so that they might all be executed for the crime. And the one who drew the shortest straw was considered the luckiest of them all, for his death came the soonest. What grinding misery must they have endured, to come to that?

And how could he comfort Cathy, who must think all day of her lover, suffering all this and more? What could he do, other than offer his own sorrow? For he too had come to love the big, red-headed Irishman, feeling a brotherhood with him deeper than any he had ever felt for any man, save Francis.

'. . . and this is where we're digging the new dam.' Matthew led Cathy through the cleared bush to show her the great cavity that had been hewn from the ground to form a watering-place for the farm. All around them lay the broken branches and scattered brushwood of the undergrowth, while at the edges of the clearing the trunks of the felled trees were stacked ready to be moved. It was arduous work, needing teams of men and oxen, and there were no fast-flowing rivers to help shift the timber, as Matthew had experienced in America. And the excavating of the new dam had meant weeks of heavy digging, shifting the earth into a great wall at its lower end and fashioning it into a barrier that could withstand even the heaviest rains.

'It'll make things a lot easier when it's full,' Cathy said. 'The summers here are so dry, and sometimes it hardly rains enough in winter to keep the wells filled. But will it stay full, d'ye think?'

Matthew shrugged. 'That depends on the amount of rain we get each year, and it seems no more certain than at home – except that it's less! It rains much harder here, it's true, but not for long enough. And heavy rain just runs away when the ground is very dry. That's why the dam should help. You see how it's shaped, so that it will collect surface water as well as that underground. We can save some of it at least.'

Cathy nodded. She enjoyed these evening walks with Matthew. They had become a little bright spot in the day's routine, when after supper they were permitted to stroll around the farm together, watching the bright parrots that flew amongst the trees, trying to spot the almost moribund clumps of fur that were koala bears, half asleep still in the forks of branches, and keeping an eye out for the kangaroos that bounced through the undergrowth.

There was always something new to see, even if it were only that day's clearance. Even then, Matthew usually had something to show her – a bird's nest, a strange animal, a flower that had blossomed overnight. If there were nothing, they would walk up to the headland and sit on a rock, gazing out over the endless blue sea. The Pacific Ocean, Matthew had told her it was called, and it stretched away to the two islands of New Zealand in the east, and northwards to China and India itself.

'So they could never really walk to China, those men who used to try?' she asked, and Matthew shook his head.

'There are thousands of miles of ocean between us and China. No, the only place you can walk to in Australia is more of Australia. Wilder parts than this – bush that's like the African jungle, or great barren deserts where no man could survive. Except the Aborigines, of course. They seem able to survive anywhere. But that's because they've grown with the land and live in harmony with it. They're almost a part of it. If we take them away from it, make them live our way of life – as is happening already – I think they will not survive.'

319

'You mean they'll die?'

'Physically, some will, I'm sure. But others – well, they'll die inside. They'll no longer be the people they are, the "noble savage" we used to talk about so romantically back in England. They'll die as a people.'

Cathy was silent, her eyes fixed on the distant horizon. Somewhere out there, a thousand miles away, lay the island where Oliver had been taken. Perhaps he was at this very moment also looking out to sea, his eyes turned towards the mainland, thinking of her as she thought of him. Perhaps he too felt this hopeless, gnawing pain inside, this longing that could never be fulfilled.

'He will survive,' Matthew said quietly, and she knew that her thoughts had been written clearly on her face. 'He's a stone man – an iron man. He'll not let them defeat him.'

'Sure, I wish I could believe ye,' Cathy said miserably. 'But I feel ashamed that I'm here, in such a good place, while he's there in such a bad one. And ye hear such tales of the island. There's some things no man can stand up to. And Oliver's not the man to knuckle under. He's not very wise in that way.'

'No, he's not.' Matthew thought of the times when Oliver would have been better to remain silent under insults or injustice, but instead let his temper get the better of him and ended up in irons, deprived even of the meagre rations Harris had dealt them, or sent for a flogging. Valour was all very well but, when you knew it could only bring worse trouble, discretion was certainly the better part. And yet he too had been tempted on many occasions to turn upon the men who guarded and goaded him. His fists had ached to pummel those sadistic faces, his feet had itched to kick them into oblivion.

'At least he would be glad to know that you were here, with a good master, and not harried in any way,' he said. 'He thought all the time of you, Cathy, and never stopped loving you. And he does so still, I know – so accept your good fortune with grace, for he'd want you to have it.'

'I know it. And I'm grateful.' She sighed, her eyes still fixed on that far horizon. 'But I can't be happy while I know he's still suffering out there.'

Matthew slipped his arm around her shoulders, drawing her close, and she rested her head against him. In the circle of his arm, she felt a safety she had never known before. Here, in this peaceful place, there was nothing, nobody to hurt her. Matthew had promised to protect her and she believed in his ability to do so. She felt a deep warmth towards him, and lifted her face towards his to show him.

Matthew was looking down at her and she felt a shock run through her at the expression in his eyes. It was an expression she had sometimes caught in Oliver's glance – a tenderness that had nothing to do with passion, the tenderness that a mother might feel for her child or an old man for the wife he had loved all his life. It was deeper than passion and went beyond its bounds, and to see it in Matthew's eyes was like a blow struck sweetly on her heart. Hardly knowing what she did, she closed her eyes and let her lips part; and a moment later she felt Matthew's lips upon them, lightly brushing, a touch as tender as his glance, as soft as the evening breeze.

For a moment after the kiss ended, both were silent, equally shaken by the unexpectedness of it. Then Matthew said quietly, 'We must go back now.' And Cathy, still unable to speak, nodded and rose with him from the rock which they had used as a seat. Together, they walked slowly back past the new dam, across the clearings and through the groves of fruit trees and vines that Simeon had planted when he had first come here. As they came within sight of the house, they saw a figure outside, waving a piece of paper.

'It's John,' Cathy said. 'His father must have sent him to look for us. Matt – he looks as if he's got some news. Saints, could it be Oliver, d'ye think? What d'ye suppose has happened?'

Her body was tense and she hurried forward, anxious to receive whatever news there was. Perhaps Oliver was coming back – perhaps someone had found mercy in their hearts for him. But as she drew nearer and saw Simeon and Rose come out of the farmhouse and stand beside their son, her anxiety quickened to fear. She stopped and turned to Matthew as he caught up with her.

'It's bad news. Sure, I know it, Matt. Look at their faces . . .'

Simeon stepped forward quickly, and took the paper from his son. He unfolded it, then glanced at Matthew.

'Perhaps you'd read it, lad. Happen it'll come better from you.'

Matthew reached out and took it. He looked at its heading and saw that it had indeed come from Norfolk Island. But it was not one of Oliver's usual letters, written in his own large, sprawling handwriting. This had been written by someone else – at Oliver's dictation.

'He's ill,' he said quickly, knowing that Cathy was past needing soft words. The truth was all that would do for her now. 'He's ill with dysentery. But he's being cared for –' that, perhaps, was not quite so true, since the letter did not say so, but Matthew hoped for it '– and he's not in danger. He asks you – us – to think of him and pray for him, and he's certain he'll be well again soon.' He glanced at the date on the letter. 'In fact, he probably is well by now. This was written a month ago.'

'A *month!*' Cathy lifted one hand to her mouth. 'Holy Jesus, he could be dead by now. All this time and I never knew . . . How can we find out? I've got to know how he is now.'

Simeon shook his head. 'All we can do is wait, lass. And I'll do my best to make enquiries. But nobody has to let us know – none of us has any rights on Oliver. It's not as if you were wed.'

'We're as good as,' Cathy whispered. She cast a quick glance at Matthew. 'That last night, when you sent us to your hut – all we needed was the priest's blessing on us. Surely in the sight of God?'

Simeon sighed. 'The authorities don't ask Him for advice. Eh, don't look so cast down, lass. We've had this letter, happen we'll have another soon to tell us he's on the mend. See, someone else wrote this for him – that shows he's got a friend. Now that's summat to think on, whichever way you look at it.'

322

'He's right,' Rose said, taking Cathy in her arms. 'And now you come in with me and we'll have a cup of tea. 'Tisn't any use worrying yourself over it – like Father says, he's more than likely well again now and sending a letter this very minute to say so.' She looked round at the three men. 'John, Matt, you'll bring in some water for us. And some kindling too, for the stove, so we can boil a kettle. Poor lass, she's had a shock, but some tea'll put that right in no time.'

She led Cathy into the house and John turned away to pick up the water pails. Matthew went with him to the well and they lowered the pails and hauled them up together.

'I don't like seeing Cathy upset,' John said suddenly. 'I reckon it'd be a good thing if this Irish cove got polished off and done with. He's never been any good to her. It was his fault she got sent here in the first place, and she's still miserable over him.'

Matthew glanced at him in surprise. John was normally a quiet young man, working hard and saying little. Now his voice sounded taut with suppressed feeling, and for the first time Matthew considered the possibility that he might be jealous of the place Oliver held in Cathy's thoughts.

Not that it would do him any good. As long as Oliver lived, Cathy would never look at another man. Even the kiss thay had shared on the headland, sweet though it had been, had no real meaning. Two people finding themselves in accord, each lonely for a love that seemed lost for ever, had shared a brief touch of understanding – no more than that. And if Oliver died it would be no different. Cathy would never forget him. Neither would she forget what they had endured together that had brought them to this place, nor the magic of that one night of love that was all they had ever known.

John said no more and they went back to the house in silence. Matthew felt his heart weigh heavy in his breast. In spite of Simeon's brave words, he felt instinctively that Oliver was doomed. The big, strong body that had endured so much physical punishment was as powerless as any other against disease.

323

*   *   *

For several weeks, Cathy lived on a knife-edge of anxiety, flying to the door or window whenever she heard the sound of someone approaching the farmhouse. There were few enough visitors normally, except from neighbouring farmers, but now there seemed even fewer and she grew pale and thin from watching and worrying.

'It'll do neither you nor him any good for you to starve yourself,' Rose told her as Cathy pushed food uninterestedly around her plate. 'You're like a ghost, and you can't even do your work properly.'

Cathy looked up in sudden fear.

'Ye'll not send me back to Parramatta?' she begged. 'Sure, I'll scrub all day and night to stay here. I never meant to –'

'Bless the lass,' Rose said, 'of course I'll not send you back. You're part of the family now. I'm just worried about you, that's all. And you're worried about your Oliver, I know that – all I'm saying is that you've got to keep things in proportion. How will he feel if he comes walking in one day and finds you looking like you do now? Why, when you came here you had roses in your cheeks and –'

'D'ye really think he'd do that?' Cathy interrupted eagerly. 'Come walking in one day? Ye – ye haven't heard anything, have ye? Ye'd tell me?'

'Of course we'd tell you, you silly besom! D'you think we'd stand by and watch you worry yourself into the ground and not tell you any news that came? But there's been none and as far as I can see there's none likely for a while. So try to eat what's put in front of you, Cathy, there's a good girl, and let your work take your mind off things. It's the best medicine there is, hard work.'

Cathy nodded and gathered some food up on her fork. But it was impossible to stop her mind travelling to Oliver. Everything about her reminded her of him. Even the knife with which she cut her meat made her think of Norfolk Island, where the men were not allowed knives at all and would have little meat to cut anyway. At every moment, he was with her, and her whole body ached for his touch.

Yet when the news eventually came, she was unprepared.

The evening sun was slanting through the trees as Simeon and Rose came home from Parramatta. Cathy had been working in the kitchen all afternoon, preparing a meal to be ready for their return. Taught by Rose, she had grown to enjoy cooking and had taken pains to make sure that the supper was equal to anything her mistress could provide. A fowl had been killed and simmered gently in a pot of vegetables until it was as tender as a newly hatched chick, some fresh bread was baking in the oven and a bowl of stewed fruit was cooling on the window-sill. The big kitchen table was laid, with a pitcher of fresh water standing by Simeon's place and, as a last touch, she was just running outside to gather a few flowers when she heard the clatter of the cart approaching along the rough track that led away from the farm.

She stood for a moment, feeling the warmth of the last rays of sun on her face, waiting until the cart appeared round the corner. And instantly she knew.

Matthew, who had been nowhere in sight a few moments before, was beside her. Blindly, she reached out and he caught her hand and held it tightly. There was no need for words. She knew that he had sensed it too, the news they had dreaded. In these last few seconds, there was nothing she could do but pray, but even as her lips shaped the words she knew it was a futile prayer.

Simeon brought the cart to a halt in front of the house. He looked down at them and Cathy saw that his face was grave. She turned her eyes to Rose and saw that she had been weeping. Trembling, she stepped forwards, her face held up as if waiting for a slap. The flowers she had picked were clutched tightly between her fingers.

Simeon climbed heavily down from the cart. He turned to help his wife down, and she came to Cathy at once, folding her in her arms, her kind face crumpled with distress. But Cathy drew herself free of the embrace.

'Tell me,' she whispered, 'tell me what's happened. It's Oliver, isn't it? He's – he's –'

'It's all over,' Simeon said quietly. He laid a gentle hand on her shoulder. 'My poor lass, it was all finished three weeks ago and more. He's been buried and out of his misery all this time.'

The flowers fell from her hand and lay unheeded on the ground. A coldness deeper than any ice crept over her body and turned it to stone. She could no longer feel the beating of her heart. The only sensations she knew were a roaring of blood in her ears and a sickness that caught her from throat to stomach.

Simeon's voice sounded from a long way off as he bade Matthew to catch her, and she felt strong arms about her, holding her steady. Dazed, unable to take in what had just been told her, she leant against Matt's broad chest and suddenly, as his hand stroked her hair, she understood the truth. Oliver was dead. Dead. Buried and out of his misery.

Her tears flowed, soaking his shirt. After a few minutes, she raised her head.

'The dysentery? He died of that?'

'In part, yes.' Simeon hesitated, glanced at his wife and Rose nodded. 'You're a brave lass, I know you'd rather have the truth. He died under the lash, Cathy. He refused to salute one of the guards who he said had been tormenting him. He was ordered a hundred lashes and died after fifty. A stone man to the last, they said.'

'A hundred lashes, for a sick man,' Matthew said. 'What are they out there, savages? Barbarians? Why do they not simply execute every one, rather than go through this charade of killing slowly? Why not just put all the convicts to sea in those old hulks and scupper them?'

Cathy could feel the anger vibrating through him. She trembled in response, thinking of Oliver being dragged out to the Triangle, so weakened by his illness that he was hardly able to stand, strapped to the wooden framework with his back, scarred from a thousand earlier lashes, laid bare by the cruel thongs. Nine of them with each blow . . . she shuddered, feeling suddenly sick to her stomach, and felt Matthew's arms close around her as he lifted her from the ground and carried her into the house.

'There, little one,' he murmured as he took her to the small room where she slept beyond the kitchen and laid her on the narrow bed. 'There, weep for him and mourn him, for he loved you to the end. But remember what Simeon said – it's been over for weeks now. He feels no more pain, Cathy, and no man can ever hurt him again. And though you will never see him again in this life, who's to say he'll not wait for you in the next?'

'And him dying without a priest?' Cathy asked through her tears. 'They say there's no such creature on Norfolk. How can he have confessed his sins? He died unshriven, Matt – he'll stay in purgatory for eternity now, and never escape.'

She knew that Matthew would not understand this. His God was different from hers, a more lenient Deity who would look forgivingly upon a suffering Irishman, thinking him more sinned against than sinning. But her God and Oliver's was a more demanding one with a harsher code, who would see no excuse in the fact that there was no priest available to administer the last rites.

'Can't you pray for him?' Matthew asked. 'To – to some saint or other?'

'I'll pray to all the saints,' Cathy vowed. 'And to the Holy Mother herself. They'll do their best for him, I know that. They'll see that none of it was his fault.' She turned her head on the pillow and the tears flowed again, spreading in a damp patch upon the white cover. Matthew held her in his arms and she felt the strength, the security of them and clung to him as she sobbed for the life that had gone. 'Oh, Matt, Matt – we niver had a chance. Oliver niver had a chance.'

'Like so many others,' he murmured as he rocked her gently against him. 'Like so many, many others, Cathy.' He hesitated. 'Do you want me to leave you now? Wouldn't you rather be alone?'

'No – no.' Her fingers tightened on his shoulders. 'No, Matt, don't leave me. Ye're all I've got now, by all the saints. Please – don't ever, ever leave me.'

She buried her face against his tear-drenched shirt and wept again. And so did not see the look that was in his face. The mixture of tenderness and dismay.

A promise made in a moment of stress, a moment of compassion. A promise that must now be met; despite all the holds that a woman far, far away kept upon his heart.

Slowly, Cathy began to recover from her first deep grief. As the months went by, she emerged tentatively from her silence; she began to eat, to sleep, to look less pale and thin. Her long, fair hair shone again and she was even seen to smile.

'I'll niver stop thinking of Oliver,' she said to Matthew as they sat on the headland one evening. 'I'll niver stop loving him. But . . . Simeon's right, 'tis over for him now. We're the ones who have to carry on.' She turned and looked at him with eyes as limpid as the sea that washed the shores beneath them. 'Matt, I'll niver forget what ye've been to me these past months.'

'I've been nothing,' he said, uncomfortably aware of his own mixed feelings. 'Nothing more than you deserve. I'm very fond of you, Cathy.'

'And I'm fond of you too, Matt,' she said softly, and lifted her face towards his.

There was a brief moment of complete stillness. Matthew remembered the kiss they had shared before, on the evening when they had first heard of Oliver's illness. He recalled the sweetness of it, as he had recalled it so often during the months that had gone by since that night. For so long he had been without the comfort of a woman's arms, renouncing all temptation for love of Rebecca. For so long he had barely realised his own hunger, like a starving man who finds it impossible to accept food when at last it is offered him. And now, with Cathy's young body trembling like a bird in his arms, with her lips so near to his, her breath as warm and soft as the evening's breeze upon his cheek, he knew a longing that could not be denied. Rebecca, Rebecca, he thought with an agony that tore at his mind, why could this not be you? Why could we not have met in another time, another place, where we would have been free to love each other as I know we should? Why do we have to be half a world apart, you in your husband's arms and I with this Irish girl, barely more than a child, as innocent, as vulnerable?

I can't hurt her, he thought, feeling her breasts move softly against him. I can't hurt her by rejecting what she offers me – and by God, I don't want to! I don't want to reject her. I want to possess her. I want to make love to her here, under the evening stars, with the sound of the waves brushing gently on the shore. I want to give her the passion I've kept within me all this time, and I want her to give me the tenderness she would have given to Oliver. And why not? What else is there for such as we?

The thoughts passed through his mind with the rapidity of summer lightning, and then he was gathering her closer against him. With one hand, he cupped the back of her head, his fingers sliding in the shimmering hair. He bent his head to hers and laid his lips upon that soft, opening mouth. It was like a rose beneath his and, like a bee, he sought its nectar with his tongue, making gentle exploration. At the same time, his hand moved to her breast and he caressed its fullness with a gentleness that belied his rising excitement. And as he felt Cathy's body quiver and heard her tiny, whimpering response, he knew that there could be no going back.

Carefully, he lifted her from the rock and laid her on the tufted grass. Her eyes reflected the rising moon as he looked down upon her, and she raised her arms and bent them around his neck, drawing him close. His heart beating hard, he covered her body with his.

Forgive me, Rebecca, he thought as he sought Cathy's mouth again. Though in truth, there is nothing to forgive, since you don't love me as I love you. But in another time, another place, you might have done. Would have done.

But we are not in that time, nor that place, and you are far away, and lost to me in this lifetime. And I am here, and Cathy is here and offering me her comfort. And I am only a man . . .

And then the kiss claimed him, and he forgot to think.

Chapter Sixteen

'Is it bad news ye have there?' Cathy asked.

Matthew raised his head and stared at her. His mind had travelled so far since he had opened Rebecca's letter that he barely knew where he was, or in what time. Slowly, he returned from the long journey his memory had taken, through the years of his captivity to this farmhouse that had become a haven to them both. For a moment, as he gazed at her, he expected to see Rebecca herself standing before him. Then the image dissolved and became Cathy, the chestnut hair paling to the colour of thick, creamy honey, the fiery eyes and determined mouth turning soft and anxious.

'Has something happened?' she asked again, and he pulled himself together and looked down again at the letter.

'Yes, it has. My friend Francis has died of the consumption. I should have expected it, I suppose – he was coughing before I left England. But there's been no mention of any illness . . . I thought he was over it.'

'Matt, I'm sorry.' Cathy crossed herself. 'I know he was a good friend of yours. And his wife too – Rebecca, did ye say she was called? So now she's a widow.'

'A widow. Yes.' He felt a sudden pain in his heart. Rebecca, a widow. Alone, in need of friendship. And he on the other side of the world, unable to lift a finger to help. Why – he glanced at the date on the letter – it had all been over months ago, Francis in his grave and the mourning period nearly half a year gone, and all without his knowing. He understood suddenly how Cathy had felt when she had heard of Oliver's death. When it was someone you loved you wanted to know at once. You wanted to share it as closely as you could.

Cathy came round the table and touched his shoulder. Automatically, he moved his hand to cover hers, but his thoughts were far away. In his imagination, he saw Rebecca dressed in black, standing at Francis's graveside. He saw the stone that would be erected, with space left below the inscription for Rebecca herself. Perhaps he would be buried with little Geoffrey; perhaps even with Jeremiah, his father.

Matthew saw Rebecca walking away from the churchyard, her head held high even though tears were falling, walking into a new life. Who had been there to stand at her side, to help her through the dark days that must have followed? Who had given her an arm to lean upon, a shoulder to weep her tears? Who would be her friend, her mainstay?

He thought of her brother Tom, stalwart and dependable. But Tom could not give her what she most desperately needed, the support of a man who loved her for herself and not because she was his sister.

He thought of Vivian.

No . . . Every instinct he possessed rose up in sharp denial. Rebecca would never, never turn to Vivian. Surely, even in the extremity of her grief, she would not look to him? But he remembered the day she and Tom had returned from London after their visit to Bessie, the day she had to be told that her son Geoffrey had been drowned. It was Vivian who had stepped forward before any other man could do so, who had taken her in his arms and broken the news. What his motives had been, Matthew had never been able to guess; but he had watched the meeting and seen Rebecca's response. And he knew that since that day she had always looked on Vivian as a friend.

Yes. If she turned to anyone now, it would be Vivian.

Matthew rose from the table, hardly knowing that he shook off Cathy's hand as he did so. In an agony of frustration, he paced to the window and stared out. The yard was a sea of mud, the trees root-deep in foaming water. The rain fell like a metallic sheet, a barrier between him and the woman he loved and needed most urgently to be with. He wanted to comfort her, to help her, to be with her during the crisis she was enduring – but even as the thoughts came into his mind, he reminded himself that the worst of the crisis was already past. By now, Rebecca must be pulling the strings of her life together again, was already facing a future without her husband. Was already making plans . . .

Plans for what? A life as a widow? Or a new life . . . as a wife?

'Matt.' Cathy's voice broke in on his thoughts. 'Matt, what is it? What's in your mind to make ye look that way?' She came close again, laid her hand on his arm. 'Please, Matt, don't go away from me.'

He looked down at her, startled by her perception, but smiled and shook his head. 'What do you mean, Cathy? You know I can't go away. Even if –' He caught his words sharply, but she took him up on them at once.

'Even if ye wanted to, Matt? And – and do ye want to?' Her glance fell on the letter. 'It's her, isn't it?' she said in a low voice. 'Ye'd like to be going to her.'

'Cathy, she's my friend. Francis was my friend. Of course I want to be with her, to help her, comfort her.'

'No.' Cathy shook her head. 'It's more than that. I can tell, Matt.' She turned away and his heart ached for her. 'I knew ye didn't love me,' she whispered. 'Not the way Oliver loved me. But –'

'And you don't love me the way you loved – still love – Oliver,' Matthew said quietly. He moved towards her and laid his hands on her shoulders, looking down at her bent head. 'Cathy, we both know he'll always be first with you. And Rebecca – there was never anything between us, but I can't help feeling the way I do about her.' Gently he turned her towards him and lifted her face with the fingertips of one hand beneath her chin. 'And there's nothing to be done about that either. Look, Cathy, my dear, we're here, together. Oliver's dead and Rebecca's eight thousand miles away. But we have each other. We have something very . . . sweet. And nothing is going to change that.'

She looked up at him and he saw that her eyes were awash with tears, like soft grey pebbles under the flowing waters of a stream. With a little shock, he realised that for Cathy this attachment was more than 'something sweet'. She had transferred to him a good deal of her deep love for Oliver. She looked to him for protection and he gave it gladly. And in return, she gave him her adoration.

He heard the sound of someone coming through the house, towards the kitchen. Swiftly, he bent and kissed Cathy's lips. He held her firmly against him for a moment and then let her go.

When Simeon came into the kitchen they were both far apart; Cathy busy at the sink and Matthew back at the table, reading yet again the letter that had brought the news of Francis's death. The letter that Rebecca had written him.

'Well, there we are then.' Simeon came out of the Governor's offices with Matthew. 'Your first ticket-of-leave. You're on your own hands now – almost a free man, Matt.'

'In some ways, yes.' Matt glanced around him. They had come to Sydney especially for this and the harbour lay spread before them, its waters as deep a blue as the great bowl of sky that hung above. The breeze had whipped off the top of the waves in tiny white flecks and the whole bay glittered and shifted in the sunlight, as if it were a carpet of jewels and the boats that swung at anchor upon it painted brooches.

'In all the best ways, surely.' Simeon clapped him on the shoulder as they turned to stroll along the wharf together. 'You can go and work for anyone in the colony now, lad. You're no longer assigned. You can earn your own money, live where you please. Isn't that freedom?'

'Oh, certainly. And I can also have every man watching me, from the constable to the boy who delivers the meat. Any one of them can denounce me and get my ticket taken away, or delayed a year.' Matthew grinned ruefully. 'I'm sorry, Simeon. You're right, I should celebrate, not cavil. But – well, in the past few weeks I've found myself almost hoping I *wouldn't* get my ticket. Does that sound strange?'

'Strange! It sounds crazy. What's amiss with you, Matt? Any

other government man's cock-a-hoop to get his ticket. Why, it's as near freedom as you can get. What prisoner in England is free to go where he pleases, work for any man and keep the money he earns? All you have to do is report to the magistrate twice a year. And you've been hoping you wouldn't get it?'

Matt grimaced. 'I can't deny it. But – well, look at it this way, Simeon. I've been happy working for you. I've been treated well, I've felt that the work I've done has been good and useful, I'm fond of you and Rose and John – and now I have to go and look for other work. I may never find a master like you again, nor a place to live as comfortably. And I'm worried about Cathy. She depends on me.'

'She does more than that,' Simeon said dryly. 'Oh, don't look embarrassed, Matt. It's been plain enough what's been happening between the pair of you and we've been glad enough to see it. In fact, we've wondered why you've never asked permission to wed – but that's your business. So long as you do right by the lass. But what's all this about finding a new master, eh? Who said you were leaving us?'

Matt stopped and stared at him. 'But you'll be assigned a new man. You won't want me.'

'Won't want you! It's the new man I don't want. Another government man, fresh out from England and the chip on his shoulder the only wood he knows owt about – nay, that's no good to me. I thought that were understood. You'll be stopping on with us – that's if you want to.'

'*Want* to? Of course I want to. But Simeon, have you thought about what it means? Until now you've only had to pay a small amount – my clothes, board and whatever overtime we agreed on. As a ticket-of-leave man . . .' He stopped, feeling suddenly embarrassed, but Simeon took over smoothly and Matthew blessed his Yorkshire commonsense.

'As a ticket-of-leave man you're entitled to proper pay for the job. Aye, I know that, and I'm ready to pay it. I told you, you'll be more value to me than a new chum off the next transport with no more idea of timber and sheep than a fly. So let's put it this way, Matt – I'm offering you a job. If you'd like to take it, well and good. If not – well, you're free to go where you like and I'll give you a good character to take with you.' He held out his hand.

Matthew looked down at it. He saw the massive palm, the thick fingers, the seams of toil that could never be washed out. Simeon had come here as a poor farmer hit by bad times in England, and had worked long and hard to build up what he had. He was a strict master who did not tolerate fools gladly, but he had given Matthew a home and friendship. Perhaps most of all, he had enabled Matthew to regain his own self-respect.

Matthew felt a flood of warmth towards the big Yorkshire-man. He placed his own hand in the other's, palm to palm, and clasped it tightly. They looked into each other's eyes, unsmiling, and Simeon gave a little nod.

'That's settled, then. You'll be coming back with me this evening and we'll go on from there.' He gazed out over the blue harbour and added casually, 'I reckon that's why Cathy looked so down in the mouth when we left, too. She thought you'd be leaving.'

'That's right.' Matthew remembered Cathy's drowned eyes as she'd gazed at him the previous morning. He remembered the way she had clung to him through the night, as if he were a rock and she about to be swept away in a stormy sea. Their loving had been tender and sweet, pierced by a yearning that neither could confess. And he had felt the fear quiver through her body as they shared their final embrace. A fear that he had tried to assuage, reassuring her that she would be well looked after by Simeon and Rose, that he would do his best to find employment nearby so that they could still remain in touch. But he knew that she still felt she was being abandoned.

'I reckon our John thought that, too,' Simeon went on, his gaze still fixed on the ships that danced on the fluttering waves. 'He's always had an eye for Cathy. You might not get such a welcome back in that quarter, Matt.'

'I wish she could love him,' Matthew said. 'It would be

far better for her – that's if you and Mrs Ackroyd could countenance it.'

'Me and Rose? Oh, aye, Cathy's a good enough lass. Mebbe not as strong as we'd like, but sensible. Aye, he could look further and fare worse, and there's none so many Yorkshire lasses in the neighbourhood to take his choice from. But she's never had eyes for nobbut you ever since you come here, and that's top and bottom of it.' Simeon took his gaze from the ships and looked Matthew squarely in the eye. 'And since you've now got your ticket – well, there's nowt to stop you doing the right thing by her, is there? Unless you've already got a wife back in England, one you've never mentioned?'

For a moment, Matthew was tempted. He could see that Simeon was presenting him with a choice – claim himself already married or take Cathy for his wife. And this was the price of keeping his place on the farm.

He thought of Rebecca, a widow now for more than a year. But how long would she remain so? For the six, seven years of his sentence that he must still serve? Was it possible that she should remain alone during all that time? Was it possible that Vivian would allow it?

No, he could not think of that. Rebecca was lost to him for ever, and he must stop this constant yearning, this hopeless desire. And he owed Cathy something, for the tender affection she had shared with him, the adoration in her eyes, the generosity with which she had given herself.

He could not lie to escape that final commitment. Even though Simeon would accept his word, even though the lie would never be discovered, he could not do it. It would live in his heart like a maggot, for ever.

'No,' he said, 'I don't have a wife. I've never been married.' And he met Simeon's direct look with one of his own, and knew that he had given a promise.

'They'll have to be properly wed,' Rose declared. 'I'll have no hole and corner affair here. No setting up home and calling themselves man and wife when the minister's been nowhere near. Besides, Cathy's the nearest I'll ever get to having a daughter of my own, and I've always had a fancy for a proper wedding in the family.'

Matthew glanced around the big kitchen table. The whole family was assembled here – Simeon and Rose, John, Cathy and himself. He looked at Cathy's face and his heart twisted a little as he saw the tremulous joy in her eyes. He had seen it first when he had returned with his ticket-of-leave and the news that he was to stay on the farm, and again when he had held her in his arms and asked her to marry him. He felt shame that he could make her so happy with so few words, shame that he could not feel the same felicity.

He knew that just as she could never come first in his heart, so he could never displace Oliver in hers. Yet there was room enough, love enough, to encompass him as well as her own first lover. And he berated himself for feeling only compassion, only tenderness, and determined to spend the rest of his days making compensation for the deep, passionate love he could never give.

He looked at Rose and Simeon. They could have been any proud parents making plans for their daughter's wedding, and he felt a wave of love for them both. They had taken Cathy and himself in, not knowing what they might be, save that they were certainly felons and he a convicted murderer. They had listened to the stories of the goose, the strike riots, and accepted them as truth. And then they had made their own assessment, without condemnation, without prejudice, and given them both the freedom of ordinary servants, a freedom few convicts were fortunate enough to possess. They had treated them like human beings and so returned them to the ranks of such.

Finally, he looked at John. The boy sat silent, his gaze fixed on the flaxen-haired girl who sat at the other side of the table, and there was a yearning in his eyes that smote at Matthew's heart; for he recognised that yearning. It held all the desire, the need, the love he had for Rebecca. It held all the hopelessness that he himself felt whenever he thought of her.

Why couldn't she have loved you in return? he asked John silently. Why couldn't it be your wedding your parents are planning now?

Rose was talking about a wedding breakfast now, and the neighbouring farmers she would invite. Matthew wondered if ever two convicts had been given such a celebration before. He glanced at Simeon, wondering if the farmer would think his wife's pleasure excessive, but Simeon's face was calm and benign, as if he approved all that she said. And Cathy looked as if she had just been handed the moon in a net. Only he and John were uneasy, the one because he loved Cathy too little and the other because he loved her too much.

A knock on the door made them all jump, and Simeon rose quickly to open it. He ushered in one of the neighbouring settlers, an ex-Army man whose farm lay a few miles to the west, and made room for him on the settle.

'You've been riding hard, Sam,' he said, pulling forward the pitcher of ale. 'Here, take a drink and wipe the sweat off your face.'

'Thank'ee.' The man filled a tankard and drank deeply. 'I've come fast – we're warning everyone in the neighbourhood. Keep your doors locked tonight, Sim, and your stock and female servants under lock and key. Jake Bellinger and three others have gone bush. Worse than that, he's shot his master, Alfred Lea, though the shot didn't kill him, thank God.'

'Gone bush? Jake? And attacked Alfred?' Simeon stared at him. 'The fool! He'd have got his ticket in another year.'

'Yes, and couldn't wait that long.' Sam Curtis glanced at Matthew. 'He's been nursing a grudge ever since Matt here got his. Reckoned he should have been ahead – and so he should but for that bit of trouble two years back. Alfred told him often enough, keep your nose clean now and you'll have your ticket the minute it's due, but that wasn't good enough for Master Bellinger and he's headed off into the bush, taking two carbines and three men with him. So I'm warning as many as I can, and came to you first because there's blood in his eye. He'll do murder before he's finished, or I'm much mistaken.'

Cathy gasped and Matthew saw her hand go to her throat. He felt a quick surge of protectiveness and rose to his feet. 'I'll go and look for him.'

'Nay.' Simeon reached out a long arm and pulled him back into his seat. 'You'll do no such thing, Matt. We'll organise this properly, if there's to be any search at all. My own advice is to wait until he shows himself. They'll want food soon; they're bound to leave signs when they take it.'

'That's true.' Sam was on his feet again. 'And meanwhile, we cower like rabbits in our burrows . . . We can't let them terrorise us, Simeon. Anyway, the main thing now is to let everyone know he's about, and I'd be glad if you could lend me your man to ride to some of the farms.'

Simeon glanced at Matthew. 'He's not my man to lend now, Sam. He's free to take his labour where he pleases. But I doubt he'll refuse you – eh, Matt?'

'Certainly I'll go.' Matthew was already strapping on his boots. 'And if I could take a gun, just in case?'

There was a tiny silence. Matthew glanced up and saw the expression on Simeon's face and for a sickening moment was transported back to that night in Kidderminster when Bill Bucknell had died. Oh God, he thought, is this to follow me all my life? But even as the thought passed through his mind, Simeon's face changed again and he went to the corner where his rifles stood.

'Take this, lad, and use it if you have to. And take Castor, he's the fastest horse.' Their eyes met as he handed the weapon over and Matthew felt a deep gratitude for the trust Simeon had placed in him. He touched the cold metal of the barrel and felt the repugnance that he always felt now in the presence of firearms. But there were times when they must be carried, times when they must be used. Please God, he would carry and use this one wisely.

As he turned away, Cathy came to the door and laid her hand on his arm. He looked down, saw the fear in her eyes and bent to give her a quick kiss, oblivious of those watching. With fingers that were suddenly gentle, he touched her face.

'Don't worry, my love. You'll be safe here, and I'll be back soon.'

'Oh, Matt, –' she whispered, and tears glimmered on the suddenly blushing cheeks. But there was no time to hesitate, no time for more. Samuel Curtis was waiting impatiently and Matt went quickly out to hear what he had to say.

'I'm going to Allsop's next, and then to Bright's. You take the road south and get word to the farms there – tell 'em to pass it on to each other. Then get back here, for I think Simeon's most at risk. Though I hope I'm wrong there, and that Jake and his gang'll just head into the bush and stay there for a while.' He gave Matthew a sharp glance. 'You weren't in the country in twenty-eight, were you, when Jack Donohoe ranged the bush? He kept a state of terror going for eighteen months or more – roamed from Parramatta to the Blue Mountains, holding up bullock drays and such. It took a squad of soldiers to capture him in the end, and they had to take him dead for as long as he was alive he'd have fought like a tiger. And they say he killed nine men in the attempt.' Curtis was checking his horse's girths as he spoke, and swung himself into the saddle with the last words. He looked gravely down at Matthew. 'And as I said, Jake's had murder in his eyes for the past month or more, ever since you came back with your ticket. So 'ware.'

'I will.' Matthew turned away to fetch his own horse. But before he was ready to ride out, he found John beside him. The boy's face was tense and pale and he too carried a gun.

'I'm coming with you, Matt. The bastard's got to be caught. I've seen him a few times, eyeing Cathy – I'll not have her hurt by any man, I'd kill him first.'

Matthew reached out and turned the gun away from him. 'Point that another way, John, or you'll be killing a friend and I can tell you what that leads to. Do you think I want Cathy hurt or frightened? Jake'll be caught all right, no error. But you're needed here now, to look after her while I'm gone.' He looked down from his horse. 'Don't do anything wild, John. I tell you, this is your place.'

John shook his head obstinately. 'Father can look after the

women. He's getting the other government men together now – they're loyal to a man. If I come with you, we can go around the farms in half the time and be back here all the faster.' He was mounting his own horse as he spoke, and looked Matthew in the eye. 'Don't tell me to stay at home, Matt,' he said quietly. 'I'm not a child any more. I'm a man, and ready to take a man's part.' He kicked his horse's sides and the beast started forwards. 'Let's go. We can ride the first part together.'

Matthew felt a sudden admiration for this boy, who was indeed a man now that the demand was being made. He nudged his own horse and followed John out of the compound, and they trotted off down the track together.

And as they went, he thought of those last few moments with Cathy, and the way her face had suddenly flushed and her eyes brimmed with tears. Why had she done that? Was it simply because he was leaving, perhaps to face danger? Or was it something else?

He heard his own voice again, making that last tender reassurance. *'Don't worry, my love. You'll be safe here . . . and I'll be back soon.'*

My love . . . He could not remember ever having called her that before. And yet, tonight, it had come easily to his tongue.

Was that why her face had taken on the colour of a wild rose, and her eyes looked like pearls washed by a soft, green sea?

It was two days before he rode back towards Simeon's farm again. Two days of hard riding, from one remote settlement to the next, passing on the message and seeing fear in the eyes of the women, angry determination in the faces of the men. Where there were enough men, or one who could be trusted, a messenger was sent from there to the more outlying stations, freeing Matthew to go on to warn another settler. And he knew that in other parts of the district, Sam Curtis and John were doing the same, so that everyone in the area would know of the danger.

Not that bushrangers were uncommon. There were many convicts who, in the past, had slipped away from their compounds or the farms where they had been assigned, and 'gone bush'. Some to attempt the long and hopeless 'walk to China', others simply to get away from the harsh servitude they were forced to endure, the lash of repeated floggings, the chain gangs. Most of them had died of starvation, thirst or the relentless heat, or had been killed by Aborigines. Some were quickly recaptured, to face worse punishment. Others, like Jack Donohoe, had managed to stay free, ranging the bush and robbing settlers and travellers alike, always staying one step ahead of police and military, living poorly or well according to their fortune. Sometimes, like Donohoe, being captured or killed at last, sometimes meeting their fate in the bush where they had chosen to live and die.

But they were always a threat, and no settler could feel at ease knowing that a desperate man lurked somewhere outside; especially one who was armed and known already to have attempted murder.

As he came nearer to the Ackroyd homestead, Matthew began to feel anxious. Nothing had been seen or heard of Bellinger at any of the farms he had visited, and as he returned he called at each one to see if there were any news. There was none. It seemed that Jake and his gang had vanished into the bush, like the snakes that slid amongst the undergrowth.

But they would not remain hidden for long. Matthew knew that Sam Curtis had been right – Jake had always seen him as a rival, and since Matthew had gained his ticket-of-leave the enmity had been there in his eyes for all to see. And Jake was the kind of man who wanted revenge and would do his utmost to get it.

Was he even now lurking about Simeon's farm, hoped to catch Matthew himself unawares, or ready to exact his revenge in a more subtle way, by attacking Cathy or even Simeon and Rose themselves? There was no knowing what went on in a twisted mind such as Jake Bellinger's. No predicting what he might do.

The sun was dipping low in the sky as he came within sight of the last farm before the final long ride to Simeon's home. Weary after his travels, he was tempted to accept lodging for the night before riding on early in the morning. But his anxiety overcame his fatigue and when the settler offered him space in the barn, he shook his head.

'I thank you, but no. I want to get back as soon as possible. Another few hours' riding will do it, and my horse is strong and as eager to be in his own stable as I am.'

'You'll stop for a meal, though.' Kit Marsh was a friend of Simeon's and knew Matthew well. 'No news is good news, they say, and we've heard of nothing amiss. It's my belief Bellinger is far away now. Or speared by Aborigines, which would be no more than he deserves.'

'You may be right, though nobody will rest much until we know certainly.' Matthew followed him into the kitchen where the family were just finishing their supper. 'Thank you, I'd be grateful for some food.'

He sat down at table, suddenly almost overcome with exhaustion, and leaned his head on his hands. Kit Marsh's wife placed a bowl of stew in front of him and he lifted his spoon with an effort. The hot broth slid down his throat, reviving him a little, and he swallowed again, gaining strength from the meat and vegetables. After a few moments, he looked up and smiled.

'I hadn't realised how tired I was. This is putting new life into me.'

'I still think you ought to stay,' Kit said. 'It's dark outside now and if Bellinger is lurking anywhere about . . . It'll do no one any good for you to be shot just for the want of a few hours.'

Matthew hesitated. The temptation was strong and he knew that Kit spoke good sense. Alone and in the dark, he would be easy prey for the bushrangers if they were about. Nevertheless, he was conscious of an uneasy feeling that all was not well at the farm, that he ought to make all speed to return as soon as possible.

He was just opening his mouth to reply when there was a commotion outside. At once, both he and Kit were on their feet and at the door, with Kit's two sons close behind them. Automatically, Matthew reached out for the rifle which he had left propped in a corner.

But it was one of Kit's stockmen who stood panting at the door. His eyes went past Kit to Matthew, and he spoke urgently, his voice quick and hoarse.

'You – Matt – there's fire over towards Ackroyds'. Bush fire – you can see the smoke and flames from here. Don't think it's reached the homestead but . . .

'*Fire!*' Matthew pushed past Kit and stared out in the direction of Simeon's farm. He could indeed see the red, angry glow and the black racing cloud of smoke that obliterated the stars. And he knew that the fire must be in the area where he and Jake had mostly recently worked on the clearing between the two farms, and that the wind must be blowing it closer and closer to the farmstead itself.

'I've got to get over there.' He thrust his way through the anxious knot of people who had gathered and ran to the stable where Castor was being given a feed. The reins were still looped over the horse's neck and he gripped them and swung himself over the broad back, pressing his knees firmly into the muscled body.

As he trotted through the yard, he saw that Kit and his sons were bringing their own horses out, but he could not wait for them to saddle up. With a clatter, he was out of the yard and galloping along the dusty track, his eyes fastened on the stormy glow ahead of him, his heart thundering as fast as Castor's hooves.

Cathy, he thought as he urged the horse onwards. Cathy . . . Please God, let her be all right. Don't let that swine have hurt her. Not poor little Cathy who has had so much already to endure.

And there were Rose and Simeon too. His friends, who had welcomed him into their home, treated him as one of the family, had sat down to plan his wedding as if he were their own son. If Jake Bellinger had harmed any of them, in any way at all . . .

I'll kill him, he thought, and understood then what it was to feel true murder in his heart. He, who was here through causing another man's death by accident, now knew how it felt to want to see another man die and know it was by his hand. He felt the full force of deep black hatred in his heart, and was shocked and sickened by it; yet could not drive it away.

He heard the other horses galloping behind him, and spurred Castor on faster. It was suddenly imperative that he reach the farm first. It must be he who saved Cathy and the others, he who took Jake Bellinger if he were there to be taken. Nobody else. These tasks were for him and him alone.

The night sky was filled now with the dark cloud of smoke, stars and moon vanished behind its menacing curtain. The acrid smell filled his nostrils, and the roar of the fire could be heard as a dull threat that seemed to rise from the earth itself. Castor hesitated in his stride and Matthew felt the fear in the big body. He bent forwards over the horse's neck, murmuring words of encouragement, and when they began to fail he abandoned all gentleness and kicked the animal roughly, yelling curses and urging it on with every ounce of energy he possessed.

They were coming closer now and he could see flames amongst the trees and undergrowth of the bush. The fire was dangerously near to the farm. If it caught the fruit trees and vines . . . if it caught the stables . . . if it touched the huts where the men slept . . .

Tiny figures appeared, beating at the flames, but Matthew could see that they had little chance of defeating them. The fire towered like a wave, high in the tops of the trees, creating its own wind which drove it on. And now there were animals on the track, kangaroos and koalas with young clinging to them, bounding and scampering in terror from the hungry beast which pursued them. And now he could feel the first scorching touch of heat on his skin, and the stifling roughness in his throat.

Castor reared and neighed, and Matthew knew that he would go no further. He slid from the horse's back and stood for a second, undecided, then let the reins go. Horses could always be recaptured, and he would go with the other animals, away from the fire, and probably end up in one of the other farms. Looking behind, he saw that Kit and his men were doing the same. They slapped the animals' rumps, though quite unnecessarily for the horses needed no urging to go, and watched them disappear into the night. Then they turned and ran towards the flames.

'You go and see that they're all right at the house,' Kit ordered as they drew nearer. 'They may need help to get away – those women ought to be out of there. We'll go and help with the beating.'

'It's useless,' Matthew panted. 'You can see what a hold it's got.' But he turned and ran towards the farm, wondering as he did so whether he would find anyone there. Perhaps they had escaped already. Perhaps . . .

The fire was at the compound fence and licking at the trees that had been left in the yard for shade. Why was nobody beating at them, trying to hold them, back? The farmhouse itself would be engulfed. Suddenly desperately afraid, he raced for the house. There were lights burning inside and he was convinced that someone must be there. But why didn't they come out?

The door resisted his attempts to open it. Furiously, he flung himself against it. Once . . . twice . . . at the third attempt it gave way and threw him into the room. He caught at the jamb, saved himself from falling, and stared around.

Cathy . . .

She was sitting in a chair beside the empty fireplace. Her eyes were wide with terror, her face as white as paper. As she turned her head towards Matthew, he saw that she was bound by the arms to the back of the chair.

Drawing in his breath, he saw that Simeon and Rose were

there too, also bound. And before them, grinning, were four men. Jake Bellinger and his gang, with the light of madness in their eyes and Jake with a gun in his hands.

At the sound of the door bursting open, Jake whipped round, his rifle held high. His mean eyes flicked over Matthew and then he smiled an evil smile.

'Well, if it ain't the ticket-of-leave man himself, brave boys. We got 'em all now. All we need do is shut 'em up together and they can roast like pork in an oven. Except they won't make such sweet meat as pigs would.' He jerked his head and snarled, 'Drop it, Farrell. Drop that gun.'

Matthew felt a deep surge of rage. He stared at the other man and knew that Jake meant to kill him, him and the others, and that he would let nothing stop him. He would prefer to leave them to face an agonising death by fire, but if forced he would simply gun them down. There was nothing, now, for Matthew to lose.

The thought took only a fraction of a second to form. Then he raised his rifle and fired.

The shot was like an explosion in the room, sounding above the roar of the fire outside. The bullet hit Jake squarely in the chest and he collapsed at once, blood gushing in a great arc that struck as far as the wall opposite. But Matthew had no time to watch as he died on the rug that Rose had made from tattered clothes during the evenings. He leapt forwards and grabbed the carbine that Jake had dropped and which had been knocked out of his hands and half across the room. Then he turned to the others, his own rifle held ready to use again.

'Which one of you is it to be? I'll take another with me, I swear. Or maybe there's no fight left in you now.'

They had no weapons to fight with anyway, he realised at once. Jake had held the only firearm they possessed and although the others were ugly enough ruffians, they were not prepared to risk their lives uselessly. They were staring now at Jake's body, at the great red stain that was spreading around it. As Matthew spoke, they raised their hands in surrender and backed away. And all became aware of the increased roar of the fire, and a crackling that told them it had caught the stables.

'Let's get out o' here,' one of the convicts pleaded. 'We're goin' to be cooked alive. Look, it wasn't us – it was Jake, he said he'd shoot if we –' His eyes showed white as he looked up at the roof, as if expecting to see the flames there at any moment. *'Let's go, Matt, for God's sake.'*

Matt glanced at Cathy. She looked sick, almost green, as if about to lose consciousness. Rose was pale too, but her face was set and determined. Simeon was hunched, as if in pain, and Matthew realised that he'd been injured, probably when the men had first broken in. He held one arm awkwardly and his hand hung useless at his side.

'Untie these people first,' Matthew snapped. 'You'll go nowhere until they're free. And jump to it!' He heard a sound at the door and turned his head slightly to see John, his face grimed with soot, framed in the broken doorway. 'John, thank God you've come. We've got to get them out of here.'

John was across the room with one stride. He barely looked at Jake's blood-soaked body as he stepped across it, and went straight to Cathy. With a few quick movements of his fingers, he had her bonds loose and lifted her into his arms. He held her close for a moment, then turned and ran from the room.

Meanwhile, the convicts were busy releasing Rose and Simeon. As they did so, Matthew stood aside and let them pass. He wasn't interested in capturing and holding them – that could come later. What mattered now was to get away from here to a safe place, and then to save as much of the farm as possible.

But as he followed them out into the yard, he felt the shock of a heat that seared through to his bones. He saw the firefighters, driven back by the thundering flames, and knew that nothing could save the farm now. It would all go; the house, the stables, the huts, the orchard, the stock. All that Simeon had worked for and built up, destroyed and lost.

John was at his side. 'They've got the cart over there. I'm

taking Mother and Father and Cathy back to Kit Marsh's place. Will you come too?'

Matthew shook his head. 'I'll stay here and do what I can. Not that there's much anyone can do.' He looked at the sky. A new light had appeared, as red as the fire, and he knew it must be the dawn. And knew that the daylight, when it came, would reveal a desolation that would break Simeon's heart. 'Yes, you get them away,' he said. 'And look after them.' He handed John the rifle and carbine he still held. 'Take these. I'll have no further use for them.'

He watched for a moment as John ran back to the cart. Cathy was there, silent and still in one corner. He looked across at her, but she did not meet his eyes.

Matthew turned and made his way across to where the firefighters were working. He had a strange feeling that something had just come to an end.

Chapter Seventeen

Once again, Matthew and Simeon came out of the government offices together, once more with cause for celebration. And yet again, the celebration was, for Matthew, marred because it still did not release him from his own personal cage. Because the bars of the cage were the principles by which he lived, and from them there was no release.

'Well, there you are, Matthew lad.' Simeon still limped a little from the injuries he had received on the night of the fire, but his arm was almost strong again and the rest of his bruises long forgotten. 'A free man. Granted a free pardon by the governor himself for saving our lives and capturing Jake Bellinger and his cronies. You can do as you like now – buy your own land, set yourself up in business, even go back to England.' His tone indicated that he thought this last unlikely but his words struck at Matthew's heart.

Go back to England . . . Yes, all he had to do was arrange for enough money for his passage to be sent – for now that he was free, his wealth was once more available to him – and he could take ship without further delay. He could be there in four, six, nine months, depending on how long it took to arrange. There with Rebecca, where he had for so long yearned to be.

And still it was impossible. For here in New South Wales was Cathy. And he could not betray her.

'I hardly captured Bellinger,' he said, thinking of that night. 'I shot him to pieces, and in front of your wife and Cathy too. I find it hard to forgive myself for that.'

'Forgive yourself?' Simeon stopped and stared at him. 'You saved our lives and you need to *forgive* yourself?'

'I should have dealt with it better than that. Seeing Jake blown apart by my gun – what did it do to those women? Cathy still hasn't recovered – she looks like a ghost. And your wife? Has she talked to you about it? It wasn't a sight for women, Simeon.'

'Nothing about that night was a sight for women,' the older man said grimly. 'That swine wasn't simply going to kill us, you know. He intended to "have some fun" first – his very words. He and his filthy ruffians – what they were going to do to my wife and little Cathy . . .' His voice shook. He paused and Matthew saw his jaw tighten until the skin turned white. 'You came in time to prevent that,' he went on after a moment. 'Do you think what they went through then could have been any worse than what Bellinger had planned for them?'

Matthew shook his head slowly. 'I suppose not. But they didn't go through that, did they? And they did see him killed. It had an effect, Simeon, and one we can't ignore. *I* can't ignore.'

'Well, you've no call to worry about Rose. She's tough, always has been, or she'd not be a Yorkshire lass. And if Cathy's still upset, Rose will see her through. You've no need to fret.' They walked on in silence for a few moments. 'And now that the court case is all over and the others sentenced – well, we can put it behind us and get back to normal. The new house will be ready soon and Rose and me can move back in. And thanks to the men who saved most of the stock that night, I've not lost so much as I expected.'

'That's good. I'm very glad.' They walked slowly along the busy main street. Matthew was deep in thought. He had known, of course, that he was likely to receive a pardon over his part in the events of that night, but he had expected it to be a conditional one, giving him the freedom to live as and how he wished in Australia, but not the right to go back to England. That changed everything – and yet, he reminded himself, it changed nothing. Because whichever way he looked, there was Cathy.

And Cathy these days was an enigma to him. His words

to Simeon had been the truth, that he felt that seeing Jake Bellinger shot down in front of her eyes had had a profound effect on her. And although he would have liked to believe that Simeon was right, and that she would soon recover from the shock, he was by no means sure it was true. It had all happened – how many months ago, now? Two, almost three? – and still she was almost silent, still her grey eyes were strangely veiled whenever she looked at him.

At first, occupied with clearing the devastation left by the fire, rounding up escaped stock and making some of the huts fit to live in again while the work proceeded, he had been too busy to notice it. He had seen little of Cathy during those early weeks anyway, for she, Rose and Simeon had been taken to Kit Marsh's farm to stay while the house was being rebuilt and the area made fit to live in again. And, he reflected, it would have been an impossible task if they had not built the new dam and so been able to carry water to protect the compound.

Even so, a good many of the huts had been destroyed and the house itself badly damaged. There was a lot to be done and it must be done before the rainy season began. Consequently, Matthew and Cathy had seen little of each other and it had been some time before he noticed the look in her eyes.

And when he had seen it he had told himself that it was natural and tried to comfort her. He remembered the first evening when they had been alone together, when he had come to the hut she shared with another female convict and found that Mary Ann was out. She had stood in the middle of the little room, almost as white as on the night when he had killed Jake, and gazed at him with eyes the size of limpet shells. Her lips had parted, but she did not speak. Perhaps in that moment she could not speak.

'Cathy.' He had stepped quickly across the room and taken her in his arms. She did not move, made no effort to escape but stood motionless within their circle. He had held her gently, looked down at her with tenderness and touched her lips with his.

'Cathy, it seems so long since we've been able to be alone

together, to talk. Tell me how you are. I've hardly seen you since – since the fire.'

She shook her head slightly, still not speaking. Her lips were cold and he lifted his head and looked searchingly into her face. It was then that he saw the darkness in her eyes, and drew back, shocked and dismayed.

'Cathy, what is it? You're surely not afraid of me? You know I'd never harm you.'

'No,' she whispered at last through colourless lips. 'I'm not afraid – not of you. But –'

'But you *are* afraid,' he insisted. 'I've seen that look before – don't try to hide it. Cathy, my love.' It was only the second time he had used that endearment, and the first time it had brought roses to her cheeks and tears to her eyes. 'Cathy, tell me what it is. What's frightening you so?'

Again, she shook her head and he drew her close, lifting one hand to her head, cradling it against his chest. He could feel her quivering like a bird in his arms and beneath his hands he could trace the shape of her fragile bones. She stood rigid against him but he told himself that it was not he whom she feared, but something else. She trusted him. She had no reason not to trust him. Yet what was it that brought that terror into her eyes?

'Cathy,' he murmured, and stroked her hair.

To his consternation, she shook her head violently, raising a hand as if to pull him away. Like a trapped animal, she began to struggle and he let her go, ashamed to use his own greater strength to keep her. As quickly as a cat, she leapt sideways away from him and stood with her back to the wall, gazing at him with those huge, frightened eyes. He felt his concern deepen to real anxiety. Had her brain been turned by all the horror she had endured? Had she lost her reason?

'Cathy –'

'No,' she gasped, looking at him as if cornered. 'Please – please, Matt, in the name of the Holy Virgin herself, please don't touch me. I – I don't know why it is. I'm not afraid of ye – I know ye'd niver hurt me. But – please, please don't touch me.'

'Cathy, what is it? Has someone hurt you? Frightened you in any way? Tell me and I'll –'

'No. Nobody's touched me. Everyone's been very kind.' She was beginning to shake. Her face was white and her hair, once so shining, hung dull and lifeless down her back. 'I just – can't. I can't . . . forget.' Her voice was barely audible and he only just caught the last word.

'You can't forget what, Cathy?' He spoke softly, gently, as if coaxing a young, timid animal into his hand. 'Is it Jake you can't forget?'

She nodded quickly, sharply.

'Did he hurt you, Cathy? Did he touch you? Was it he who tied you up?'

'No – no, that was one of the others, God forgive him. No, he didn't touch me. He just . . . looked at me.' She covered her eyes with her hands. Matt made an involuntary movement, wanting instinctively to go to her and take her in his arms, try to comfort her, to still that dreadful trembling. But he forced himself to remain still, afraid to distress her any more. 'And then – and then you came. And – and . . .' But she could not go on. She stood shaking, her head bent, her hands clutching her hair, and he saw the tears flow between her fingers. Oh Cathy, Cathy, he thought, what can I do to ease your pain? If only I could take it away – bear it for you.

Ever since that evening, he had been trying gently, slowly, to win back her confidence. And by now, he was afraid that he might never succeed. It wasn't just fear he saw in her eyes. Fear could eventually have been overcome. However, slowly, Cathy would have forgotten the sharpness of it and begun to put it behind her, to live again. But there was more than fear, and he believed that he knew now what it was.

It was repugnance. Repugnance for him, for what he had done. And that was something he did not know how to fight.

Simeon stopped at one of the shops and looked through the window. From being a purely penal colony, with only the military stores from which to obtain goods, New South Wales had grown into a community of farmers, shopkeepers, blacksmiths, clerks – all the people, in fact, who found their place naturally in any town or village. Many were old soldiers, their service finished, who had stayed because there was nothing to go back to England for; others had returned from the Napoleonic Wars to find themselves unwanted, an embarrassment to the society they had fought to protect. Some were settlers who had come out in the hope of a better life and found a harder one – for starting up a new colony was no easy task, and although many succeeded, many others foundered along the way. And many were those convicts who had come expecting a harder life and found a better, Emancipists who had gained their pardon and been granted land of their own, or had started their own business.

And so from a medley of felons, soldiers and pioneers the colony that had been intended to serve only as a prison had become an outpost of their homeland, the beginning of a nation that depended still on its parent but was already, however slowly, growing away from it.

'Women's clothes,' Simeon remarked. 'Rose is beginning to talk about yon wedding again, Matt. But this pardon of yours makes a difference. Happen you are making plans to go back home, after all.'

'No. It's out of the question.' Matthew spoke quickly, almost roughly. Even if Cathy were to be granted her own pardon on marriage, as sometimes happened, he would never take her back to England. Never take her to Kidderminster, where Rebecca lived. 'No, I shan't let Cathy down. I've promised to marry her and marry her I will.' Only as the words left his lips did he realise how they had betrayed him, and he met Simeon's eyes and saw the understanding in them. 'Not exactly the speech of a lover, is it?' he said wryly.

Simeon shook his head. 'What's between you and Cathy is your business. And there's been many a good marriage made without "love" – whatever that is. They say it comes later, if you're lucky, and I must say me and Rose have been lucky there. She's been a good wife to me, Matt, and happen young

356

Cathy'll be a good wife to you too. Loyalty, devotion, right thinking – what more does anyone want?'

What indeed? Matt thought. Passion, perhaps, that might wane with the passing years? A bond that held two people in a grip that had nothing to do with mundane qualities but from which all must follow? Or the tender affection that he knew had existed between Cathy and himself, before the night of the fire?

And what hope was there for marriage between them, if that tenderness had gone and been replaced by fear and disgust?

'I'll have to decide what I'm to do first,' he said, speaking his thoughts aloud. 'I have money in England. I can afford to buy some good land to add to my grant and start my own farm. Or I could begin a business.' But what did he know of business, save what he had learned from Francis about carpet-making? Perhaps he could begin a new industry here, in making carpets. But the climate in Australia did not call for warm floor coverings, and those people who wanted and could afford such shows of wealth and status preferred to have them sent out from England. 'I hadn't expected to be thinking of such things for many years to come,' he said with a grin.

Simeon gave him a thoughtful glance. 'I daresay you didn't, lad. But here it is, and if you'd like to take a drink with me I've got summat I'd like to suggest to you.' He nodded towards a tavern. 'Let's go in here, out of the sun.'

The tavern was quiet inside and they settled themselves in a corner with drinks in front of them. Matthew waited, wondering what Simeon was about to propose. His offer of continuing work had been welcome when Matthew had gained his ticket-of-leave – was it really only a few months ago? – but a free pardon changed the situation substantially. And Simeon's own circumstances were different now, with the damage to his farm. He wouldn't be able to afford to employ Matthew as he had before; he would need assigned government men again.

For a few minutes they drank in silence, each occupied with his own thoughts. Then Simeon set down his glass and said, 'I've been thinking, Matt. I knew you'd get your pardon, of course, though I did think it would probably be just a conditional and you'd not be able to go back to England. But if you say you're staying here anyway – well, that don't make so much difference. And what I've been thinking is this, and you can say no if you don't like the idea – but give it a bit of thought yourself before you say owt.'

He paused, clearly trying to collect his thoughts after saying so much. 'Happen you might think about coming into partnership with me,' he said at last, abruptly. 'Put your grant together with my farm and make summat bigger and better out of both. I know mine's a bit of a mess at the moment, but that'll improve with time. And we work well together.' He paused. 'Rose and Cathy get on well, too. Like mother and daughter, they are. I reckon it'd work, but you see what you think.' He lifted his glass again. 'Well, that's it. You don't have to answer now.'

Slowly, Matthew raised his own glass. He sipped his ale, tasting the cool liquid as it ran down his throat. His mind, already shaken by the new possibilities opened up to him that morning, considered this new suggestion, turning it this way and that, trying to see all sides and take account of all its facets.

A partnership with Simeon. Working as a free man, on his own farm – but alongside the man who had treated him like a human being, who had trusted and respected him. Married to Cathy, starting their own family, seeing their children grow in this new country which was still so raw, yet was beginning at last to create its own excitement.

He had felt that excitement in America, where they had had time now to consider themselves a nation, yet were still pioneers. That could begin now to happen in Australia, as more and more free settlers realised its possibilities and came to make their fortunes, or at least their livelihoods, here. And if the transports were abolished, as was now beginning to be discussed, the excitement would grow – and the colony with it.

To have been here in the earlier days, establishing a farm or business, could only be an advantage. And to be working with a man he trusted and respected and most of all liked, could be an even bigger one.

Was he likely to have such good fortune in England? Where industries such as the carpet-making business were still struggling to recover from the Napoleonic wars, where he had never found his own true niche, where Rebecca would still be denied him by reason this time of his own marriage? He shook his head. There was nothing, could never be anything, for him to go back for in England.

'Yes,' he said, and set his own glass alongside Simeon's. 'I think it would work very well. And I'd like to give you my answer now.' He took the two glasses to the bar and asked for both to be refilled, then carried them back. Still standing, he handed one to Simeon and touched it with his own. 'To our future partnership,' he said, and drank deeply once again.

And knew exactly what it meant to have burnt one's boats.

The new farmhouse was almost ready. Built from the foundations of the first, it was larger, with more and bigger rooms. Rose spent all her time now in choosing new furnishings, and she and Cathy spent long hours poring over pattern books, sending for fabrics, many of which must come from England, and sewing new curtains and covers for chairs and sofas. Cathy, who had seldom plied a needle before, learned her new skills quickly and soon embarked on a patchwork quilt. But she was shy when asked to show it to Matthew, and produced her coloured scraps reluctantly.

'All the brides in my family made their own quilts,' Rose remarked, and the words brought a blush to Cathy's cheeks. 'Mind you, we had a sort of tradition that there'd be no wedding till the quilt was done. In fact, I had one aunt who never did finish hers – and stayed a spinster to the end of her days.'

Matthew smiled and took up the little coloured shapes, holding them against each other and admiring the effect. 'It's going to be very pretty,' he declared. 'How long do you think it will take you?'

'Oh, a long time,' Cathy said instantly, and blushed deeper still. 'I mean – I don't have much time, ye see, what with the curtains and such, and all me work for Mrs Marsh. And I'm not a quick worker, not with me needle, niver having done it before.'

'Nonsense,' Rose said roundly. 'You know we've nearly finished the curtains and things, and once they're done you'll have plenty of time. Joan Marsh isn't a slave driver and she knows you're anxious to wed. Would've been all over by now, and you with your first on the way, I daresay, if it hadn't been for that blessed Jake Bellinger.'

Matthew cast a glance of amusement at Cathy but to his dismay saw that her blush had deepened to a scarlet so fiery it surely must burn her skin. There was real distress in her eyes, and he quickly laid down the pieces of patchwork and searched for a change of subject.

'You'll be moving into the new house soon,' he said. 'You'll be glad to be in your own home again.'

'Aye, happen we will. Not that Joan Marsh hasn't been kindness itself, a right good neighbour, good as a Yorkshire lass she is. But it's better to be in your own place.' Rose glanced up at Matthew. 'You'll be thinking that yourself, I don't doubt. How's your building work coming along?'

'Oh, pretty well.' Again, he glanced at Cathy, hoping to see some sign of eagerness in her face, but her head was bent over her work and turned slightly away, so that it was hidden. 'I want Cathy to come with me to see it tomorrow, if you can spare her. There are things she ought to decide, if it's to be her home.'

'Of course I can spare her.' Rose might have been at home in England, offering to lend her maid for the day, rather than the mistress of an assigned convict woman. Matthew thought of so many others, treated like slaves or worse, kept as poorly as any scullery girl with barely enough to eat and only rough convict clothes to wear. At least Cathy, after all her early despair, had come into this safe harbour. And, once married to him, she would be as free as any settler's wife, with her own home. He felt his old tenderness sweep over him and reached forward to touch her cheek with gentle fingertips.

She flinched only slightly this time, and he felt a pang of hope. Perhaps she was recovering at last from her terror, and willing to look ahead again. Perhaps she would even learn to look at him again with affection, if not the adoration she had given him before.

The responsibility lay with him. Cathy could not help her feelings. If she looked on him with disgust, it was because he disgusted her. If he wanted her to look at him with trust and affection, he must earn that trust. Most of all, he must go gently, for Cathy was like a wild fawn, ready to leap away at the slightest false move. And once gone, she might never be caught again.

'Come and look at the house with me tomorrow,' he said softly. 'It will soon be time to start thinking of curtains of your own. As for the quilt – you shall decide whether we wait for it to be finished or not. And you may take your own time to do the work.'

Cathy looked up at him. She rarely met his eyes now and he felt a flicker of hope, for there was gratitude in her glance. Well, that was better than what he had become accustomed to seeing there. And surely gratitude might turn to trust, and trust to love?

He stood up, feeling more optimistic than he had done for weeks. 'I'll call tomorrow morning,' he said, like any swain, and Rose smiled and nodded. Cathy's head was bent once more over her work and she did not look up again. But he went out with a spring in his step, nevertheless, and a feeling of hopefulness for the future.

The new house was being built on the land Matthew had been granted close to Simeon's. To make the farm larger still, he had bought another parcel adjoining it and the entire holding now ranged over several hundred acres. Simeon's stock, saved from the fire, roamed on the unburned pastures and clearing had already begun on the new land.

Matthew reined in the horse and the cart came to a halt. He sat for a moment, looking at the dell where he had positioned his new home. It nestled into the curve of a low hill, sheltered by tall eucalypts, facing south so that it might be sheltered from the worst of the sun's heat. Before it lay a stretch of natural pasture, green after the recent rains, and a creek that would dry up in summer but now ran with tumbling brown water.

It looked idyllic, he thought. A place any man would be proud to bring his wife. A place he would have liked to bring Rebecca – but no. He must not think of her now. He was promised to Cathy and must give her all his allegiance.

'Do you like it?' he asked, a little anxiously. 'You can plant a garden in front of the house if you like, running down to the creek. And we can have a seat outside, to sit in the evenings. Will you like that?'

'Yes, if ye think so,' Cathy answered and he suppressed a sigh. Her voice was so small, so timid still, as if she were a beaten dog afraid of being kicked. He tried gently to encourage her.

'Cathy, it's for you to say. You'll be mistress of your own house. You must have things the way you want them.' He urged the horse on again. 'Let's look around and you can tell me how you'd like the rooms.'

But it was hard work. The house was half built now, and it was possible to visualise it as it would be when finished. And there were drawings, made by Matthew when he had first begun to consider the full implications of his partnership with Simeon. Most women, he thought with a hint of quickly suppressed exasperation, would have been excited by the prospect of planning their new home.

But Cathy followed him around the house as if she were an untamed deer, looking only for an opportunity to escape. She gazed at everything with wide eyes, nodded or shook her head as required, trembled if asked to make a decision. In the end, Matthew was driven to make a more positive demand on her. He laid his hands on her shoulders, ignoring the quiver that ran through her body, and spoke firmly.

'Cathy, please tell me what it is that ails you? You behave as though you're afraid of me – as if you think I'll do you harm. You must know I'd never hurt a single hair of your head. Please, tell me what has upset you so much and why you shudder when I touch you. Because if you don't, if you're going to live in fear of me, how can we ever be happy together? How can we ever have a true marriage?'

Cathy stood quite still under his hands, her eyes cast down. Feeling a tremor of impatience, Matthew put his fingers under her chin and lifted her face so that she was compelled to look into his eyes. His heart smote him at the expression in hers but he forced himself to continue. She must not be allowed to go on in this way. It was damaging them both.

'Don't you love me at all?' he asked. 'I know I can never be what Oliver was to you – but we used to be happy together, you used to trust me. Why don't you trust me now? What's changed you?'

He hoped she would tell him of her own free will. At least he would know that she wasn't concealing the truth from herself. But when she still remained mute, he was forced to make her face it.

'It was the night I killed Jake, wasn't it?' he said quietly. 'No, don't turn away, Cathy. Don't try to hide from it. What was it that left you so afraid? Was it what he did to you . . . or was it what I did to him?'

There was a long silence. He waited, knowing there was no more he could say, no more he could do. If Cathy still refused to accept what had happened, if she preferred to spend the rest of her life with her mind closed, her memory obstinately darkened, there was nothing he or anyone else could do about it. And although he would never go back on his promise to marry her, to protect and look after her for the rest of her life, their life together would be no more than a shadow.

But if only she could summon the courage to look at it, talk about it – then, he knew instinctively, there was a chance that she might recover, might become again the old Cathy. Timid always, but happy in her own quiet way, devoted to him and whatever family they might have, growing old in contentment. The Cathy she could be, deserved to be.

'What did he do to you, Cathy?' he asked. 'Is it that which haunts you?' And when, with a sinking heart, he saw her give a very slight shake of her head, he said in a lower tone still, 'Then it must have been me.'

At last she looked up at him. Her eyes had the drowned look he had seen so often, and which always moved him to pity. She had suffered so much, this girl who still seemed more child than woman, had seen so many horrors. She had lived in poverty and starvation, had endured the abominations of the hulks and the transport ship, had known helplessness at the hands of the authorities here in Australia.

And although she had known kindness too, and had begun to emerge from her morass of fear, the events of that last night at Simeon's farm had knocked her back again into its clinging mire, just as a heavy blow might send her reeling into the midden in a farmyard.

'Is it because I killed him?' Matthew asked.

'I've niver seen anything like it,' she whispered. 'In all me days. It was the blood. I've seen blood before, but niver like that, all spouting and gushing. It was on me face, I could feel it running down like tears . . .' She shuddered violently and he put his arms around her. 'It was all over me clothes, all on the walls, everywhere . . . I niver knew shooting a man could be like that.'

I did, Matthew thought. I knew, because I've seen it before. I've done it before. He felt sickened, seeing it suddenly through Cathy's eyes, knowing now why she looked at him with such fear, such involuntary loathing. She knew he had had no choice. She knew there was nothing else he could have done to save them all that night. And yet she could not help the repugnance she felt.

'And ye just seemed to take it for granted,' she went on. 'Ye didn't seem to notice the – the blood and all. It – it was nothin' to you, nothin'.'

'That's not true, Cathy. I don't like killing any more than you do. I've never before killed deliberately like that – not even a dog. And there was no time to say prayers for his soul – the house was about to catch fire. We would all have died like Jake if John and I hadn't got you out of there, fast. Cathy, you know it had to happen that way.'

'I know,' she whispered. 'And I'm sorry. I – I'll try to make ye a good wife, Matt. I just – can't –'

She turned away, and he let her go, knowing that she needed her tears. Knowing too that she needed time to recover, to regain her old trust and affection for him, even though she might never feel again the same adoration. But he didn't want adoration anyway, he told himself. He didn't want hero-worship. Just good, honest, everyday love.

And how could he ask even that, when he knew he couldn't give it himself?

'We need some new stock,' Simeon said as he and Matthew sat poring over their plans for the new farm. 'That's agreed. Five hundred sheep would be a handy number, and the present price is a pound each. Can we run to that? That should bring us an annual income of, say, two hundred and fifty, maybe three hundred a year. The horses are doing well. My best mare will foal again next year and that'll bring us up to four mares, two stallions, three colts, a filly and whatever she produces. We'll sell one of the colts and geld the other. I'm not sure we need two stallions either – Castor can handle what we've got and he's sired some grand foals.'

Matthew nodded. 'I think you're right. And we should get a good price for Pollux, he's done well too. What do you think about more cows? We've only got five for our own use.'

'Enough. We can graze forty or fifty on shares with Kit and one or two others. Better than sinking our own money into a herd. I'm not a cow man, never have been.' Simeon gazed at the figures. 'Well, it looks all right to me, lad, but you're putting money into it, so you must say what you think.'

'I think it looks very good.' Matthew nodded. 'We'll do well together, Simeon.'

'Aye, I think we will that.' The older man stood up and went to a cupboard. He took out a bottle of rum and poured a measure into each of two glasses. 'To our new venture, Matt.'

Matthew lifted his glass. 'To our new ve –' He stopped and turned his head. 'Hullo, what's that?'

'Sounds like a visitor.' Simeon peered through the window. 'Aye, Sam Curtis. He said he was going to Parramatta, he must have collected some letters for us. News of some sort, maybe. Let's go and see. Maybe summat from home.'

Matthew set down his glass, the toast forgotten. He felt a sudden tautness grip his heart, as if someone had just pulled its strings tightly together. An odd breathlessness caught at his lungs as he followed Simeon out of the house and saw Rose and Cathy already there, greeting the man who had just ridden into the yard. He saw Sam taking packages from his leather pouch, and stopped. For a moment, he didn't want to know.

And then Cathy turned and saw him. He met her eyes and knew that she too had this strange presage of doom.

Kit and Joan Marsh were there too, reaching out for the letters that had been brought. And there were others – young John, the Marsh's own daughter and two sons, the government men who were working about the compound. Excitement crackled in the air; everyone wanted letters, especially if they were from England.

'Something here for you, Matt,' Kit said, tossing a package over to him. 'Oh, and another one too – confirming your grant, I daresay. You'll be a landowner just like the rest of us now!'

Matthew smiled absently. He was staring at the first packet that Kit had thrown him. It was addressed in Rebecca's handwriting and, for the first time in his life, he did not want to know what she said. He did not want to open it.

He was aware of Cathy coming close to him. He looked down and saw her face, but he could not analyse her expression. It was tinged with apprehension, but there was something else besides and he did not know what it was.

'It's from England, isn't it,?' she said in a low voice. 'From Kidderminster. From . . . her.'

He nodded, and began to tear the packet open. The letter fell out – not her usual five or six sheets, closely written, but a single sheet, with only a few words upon it. And as he stared, his heart grew tighter and he knew as certainly as if her voice had sounded from the page, that Rebecca needed him. And that her need arose from a love he had never dared hope for.

Rebecca needed him. She loved him. And he had only a week ago written to tell her of his betrothal to Cathy . . .

Rose came to him late that evening, as he sat out on the porch watching the sun go down behind the mountains. She sat down on the bench beside him and touched his hand.

'What is it, Matt?'

He shook his head. 'Nothing that anyone can do anything about, Rose.' He was silent for a few moments, then asked with passion in his voice, 'Why does everything have to happen at the wrong time, Rose? Why can't life go smoothly – at least some of the time? Why does it have to twist and turn, like a corkscrew, so that when you are offered what you want, you can't take it – and when you can take it, you aren't offered it?'

Rose did not answer at once. Then she said, 'Have you been offered what you want, Matt?'

'No,' he said moodily. 'Not offered. I just know it's there. If *I* were there too, and not eight thousand miles away.'

'Rebecca?'

He nodded. 'I'm sorry, Rose, I can't help it. I've always loved her. I always will. But I thought there was no chance. I thought I'd never even be able to see her again. And then –'

'And then her husband died. But she's been a widow for over a year now. You've known she was free and that you couldn't go to her. And even when you had your pardon, you never seemed to consider the idea of going back.'

'Because there was Cathy! How could I abandon that child? She trusted me – once. I've hurt that trust through what I did to Jake, even though it had to be done. But in time she'll forget that. She'd never forget it if I betrayed her again, by leaving her alone. I can't do that to her.'

'So why is it different now? What was in that letter that made you look as you did? What is making you sit out here as if the world were about to end?'

Matthew took the letter from his pocket. He read it again, even though he now knew it by heart. He looked at Rose and saw the concern in her face, the willingness to understand without condemnation, and he felt a warm rush of gratitude.

'Rebecca has lost her business,' he said tonelessly. 'The factory – the workshops, where the carpets are woven, have been burned down. They're having to close. She doesn't even have enough money to educate the boys, barely enough to feed them. She needs my help, Rose. And it's not just money – she needs *me*. To be with her. To stand beside her.'

'Is that what she says? Is she asking you to go to her?'

He shook his head. 'She tells me only about the business. But I know that's what she needs.'

Rose looked into his eyes. He wanted to look away, but could not. In honesty, he had to let her examine his soul through its windows and read what was written there.

'And will you go to her?'

Matthew stared at her. 'Go to her? How can I? I've just agreed to join Simeon in his farm – in *our* farm. The wedding's being planned.' He looked down at the letter. 'I've even written to Rebecca to tell her so. She'll know soon that I can't help her. It's too late even for money – it's now she needs it, not in the five or six months it would take to arrange it. And she'll know . . .' *That I've betrayed her*, his mind added, but he could not speak the words aloud. Not even to Rose.

She looked at him thoughtfully, then laid her hand over his again and held it in a warm clasp.

'Don't worry too much, Matt,' she said in a careful voice, as if she wanted him to hear and take note of every word she said. 'You've told me often enough what a beautiful woman she is, how warm, how loving, how much liked. I daresay she'll marry again quite soon, and then all her troubles will be at an end. And you can stay here and be content.'

She gave him a long, intent look, then got up and went back into the house, leaving him alone with the mountains and the sunset. And his thoughts.

Rebecca, married again? And he content, in Australia – without her?

No. No. *No!*

The moon slanted through the wire screens of the windows as Cathy crept silently from the room she shared with the Marshes' two house servants. On the landing, she paused and peeped down into the yard. The tall eucalyptus trees stretched twisted fingers towards the sky, as if calling the heavens to witness her secret ramblings, and outside she could hear the hoot of the owls who hunted by night, and the occasional distant boom of a kangaroo.

Indoors, no one else stirred. From Simeon's and Rose's room came the faint rumbling of Simeon's snoring. Soon, the Ackroyds would be moving into their new home; and soon after that, Matthew's farmhouse would be finished. And then the wedding would be held . . .

Shivering, although it could not be cold, Cathy slipped through the house, her bare feet making no sound. She came to the door which led to the porch, and opened it quietly, fastening back the hook so that she would be able to come in again. Then she turned the corner of the house and tapped softly on the door of the little lean-to hut occupied by Matthew.

It was a few moments before he heard her and came. He opened the door and stood there, bare-chested, gazing down at her.

'Cathy!'

'Ssh.' She glanced anxiously about her. 'Matt, please can I come in?'

'Of course you can.' He stood aside and closed the door behind her. The tiny space was lit only by a shaft of moonlight

369

which came through the small window. It shone on the narrow bed, its rough sheets thrown back. Cathy looked down at it and thought of the times she and Matt had shared a similar bed, back on Simeon's farm. Tender, sweet, loving times.

Times she could never repeat.

'Matt.' She spoke rapidly. 'Matt, I've got to talk to ye. There's niver any time during the day, niver a moment when there's not others about. And it can't be left any longer.'

He came close but didn't touch her, and she felt grateful for that. He understood so much of what she felt, and the tears came hot to her eyes because his understanding had made no difference to the shaking of her body, the prickling on her skin, whenever she had thought of the night he had shot Jake Bellinger, the noise, the blood. If it had, they might have been married by now. But out of consideration for her, he had agreed to wait. And now . . .

Somewhere inside, her feelings for Matt had never changed. But it had taken a letter from England to make her realise it. And now, as Matt had said to Rose, it was the wrong time.

He spoke gently. 'Tell me what it is, Cathy.'

She turned to face him. 'Matt, I cannot marry ye. I've been trying to tell meself it's all right, that I'll get over it . . . but it niver will be, and I won't. I'll niver be able to be the wife that ye want, and we both know it, don't we?' She met his eyes and her own, though wet with tears, were steady. 'Don't we?'

'Cathy, I'm sure –'

'No, Matt.' With an effort, she raised her hand and placed one finger against his lips. 'Don't say anything ye don't truly believe. Not now.' She waited, and he was silent. 'Ye see?' she said, and there was a wealth of sadness in her voice as she thought of what might have been. But even now, she knew that he might try to persuade her and if he did, she would be lost. Here, in the tiny room, lit now by a flood of moonlight, she would be truly lost. 'Besides,' she said with an even greater effort, 'there's somethin' else.'

'Something else? Isn't it enough that you loathe me for what I did? What else can there be?'

'It's John,' she said in a low voice. 'Matt, he's loved me for a long time and – and I think I love him too.' She closed her eyes, swallowed and then went on. 'I think if I just . . . look at him the right way, he'll ask me to marry him. If he thinks that you – if you're not –'

'Not here,' Matt said. 'That's what you mean, isn't it, Cathy? He'll not ask you while I'm about. And if he does ask you, you'll say yes.'

The ache in her throat prevented her from answering. She cast her eyes down and waited. Her heart was beating very fast.

'Tell me the truth, Cathy,' Matt said. 'Do you really believe you love him? Because if you do, I'll let you go. I want you to be happy, Cathy.' He lifted her chin, forced her to meet his eyes. 'Look at me and tell me. I know you well enough – you could never look at me and lie. So –?'

Cathy looked at him. Almost, she wavered. And then, steadily and without a tremor, she lied.

'I do believe I love him. And I want to marry him.'

Matt stared at her. Then he let her go. He walked to the door and opened it, then closed it again.

'Cathy. Don't – don't leave me without one last kiss. For the sake of all we shared.'

No, she wanted to scream, no. For if I kiss you, you'll know the truth . . . But she could not refuse. She let him take her in his arms, lifted her face to his, and parted her soft, trembling lips.

Matt laid his mouth upon hers and she felt the sweetness of it, the tenderness. With the tiniest of whimpers, she clung to him, her senses reeling. And then, swiftly, she tore herself away and wrenched open the door.

'Cathy!'

'I must go – they might miss me.' Breathless, as panic-stricken as if dingoes were after her, she ran from the hut and along the porch. She felt Matthew's hand on her arm, shook it off and found the hook that held the porch door open for her. In seconds, she was inside and leaning against the wall, shuddering.

Why does everything happen at the wrong time? he had asked Rose. And she could only echo his words in her own weeping heart.

'So that's it.' Simeon rode back into the yard and climbed down from the cart. He moved like an old man, Cathy thought, looking at him with pity. He and Rose felt this loss as much as she did. But they did not have the added burden of guilt that she carried. They had not sent Matt away, back to England. 'He's gone. I watched the ship sail myself. In a few weeks he'll be back in England and it'll all be as if he'd never been away.'

'No, it won't. He'll never forget Australia – nor you and Mrs Ackroyd.' Soon enough, Cathy would have to accustom herself to calling Rose 'Mother' but the idea was still strange in her mind. And it would be even stranger, living in the new house with John instead of Matt. 'And he says he'll come back, someday,' she said, trying to offer hope. 'After all, the farm's still partly his. He'll want to come back and work it.'

'Aye, happen.' Simeon sounded unconvinced. He looked around. 'It won't be the same, working it without him. I was looking forward to that.'

Cathy turned away. She could not bear the sadness in his voice, the stoop of his shoulders, and all caused by her. And yet, she'd wanted Matt to go. She'd known he would never be happy here, knowing that his Rebecca was in need of him. She couldn't have forced him to stay.

Simeon was pulling something from his pocket. 'There was a letter for him at the office there. It must have been mislaid. We called in before the ship sailed, and it wasn't there then. I don't rightly know what to do with it.'

Cathy looked at it. 'It's from Kidderminster. It must be from –'

'From her. Rebecca. Aye, that's what I thought.' He glanced

round as Rose came out of the farmhouse, and showed it to her. 'What d'you think we should do with it, lass? I don't rightly like to open it, but happen it ought to be answered. He didn't write to her before he went, you know. And a letter sent now might easily arrive before he does, the way ships get blown about.'

Rose took the letter and gazed at it thoughtfully. Then she said, 'I think we'd better open it, Simeon. It might be important, after all. Open it now. See what it says.'

Simeon hesitated, glanced at his wife, then at Cathy. She stared back. Her heart was thumping. There was a strange, gnawing pain somewhere deep in her stomach. When she spoke, it was more loudly and roughly than she had ever spoken in her life, and the Ackroyds looked at her in astonishment.

'Open it,' she said. 'For the sake of Michael and all his angels, open the damned thing!'

Simeon opened his mouth, then closed it again. He took his knife from his belt and slit the paper. He unfolded the sheets inside and scanned them quickly.

'Well?' Rose said, and her voice was as anxious as Cathy's. 'For God's sake, Simeon, tell us what it says!'

'It says she's to be wed,' Simeon said slowly. 'It says she's to marry the cousin – Vivian Pagnel. The one Matt never liked.' He crumpled the letter in his hand and stared at the two women, and there was a baffled anger in his face and in his voice. 'He's going all that way, and he'll find her wed.'

Rose turned impulsively to Cathy and reached out her arms. 'Oh, my dear,' she said compassionately. 'Oh, my dear . . .'

But Cathy turned away. At this moment, compassion, pity, even kindness would be too much for her to bear. She walked away and stood in the middle of the yard, staring with aching eyes out over the vast expanse of bush, the clearings, the pastures far away, the distant blue peaks of the mountains.

And Matthew's own phrase, heard as she sat out of sight near the darkened porch, came once again into her mind.

Why does everything have to happen at the wrong time?

REBECCA
AND
MATTHEW

Chapter Eighteen

'I tell you, Rebecca, I will *not* have our marriage postponed. Why should we let two foolish, headstrong children upset our plans? They obviously care nothing for us – in three months, we've heard not a word – so why should we delay any longer?' Vivian paced backwards and forwards across the room. His face was flushed with anger, his body taut, hands clenched into fists as if ready to fight. If Daniel were to walk into the room now, Rebecca thought, he would be felled at once with one blow from those fists. And Vivian would be glad of the chance to do it.

Sadly, she glanced out of the window. The snowdrops were fading now and the purple and gold of crocuses taking their place. The daffodils were in bud, a few brave trumpets already open, and the grass had begun to grow again. Signs and symbols of hope, but there was little hope in her heart.

'If only we could find out where they've gone,' she began, but Vivian cut in angrily.

'For God's sake, Rebecca, haven't I tried? Haven't I sent detectives scouring the country, from London to Liverpool? What more can I do? They left no hint – even William had no idea what they planned, even though the young rogue connived at their escape.' He scowled and Rebecca knew he had still not forgiven William his part in the elopement. 'All we know is that Lucy's sisters remember hearing her speak of America. And what use is that? We can't watch every ship that leaves the country. London, Bristol, Liverpool – where would we start? Am I to post myself at the foot of the gangway every time a ship sails? They'll almost certainly use false names, anyway – even supposing that it *is* their intention. It's the faintest chance possible.'

'But it *is* a chance. Vivian, is there nothing else we can do?' She rose to her feet and went to him, laying her hand on his sleeve. 'The thought of them, homeless and without money . . . Vivian, I *know* what it's like. I've hardly slept since they went. I lie there at night, picturing them in London, roaming those dreadful streets, sleeping in doorways and corners . . . And the dangers to Lucy! You know what they are. Don't you worry about her, day and night?'

'The chit's asked for whatever comes to her,' he said brutally. 'I'm sorry, Rebecca, but I've had more trouble than I'm prepared to tolerate from that wilful minx. She was always over fond of her own way – well, now she's got it and she must tread it herself. I wash my hands of her. And I advise you to do the same with Daniel.'

'I can't do that! He's my son – my flesh and blood. How can I forget the months I carried him in my body? How can I forget the day he was born, all the days and years since? He's part of me, Vivian, and I'll never put him out of my life, whatever he does.'

'Then you must live with the pain of it. You choose it.'

'I choose it only because I *have* no choice,' she answered in a low voice. 'No mother can do otherwise.' She looked up at him, her face pale. 'Vivian, if we differ so much on this, how can we ever make a happy marriage together? Don't you think we should consider carefully what we're doing? And if we decide not to marry after all, they might come back and –'

'Decide not to marry? I've told you, Rebecca, I won't postpone our wedding. The date's been settled – June the first. And it's not so very long now. You should be making arrangements, sending out invitations. You must put this worry aside.'

'But I *can't do that!* Don't you understand?' Rebecca turned away and began to pace the room as he had done, twisting her hands in front of her. 'And I'm not suggesting a postponement. I'm asking whether we should marry at all – when we hold such different views?' She turned and faced him. 'I think I'm telling you, Vivian, that I can't marry you. Ever.'

He stared at her. His eyes narrowed, his jaw tightened and a muscle in his cheek began to twitch. He took a step towards her, and Rebecca flinched but stood quite still. She could not allow him to intimidate her now.

'You're telling me you can't marry me? *Won't* marry me? You imagine that you can do that – that you can stand there and casually break off our engagement?'

'Vivian, there's nothing casual –'

'You really believe that you can humiliate me in front of the whole of Kidderminster? That you can make me look a fool in front of all my friends and acquaintances – in front of all my *enemies*?'

'Vivian, I don't want to make you look a fool. I don't want to humiliate you –'

'And just what else would you be doing?' he demanded harshly. 'How else do you expect me to feel, other than humiliated?'

Rebecca looked at him and moved her hands helplessly. He watched her for a moment and then went on.

'You understand, don't you, what you've done? You've stood with me in front of everyone who matters in this town, and promised to marry me. You've accepted my ring.' He moved suddenly and gripped her wrist between hard fingers. 'You're wearing it now. You do realise that if you persist in this idiotic course I can sue you for breach of promise? I can humiliate you as you've humiliated me. I can take you through the courts and I can claim compensation.' He glanced around the room. 'I could claim this house, which is rightfully mine far more than yours.'

Rebecca stared at him. 'You wouldn't . . .'

'And why not? I've waited years for you, Rebecca – yes, even before Francis died, when he was ill, I knew that one day you'd be mine. I exercised all the patience I possessed. I watched you mourn him, I watched you struggle with that damned business of yours, I watched you gallivant around the country on that ridiculous journey to gain new customers –'

'Which I did!'

'Which you did —'

'And from which you have benefited.'

'And from which I have benefited,' he acknowledged. 'But Rebecca, my dear, it did *you* no good, did it? You still lost your business.'

'Only through fire,' she interrupted again. 'If it hadn't been for that –'

'You would still have failed,' he said bluntly. 'No, I know I can't prove that now – but I know it and, if you'd only let yourself admit it, you'd know it too. Your burdens were too great. You had debts, responsibilities.'

'I seem always to have had burdens and responsibilities,' she said hopelessly, and turned away. 'And now you're adding to them.'

Vivian stood still for a moment. Then he came towards her and laid his hands on her shoulders. Rebecca felt the warmth of his body just behind her, but her head was bent and she would not turn and let him see her tears.

'Rebecca, the last thing I want is to add to your burdens. And how can you say I'm doing that? I want to marry you – I want to take them from your shoulders. Haven't I already done it? Haven't I taken on the rebuilding of the factory? Haven't I given or promised jobs to all your weavers?' He paused, then added quietly, 'Are you being quite fair to me, Rebecca?'

'No,' she said after a minute, 'I'm probably not.' She turned again and faced him. 'But how can I marry you, Vivian, knowing the way you feel about Daniel and Lucy? I'll never even be able to mention their names. It will be a part of life we can never share.'

'There are many parts of life that people don't share,' he said soberly. His face softened. 'Rebecca, I understand what you say. You have a mother's feeling for her child and that's natural. But those feelings don't have to come between us – they can't be allowed to. We still have our lives to lead. And what Lucy and Daniel do with theirs – whether they ever come back, or whether we never see them again – can't be permitted to interfere.' His voice was wry as he added, 'They haven't allowed us to interfere with them, after all.'

There was a short silence, then he drew her into his arms. 'Rebecca, my dear, I hate to see you so unhappy. Why don't you let me help? You talk about sleepless nights – why not let me share those nights? Let me lull you to sleep, as a husband should. Let me share every part of your life – yes, even your worries about the children. Tell me our marriage will go ahead, and I promise I'll do all in my power to find them.' He tipped her face towards his with one finger, and bent his head, and she felt that dark flame of excitement ignite within her. 'Give me a kiss now, sweetheart, and let's forget the rest of the world for a while.'

Rebecca sighed, then resisted no more. She laid her hands on his shoulders and received his kiss.

She had walked into her cage by her own choice, and there was no way out.

The wedding plans went on. Invitations, arrangements for the service, the wedding breakfast, the bridal gown and the dresses of her attendants. Vivian's unmarried daughters, Mary, Margaret and Jane, were in a fever of excitement as they were fitted for gowns more elaborate than any they had yet owned. Both houses were to be completely refurbished: Vivian's because it was there that the wedding breakfast was to be held, Pagnel House because it was where the couple were to live. And with so short a time to go, the flurry spread into every corner, so that there was almost nowhere to find peace and quiet.

'The old schoolroom's the only place fit to live in,' William complained, and took himself there whenever he was at home, But between school and the factory he seemed to be at home only to sleep anyway, as Rebecca told him when she caught him one morning in the hall.

'William, do wait a minute. I need to talk to you. You're never here these days, and there are things to be decided.'

'What things?' He submitted to having his collar straightened. 'Mother, I'll be late.'

'Well, that shouldn't bother you. You've never worried about missing your studies before. No, don't go rushing off. Listen to me. We have to talk about your giving me away at the service. You will do it, won't you? There's no one else except your Uncle Tom.'

William shrugged. 'Well, I suppose I've no choice,' he said ungraciously. 'I'll do it if you want, though I'll feel a fool.'

'There's really no need.' Rebecca's tone betrayed her exasperation. 'All you have to do is walk me up the aisle and then give my hand to the vicar when he asks. Then you just step back.' She gazed at him, a small frown on her forehead. 'If only you were a little older. Of course, if Daniel's back by then . . .'

'He won't be,' William told her. 'And even if he were, he wouldn't do it. He doesn't *want* you to marry Uncle Vivian, don't you realise that? He's hardly likely to take part in a ritual to hand you over. And I'm sorry, but with only a couple of months to go I'm not likely to get much older. So perhaps it had better be Uncle Tom. He seems to age five years every time I see him.'

'I know,' Rebecca sighed. 'He's still brooding over Nancy – and can you blame him? It's less than a year . . . No, William, you know I can't ask him. He's still convinced Vivian was responsible for the fire, and he won't even speak to me. I doubt very much if he'll come to the wedding.'

'Unless to declare some just cause or impediment,' William said with a grin, and Rebecca shuddered.

'Don't, William. It's not a joke. And what "impediment" could there be, after all? Vivian and I are both widowed. There are no wives or husbands hidden away – no former lovers.' She stopped suddenly. Who knew what lovers Vivian might have had? But there were none who could come forward and prevent his marriage, of that she was sure. And in her own case?

There had been no lover for her, save Francis. And no other

man who had even touched her heart, save for one. And that one was far away, working his time out in Australia.

If Matthew should return ... But that was impossible. It would be years before he could come back, and unlikely that he ever would. Murderers were rarely granted the unconditonial pardon that gave them the right to come back to England. And even if he did – even if he walked through the door at this very minute – what could she do? She was committed now to marrying Vivian. And he had made it very clear that she would not be permitted to break that commitment.

'You'll give me away, William,' she said firmly, pushing away the dangerous thoughts. 'And you'll do it very well. If you look even half as handsome as you did at the Christmas ball, you'll have every young lady in Kidderminster swooning after you.'

William grimaced. 'Heaven forbid! They were bad enough that night, and I've had nothing but invitations to tea ever since. Really, Mother, I can't understand why everyone makes such a fuss about this business of love and marriage. I shall never get married. I've got more sense.'

Rebecca laughed. 'Wait a year or two before you take any monastic vows,' she advised. 'And come home early this evening – you'll need a new suit, and the tailor will be here today. There's no time to lose now.'

William ran off, his books under his arm, and Rebecca went to the window to watch him go. And after he was out of sight, she stayed, gazing down the hill at the road that climbed up from the town.

For a moment, she was back in Unicorn Street on a blustery March morning not long before William was born. A bright, auburn head, hair blown like autumn leaves before the wind, was lighting the shadows outside her front door. And Matthew Farrell was waiting for her, eyes dancing in his lean, tanned face.

Her own eyes misted suddenly with tears. She blinked them away and the vision was gone. The street was empty, and Matthew was still in Australia, and lost to her for ever.

* * *

On that same day, somewhere at sea, Matthew's ship lay almost motionless on the slowly heaving swell of the Doldrums. The wind had dropped days ago and was not expected to blow until everyone aboard had given up all hope of ever moving again. The heat pressed down as stifling as a woollen blanket, and even the most ardent gamblers amongst the sailors had dropped their cards on the deck.

Matthew stared at the horizon until his eyes ached. He gazed up at the drooping pennant on top of the mast until his neck felt ready to break. And his mind sent constant messages to Rebecca, begging her not to forget him.

And in Australia, Cathy and John were married in the little wooden church near Simeon's farm. As she laid her hand in his, Cathy was conscious of a deep sadness that this could not have been Oliver, who had loved her so long and so passionately. Or Matthew, who had never loved her but had cherished and comforted her. And then, as she looked up into the eyes of the young man who had loved her silently ever since he had first seen her, she felt a letting go. A releasing of old ties. And a sense of going forward.

Perhaps, after all, some things did happen at the right time . . .

May came and still there was no news of Lucy and Daniel. Rebecca had almost given up hope of ever seeing her son again, and alternated between misery and anger. How could he have done this to her? How could he just disappear, leaving her abandoned, when she had already lost so much? Why, at least, did he not send word that he and Lucy were well – even just that they were still alive?

'Of course they're alive,' Vivian snorted when she confided her fears. 'They're simply selfish and inconsiderate, no more than that. They'll be back, Rebecca, mark my words, they'll come snivelling home one of these fine days with their tails between their legs. You've no cause to worry.'

But Rebecca did worry. She knew all too well what it was

like to be homeless in London – for she was convinced that was where they must have gone, didn't every runaway seeking his fortune go to London? She had been there herself, alone and frightened with nowhere to go, no one to turn to. And Tom and Bessie had been there before her, desperate for money, forced to degrade themselves simply to live. Was this what was happening now to Daniel and Lucy?

She pictured them, wandering hand in hand through the teeming streets around Covent Garden. Huddled together in a doorway at night, trying to snatch what sleep they could during the long, cold hours. Trying to find work to earn enough money for a crust of bread, a cup of milk.

'But they weren't penniless,' Vivian pointed out. 'They both had money – not much, perhaps, but enough to help them through the first days. And Lucy had some jewellery, nothing valuable but certainly good enough to pawn. They had clothes that could be sold, the sort of knick-knacks that have a market in the streets.'

'Vivian, do you know what you're saying? Doesn't it tear at your heart to think of them selling their few possessions – the watch Daniel's father gave him, the few pieces of jewellery that Lucy had from her mother? And then their clothes – until they've nothing left but what they're wearing? Doesn't it touch you at all, to think of it?'

'Aye, it does.' But Vivian's voice was grim. 'But they get none of my pity, Rebecca, they deserve none. They brought this on themselves and I tell you again, when it gets too hard they'll come home. What else can they do? Neither of them is accustomed to poor living as your brother and sister were – they'll not be able to stand it. They'll come back.'

Rebecca was silent. Perhaps he was right. It was true that neither of them was used to the sort of life that Bessie and Tom had known since birth. Lucy had been brought up in the lap of luxury, wanting for nothing. And even though Rebecca had never allowed Daniel to take his advantages for granted, he had never known hunger or cold, the kind of deprivation that she had suffered as a child. Perhaps, as Vivian said, when life became too hard, they would come home.

But with summer coming, and the nights less cold, when would that be? And Daniel might, after all, have found employment. He could have found a position as a clerk, even a teacher. Even Lucy might have found work as a governess.

'Stop worrying about them, Rebecca,' Vivian said gently. 'I know it's hard, but all your worrying won't bring them back, nor do them any good. And it's making you ill. You've got thinner, you look pale. And I want you to look radiant on the day you become my wife.'

Rebecca smiled faintly. 'I'm sorry. But Daniel's my son, my firstborn. And Lucy's been almost a daughter to me, all these years.'

'And is still,' he said. 'They'll not have forgotten you, Rebecca, and I really do believe they'll come home one day.'

'And to what welcome?' she asked wistfully. 'You're so angry with them, Vivian. Can you promise me you won't turn them away again?'

He shook his head. 'I know I said harsh things when they first disappeared. But time's gone by since then – no, I wouldn't turn them away. I'd expect an apology, mind,' he added with a return to his former grim tone. 'I'd want an explanation and a promise that nothing of the like would happen again. And I'd send Lucy away, to one of her married sisters, and then see if I could find some position for her somewhere as companion, or governess, for nobody would take her as a wife after this. But, no, I won't turn them out. Not if it will keep that smile on your face, my dear. And now, let's forget them for a while and consider our wedding trip. Would you like to know where we're going?'

Rebecca looked at him in surprise. 'I thought you wanted to keep it a secret.'

'I did, but I think you need cheering up.' He smiled at her, and she felt a sudden warmth towards him. This was Vivian as she liked him best – friendly, natural, without any of the deviousness she so often sensed in him. Like this, she thought, she could almost love him. Could – *would* – learn to love him.

'Where are you taking me then?' she asked. They had agreed on a month after the wedding, to go away and give the servants time to bring both houses back to normal and transfer those furnishings and belongings of Vivian's that he wanted moved to Pagnel House. 'What is the surprise to be?'

'Paris!' he said with an air of triumph, and laughed at her expression. 'Yes, a journey to France for your honeymoon trip. There are such sights to see there. The Cathedral of Notre-Dame. The Seine. The Louvre. Montmartre . . . oh, all the things you never dreamed you'd see.' He pulled her to him and spoke exuberantly. 'We'll have a real holiday, Rebecca, and forget all the worries and troubles you've suffered over the past few years. And when we come back, we'll start our new life together. I shall be Mayor then. There'll be balls, soirées, functions of all kinds to attend and to give. It's going to be very different for you then, Rebecca.'

'Yes.' She felt a sinking qualm. Was she going to be able to rise to all these occasions? Was she really going to be able to stand by Vivian's side and hold her head high, knowing that the whole of Kidderminster knew her origins?

And then she remembered her father, Will Himley, and the pride he had always taken in himself, in his family, in his trade. 'We're weavers, Becky,' he would say to her as she stood by his side at the loom, drawing first the sword and then the wire. 'And weavers don't have nothing to be ashamed of. We're independent people, weavers are, and as good as any man. And don't you ever forget it.'

No, Father, I won't, she thought now as Vivian painted the picture of her future life. This isn't what I ever expected, and you would never have dreamed of it. But I won't forget my early days. I won't forget you and my mother. And I won't forget the things you told me.

The ship had come through the Doldrums at last and was making good speed across the oceans. Matthew's hopes began to rise with the winds and he spent hours standing in the bow, watching the foam under the foot of the boat. Above his head the sails billowed, stained with salt and much mended but still able to fill with wind and drive the ship forward. Now and then they passed land – an island, like a jewel in the limitless sea – and sometimes they hove to and sent boats ashore for water and other supplies. And Matthew would watch in feverish impatience, anxious only to be on his way again.

'Only a week to go now,' Polly said as she came upon Rebecca sewing in the garden. 'Feeling nervous?'

Rebecca laid down her work. 'I seem to have been sewing for weeks,' she observed. 'There's no end to the undergarments I seem to need – chemises and petticoats, each trimmed with ribbons and lace and some even embroidered. I've never had so many in my life.'

'Well, you need 'em,' Polly said. 'Look at all the new duds you've got – a whole new wardrobe. You've bin in widow's weeds the last couple of years, after all. Can't expect Mr Vivian to want you to go about in black any more.'

'No, that's true. And fashion changes so quickly. I've ordered two of the new stiffened crinoline petticoats as well as some bustles. Skirts seemed to grow wider every year and look dreadful without the proper support underneath. If it goes on like this, we won't be able to get through doorways.'

Polly laughed. 'I've just seen your wedding dress. It looks lovely – you'll be a real beautiful bride. All that lace and satin – like summat out of a fairy-tale.'

Rebecca smiled, but there was a touch of sadness in her eyes and Polly sat down beside her and took her hands. 'Here, what's the matter? You ent heving second thoughts, are you?'

'No, not second thoughts. I just – well, I can't help remembering my first wedding. It was so different from this. That dark little church in London, and only Tom and Bessie and old Sal to witness it. And myself already heavy with Daniel ... And yet, there was so much love between Francis and me, it was as if we lit the church ourselves. We didn't need lamps or candles.' She looked down at the froth of lace in her lap and bit her lip. Where was the light and the warmth to come from in this marriage? It was true that Vivian could, on occasion, be warm and caring, as gentle as any woman could wish. Yet there was always that hint of darkness about him, that suggestion of forces it was better not to unleash. And there was the darkness of her own spirit too, the darkness he seemed to call forth. The sultriness of the flame that burned between them, whereas between her and Francis it had been so light.

'I'm being foolish,' she said at last, picking up her needle again. 'I expect it's what you said just now – I'm feeling nervous. Being married again . . . And Vivian is so different. But it's too late to back out now.'

Polly gave her a shrewd glance. 'It's never too late to back out, not if you thinks it's right to. What you've got to decide is whether it's just nerves or if you really feel worried about it. And if you do . . .'

'I thought you felt I was doing the right thing,' Rebecca said. 'When we talked a few weeks ago, you seemed quite positive about it.'

'Well, so I might be. But it's *you* has got to be sure, ent it? What I said was, nobody else can live your life for you. So you got to be sure yourself.' Polly cocked her head on one side, examining Rebecca's face. 'What is it, Becky? What's on your mind? Come on, we bin friends too long, you can't fool me.'

Rebecca laughed ruefully. 'No, I can't, can I? Oh, Polly, I don't know – it *is* just foolishness. It's not as if anything was ever said but – well, all these past few weeks I've had this strange feeling. A sense of – of something about to happen.'

'Well, so it is,' Polly said practically. 'You're getting married.'

'Yes, of course, but – well, it's something more than that. Something different. Something unexpected.'

'Well, let's hope it don't then. We've had enough unexpected things happen around here. Anyway, that's just spring. Always has that effect. It's all these flowers coming out and leaves on the trees and all that.' She looked around the garden.

'Your blood changes too. Enough to make anyone restless. I reckon that's all that is.'

'Perhaps.' Rebecca broke off a length of silk and threaded her needle. She hesitated. 'There's something else. You see, just lately I find myself thinking more and more about Matthew Farrell.' She gave her friend an apologetic glance. 'I told you it was foolish.'

'Mr Farrell?' Polly echoed. 'Him that was sent to Australia? But there weren't nothing between you and him, surely? He was Mr Francis's friend.'

'I know. And mine. And no, there was nothing *between* us – nothing but friendship. Nor ever would have been, I'm sure. And yet . . .'

'Yes?' Polly said.

'And yet . . . There was *something*. Some closeness – something that might, perhaps, have developed now. It never could while Francis was alive and neither of us would ever have wanted it to. But now . . . If only I could know, Polly,' she said, looking at the housekeeper with eyes as dark as chestnuts. 'If only I could know if it was really there, or if it's just in my imagination. It's so long since I saw him.'

'Aye, and what do they say? Absence makes the heart grow fonder,' Polly said. 'Look, Becky, don't you think it's just because he's so far away and you're never going to see him again? You liked him, and why not? Any woman would. And he liked you. But it might never hev bin any more than that. And now it *can't* be.'

'So why do I think of him? Why do I wonder – and wish? And what about this feeling I have, of something about to happen?' She moved restlessly. 'What does it all mean?'

'Wedding nerves,' Polly said firmly. 'No more'n that. Here you are, getting married to Mr Vivian and feeling a mite scared about it, just as anyone would. And there he is, away on the other side of the world so you can think about him, and wish, and still be safe –'

'Safe? Whatever do you mean – why safe?'

'Why,' Polly said, 'if he was here it'd be a different kettle of fish, wouldn't it? You'd hev to face up to it then, if there was anything. You'd hev to think about it and worry about it and make decisions. But as it is, you can't do nothing about it, so you'll go to the altar next Saturday and wed Mr Vivian and live as you know you're going to live. And you'll always hev that little bit of romance in the back of your mind, to give you summat to play with.' She shook her head. 'I told you, Becky, you can't fool me. I know you too well. You need your bit of romance, and why not? Don't do no harm.'

Rebecca gazed at her. Was Polly right? Was this the only reason why her mind went more and more often to Matthew, why her heart was so uncertain? Did this longing for something that might have been exist only because she knew it could never be – to give her something that, deep down, she knew she would never have with Vivian?

A 'little bit of romance to play with'? Was that really all it was?

The ship docked at last in Portsmouth Harbour, and Matthew stared out at the dancing blue waters. After Sydney, it seemed a tiny space, a minute haven, yet it was one of the most important harbours in the country, one of the havens from which the ships of Her Majesty's Navy sailed. He could see their masts now, a black tracery against the May sky. And he could see the prison hulks, rotting where they lay yet still housing a seething mass of despairing humanity. The 'criminal class' which transportation was supposed to end, yet which still came heaving to the surface of the society which bred it.

It was difficult to believe that he was here again, a free man instead of the shamed convict who had shambled in chains through the streets to the jeers of those who had come to stare. Difficult to believe in the years that had passed since then. The long voyage, so much of it cramped below decks in stinking darkness. The arrival in Sydney, the toiling in the bush, the floggings, the hangings, the transportations to Norfolk Island. Oliver . . . Cathy . . . A life gone by, a life in the past. Difficult to believe that they were still there, eight thousand miles away, going on with the life he had abandoned. Simeon and Rose were still working the farm, Cathy and John probably married by now. And he?

Why had he come all this way? He had felt Rebecca's need reaching out to him across the oceans, had known he must answer that need. But why should he suppose that she needed him still? Her letter had been written months before – a hundred things might have happened since then. The business in collapse, as she had feared, and by now beyond all help. Or some other rescuer come forward, setting the business on its feet and even now taking his place at Rebecca's side . . .

Matthew recalled Rose's words, spoken one evening on the verandah. Rebecca might marry again, she had said, might find some other man willing to take on her burdens. At this very moment, she might be wife to some other man, and once again out of Matthew's reach.

Hastily though he had travelled, he might yet have been too slow.

Almost mechanically, Matthew set about arranging his journey to Kidderminster. His heart, which had never quite ceased to hope during all the long, weary voyage, seemed to have lost its vitality, yet he could not turn back now. There was still a chance. It was only a few days to Kidderminster now. In a few days, he would be there.

He would know the truth as soon as he saw her. He would know at once if she loved him.

'So,' Vivian said, 'this is to be our last day apart. Tomorrow we'll be husband and wife.'

Rebecca gave him a quick smile, then looked away across the fields where they were walking. The last day of May . . . The sense of anticipation she'd had all month seemed after all to have been her imagination. Nothing had happened. Only the preparations for her wedding, going forward as inexorably as the seasons themselves, immutable, unchangeable.

If only there had been a letter. If only she could have had Matthew's good wishes. She had a sense now of something unfinished, of words left unspoken. And the helplessness of knowing there was nothing she could do about it.

'Rebecca, you're not listening,' Vivian said, and she jerked back with a start to the present. 'I was asking if you had everything prepared for the journey? We'll be leaving early on Sunday morning.'

'Oh, yes. Yes, everything's ready and Polly will take care of the last-minute details.' She frowned and gave him a hesitant glance. 'Vivian, I still can't feel happy about it. Leaving the country when we still don't know where Daniel and Lucy –'

He flicked his hand in exasperation. 'And what difference does it make which country we're in? We won't know where they are whether we're here or on the moon. We don't even know which country *they're* in – why, we might walk down a street in Paris and find them there! It's as likely as running into them in London.'

'I know.' She said no more, not wishing to anger him. It was weeks now since they had talked properly about the two runaways. Indeed, there was nothing more to be said. Vivian had, she knew, made every effort to trace them, without success. He could hardly scour the entire country.

For a little while longer she and Vivian walked together, but soon it was time to turn back for home. For the last time, they parted at Rebecca's door, to go to separate homes. Tomorrow, they would be husband and wife, bound until death.

Rebecca stood at the window watching Vivian walk away down the hill. And once again had that sensation of something about to happen.

'A last touch here, madam.' The dressmaker twitched a fold of material into place and then stood back, regarding Rebecca critically. 'Yes, that's perfect. Perfect.'

Rebecca looked into the long mirror. Her face looked back at her, strange in its setting of satin and lace. As a widow, she had chosen pale, silvery grey rather than bridal white. Against it her tawny hair was a rich, glowing bronze. Her face was pale and her eyes burning brightly, almost as if she had a fever. But when Polly laid a hand on her forehead she shook her head.

'You're as cold as ice. You look lovely, but you need some colour in those cheeks. Wait a minute –'

'Not rouge,' Rebecca protested as Polly picked up a small pot. 'Vivian will hate it.'

'Vivian's not your husband yet,' Polly said grimly. 'And if you take my advice, you'll not let him rule you – not about the way you look. It's the only thing you'll hev left. Anyway, he'll never know. Just a spot here and here, well rubbed in . . . there, now don't that look better?'

'Yes, it does,' Rebecca admitted, looking again into the mirror. 'I don't look quite so much like a ghost.'

'And he'd rather hev you looking like that, I'll wager. Here, a touch on your lips'll make a difference too. And now I can hear the carriage at the door. It's time to go.'

The two friends stood quite still for a moment, looking at each other. Suddenly, Rebecca was aware that this too marked the end of an era. She and Polly had been friends for so many years – ever since that first day when she had come as a frightened little scullerymaid into the very kitchen where Polly now ruled. And they had maintained their friendship even though Rebecca was now Polly's mistress. They had never lost their easy familiarity, their plain speaking together. And Rebecca had never seen any need to change in her manner towards the other woman.

But now, things were going to be different. Vivian would be here, master of the house. He would not look kindly on Rebecca's friendship with a servant, even if it were the housekeeper. He would expect a certain formality.

There would be fewer easy chats by the fire. Fewer confidences made, less advice given. Their talks together would be concerned more with household matters, less with intimate ones.

Rebecca felt suddenly frightened. What would she do without Polly's sturdy commonsense? How would she manage without Polly to laugh her out of her anxieties?

'Now don't look like that,' Polly said roughly. 'I know just what you're thinking, and it's daft. I'll still be here, same as always, and there'll be plenty of chances to hev a chinwag. You go off, now, and get yourself wed and I'll be there in the church to make sure you do.'

Rebecca laughed a little shakily. 'You're very good for me, Polly,' she said, and leaned forward to kiss her friend's cheek. 'You always have been – ever since that first day.' She stopped, knowing that tears were threatening, and managed a watery smile. 'You'd better go at once, if you mean to be in church before me. And – wish me happiness.'

'You know I do,' Polly said, and her mouth twisted downwards suddenly. With a quick, jerky movement, she turned away and went to the door. And then stopped and looked back, and Rebecca saw that there were tears in her eyes too.

'I wish you all the happiness in the world,' she said. 'I always hev.'

Matthew heard the bells pealing as his hired carriage rolled at last into the square in Kidderminster. Barely noticing them, he leaned out to give the driver instructions for finding Mount Pleasant and the house that stood at the top. He scarcely registered the number of carriages that stood outside the church. Some society wedding, no doubt. Some pretty young girl, being married to a bachelor she had hardly spoken to, chosen for her by her father. Or maybe some couple who truly loved each other, who were setting out to be partners on a journey through life together. As might he and Rebecca be doing, as soon as he could convince her that it was right.

Would she be difficult to convince? He smiled a little, thinking of the pleasures of courtship. And then frowned. There would be other things to consider before that. Rescuing her business, helping her to find her feet again in a world that had knocked her down too often. Giving her the help and support he ought to have been giving her all these years, if only it hadn't been for that disastrous night when Bill Bucknell had been killed. The night when everything began to go wrong.

And now at last he was at the top of Mount Pleasant. The carriage turned up the drive, came to a halt at the steps. Matthew leapt out and bounded up to the door.

His pounding was answered by a housemaid he had never seen before. She stared at him.

'Oh, sir, you shouldn't hev come here yet. They're all still down at the church. Madam's only just left.'

'The church?' he repeated. 'Why at the church?' He remembered the bells, scarcely heard, the carriages he had ignored. 'Is – is there a wedding?' One of Vivian's daughters, he thought. Susan – hadn't Rebecca mentioned her engagement in one of her letters? Or Lucy. 'Who's being married?'

The girl's eyes opened wide. 'Don't you know, sir? Isn't that why you're here?'

'Why I'm here? Of course it isn't – I knew nothing of any wedding.' Behind her, he glimpsed a hall filled with flowers, with decorations. Other servants, hovering in the background, listening. And a terrible suspicion gripped his heart. '*Who is being married?*' he demanded, fighting a desire to shake the information from her. 'Tell me – tell me quickly, for God's sake!'

The housemaid took a step backwards, clearly afraid that she was dealing with a madman, and an older woman came to take her place. She looked at Matthew and he stared back, dimly recognising her. But she hadn't been as stout as this when he had seen her last. She hadn't been as grey . . . '*Polly!* Thank God for someone with some sense. Now, tell me, *who is being married?*'

'Oh, sir,' Polly said, and her hand went to her throat as she stared at him with eyes that were filled with pity. 'Oh, sir, I'm that sorry. It's Becky that's being married, sir. Rebecca. She's marrying Mr Vivian – and I ought to be there to see her do it. Would hev bin too, if it hadn't bin for summat going wrong in the kitchen . . .' She gazed at him and he saw the tears blur her eyes.

Matthew barely heard her words, let alone understood them. With a terrible feeling of doom and loss in his heart, he swung round and hurled himself back down the steps and into the carriage. Polly followed him and he leaned out and gripped her arm, hauling her into the carriage with him with as much ceremony as if she were a bag of coal. He leaned out again and shouted at the driver. 'Back down the hill, as fast as you can make it. To the church – we may yet be in time!'

'And what do you mean to do?' Polly asked from the corner where he had flung her. 'Take her by force? Because he won't let her go now, you know. Not now he's got her at last.'

Matthew turned and stared at her. 'Not let her go?' he demanded. 'When she belongs with me? We'll see about that, Polly – mark my words, we'll see about that.'

Rebecca walked slowly up the aisle. Her hand was on William's arm, her eyes fixed on the man who stood in the front pew. She was scarcely aware of the people who thronged the church, of the colours of the women's gowns, the sombre black of the men's coats. The thunder of the organ sounded in her ears but she barely heard it. She was aware only of the thumping of her heart and the feel of William's sleeve beneath her fingers.

As she approached, Vivian turned and stood tall and dark, looking down into her eyes. She felt a qualm within her and quelled it, returning his look with her own steady gaze. Softly, she laid her hand in his and knew it was a promise, and then the wedding service began.

It was done almost before she knew it. The words, the prayers, the hymns. The signing of the register – a new innovation since her first marriage, when there had been no such thing. The certificate that was given to her, to prove her marriage. And then Vivian's kiss, his first as a husband – and the walk down the aisle as a different person. As Mrs Pagnel still – but Mrs Vivian Pagnel. No longer Mrs Francis.

She felt a sense of grief, of betrayal. But what else could I have done? she asked her dead husband. What else, to keep the business, to give the weavers employment, to keep a roof over my head and the boys'?

And even that had not been achieved. Even this morning,

she had still hoped that Daniel might appear, that he might have forgiven her and returned to lead her up the aisle in place of William. Even now, as she came out of the church on Vivian's arm, a little dazzled by the sunlight, she searched the faces of the crowd, hoping to see him amongst them.

And found herself looking instead into a different pair of eyes. Bright blue eyes in a lean, tanned face. Eyes that were accustomed to dancing but were now wide with shock. Eyes she had never expected to see again in this world.

Matthew . . .

Chapter Nineteen

'The truth! I want the *truth* – not a set of half-lies and evasions.'
Vivian paced the room, then swung back from the window
and confronted her. Outside, Paris bustled past, a medley of
sights and sounds that should have been exciting but were
now terrifyingly alien. They had nothing to do with Rebecca,
nothing to offer her. If she ran out of this room, this strange
hotel, there would be nowhere to go, no one to turn to.

'Vivian, I've *told* you the truth – I swear it. Matthew and I
were never more than friends.'

'Friends? You expect me to believe that, after the way you
looked at him on our wedding day? Our *wedding* day, Rebecca!
You'd not been married to me above twenty minutes and yet
you could look at another man with your heart in your eyes,
and tremble at the sight. And you expect me to believe that
you were never more than friends – never lovers?'

'It's true,' she whispered, too exhausted to raise her voice
any more. It seemed that this quarrel had been going on for
as long as she could remember. Certainly it had begun as soon
as they had taken leave of their last guest and turned back into
the house together to start their married life. It had started that
night, continued as they began their journey next morning,
and followed them down to Dover, across the Channel and
here to Paris. And still Vivian would not believe her. Still, he
accused her of having betrayed Francis with Matthew.

'As if I'd ever have done such a thing,' she had protested
when he first made the terrible accusation. 'I loved Francis – I
would never have been unfaithful to him. How can you even
think such a thing, Vivian?'

'I can think it because it's obviously the truth,' he had retorted. 'Oh, you were very clever, Rebecca, very devious, I'll admit that. Nobody could have suspected at the time, though you were alone with him often enough, in all conscience. And helped him plan and furnish his house, too. Why Frank himself never realised, I don't know. And that's not all.' He stared at her. 'You had your own sister installed as his housekeeper – so that you could play your vile games with him secure in the knowledge that nothing would ever be said. Oh yes, I see it all now. Very, very clever indeed. But not quite clever enough.'

'It's not true,' she gasped. 'There was never anything improper between Matthew and me.'

'Then why did he come rushing back from the other end of the world to claim you?' he demanded. 'Why did he come to the church, as if he thought he could stop you marrying me? Why did he look as if you'd betrayed him? *And why did you look at him in the way that you did?*'

Rebecca gazed back at him and shook her head speechlessly. She could not answer his questions. She barely knew the answers to them herself. Why *had* Matthew come back? Why had he arrived at the church just as she has emerged as Vivian's wife? Why had he looked at her, as Vivian had noted, as if she had broken some sacred vow?

And why had she felt as if that indeed was just what she had done?

I never made Matthew any promises, she thought, but something inside her told her this wasn't true. Matthew and she had never been lovers, never even acknowledged or admitted to themselves that there might ever be love between them. But at some deep, unspoken level, each had known. A promise had been made, somewhere where their instincts had met. And that was why she had been so uneasy about her marriage. Why she had had that feeling of waiting, that sensation that something was going to happen. Somehow, she had known Matthew would come. Something inside her had known that she should wait.

'Vivian,' she said now, 'what is the point of questioning

me like this? I can never give you any other answer, because there's no answer to give. And in any case, I'm married to you now. What possible threat can Matthew pose?' She moved towards him, hands outstretched. 'Vivian, he came back to Kidderminster simply because he was given a pardon. It's his home. Why should he not come back?'

'I thought he was staying in Australia. You told me you never expected to see him again.' Vivian twisted away from her and scowled down into the narrow street. 'A fine way to begin a new marriage!' he said bitterly, 'with the knowledge that my wife is a whore.'

'*Vivian!*' Sudden fury gripped her and she gripped his arm, pulling him to face her. Startled, he made no resistance and she confronted him with blazing eyes. 'How *dare* you call me that!' And with her other hand she slapped him hard on the cheek.

The sound of the slap was like the crack of a gunshot in the room. It was followed by a silence as they stared at each other. Vivian's face was white, the red marks on her fingers standing out like weals across the ashen skin. For a moment, his eyes were blank with shock. Then a glitter appeared and he reached towards her.

Rebecca backed away, suddenly afraid. She had always known that Vivian could be violent – she had experienced it herself as a young housemaid, when he had caught her in a dark corner and tried to force himself upon her. But she had thought those days past. Vivian had grown up, matured, become civilised. Was it no more than a veneer?

'You little wildcat,' he breathed. 'You little firebrand. Hit me, would you? Well, you'll find when it comes to strength of arm I can best you any day, my pretty little wife. My pretty little *whore* . . .' His narrowed eyes dared her to react with a second slap, but she didn't move. Her back was against the wall now and she could only stand there, looking up at him, helplessly pinioned. And as she watched his face, a new fear trembled through her body, and she knew that there was more than one kind of violence, and Vivian would be willing to use them all. And she knew just what kind he would employ to tame her now.

Oh no, she thought, not that. But as she gazed imploringly into his eyes she saw no mercy there.

Vivian laughed, as if he understood exactly what she was thinking. 'It's no use looking at me like that, Rebecca. I'm your husband now. Your body is mine to do as I like with, and no one is going to say me nay. Love you or beat you, it's all the same to me, and there's no one to hear you scream or come running to save you. So stay quiet, my love, while I take what is rightfully mine.' He shot out a hand and gripped her by the neck, his fingers and thumb pressing lightly but with menace into the soft flesh. 'And since you like to play the whore with other men, you'll play it with me too. No acting the prim little wife, lying still and submissive. I see no reason why I should miss the pleasures you can undoubtedly offer.'

He dragged her against him and one hand caught at her hair, dragging it back painfully so that her head was tilted towards his. As she opened her mouth in a gasp, he laid his own roughly upon it, grazing the softness of her lips with his teeth, forcing his tongue against hers. Rebecca whimpered and struggled in his arms, but he tightened his grip and shifted one hand to her breasts, squeezing them cruelly. His body was hard against hers, a barrier she could not escape, and as the assault of his mouth increased, she could taste her own blood.

'Vivian, please!' she gasped when he took his mouth away at last. 'You're hurting me – please let me go.'

'Let you go?' He laughed a harsh laugh. 'But I'm your husband now, Rebecca, remember? I'll *never* let you go. You're mine now – *mine*. After all these years, watching you with my mealy-mouthed cousin, thinking of you in his bed, in his arms, having to endure seeing you bear his sons – after all this time, you're mine! And I'll make sure you know it too.' He swept her suddenly into his arms and carried her through into the bedroom. He dropped her on the bed and she lay sprawled and breathless, staring up at him, gripped by a fear that threatened to choke her but conscious too of a fury that scorched her shuddering body. Trembling, she raised herself on one elbow and spoke through swelling lips.

'Don't you dare talk of my husband like that, Vivian! Yes – Francis, my husband, for so he was and a better one than you'll ever be. And a true gentleman too, which you'll *never* be, for under all your grand clothes and fine talk you're nothing but a brute, an animal.' He lunged towards her but she was crouching now and slid back on the bed, holding him at bay with outstretched hands, her fingers held out like talons. '*Don't come near me!* If I'm a whore, it's becoming your wife that has made me so, for I've never sold myself to any man before. Nor have I ever lain with any man but my husband.'

'Which you'll do again!' he snarled, catching her wrists and holding them up so that she could not reach him with her nails. 'And again, and again, as often as I please. *I'm* your husband now, Rebecca, which is something you seem to need reminding of. And I've rights over you and your body, rights you'll grant me whenever I demand them. As I'm demanding them now.' He stood over her, his bulk immense against the dim light, and she knew she had no armour against his strength. Nor would anyone agree that he was wrong to use it in the way he threatened. He was indeed her husband, and had every right to use her as he wished. It was her duty to submit.

Submit! Mere knowledge of the law was not enough for Rebecca's mind and body. Furiously, like the wildcat he had called her, she fought back, knowing that even though she must eventually lose the battle neither her pride nor her instinct would allow her to give it up. And so it was not until she lay exhausted and helpless beneath him that she finally succumbed, turning her head to one side and letting the tears ooze between her tight-closed eyes as Vivian thrust home his final assault.

It had never been like this with Francis, she thought. Never so rough, so angry. When Francis had kissed her, when his fingertips had moved over her body finding all the secret places that came to life at his lightest touch, it had been with a feathery gentleness that had brought its own excitement. Not this brutal handling that Vivian was giving her now, this painful squeezing and probing. And when Francis had covered her body with his, he had done so with a tender passion that had found its echo in her own eager response. Not this sudden onslaught, this cruel invasion that threatened to tear her body as childbearing had never done. Not this violent thrusting that scraped at dry, sensitive flesh; not this snarling desperation before he wrenched himself away and lay panting above her.

Rebecca lay still, feeling the tears trickle hotly from the corners of her eyes and into her tumbled hair. So this was to be her life from now on – this callous brutality, this savage onslaught that paraded as loving. Loving? No, the word had no place in Vivian's vocabulary. She doubted if he had ever felt love in his life.

And she had gone into this of her own volition. Never realising that in giving herself to him, she had cut herself off for ever from the man she really loved. Never realising that in making a promise to Vivian she was breaking a much deeper, more lasting vow.

Vivian's breathing quietened. He raised his head and she trembled, fearing another assault. Instead, he spoke, and his voice was harsh and bitter.

'You little bitch,' he growled. 'You think you can escape me, don't you? You think you can lie there and get the better of me. A whore? I've known better in the kindergarten. And don't stare at me with those great eyes, pretending you don't know what I'm talking about – *you* know well enough.' He lifted himself above her and she stared up at him, tensing herself for his invasion, knowing that already her flesh must be torn and bleeding. 'No,' he said, and smiled mockingly, 'you're safe for the moment, little bird. But I'll be back. And next time, you'd better remember a few of your old tricks, for I've not had to put up with a flour-bag in my bed since Maria died. And I don't intend to tolerate it now.' He lifted one hand, laughing as he saw her flinch, and stroked her cheek with a gentleness that was almost more frightening than the cruelty he had shown earlier. 'Not when I know there's a tigress lurking inside you,' he murmured softly. 'And there is . . . isn't there, Rebecca, my sweet? Or do I have to ask Farrell about that?'

He lifted himself away from her and stood up. His naked body gleamed with perspiration, the dark hair of his chest matted and wet. Rebecca watched as he went to the washstand and poured water into the bowl, sluicing it over his body. He rubbed himself with a towel and turned back to face her.

'Well? Admiring your husband? Proud to have married such a man?' He glanced casually into the long cheval mirror in the corner. 'A better body than Frank's, eh? He was always a skinny fellow, no more than a yard of pump-water when he was a boy. I never could understand what it was drew you to him – mealy-mouthed . . .'

'*I told you!*' Rebecca was up again, ignoring the soreness of her body, crouching on the bed. 'Don't talk of Francis again in that way or I swear I'll tear your eyes out. And be glad to do it too. He was my husband and I loved him – and he loved me too, which is something you know nothing about. Yes, love. Francis could love me so that I thought I was flying. He could touch me and take me to the stars. He could kiss me and make me melt. And you can do none of those things!' Her eyes blazed with scorn, raking the body of which Vivian was so vain. 'Big and strong you may be,' she said, and her tongue lashed him like a whip. 'Big enough to beat me and crush me, if that's what you want to do. But you'll never tame me, Vivian Pagnel. And you'll never make me love you. Because you don't know how. And you never, never will.'

Vivian stared at her. His face was suffused with anger. He took a step towards her and she forced herself not to cringe. Fear was what he wanted from her, she realised, not love. And she was determined now to give him nothing, nothing beyond her wifely duty. Submission, yes, for that was what she had promised him when she had signed her marriage certificate. But fear – no.

Vivian halted, almost as if something in her face, her proud bearing, stopped him. He hesitated, then turned away.

'Whore's talk!' he sneered, and began to drag on his clothes. 'Just what I might have expected from a woman who grew up in the slums. Well, I'll tell you what I'm going to do. I'm going to go out and find myself a *real* whore. A nice willing doxy who knows what a man wants and knows how to give it to him. Paris is the place for them, so they say, and I mean to find out for myself.' He came over to the bed and pushed her so that she fell back on the tumbled sheets. 'And then I'll tell you exactly what I expect of you. And you'll do it! Make no mistake, Rebecca, you'll do it.'

He slammed out of the room and she turned, burying her face in the sweat-stained pillow. She let the tears come again, soaking the already damp sheets, and sobbed out all the turmoil and pain of the past few days. Of the months; of the years.

What had she done with her life? Francis was lost to her and Matthew come back too late. And she was trapped, locked into a cage with a man she hated and feared, a man who had shown himself now in colours more terrible than any she had imagined. She had condemned herself to a life of misery, and for what?

The weavers would have found work. William could have gained a position with any of the other manufacturers. And Daniel would never have run away. He and Lucy would have been in Kidderminster still, with their own happiness ahead of them.

And if she had been forced to sell Pagnel House, if they had been reduced to living in a smaller house, with fewer servants, with none of the luxuries they had grown accustomed to – would it really have mattered? She and Francis had lived modestly in London and been happier than at any time since. Had she forgotten that contentment came from other things than wealth?

Why had she not listened to her heart – to those instincts which told her to wait, that something else, something better and truer, was on its way? Why had she not waited for Matthew?

But she had never known he was hers to wait for. She had never known he would return.

Matthew used the month while Rebecca was in France to open up his own house. It had been closed all the years he had been in Australia, with only a caretaker to look after it, and was sadly in need of repair and refurbishment. Dealing with this took up much of his time, but there was plenty left for brooding and for wondering just what had been happening, and he went to Polly to find out.

'It's all my fault,' the housekeeper told him miserably. 'She *said* she weren't sure. She said she felt she ought to wait. And I told her it was just wedding nerves. She was doing the right thing by everyone, I said, and Mr Vivian was a fine figure of a man, she'd be the envy of Kidderminster. And when I saw her look at you when she come out of the church and saw you there . . .' She shook her head and the tears rolled down her cheeks. 'A fine friend I bin to her,' she said bitterly. 'I ruined her life once by letting her little boy drown and now I've done it again.'

'Polly, I'm sure you don't need to blame yourself,' Matthew said gently. 'If Rebecca is as I remember her, she'll have made up her own mind. And not just for her own benefit, either.' He hesitated, then asked, 'Did – did she seem as if she loved Vivian?'

'I dunno. I really don't. He's bin a good friend to her over the years, I can't say he hasn't, and I think that was all a part of it. But love?' Polly shook her head again. 'We did talk about it once. I told her she had to forget all that and settle for what most women got out of their marriages – she just wanted a bit of romance to play with.'

'I probably would never have been able to return, if it hadn't been for a man who had a grudge against me,' said Matthew. 'Life works in a very strange way, Polly. I was sent to Australia for killing one man by accident, and I came back through killing another quite deliberately. But tell me about the fire, Polly. How did that happen? And was the business really failing before then?'

'Oh, yes, though Becky'd never admit it.' Polly told him about Rebecca's struggles to keep the co-operative going, the strange loss of orders for which Tom had blamed Vivian. Her journeys to gain new orders and better terms for raw materials. Her return to find Tom and Vivian at loggerheads. And, finally, the fire itself.

'That was the last straw,' she said sadly. 'She still tried, of course, Becky was never one to give in. And the men tried too – all turned to and cleared the mess up and started to build the place up again. But anyone could see Becky couldn't go on like that for long, paying them with no money coming in. And she wanted to do right by them, so when Mr Vivian made his offer . . .'

'You mean he offered work for the men, if she would marry him?'

Polly looked at him, startled by the tone of his voice. 'Well, I suppose it did amount to that,' she admitted. 'But he wrapped it up different, like. And there was the boys too, and Tom – not that Tom would give him the time of day, see him in prison first.' She paused. 'You did hear as Tom blames Mr Vivian for the fire? Swears he saw him there – reckons he started it deliberate.'

'*Deliberately?*'

'That's right. Tom was just going round by the building that night, see – saw the fire get hold and says he saw someone nipping off down the alley away from it. And he reckons that must hev been the man who started it, otherwise why not raise the alarm? Nobody else did, only Tom.'

'And he thinks that was Vivian?'

'Swears it was. Only he's bin so affected by it – losing his Nancy and all – that everyone just thinks he's raving. He and Mr Vivian hev always bin a bit at loggerheads, anyway. You know Tom didn't ever want to come back to Kidder, not really, on account of what Mr Vivian might do.'

Matthew stared at her. 'But why was Nancy there?'

'Well, that's another thing, ent it? Tom blames hisself for that. Says he stopped overlong in the tavern and Nancy was round looking for him, thinking he was still at work. If he'd gone straight home, see, she'd never hev bin there. So he's got all that eating at him too.' Polly sighed. 'I don't reckon he'll ever get over it. He's going to carry it to the end of his days.'

And when Matthew talked with Tom himself, he agreed with her. He was shocked by the change in Rebecca's brother. Once big and broad, he seemed to have shrunk, his skin hanging on him as if it were an oversized suit of clothes, his eyes sunk into deep hollows in a sagging and wrinkled face. He moved lifelessly, as if nothing were worth doing, and it was only when Matthew mentioned Vivian that he came to life.

'That bastard! Done for my Nancy, he did, killed her as sure as if he'd strangled her with his own bare hands. Ought to be strung up, only hanging's too good for such as him. If only I had the chance, I'd show him.' His hands clenched and unclenched convulsively and Matthew watched him with dismay. It was easy to understand why Tom had been dismissed as a madman. There was an unnerving light in his eyes and a frightening wildness in his voice. Matthew could well believe that Tom might do murder if he came upon Vivian in the right circumstances.

But what of Rebecca? Polly had told him that Tom had refused to go to the wedding. Did he feel the same enmity towards her?

'Becky? She's no sister of mine,' Tom said shortly. 'Let us all down, she hev, marrying that bastard. I thought better of her than that. But she's like all the rest – eye out for the main chance, selling herself to the highest bidder. Saying it was all for the weavers and the boys – and me. *Me!* As if I couldn't look out for meself. As if I couldn't hev found good work with any manufacturer in Kidder. I told her, I don't need no sister fixing my life up for me. Nor did none of the others either, for all they thought she was a queen. They'd all hev bin all right.

Whoever bought the carpet-shop would hev taken 'em all on, stands to reason.'

It didn't stand to reason, Matthew thought. There were still plenty of weavers out of work in Kidderminster, just as in every other carpet manufacturing town in England, and in Scotland too. And neither Vivian nor any of the others were likely to employ a man out of sentiment.

But it was useless to argue with Tom. He was clearly in the grip of a gnawing bitterness that he would not let go. Or perhaps he didn't want to let it go. Perhaps, without Nancy and without the carpet-shop, it was all he had left to live for.

Matthew sighed and left him, thinking again how strangely life worked. If Tom had not feared and hated Vivian for what had happened all those years ago, when he and Bessie had fled to London, he would not feel this bitterness now, not be so ready to accuse Vivian of setting fire to the carpet factory. If Jabez Gast had not been killed – if he hadn't raped Bessie that night – there would have been no cause to flee. And if it had not been for the conditions in the carpet factory, the twelve and twelve system that forced young girls to work the night through, none of it would have happened.

Like so much else, he thought as he walked slowly by the turbid river, it all came down in the end to greed. The greed that incited manufacturers to extort every last ounce of work from their employees, while paying them as little as possible. The greed that kept the wealth of the country in just a few pockets, while the masses starved and were forced into crime in order to live at all. The greed that had transported thousands of petty criminals to Australia, to leave England a 'cleaner' place to live.

And we are all victims of it, he thought. Tom, feeding on the anger that he's carried inside him since he was a young man, forced to live upon his sister's earnings from prostitution. Rebecca, impelled into a marriage that must be a disaster, because she carried the responsibility for so many lives. And myself, driven to commit murder and then returning at last to find the only woman I have ever loved, lost to me . . .

He turned his steps back towards his own house, the house he and Rebecca had planned together. What was the use of opening it up, making it fit to live in again? Did he intend to stay in Kidderminster, watching Rebecca as she moved through life belonging to another man? Wouldn't it be too painful to bear, knowing that she loved him as he loved her, knowing that their love could never be?

He thought of the day of her wedding, when he had arrived in a breathless agony at the church door only to find that it was closed against him. The wedding had begun, and he had no way of stopping it. He could not declare an impediment, for in law there was none. He could only wait, staring with anguished eyes at the big wooden door, waiting for it to open and Rebecca emerge.

As all too soon it did. He watched it swing inwards, saw the darkness inside lit with the colours of the women's gowns; saw the centre of all attention – the newly married couple. Vivian, tall and complacent in his black frock coat, his top hat held under his arm. And, on his other arm, Rebecca in silver grey, her tawny hair piled high upon her head.

Their eyes had met at once. It was as if she had known he must be there, as if her gaze was drawn immediately in his direction. He saw the shock on her face, almost heard her quick intake of breath. He saw those great dark eyes widen, grow darker still. He saw the awakening in them; the recognition and the realisation of love.

And he had seen Vivian turn to her, aware that something had happened. He had seen Vivian's eyes too turn in his direction, and had seen the dawning knowledge there too.

Matthew sighed and stopped on the little bridge, watching the murky waters flow beneath bearing silt and sediment from so many industries that let their waste flow into it. It would have been so much better if Vivian had never known. Matthew had seen the expression in the other man's eyes as he looked from his new wife's face to Matthew, and he had feared for Rebecca.

What was happening to her now?

411

* * *

Rebecca and Vivian returned to Kidderminster on a hot day in early July. The streets were quiet as the coach rattled into the square, and their luggage was transferred quickly to their own carriage, already waiting for them. There was no unexpected arrival here; Vivian had sent word ahead and all would be in readiness.

Rebecca gazed out of the window as the carriage mounted the hill. Kidderminster looked much as usual, and why should it not? They had been away only a month. But somehow she felt as if a lifetime had passed since the day they had been married. She felt older, as if she had passed through an experience that had changed her for all time. And so it probably had, she thought ruefully, and wondered what a lifetime with Vivian would do, if this was the result of the first month.

Well, she was likely to find out – if she survived it. And that itself seemed doubtful, since Vivian was determined that she should bear him a son.

'Why else do you think I married you?' he had taunted her one night as she lay in the bed that had become a battleground. 'You're a good breeder – you've had three lusty sons, with no trouble. Fine, well-grown, intelligent sons too, though headstrong and foolish in Daniel's case. But that can be beaten out of them early enough. While that whey-faced Maria could never manage more than simpering girls. And if you could do it for Frank, you can do it for me, aye, and more. Proud as you are of his sons, mine will be twice the men and worth twice the pride.'

'Even though they won't be true Pagnels?' Rebecca reminded him. 'Daniel and William are descended from Jeremiah – they have Pagnel blood in their veins as well as Himley. Your sons will be half Himley too – common weavers.'

'That's enough!' His hand caught her a stinging blow on the cheek. 'My family is as good as any Pagnel. My mother's family have titles – what Pagnel has ever achieved that? As for the Himley part –' his teeth bared in a grin '–

I've told you, that can be beaten out of them. And will be.'

Rebecca was silent. The thought of Vivian fathering her children sickened her. She said quietly, 'I did not expect you to want more children, Vivian. I thought you were content with my own sons.'

'Your sons? Have you forgotten that Daniel has run away with my daughter – ruined her? Do you really expect me to offer him the advantages I was ready to give him, if he had shown himself responsible enough?' Vivian gave a short, harsh laugh. 'I'm afraid that young man has queered his pitch for ever, Rebecca. He'll never be welcome under my roof again.'

And under mine? Rebecca thought, but she only said, 'There's still William.'

'Aye, and a good enough worker,' Vivian acknowledged. 'But as headstrong as his brother, I've no doubt, when it suits him. Suppose he takes a fancy to one of my other daughters? Do I have to go through all this again? Or perhaps some other wild idea will enter his head. No, Rebecca, your sons have been brought up with too much laxity. They've been allowed their own way too much, and we now see the results. *My* sons will be taught correctly from the beginning.'

'But, Vivian.' She stopped. It seemed impossible now, but the thought of children had never occurred to her. At Vivian's age, with a quiverful of daughters, she had not expected him to want more. If he had, she would have expected him to look for a younger wife. And with her own sons already grown, their ability proven . . .

'Well?' he demanded. 'What were you going to say, Rebecca? Out with it – there should be no secrets between husband and wife.'

The irony of the remark twisted Rebecca's heart. No, there should indeed be no secrets between husband and wife – but that implied a loving relationship, not the legal ownership that Vivian seemed to think comprised a marriage. And even between lovers, she thought sadly, there were still sometimes

413

secrets. This very matter had almost driven her and Francis apart once.

'I'm sorry,' she said. 'I truly never thought you would want more children, Vivian, or I would have told you. But –'

'Told me what?' he demanded, and raised himself on one elbow to stare into her face. 'What have you kept from me, Rebecca?'

'I kept nothing from you deliberately,' she said. 'If I had known . . . Vivian, I had a difficult time when William was born. We thought we would lose him – for a time the doctor even feared for my life. And when it was all over, he told Francis that it was unlikely I would ever conceive again. And that if I did, it might kill me.'

She looked up at him and as she saw the expression on his face, her heart sank.

'He told you *what*?' Vivian said slowly. 'He said you would never conceive again? And you married me, knowing this, and never said a word? You let me give you a ring, give you my *name*, knowing you could never provide me with children – with *sons*?'

'I never thought you expected them,' she said desperately. 'Vivian, I'm not a young girl, with years of child-bearing ahead of me. I've had my family, and so have you. I thought –'

'You thought I would provide you and your boys with security. An inheritance for them to grow into, little though they deserve it. You thought I would give you comfort, put your business back on its feet, employ all your precious weavers, and call your sons mine, and never want any return for it all. You thought you could take what you liked and never give a thing. Well? Didn't you?' He gripped her bare shoulders, his fingers biting into her flesh, and shook her roughly. 'Isn't that what you thought?'

'No! No, it wasn't like that. Vivian, you begged me to marry you, you asked me over and over again.'

'*Begged* you? I've never begged any woman. I offered you marriage, Rebecca, *offered* it I say, because I pitied you. Yes, God help me, I pitied you. And I thought we could do well together. I thought you would give me what I wanted and in return I would look after you. Yes, and your blasted sons as well. And what have I got?' He shook her again and his face was distorted with his rage. 'I've got a virago who lets her temper fly when it suits her, but holds back from me in bed. I expected a tigress who I would enjoy subduing – and subduing again and again. I've got a bag of flour. I expected a woman who would look up to me, respect me, treat me as a wife should treat a husband – and I've got an iceberg who looks at me with contempt. As if you were better than me, Rebecca – you, a weaver's daughter who grew up in a hovel. You seem to think you've more cause to be proud than the man who has saved you from going back to that very hovel.'

'And perhaps I'd have been better off if I had,' she retorted. 'If there's one thing marriage has taught me, Vivian, it's that there are more important things than wealth and position, and having children just to carry on a line. I had my children for love, Vivian, because I loved Francis. Our sons grew from that love.' Afraid though she was, her eyes still burned with scorn. 'I thank God I shall never conceive your sons,' she told him. 'For they would come from hatred, not love, and that's a terrible legacy to hand on to a child.'

Vivian stared at her. His eyes were narrowed almost to slits, through which she could see the gleam of a fury so deep that she was struck with terror. His face was darkened with the blood that suffused his skin; his lips drew back, his nostrils flared wide and his breath came slowly and heavily.

'Never conceive?' he snarled. 'Never conceive my sons? We'll see about that, Rebecca. We'll see if that fool of a doctor was right. We'll try, shall we? We'll try to make you conceive.' She gasped as she felt his hardness against her and then cried out as he forced his way into her, thrusting against the tight, dry muscles that resisted him, battering himself into her body. 'I'll make you conceive, Rebecca,' he growled, shifting his grip to her buttocks and pulling her hard against him so that he could drive even deeper. 'I'll prove that doctor wrong. You *will* give me a son – you will – you will – you *will* . . .'

* * *

Polly was at the door to receive them when they arrived, with the rest of the servants lined up in the hall. They bobbed and curtseyed, the men bowing their heads as Rebecca and Vivian entered. Rebecca smiled at them and asked after their welfare as if she had been away for months; but Vivian was impatient, giving no more than a cursory nod, and ordered that the luggage should be unpacked and tea brought to the drawing room at once.

'I'm not satisfied with these people,' he said as soon as he and Rebecca were ensconced in the newly decorated room. 'You'll have to make some changes.'

Rebecca stared at him. 'Not satisfied? But they've served me well enough, all of them. What possible complaint can you have?'

'They're slack. You can see it in the way they move. I like a servant to move smartly, quickly, eager to do my bidding. Not the idle slouch that these fellows affect. And the maids – far too pert. A maid should be modest. Why, that little housemaid looked me straight in the eye, bold as a monkey, and as for the parlourmaid – she seemed to think me below consideration at all.'

'That isn't true! She was as modest as you could wish, that's all. As for the maids being pert – well, I'm surprised to hear you, of all people, complaining about that, even if it were so. I thought you liked a maid with a touch of fire in her eyes.'

Vivian gave her a cold glance. 'You forget yourself, Rebecca. You're not an independent woman now, free to utter any vulgarity you choose. You're my wife and I don't care to hear you speak in that way. I'll be glad if you give that maid her notice at once.'

Rebecca gasped. 'Her notice? But why? She's done nothing wrong.'

'Do we know that? In any case, we'll not take the risk. You've a son fast approaching the age at which a young man can easily be swayed by a pair of bright, saucy eyes, and I'm surprised you don't realise the dangers.'

'To her, rather than him,' Rebecca said with bitterness. 'Though I don't expect my son to behave in a manner –'

'One of your sons has already done so,' Vivian pointed out cruelly. 'And William's a lusty youth, he'll be no different. You seem to have scales on your eyes where those two young men are concerned, Rebecca.'

She was silent. Still nothing had been heard of Daniel, though she had hoped to find news of him on their return. She was beginning to give up hope now. Perhaps one day he and Lucy would return, or even write, but it would be in their own time and for their own reasons. They had hidden themselves well and did not intend to be found.

'So you'll dismiss the maid,' Vivian was saying. 'And engage one with a more modest demeanour. And you may as well warn the rest of the staff that I shall have my eye on them from now on. There have been several things I've noticed over the past few months and would like to see improved.'

'I've always been perfectly satisfied.'

'But you weren't brought up to this life, were you, my dear? You've learned well, I admit, but there are still a few rough edges which need to be smoothed.' He spoke with a certain relish, as though he looked forward to doing the smoothing. 'And it will help you to have the right servants, properly trained by a mistress who *does* understand these things.'

'So you are going to expect me to replace other servants as well,' Rebecca said tightly.

'Possibly, very possibly.' He smiled at her and she wondered how she could ever have been so mistaken as to take his smile for kindness. 'But we'll do nothing in a hurry. Just wait for a while, and watch. It may only be necessary to replace one or two of the key staff. The butler, for instance. The housekeeper –'

'But Polly's my friend! We've been friends ever since we first met.'

'And that was when?' Vivian asked smoothly, and Rebecca saw the trap he had driven her into.

'You know when it was,' she whispered, and then, defiantly,

417

'since we were servants together. Since I came to this very house as a scullerymaid.'

Vivian leaned back as if satisfied. 'Exactly. She's too familiar with you, Rebecca. How can she possibly treat you with the deference appropriate between a servant and her mistress, when she's seen you standing at a sink scrubbing dishes? *Friend!* It's ludicrous.'

Rebecca sat silent, trying to calm her thumping heart. She wanted to defy him, to tell him that this was her house, that she had been mistress in it for too long, that she would never dismiss a servant simply because he told her to do so. But she knew it was useless. The house was no longer hers – it was Vivian's. As were all the things in it. As were the servants. As was she herself.

Chattels, all of us, she thought despairingly. And whatever Vivian thinks I like best, he will destroy, because he's always wanted to possess me and he thought marriage would give him that right. And now he knows he never will.

Marriage might have given him her house, her body, all her worldly possessions. But nothing could give him her spirit.

'But why did you never write and ask my help?' Matthew asked. 'Why did you never apply for money?'

He had called one morning, hoping that it was safe to do so and knowing that Vivian was at his factory, where he spent every morning. The maid who had opened the door had looked uncertain but Polly herself had been passing through the hall at that moment and had taken him straight into the garden, where Rebecca was sitting in the shade of a large pear tree. And he had stood at the edge of the lawn for a moment before Rebecca saw him, gazing upon her with hungry eyes.

There was a book on Rebecca's lap but she was not reading it. Instead, she was sitting with closed eyes, a faint frown creasing her brow as if already she were weary. She leaned her elbow on the arm of her seat and her forehead on her hand, and her neck was bent as if it had no more strength to hold up her head. Her whole attitude was of dejection, and

Matthew felt a surge of love, tenderness and regret. Why had nothing come right for them?

He went forward quietly, but a small stick cracked under his boot and Rebecca jumped and looked round. For a moment, she stared at him, as unbelieving as if she had still thought him in Australia. Then he saw the shock in her eyes replaced by joy – and, as quickly, by fear.

'Matthew!' She glanced rapidly about the garden. 'What are you doing here?'

'I've come to visit a friend,' he said quietly. 'My dearest, most valued friend. Is there any harm in that?'

'No – yes – I don't know. Oh, Matthew . . .' She gazed up at him with luminous eyes. 'Matthew, I've wanted you so much . . . Does anyone know you are here?'

'Only the maid. And Polly.'

'Polly knows?' She relaxed. 'Then she'll make sure – I mean, if Vivian comes home she'll – oh, it's all so difficult. Matthew, I don't know how to tell you –'

'You mean your husband will be angry if he finds me here,' he stated. 'Then I shan't allow him to find me. But, Rebecca, do you really mean to say you're not allowed to receive your friends?'

'Only some of them,' she said wryly. 'Those he doesn't approve of – which means almost all my old friends. And especially you, Matthew.' She gazed at him, her eyes moving over his face as if searching, as if trying to store up every detail. 'But I can't give up my friends,' she said desolately. 'I can't give up . . . you. Not now that you're back. Oh – sit down here, beside me, and tell me how you are. How is it you were able to come back? How just at that time?' She caught his hands in hers, her eyes burning into his. 'It was almost as if I knew – as if *you* knew I needed you. If only you'd come sooner!'

He looked at her. 'I was right, wasn't I, Rebecca?' he said in a low voice. 'All those years I was away, whenever I thought of you – and it was often – I knew that I loved you. And slowly, gradually, after Francis had died, I began to feel that you loved me too. I told myself it was nonsense – my imagination – and in any case I didn't believe I'd ever be allowed to come back. But I was right, wasn't I? You feel it too.'

She nodded. 'I thought it was my imagination too,' she said softly. 'I didn't know what it was – just a sensation that something was going to happen, that I ought to wait. But I could find no reason for it. I couldn't see anything else to do but marry him. And then, on the very day, when it was all too late –'

'I came as fast as I could,' Matthew said, and she nodded again. 'Oh, Rebecca, Rebecca . . .' He caught her in his arms and she rested her head on his shoulder as if she had done so all her life. He felt her slightness against him, the shape of her body fitting against his as though it had been made for that purpose, and he seemed to know it as if they had always been as close, as if they had known and loved each other before. In another life, perhaps; in a series of other lives.

Suddenly Rebecca drew away from him. 'Matthew, we mustn't.' Her eyes went to the house, to the windows that looked down over the garden. She took a breath, then went on rapidly, 'Tell me what's been happening to you, Matthew. Tell me about Australia.'

'No,' he said, 'you tell me first. Tell me what happened after Francis died. Tell me how you came to marry Vivian.'

She hesitated, and then began. He heard of Francis's death, of the difficulties she had begun to face, of Vivian's help and then his suggestion that he should adopt Daniel as his son. And, finally, of his proposal and their marriage.

And he asked her why she had never written to him for help. Why she had never asked him for money.

Rebecca gazed at him. 'Apply for money? But how could I? You were so far away – I didn't think you had access to your money.'

'Rebecca, I had a lawyer. Richard Godson, the man who should have defended me at my trial. He would have helped.'

'Mr Godson's a Member of Parliament now. He has been ever since 1832, when they reformed Parliament.'

'His partner, then,' Matthew said in exasperation. 'His firm still exists, doesn't it? Then he would still have helped you. Dammit, Rebecca – forgive me – he had my *instructions* to help you, should you ever need it. Francis knew.'

'But Francis was dead. And I didn't know.' She met his eyes and he saw that hers were drowned in tears, dark as forest pools shaded by the trees of autumn. 'If only we had understood each other, instead of only wondering.'

'If only either of us had had courage to speak the truth,' he said, and longed to take her in his arms again. 'Rebecca, tell me this, does he make you happy?'

He knew the answer even as he spoke. It was in her look, in her face, in the hands that he still held close in his own. It was in the fact that she could not receive her friends; the fear that sprang to her eyes whenever Vivian's name was mentioned. It was in the trembling of her lips.

A terrible despair gripped Matthew's heart. He wanted to carry her away, sweep her out of Kidderminster for ever. But all he could do was stroke her fingers, and tell her with his eyes all that his heart wanted her to know.

'I would have made you happy, Rebecca,' he said, and in the tremor of his voice heard all the yearning of his own heart. 'I would have lived only to make you happy.'

Chapter Twenty

'She's no sister of mine.' Tom started up out of his chair. 'I've told her that and she knows I mean it. 'Tis no use you coming here begging for her –'

'I'm not begging.' Matthew kept his voice quiet, knowing that it would do no good to anger Tom further. 'And Rebecca doesn't know I've come. I simply wanted to talk to you, Tom. We were friends, and it's a long time since I saw you. Sit down again, for God's sake.'

Tom glowered at him for a moment, then slowly resumed his seat. He looked at the empty grate, huffed a little, then spoke grudgingly.

'Well, I suppose I've no quarrel with you, after all. You did your best for us when you were here before, though it didn't do no one much good. How was it in Australia, then?'

'Not so bad, all things considered.' Matthew thought briefly of all that he had seen, suffered, even enjoyed, and knew that he could scarcely begin to recount it all to Tom. 'But it's you I came to talk about. How are you, Tom? I don't have to tell you how shocked and sorry I was to hear about Nancy.'

'Aye, 'twas a shocking affair right enough. A crime, that's what it was. Murder. And if I could prove it, if I could get anyone just to *listen* to me . . .' He stopped and fixed Matthew with a feverish stare. 'But they won't. They tell me I'm mistaken, I never saw anyone, I'm imagining it. But I'm not, I tell you. I know what I saw and I know who I saw, and one of these days I'll see justice done.' He lowered his voice and spoke as if confiding a secret. 'I'll tell you summat, Matt. I bin going to Town Bridge Chapel, down by Bull Ring

Street. And I learned a thing or two there.' He nodded sagely. 'Retribution. That's what Mr Vivian Pagnel got coming to him. Retribution.'

'You think so?' Matthew looked at him with concern. He knew that Tom had become a little strange – confused, Rebecca had said, downright mad had been Polly's opinion – but there was something more worrying in Tom's manner. He caught a flicker in Tom's eye and reminded himself to tread carefully. Tom was clearly very sensitive to his listener's reactions.

'You think I'm mad, don't you?' Tom accused him. 'Aye, I know, they all do. They'll have told you. Cracked as an old teapot, that's Tom. Well, and haven't I a right to be, seeing what's bin done to me and my poor Nancy? You didn't see her that night, all burnt and black. I did. I saw her.' His voice wavered and broke. 'I seen her every night since,' he said. 'I see her every time I shut me eyes.'

Matthew felt a wave of pity. Tom was right, he thought – he did have a right to be maddened by what had happened. And it was natural that he should look for someone to blame. But hadn't he mourned for long enough now? Wasn't it time he began to calm down, to accept the situation? It couldn't be changed, after all – was he to go on being mad for the rest of his life?

As Matthew's old nanny had told him when he was in a sulky mood – 'you'll get stuck like that one day if you're not careful'. Tom might 'get stuck' like this. And that would be another tragedy.

'Have you got work, Tom?' he asked. 'Rebecca's been worrying.'

'I told you, she's no sister of mine!' The fever was in his eyes again. 'And she's got no cause to worry about me, neither. She knows very well that if it weren't for her I'd still have me position in the co-operative. I wouldn't *need* to look for work.'

'But the co-operative factory was burned down,' Matthew said, and then bit his lip. He hardly needed to remind Tom of that.

But this time, mention of the fire did not remind Tom of Nancy. Instead, he leaned forward and said, 'And why did he hev to do that, eh? Why did he set fire to it? To get Rebecca to marry him, of course! That carpet factory would hev bin worth more to him standing than in ruins, but it were Becky he wanted. And as long as she had that, she could manage without him. Proved it, didn't she, by going off and getting all those orders?' He sat back and gave Vivian a triumphant look. 'Aye, there were only one way he could get her and that was by making sure she'd never weave another carpet.' He nodded, as if he had proved his case, and closed his lips.

Matthew stared at him. The trouble was that in all Tom's ravings there was a kernel of something that could very well be the truth. 'But why did he want Rebecca so badly?' he asked, thinking wryly that this was a question which he himself could answer with ease.

'Why? Why, she had everything he wanted, didn't she? Pagnel House, what he allus thought should be his, two sons already Pagnels, and a lot of customers he'd hev give his eye teeth for. Marry her and he'd get the lot. Simple as that.'

Yes, it certainly was simple – and Matthew found himself chilled by the thought. And Rebecca? She had married Vivian because there was no other choice. If only she'd known, he thought, what choice there was . . .'

'Tom,' he said, 'do you know how unhappy your sister is?'

Tom looked at him. 'Unhappy? Becky? When she's got everything anyone could ask for? Don't make me laugh!'

'She is,' Matthew insisted. 'Tom, you know she didn't marry Vivian Pagnel for love. She married him because she could think of no other way to keep her weavers in work and her sons fed and clothed. There was nothing left for her to do, Tom. She would have lost the house, everything.'

'She could hev come here,' Tom said. 'I would hev looked after her. I can still work, Matt – there's half a dozen manufacturers at this very minute after me to work for them. Head weaver, overseer – take me pick, I could. Becky wouldn't hev starved.'

Matthew looked at him helplessly. Were all these offers more figments of Tom's imagination? His pity increased. Was Tom to go on living here until his savings ran out – and then what? Who would employ him while he was still raving about Vivian Pagnel being a murderer, about retribution?

'Rebecca might not have starved,' he said quietly, 'but her weavers would have done. And that was her main concern.'

'And are they any better off now?' Tom demanded with an abrupt return to rationality. 'He's only took on half of them, from what I hear. What are the others doing, eh? Tell me that. Or ask Becky. She ought to know, seeing as she's so worried about them.'

Matthew rose to his feet. There was little more he could say. He looked soberly at Tom, who was staring once more at the empty fireplace.

'I have to go now,' he said gently. 'But I'll come again, if I may.'

'Aye,' Tom muttered without looking up. 'Come in any time, Matt. We was allus good mates. And I don't go out much these days, 'cept down the chapel. Does me good to hev a bit of a chinwag.'

Matthew moved to the door, then hesitated. But he could find nothing else to say and he turned to go, heavy at heart.

As he opened the door, he heard Tom's voice.

'Here,' he said roughly, 'you said Becky was a bit low. She – she's all right, ent she? I mean, she is, *really*?'

Matthew turned back and gave him a serious look.

'I don't know,' he said slowly. 'But I hope so. I very much hope so.'

'I'm sorry,' Rebecca said tensely, 'but you mustn't come here any more, Matthew. Vivian –'

'Has he forbidden you to see me?' Matthew reached out, but she moved quickly out of his reach. 'Rebecca, tell me the truth.'

She looked at him helplessly. 'He hasn't forbidden me, no. But I know that if he were to find you here – Matthew, he never stops asking me about you. Whether we were lovers before you went away. And when I tell him we weren't, he doesn't believe me. He asks why I spent so much time with you, why I helped you plan your house.'

'You helped him too. Don't you remind him of that?'

'Of course I do. But he says that was different, we were family, he'd been widowed. You're a bachelor and it was *unfitting* that I should behave in the way I did.'

'But it was none of his business!' Matthew said explosively. 'You were married to Francis – and he had no objection, he encouraged our friendship.'

'I know. But it's Vivian's business now,' Rebecca said dully. 'At least he considers it so. And if he came in and found us together . . .' She fell silent.

'Yes?' Matthew asked quickly. 'What would happen, Rebecca? What would he do?' He crossed the room swiftly and caught her before she could turn away, gripping her hands, looking down into her face. *'Tell me what he would do, Rebecca.'*

There was a long silence. Rebecca's eyes filled with tears. She turned her head away and he let go of her hand to turn it back. She met his eyes unwillingly, and the tears brimmed over. Her lips trembled.

'Rebecca,' Matthew said quietly, 'please tell me. Does Vivian ill treat you?'

She gave a little gasp, then said, 'You must understand, Matthew, Vivian has a different idea of marriage. He's not like Francis –'

'You mean he sees you as his possession, to do with as he pleases.'

'Most husbands do,' she said faintly. 'Most wives believe it too. We depend upon our husbands' kindness, Matthew.'

'And if they have no spark of kindness in them?' he demanded. 'If they don't even know the meaning of the word? Rebecca, *tell* me – does he ill treat you?'

'He does no more than a husband has right to do.'

'Rebecca!'

She flinched and he felt a spasm of remorse. As if she had

427

not enough to endure, without his haranguing. But he had to know.

'Please, Rebecca,' he repeated more gently and, with an agonised glance at him, she pushed back her right sleeve.

Matthew stared. The bruises were livid on her arm, the clear impression of fingers and a thumb. As he watched, Rebecca let the sleeve fall again and then raised her hand to her neck. She pulled the silk away from her skin and he saw the angry marks on her breast.

'The swine! The *bastard!*'

'Please,' Rebecca said quickly. 'Please, Matthew, you mustn't say anything. Not to Vivian – nor to anybody. There's nothing anyone can do. He has a right to beat me if he thinks I warrant it.'

'*Warrant* it? Rebecca, that's ridiculous! How could you possibly warrant –'

'Vivian believes I do,' she said simply. 'And no one would deny him the right to correct me.'

'*Correct* you? But what have you done? How can you need "correction"? The whole thing is outrageous.'

Rebecca looked at him sadly. 'I'm being corrected for my behaviour with you,' she said. 'Because you were outside the church on my wedding day, and Vivian saw the way we looked at each other. And he knew.' She laid her hands on his shoulders. 'We may never have been lovers in any worldly sense,' she said, 'but in the most real sense of all – the spiritual sense, the sense that lies in our hearts, in the very centre of our beings – we have always been lovers. And although Vivian would never understand it in those terms, he knows.'

'So he believes we must have been lovers in his sense,' Matthew said, and she nodded. 'And are – or would be – still.'

'And that,' she said, 'is why you must never come here again.' She glanced down at her arm, slipping the sleeve back again to show the bruises. 'Oh, not for these. These are nothing. But Vivian can hurt me in other ways, Matthew. He's already threatened to dismiss Polly. Or rather, to force me to dismiss her.'

'Polly? But why? What has she done?'

'Nothing, except be my friend. That's enough. You see, Vivian doesn't like me to have friends.' She turned away but not before he had seen fresh tears fall. 'I haven't done it yet. I've told him I won't do it without good reason. But I don't know how long I can defy him, Matthew. I thought I was strong, but –' Her voice shook and she covered her face with her hands.

Matthew put his hands on her shoulders and drew her back against him. 'Rebecca, what is it? There's more, isn't there? Tell me, my darling, for God's sake.'

She turned in his arms and he held her against him, gently for he knew there must be bruises she had not shown him. 'I must know, Rebecca,' he said, his cheek against her hair.

He felt her shudder against his body, and a rage filled him against the man who could make her fear like this. Not come here again! he thought furiously. Why, if Vivian were to walk in here now I'd kill him. I swear I would kill him.

'He wants a son,' Rebecca said tonelessly. 'He means to have a son, Matthew.' She looked up at him and he saw the whiteness of her face. 'That's why he wanted to marry me – apart from all the other things I had. He thinks I will give him a son, and he's doing his best to ensure it.'

There was no mistaking the horror in her eyes, and Matthew needed no imagination to picture what she was enduring night after night. He held her more closely, afraid to let her see the black fury in his face as he thought of it. It must be nothing short of rape – and she had known nothing but love before, nothing but tenderness.

'Leave him, Rebecca,' he said urgently. 'Come away with me. We'll go right away – to the Continent. Or back to Australia. It can be a good life there, Rebecca. I have my share in Simeon's farm still. We can be together, and I'll look after you well, I swear it.'

She drew away slightly and smiled but her eyes still swam with tears. 'I know you would. But how can I leave? There's William – and Tom. And all the others – Polly, the servants, the weavers. I can't do it. Vivian would take his revenge on every one. And perhaps I'll conceive after all, and bear him his son, and then he'll leave me alone.' Matthew gazed at her and knew she meant it. She still cared first and foremost for those whom she believed depended on her. She would not leave Vivian while he still wielded such power.

'Then is there nothing I can do for you?' he asked hopelessly, and wondered how he was to spend the rest of his life. If he were not to see Rebecca, except at a distance about the town . . . wouldn't it be better if he left Kidderminster, if he did indeed return to Australia?

Yet he knew he could not. While Rebecca lived, he must be near her. One day, she would be in need again, and this time he would be at hand.

'Yes,' Rebecca said, 'there is one thing you could do for me, Matthew. Or try to do.' Her eyes were sad as she said in a low voice, 'Find Daniel for me. Find Daniel and Lucy. And if you can't bring them home, at least make sure they are well.'

'You don't really believe she's betraying you?' Ben Messinger sipped his port and gave Vivian a sceptical glance. 'Why, you've not been married above three months. Surely you can keep a woman satisfied that long, Vivian?'

He flushed a dark, angry red. 'I'll thank you to keep your coarse comments to yourself, Ben. This is my wife you're talking about, not some slut from the streets. And this is no ordinary escapade. It was going on before he was transported.'

'But that was – how many years ago? Eight, nine? She was married to your cousin then.'

'Does that make a difference?' Vivian demanded. 'If a woman will betray one man, she'll betray another.'

'I still find it hard to believe.' Ben helped himself to a second glass of port. 'She doesn't seem the sort.'

'Not the sort!' Vivian snorted. 'Ben, you don't know Rebecca – she's deep. Devious. She'll look straight at you and tell you lies. I don't believe a word she says any more.'

Ben stared at him. 'But, Vivian, only three months wed.'

'I know. I made a mistake. I was sorry for her, I felt an obligation towards her. I wanted to help her.'

'And couldn't you have done that without marrying her?'

Vivian lifted his hands. 'With hindsight, yes, probably. But we do what seems best at the time, don't we? If I'd known Farrell was on his way back – if I'd known what had happened before – well, obviously I'd have acted differently. But there it is, what's done is done and now I have her on my hands and nothing to be done about it.'

'You won't allow her to cuckold you, though, surely?'

'I don't *allow* her to do anything,' Vivian said. 'She's my wife now and does as I say. As she's beginning to discover.'

They went into the drawing room where Rebecca was pouring coffee. She looked up and smiled, but Ben noticed the shadows in her eyes. He accepted the coffee, watching her and wondering.

Ben Messinger had known Vivian for a long time. He knew more about Vivian than any person living. He knew what Vivian had done as a boy, as a young man. He had been regaled with tales of seduction since they were old enough to know the meaning of the word.

He did not see Vivian as a cuckold, and he did not see Rebecca as an unfaithful wife. But he did see the darkness in her eyes, he did see the way she kept clear of Vivian as she moved about the room, and he saw the tremor in her fingers as she handed him his coffee.

If anything, he would have thought that Rebecca feared her husband – feared and yet despised him. And he wondered just why Vivian, who rarely admitted a rejection, should have taken such trouble to make sure that Ben knew of Rebecca's perfidy.

'Where could they have gone?' Once again, Matthew was in Unicorn Street with Tom. 'Have you no idea at all? Didn't they leave any clues?'

'If they did, I don't know what they were. I tell you, they just slipped away.' Tom shook his head. 'Mind, I don't blame 'em.

They knew what it'd be like once he married Becky. And they wanted to get wed themselves – thought it'd be impossible once they was brother and sister, in a manner of speaking.'

'They wouldn't have been brother and sister,' Matthew said impatiently. 'Would William know? He seemed to know they were going – didn't he have any idea where?'

'He wouldn't say.' Tom looked up at Matthew. 'I'm going to miss that boy, you know. Sending him off to school, they are – be gone in a week. School!' He snorted his disgust. 'What's wrong with the school here? He bin doing all right there. Any road, school ent no good for a boy like him. He wants to be in the factory, not behind a desk. His mother's right hand, he was, aye and mine too, afore that Vivian Pagnel stuck his oar in.'

'Perhaps I'd better talk to him. If he's going away in a week ...' Matthew got up. 'I'll go and find him at once. Where is he likely to be, in the factory?'

'Not likely – Vivian won't let him near the place now. You might as well sit down again.' Tom looked up as Matthew stood irresolute. 'Sit down, I tell you. You'll see him soon enough – allus comes in to see me of an afternoon. Didn't I say I'd miss him?'

'He's coming here?' Matthew took his seat again. 'Well, why didn't you say so?'

'I did, soon as I could,' Tom pointed out. He gave Matthew a sharp glance. 'Why are you so interested in them two anyway?'

'Because Rebecca asked me to try to find them. She's desperately worried about them, and naturally so – she knows all too well what it's like to be in a strange place without money or friends. As you do yourself,' he added.

'Aye, I knows what it's like. And I'd not like young Lucy to go through what our Bess did.' Tom was silent for a moment, then said musingly, 'It's funny what happens, ent it? Me and Bess driven away all them years ago and now Dan and Lucy running off just the same. Only they can come back any time, of course, and not be afraid they'll get a noose round their neck. And our Becky turning her back on all of us –'

'Tom, that isn't true! Rebecca hasn't turned her back on you. It's the other way about. You've turned your back on her, Tom, and just when she needs you most.'

'Needs me? Our Becky don't need me – not now she's one of the most important women in Kidder. She don't need no one now.'

'She does need you,' Matthew insisted. 'Tom, don't you know what's happening to her? Vivian's keeping her almost under lock and key. She's not allowed to go to the factory, she mustn't walk alone out of doors, her own friends are not even allowed to visit her. He's even pressing her to dismiss Polly – Polly, her friend from childhood. And you think she's turned her back on you all and doesn't need you? Tom, she's little more than a prisoner!'

'A prisoner? Don't make me laugh. Why, she could walk out of there any day she chose. She could tell Vivian Pagnel just what to do with his fine house and his fine servants. It's her house anyway, ent it? Left her by her husband.'

'And now Vivian's her husband. And owns everything that was hers. And that isn't all, Tom.'

Tom looked at him, evidently shaken by what Matthew had told him. In his world, husbands and wives were partners; there had never been any possessions to own anyway, beyond those needed for survival. And he and Nancy had followed the same pattern. To them, marriage had meant sharing.

'What else is there?' he asked a trifle sullenly.

'He's ill treating her,' Matthew said quietly. 'He forces himself upon her and he beats her, Tom. I've seen the bruises.' He took a small breath. 'I've seen *some* of them.'

There was a long silence. Tom stared at him. Matthew could sense the information clicking over in his brain, slotting in with the opinions already there, with information and misunderstandings that had tangled together over months, perhaps years.

'He knocks her about?' Tom said at last. 'Our Becky?' And

his eyes glittered suddenly, and his voice rose. And Matthew knew that he had made progress at last.

'I don't know where they went,' William said. He had come in half an hour later, surprised and pleased to find Matthew there and even more startled to discover the change in his uncle. Tom seemed to have come to life again. Gone were the sullen apathy, the resentful truculence. The anger was still there – the anger over Nancy's death, the talk of retribution. But instead of refusing to talk about his sister or her missing son, he was eager and anxious to hear what William had to say, peppering him with questions before the boy had even taken off his cap.

'You must have some idea,' he persisted. 'Dan talked to you. You knew he was planning to run off. Didn't he say nothing at all?'

'He mentioned America,' William said. 'I mean, he often talked about going there one day. He didn't say he meant to go with Lucy. I thought it was just an idea – I never thought he'd really go.'

'America?' Matthew said thoughtfully. 'Well, it's an idea. I wonder if they did. Would they have had enough money for the passage?'

William shrugged. 'I don't know how much they'd need. I don't think he had much money, anyway. I don't know about Lucy.'

'Rebecca seems to think not. Anyway, it ought to be possible to find out. But there's something else I think they'd have done first.'

Tom and William looked at him. 'What's that, then?'

'Why get married, of course. Wasn't that what they wanted? And weren't they afraid that once their parents had married, it would be forbidden? Surely that's the first thing they'd take care of. And in that case –'

'But they're too young to get wed!' Tom said. 'They'd need consent. No priest'd do it.'

'No,' Matthew said, 'not in England. But in Scotland . . .'

'*Scotland?*'

'In Scotland,' Matthew said, 'two people can marry at sixteen without their parents' consent. They have to live there for a while, if I remember rightly – a few weeks, no more. If Daniel and Lucy did that –'

'They could be man and wife by now,' Tom said. 'And on the other side of the Atlantic.' He shook his head. 'You'll never track 'em down now.'

'Perhaps not,' Matthew said. 'But I mean to try.'

'He's been here again,' Vivian said. He gripped Rebecca's arm and twisted her to face him. 'Tell me the truth! He's been here, hasn't he – you've been together, the two of you, laughing at me behind my back?'

Rebecca shook her head and tried to free her arm but he grasped it all the harder.

'Vivian, I don't know what you mean.'

'You know well enough, madam. That convict paramour of yours, Farrell. You've had him here again. D'you think I don't know when a man's been in my house? D'you think I can't smell him – his tobacco, the macassar he uses on his hair, the very stench of him? It's in the air I breathe.'

'Vivian, I swear to you that Matthew hasn't been in this house for weeks. It was Tom who came here this afternoon.'

'Tom? Your *brother*? But he's not spoken to you since before we were married.'

'Well, he's spoken to me now,' she said. 'He came to tell me he wanted to make up our quarrel.'

'And you, of course, were only too pleased to do so.'

'Of course I was. I've few enough friends left now.'

'And I suppose that's my fault?'

'Well, isn't it?' she flashed. 'Haven't you driven them all away – Matthew, Louisa, Margaret, all my friends? Even my son's being sent away to school. Do you begrudge me my brother too?'

Vivian jerked her wrist and brought her tumbling against him.

435

'I begrudge anything that keeps you from me,' he muttered, and spread his other hand upon her breast. 'I begrudge every moment of the day when you're not with me. I begrudge anything that might take your mind off me and prevent you from conceiving our son.'

'Vivian! I can't *think* myself into conceiving. I can't will it.'

'Can't you?' he snarled. 'You certainly seem to be successful enough in willing it *not* to happen!'

'I'm not –'

'Well,' he said, 'you're doing something to stop it. Or you'd have conceived by now and be swelling with him, and that would put an end to your capers. And I'll have no more of it, do you hear?' he shouted suddenly and thrust her suddenly from him, so that she stumbled and fell against a small table. 'I'll have no more of your games – you'll give me what I want, madam, even if it does kill you in the giving. Aye, and why not? Maria died for me that way – so shall you, if it has to be, but *you'll* do it giving me my son!'

Rebecca tried to rise but her back had been hurt by the corner of the table and the pain caught her unexpectedly. Before she could recover, Vivian had pushed her again and she slipped to the floor and lay headlong on the carpet. With a sound somewhere between a growl and a shout of triumph, he leapt forwards and straddled her, his hands at his belt.

Rebecca shrank and tried to wriggle away, but her clothes hampered her, the folds of her skirt tangling about her legs. She looked up, terrified, and saw Vivian kneeling over her now, his shirt loose about his thighs. He bent and fumbled with her skirts, ripping them above her waist, and she cried out as his fingers tore at her flesh. He mounted her and began the thrusting she dreaded so much.

'*Becky!*'

The name stopped Vivian short. He wrenched himself away from her, causing a tearing pain that she knew would bring blood and soreness later, and turned his head.

From her position on the floor, Rebecca could not see who had come into the room. But she knew the voice well enough and closed her eyes, knowing that her last source of support was now to be taken from her.

'What in hell's name are you doing here?' Vivian growled, and Rebecca heard Polly's answer.

'I came in to see what orders madam had for supper tonight.' Polly came forwards into Rebecca's view. 'Is everything all right? Has there been an accident? You're not hurt, are you?'

'No, she's not hurt,' Vivian snapped. 'Nor is she concerned about supper at the moment. Is there no privacy to be had in this house, without servants blundering in at any moment? I'd have thought you'd know better, Mrs Barlow, in your position.'

'And I'd hev thought you'd know better too, sir, in yours,' Polly retorted, with a look that told him she knew exactly what his position had been. She bent and helped Rebecca to her feet. 'You all right, Becky? You're all shaky. Let me help you to bed.'

'Leave her alone!' Vivian said furiously. 'And stop calling her by that ridiculous name. She's your mistress, have you no respect for her?' He turned on Rebecca. 'I told you the woman was too familiar. In fact, I told you to get rid of her. Why haven't you done so?'

Rebecca shook her head. 'Polly's the only friend you've left me. I can't –'

'Can't? *Can't*? Has she some kind of hold over you, is that it? Does she know something about you – something about your cavortings with your lover, perhaps? Does she connive at your meetings? Is that why you won't get rid of her? Well, if you won't do it, I will.' He turned to Polly. 'You'll pack your bags now and leave this house, d'you hear me? And there'll be no more whining about friendship. I'll not have you through the door again. Do you hear?' He took a step towards her and swung a large hand towards her face. '*Out!*'

Polly stared at him. 'You're mad,' she whispered. 'You've gone stark, staring mad.' She turned to Rebecca. 'I can't leave you here with him.'

'You'll have to, I'm afraid.' Rebecca summoned up the ghost

of a smile. 'Don't look so stricken, Polly. I'll be all right. What you saw wasn't so bad as it looked – just a part of married life, really.' Her smile trembled and her mouth turned down as if she were about to cry. 'Oh, Polly!'

Ignoring her employer, Polly stepped forward and took Rebecca in her arms. She held her close, murmuring words of comfort, soothing her with her hands. Her own tears flowed as well, soaking into Rebecca's hair.

'Where will you go?' Rebecca whispered at last. 'What will you do?'

'Don't you fret,' Polly said. 'I'll be all right. It's you I'm worried about.'

'Then you can stop worrying at once.' Vivian laid a hand on each woman's shoulder and dragged them apart. 'My wife will be well enough in my care. And I'll bring my own housekeeper over from the other house. We'll manage very well without you, Mrs Barlow. And now I'll be glad if you'd get out.' He pulled his watch from his waistcoat pocket. 'You have one hour. After that, I'll fetch the constable.'

'Vivian –' Rebecca began protestingly, but he turned on her and she was silenced by the threat in his eyes.

'It's time you knew,' he said softly, menacingly, 'that I mean to be master in my own house. Or do you want me to show you in some other way?'

'Tom, I'm glad you came.' Matthew lifted the decanter of brandy. 'Is it too early for you? You've had a long walk for a cold evening.'

'Aye, nights are drawing in now right enough.' Tom came over to the fire. He looked pitifully thin, Matthew thought, his trousers hanging loose on his shanks and his hands bony as he rubbed them together. He still spent most of his time alone in his house, brooding, and Matthew did not know whether he had looked for work or not. 'I came to tell you I bin to see Becky,' he said, warming his hands. 'This morning. I thought about what you said – thought about it a lot. And I reckon I was wrong.'

'Well, that's very handsome of you,' Matthew said. 'And I'm very pleased. We'll drink to it, eh?' He poured brandy for them both. 'And I've some news for you too. Good news.'

Tom sipped his brandy and coughed. He began to wander around the room, picking up oddments and examining them. Matthew watched tolerantly. He had noticed already that Tom's attention span was shorter these days. Shortened by shock and grief, he thought, and prepared himself to wait until the other man was ready.

'What's this? Summat from Australia?' Tom was staring at a large, heavy object that could have been wood but might as easily have been some strange, rough stone. It was pocked all over with what appeared to be eyelets. 'Looks like a giant bullet.'

'Yes, it does, rather.' Matthew took it from him. 'It's a seed-pod from a tree. See, all these small pods hold seeds and when they're ready they pop out. On the tree it's a large flower, like a brush, covered with narrow red or yellow petals. Quite attractive.'

Tom stared at it, then lost interest. He moved on around the room, touching the assortment of souvenirs that Matthew had brought back from his travels. A miniature totem pole from America. A piece of glass from Venice. A lump of volcanic lava from some Italian mountain. And a case in which lay two silver pistols.

'Here,' Tom said, 'this ent the gun you –'

'Shot Bill Bucknell with,' Matthew said quietly. 'Yes, I'm afraid they are. Or one of them is. Don't touch them, please, Tom. I still keep them loaded – just in case. But I don't intend ever to use them again, and I don't like them to be taken out of their case.'

'Better if they was kept under lock and key then,' Tom commented, and put the case down again. 'So what's this news you got for me then?'

'Ah, now that's something of real interest.' Matthew's face lit up and he drew Tom away from the little table and over to his big bureau. 'Look at this. You know I've sent out enquiries for Daniel and Lucy? I've written to old friends and contacts all over the north of England and in Scotland – a man in Edinburgh I knew years ago, and another two or three in Glasgow and along the borders. With most of them, of course, I've drawn a blank – but today I received this letter.'

He took out a sheet of paper and flourished it before Tom's eyes. 'Read that.'

Tom took the letter and perused it slowly, his lips moving silently with the words, while Matthew waited impatiently. At last he looked up.

'It says here he knows our Dan,' he said in a tone of wonder. 'Says he met him *and* young Lucy, when they was staying in a village nearby. He says they got themselves wed in the local kirk – what's a kirk? – and then set off down to Liverpool to wait for a passage to America.' He laid the paper down and stared at Matthew. 'Got wed in a kirk? Would that be legal, Matt?'

'Legal enough, I think,' Matthew said with a grin. 'A kirk is a church, Tom. So we know they're well enough – and as I thought, not in London at all. Vivian was looking in the wrong place all the time. No wonder he never found any sign of them.'

'And then they went to Liverpool. Well, they'll be gone by now – off across the Atlantic. We'll never find them.'

'But look at the dates, Tom! They stayed a long time in Scotland. See, my friend says they found themselves positions in a family – the minister recommended them and they were taken on as tutor and governess to the children. They earned enough money to set them on their way again, and they left for Liverpool less than a month ago. A month! They could still be there, Tom, waiting for a passage. We could still catch up with them!'

Tom gaped at him, but before he could speak there was a commotion at the door. Matthew whipped round but it was thrust open before he could reach it and Polly Barlow burst into the room, her bonnet half off and her shawl flying from her shoulders. Her plump face was red and her eyes swollen. She dropped into a chair and sat breathing heavily, while Matthew and Tom bent over her in concern and the housemaid fluttered round in panic.

'She would come in, sir! Seems there's bin trouble – says she's been thrown out. Mrs Barlow, thrown out! I can't hardly believe it.'

'Fetch her a glass of brandy,' Matthew ordered curtly. 'She's obviously in distress. Here, Polly, drink this.' He held the glass to her lips. 'That's better. Now, take your time and tell us what's happened.'

'Is it Becky?' Tom demanded. 'Has aught happened to our Becky?'

Polly nodded and choked on the brandy. Matthew patted her shoulder and took the glass, then gave it back to her. She recovered and sipped again.

'I just went in, not thinking anything, and I found them on the floor. He was – he was – well, you'll know, sir. And he was hurting her, I could see that. I'd already heard her cry out a bit, before I went in. That's why I did it – couldn't stand it no longer, I couldn't. I know what he's bin doing to her. Poor Becky . . . Anyway, he just let fly at me. Said I was con-conniving. He thought you were coming to the house when he was out, sir. He thought you and she –'

'I know what he thought,' Matthew said grimly. 'And then?'

'He told me to pack my things and go, sir. Said he'd been telling her to get rid of me long enough and he'd get his own housekeeper over.' Polly began to weep again. 'I had to do it, sir. He said he'd fetch the constable if I didn't. And Becky – she said I'd hev to go.' She looked wildly at the two men. 'She said she'd be all right, sir, but I don't believe it. He hits her, I know that, and he treats her something cruel. He was looking at her like murder when I last saw them. And she ent got no one in that house now to help her.'

Matthew and Tom looked at each other.

'We've got to get her out of there,' Matthew said. 'I've already asked her to come away with me. Now she'll have to. I won't stand by and let him abuse her in this way. I'll go now, and bring her back here with me, no matter what Vivian says or threatens.'

'I'll come too,' Tom said, but Matthew shook his head.

'It'll be better if I go alone. You stay here and look after Polly. See that she has something hot to drink, and a meal, and get the housekeeper to give her a room. She'll stay here until we get this sorted out.' He paused then said, 'It may be best if I don't bring Rebecca back here after all. It's the first place Vivian will look. Tom, get the maid to pack some clothes for me and have the carriage brought round. No, have it driven down to the square in front of the church. Rebecca and I can come down the hill and meet it there, and drive straight away.'

'But where will you go?' Tom followed him to the door, watching as he shrugged into a coat. 'Where do you mean to take her?'

Matthew stopped and looked at him.

'Best if you don't know that, Tom,' he said quietly. 'But I'll take care of her, never fear. And I'll write as soon as it's safe. Now, there's just one more thing . . .'

He ran back into the drawing room, then came out with a wallet which he slipped into his coat pocket. 'Fortunate I had some money in the house,' he said with a faint smile. 'Take care of things for me, Tom.'

He ran out of the house and Tom heard his footsteps go rapidly away along the drive. Then he returned to the room where Polly was recovering and stood gazing at her for a moment.

'Hitting our Becky, was he?' he said. 'Knocking her about? Well, I'm her brother and I got summat to say about that, too . . .'

Rebecca was alone when Matthew arrived. Shaken and bruised, still weeping for Polly, she shook her head when the parlour-maid came into the drawing room and told her that there was a gentleman to see her. But Matthew pushed his way past the girl and then gently eased her from the room. He closed the door and came swiftly across to where Rebecca sat.

'My darling, what's he done to you?' He knelt before her, catching her hands in his. 'What's been happening? Don't try to be brave, Rebecca! Polly came to me. She told me everything.' He looked into her face. 'Rebecca, you can't stay here any longer. The man's mad – he's evil. He'll kill you if you let him. Where is he now?'

'He went out. He said he needed to get away from me . . .' She looked at him with eyes that seemed almost to fill her face. 'I – I think sometimes he is afraid he *will* kill me, Matthew. And at other times, he wants to. But I don't believe he ever will.'

'Not deliberately, perhaps. He has too much to lose. But in the way he treats you – no woman can stand up to that for ever.' He held her close against him. 'You've got to come away with me,' he murmured. 'Come now, Rebecca. Leave him. We'll go anywhere you like. But I can't leave you here with that man.'

'Oh, how I want to come,' she breathed against his cheek. 'If only I could . . .'

'But you can! What stops you, Rebecca? You surely have no loyalty towards him? He's thrown away all right to that. As for money, you need have no fears, I have enough to set up home anywhere we like.'

'Matthew, stop,' she interrupted. 'I can't come with you. How can I? I can't leave William. And there's Daniel – how can I run away, still not knowing where he is?'

'But I have news of Daniel.' Rapidly, he told her about the letter he had received that very day. 'If he's in Liverpool still, we can find him. We'll go there first. And William's safe enough at school – we can fetch him too. I'll look after them both, Rebecca, and Lucy as well.'

'Matthew, I can't. Vivian will have every constable in the country searching for us if I take William. Don't you know that a mother has no rights over her children? And they're his now, just as much as if they had been born his. He could have me imprisoned!' She shook her head. 'It's as impossible as it ever was. And it isn't so bad, after all. If I just submit to his will – do as he wants. And if I can give him his son . . .'

'At risk of your life?' Matthew said bitterly. 'Rebecca, at least think of this. If I go to Liverpool – if I find Daniel and bring him back to you – *then* will you think of coming away with me? Daniel is a grown man now – a married man. He could be made William's guardian. There would be nothing then to give Vivian any hold over you. If I did that?'

'If you did that – if there were really nothing he could do to harm any one of us – then yes, I'll come away with you.' Rebecca touched his cheek and he bent forward and kissed her. Then she stiffened in his arms.

'The carriage! I can hear him coming. Matthew, go now please. I don't know what Vivian will do if he finds you here. Quickly, slip out the back way. The servants will never tell.'

'One more kiss,' he muttered and drew her swiftly against him. Then he was gone, out of the room, and she heard his footsteps go quickly through the hall.

There was a moment's silence. Rebecca waited, conscious of a strange feeling that something was about to happen.

She heard the carriage halt before the door. Vivian's footsteps sounded on the drive. His voice gave a curt order, and she heard the carriage move away.

And then there was the crack of a pistol. And the sound of running feet.

Rebecca was out of the room and running to the hall. The footman was already at the front door, dragging it open. His white face and wide eyes told her that he had heard it too. Together, they ran down the steps and stared in horror at what lay on the gravel at their feet.

Vivian's eyes were still open, glaring with malevolence at the impassive stars. The bullet had made a neat hole in his forehead. It had made a much larger and less neat one through the back of his head.

Chapter Twenty-one

The docks at Liverpool were a maze of wharves and jetties, the sky a network of tall masts, a complex graph of black against the scudding clouds. Out in the deep water great ships moved with slow majesty, their sails flapping as they rose, billowing as the wind caught and tugged them. Ships bound for the Far East, for India and China; for the sugar islands of the West Indies; for America. There were even a few steamships, though none were yet crossing the Atlantic from Liverpool. It was only two years since the *Great Western* had made her famous voyage from London, entirely under power. It would come, Matthew thought. Soon all these great masts would be a thing of the past.

The breeze blew stiff with salt and thick with a thousand smells; the sweet, nauseous tints of rotting vegetables, the throat-catching stench of dead fish, the headiness of beer spilled from burst kegs and all the other odours, some homely and familiar, others strange and exotic, of a dockyard.

Matthew wandered amongst the throngs of busy people. In the years since he had last docked here from America, the place had grown out of all recognition. Everyone seemed to have a purpose, hurrying with boxes and trunks, hampers and baskets of vegetables and fruit, crates of meat and huge barrels of water. Everyone knew where they were going and were impatient of the man who did not.

How would he ever find Daniel and Lucy amongst this crowd? For the first time, Matthew wondered if he had acted too hastily. He ought to have engaged someone more accustomed to such work. But he had been too distressed by Rebecca's situation, too determined to get her away from Vivian, to think clearly. And he knew that if he had the chance again, he would do exactly the same. What other course was there, after all? Vivian could not be allowed to go on ill treating her. And now Daniel had to be found.

If he were here to be found . . . Matthew stopped and gazed hopelessly about him. Somewhere in all this apparent chaos there must be some kind of order. Ships couldn't just arrive and moor to any jetty – there must be wharves assigned to cargo ships, to passenger ships, to ships from different parts of the world. What he must do was find those bound for America. And to do that, he must ask someone. Wandering about hoping to find them for himself would only waste time.

Reaching out, he grabbed one of the urchins who were running about on the chance of pickings or an odd job. The boy was about twelve, he guessed, though small; in Matthew's grasp he was like a piece of wire and as easy to hold as an eel. Matthew shifted his grip to the ragged collar and the boy stopped squirming and looked at him with bright, dark eyes.

'What d'yow want, then?' His accent was almost too thick to be understood, but Matthew had had years of practice with strange accents and quickly deciphered the words. 'I ain't done nothin'.'

'Then do something now,' Matthew said pleasantly, and produced a halfpenny. 'Show me where the American ships berth and there'll be another of these for you when we get there.'

The boy looked at the coin and his eyes widened. A penny, just for showing a gent what he could see for himself if he turned his head! But he had more sense than to say so. Pocketing the halfpenny, he set off at a run, slipping between porters, sailors and stevedores, leaping bollards and skimming along the caissons without any apparent thought of danger. Matthew, unsure whether the boy intended him to follow or was simply running away with the halfpenny, made slower progress. Porters and stevedores were not so willing to let him push past them, and the narrow gaps an urchin could slither through were barriers to Matthew. But every now and then he caught sight of the impudent face grinning back at him, and did his best to keep pace.

He caught up with the boy after about ten minutes, finding him on a wharf where several tall ships were being loaded. He glanced up at them, then around at his surroundings, and his mouth twitched.

'Here yow are then, mister,' the boy said. 'Ships goin' to America. Yow goin' there too?'

Matthew shook his head. 'I've seen it, years ago, though I daresay it's different now.' Absently, he took another halfpenny from his pocket and handed it to the boy, then glanced at him with a twinkle in his eye. 'Though I'm not sure you deserve it, you scallywag – you brought me the long way round, didn't you!'

The urchin grinned. 'Well, I 'ad to earn it, didn't I? And I didn't reckon yow'd know anyway.'

'With that great figurehead staring down at me?' Matthew laughed. 'Well, I don't blame you. You're a bright lad, you deserve to do well, though I daresay you'll end up in jail one of these days.' He sighed a little, but the boy seemed unconcerned and let his grin widen.

'Yow want anythin' else then, mister? Any messages, like? I know the place like the back of me 'and. Yow want owt, yow just tell Micky O'Brien, see?'

Matthew laughed, then paused. Maybe the boy could be useful, after all. 'Very well, Micky O'Brien,' he said, 'see if you can do this for me. Find out if a young married couple called Pagnel are sailing on any of these ships. Or if anyone's ever heard the name. There'll be more than a penny in it this time if you can do that – but no tricks, mind. I know the couple concerned and I want to see them in person before I hand over any money.' He nodded his head in indication. 'Go down to the far end of the wharf and start there. I'll start at this end. And find me the minute you have any news.'

'Pagnel, is it?' the boy said. 'Tell yow what, I'll find 'em all right if they're on any o' these ships. Yow just leave it to me, mister.'

He was off again, streaking away down the wharf, and Matthew watched him go, wondering if he would ever see him again. Well, if he were to be trusted he would be another pair of ears and eyes on the job, and if he disappeared there would be no harm done.

He turned to the first of the ships. It was due to sail soon, by the stores being carried aboard now – perishables like fresh fruit, vegetables and meat were always last. There was an officer standing at the foot of the gangway, watching the loading, and Matthew approached him.

'I'm looking for some friends of mine – a young couple, just off to America. I want to wish them goodbye, but I've mislaid the name of the ship they were to sail on. Do you have any list of passengers?'

The officer looked him up and down. He was a poor specimen, Matthew thought, his uniform stained and scruffy, and he smelt strongly of rum. But what matter, if he could help find Lucy and Daniel?

'What's it worth? You can see I'm busy.'

Matthew thought quickly. It was no use offering pennies to a man like this, nor was there any guarantee that he would be able to give any useful information, but the cost could not be counted now. 'A sovereign if you consult your lists,' he said, 'and another if my friends are found.'

The man raised his eyebrows. 'Keen to say goodbye, ain't you?' he commented, but called a sailor over. 'Watch this lot, and see there's no pilfering. It'll be off your rations if there is, mind.' He jerked his head at Matthew. 'Come on, then.'

Matthew followed him up the gangway. His heart was beating fast. Suppose he were to strike lucky – suppose Daniel and Lucy were aboard the ship at this moment, or arriving soon? He thought of Rebecca's face as he arrived home with her son. With all obstacles then removed, she surely wouldn't refuse him again . . .

The officer led him into a small cabin below the top deck.

A narrow cot took up one bulkhead and opposite were a narrow cupboard and a desk with drawers. The man pulled one of these open and produced a stack of papers, stained and dog-eared.

'Passenger list,' he explained laconically. 'Mind, these are only the ones that have booked cabins. Steerage is first come, first served. There's always enough to fill the places and it's up to them to let their friends and family know they'll be aboard.' He gave Matthew a sharp glance. 'What names?'

'Pagnel. Mr and Mrs Pagnel.' Matthew watched anxiously as the man ran a tobacco-stained finger down the list. They seemed to be in no particular order, and he had perused several pages before he shook his head.

'Not sailing with us. Not unless they're steerage.' He glanced again at Matthew, clearly assessing the value of his clothes. 'Don't reckon that's where they'd be, do you?'

Matthew shook his head. 'I've no idea. They might be. How could I find out?' In fact, he thought it more than likely that Daniel and Lucy would be forced to travel by the cheapest way possible.

The officer shrugged. 'Stand at the bottom of the gangway as the passengers come aboard. That's the only way. It's a fair scrum, mind.'

'Well, I suppose that's what I'll have to do.' Matthew felt depressed. With several ships preparing to sail, how could he be sure of catching the pair? While he was watching one ship, they might be boarding another. And he couldn't enlist any help – nobody else knew what Daniel and Lucy looked like.

'I suppose there's a chance they're on another list,' he said, and fished in his pocket for the sovereign he had promised. 'Thanks for your help, anyway.' He hesitated. 'If you should hear of anything – from some other ship, or perhaps a last-minute change in the passenger list – I'm staying at the Cock and Dolphin. You know it?'

'I know it.' The officer pocketed the money and they moved out of the cabin. 'What I don't know, mister, is your name.'

'Farrell.' Matthew realised suddenly what the man was

449

thinking. 'There's no trouble involved in this,' he said. 'They're not being hunted by police, or anything like that. You'll not be involved in anything of that kind.'

The officer nodded. 'I don't want to be called as a witness, that's all.'

'You won't be.' They were on deck now and Matthew paused to look down from the deck at the bustling wharves. He felt hopelessness descend like a cloud about him. How could he ever expect to find Daniel and Lucy in this chaos?

He continued his search for the rest of that day. Each ship operated in much the same way – a passenger list, sometimes neatly filled in, more often a welter of scratchings-out and almost unreadably scribbled names, for those who had booked cabins. Nothing for the greater number who would travel steerage. Generally numbers were counted and tickets given out, so that those who had paid in advance could be sure of a place, but no names were kept. And when Matthew counted up the number of people travelling to America, he felt his hopelessness grow. Worse still, several of the ships had more than one gangway. He couldn't possibly watch them all.

He saw nothing more of Micky O'Brien, and went back to his hotel at last, despondent and almost ready to give up.

'Look,' Polly said, 'I told you to stay in bed. You're not fit to be down here, wandering about.'

'I can't stay in bed.' Rebecca moved restlessly about the room. 'It keeps coming back to me. Vivian lying there, his head –' she shuddered. 'Polly, who could have done such a thing? I won't believe it was Matthew.'

'It's what the police think. Mr Merrefield himself told me that. He's bin and searched the house and found a case for two pistols – and only one in it. And he reckons the bullet could hev come from that.' Polly sighed. 'And o' course, he remembers Mr Matthew being transported, even though there weren't no police force here then. He's local, see.'

'I know.' William Merrefield had been appointed Chief of the Borough Police Force when it was first formed five years

450

earlier, and Rebecca had met him several times. Several years older than she, he was a conscientious man and generally respected. 'But he's wrong,' she said passionately. 'He must be. Matthew hated killing – he had reason to. He wouldn't have done it.'

Polly was silent for a moment. Then she said, 'I've never seen him so lit up as he was that night. He and your brother, both of them. And the case was in the room then – I saw it with me own eyes.'

'With both pistols in it?' Rebecca demanded, and Polly shook her head.

'It was closed when I saw it. But if it weren't Mr Matthew, who else could it hev bin?' She glanced at Rebecca. 'There were only Tom there with him.'

'*Tom*?' Rebecca shook her head at once. 'No. Never. Oh, I know he hated Vivian – but he would never – surely –'

'I told you,' Polly said quietly, 'they was both almost beside themselves over what I told them. And . . . if they had nothing to be frightened of, why hev they both disappeared?'

Rebecca wheeled and faced her. 'I told you that! I told Mr Merrefield – they've gone to Liverpool to look for Daniel and Lucy. If he sends his men there, they'll find them both, searching on the ships bound for America. I asked Matthew to go – I *begged* him – and he must have gone straight to fetch Tom and left at once. And then, in all the flurry –'

'They got a good start,' Polly said. 'But Will Merrefield's constables will catch up with them soon enough. And then let's hope we'll find out the truth. But they'll hev a hard job convincing him. He's made up his mind, I reckon, and when Will's certain sure he's right he takes a deal of persuading.'

Rebecca sank into a chair and rested her head in her hands.

'What's going to happen, Polly?' she asked hopelessly. 'It's like a nightmare. I feel I've been through all this before. Is Matthew going to be charged with murder all over again? Does this mean he'll be transported back to Australia – and Tom with him this time?'

Polly looked at her gravely. There would be no transportation this time, she thought, if Matthew were to be found guilty. No, this time he would swing, and make a public spectacle for the citizens of Kidderminster to enjoy.

And Tom with him.

Matthew was finishing his breakfast next morning when the waiter came to his table and murmured a few words in his ear.

'To see me?' Matthew said. 'Why, bring him in. And bring him some breakfast too – eggs, kidneys, bacon, as much as you can get on the plate.'

The waiter looked down his nose but went out again, and a moment later Micky O'Brien sauntered in, hands in pockets, as jaunty as a starling and staring at the other guests as coldly as they stared him. He spotted Matthew in his corner and came over, grinning cheekily, then his eyes widened as the waiter placed a loaded plate in front of him.

'Hey up, is this for me then?' He grabbed his knife and fork and began wielding them with more energy than finesse. 'Do yow eat like this every mornin'? And dinner and supper too?' The food was crammed into his mouth as if he were afraid that someone would snatch it away. Matthew watched, his amusement tempered by pity. The youngster was clearly hungry. And it was almost certainly his normal state.

'Eat as much as you like,' he said. 'There's more if you want it. Now, what have you got to tell me?'

'Those two yow're lookin' for,' the boy said through a full mouth, 'I reckon I've found out which ship they mean to sail on.'

'You have?' Matthew stared at him, conscious of a rising excitement. 'You're sure it's them?'

'Sure's I can be. Course, it could be someone with the same name, but I don't know what they look like, do I? Yow'll have to see for yerself.'

'Of course! Which ship is it? When does it sail?'

'Well,' Micky said, wiping his plate with a slab of bread,

'that's the trouble, see. Ten o'clock this mornin's the time, and all passengers have to be aboard by nine and the gangplanks up. And –'

'But it's almost eight now!' Matthew was on his feet. 'Leave that – there'll be another for you if we catch them in time. Why didn't you tell me it was so close?'

'And miss a breakfast like that? Yow don't have to worry, mister. It'll only take us a quarter of an hour to get there. That gives us –'

'Almost no time at all!' Matthew dragged him from the room. 'We've got to find them, for God's sake. How are they travelling – steerage?' He thrust his way past two men who were coming into the hotel and leapt into the cab they had just vacated. 'What's the name of the ship? The *Lady Anne*?' He stared at Micky. 'Are you sure? It's the first one I tried.'

'And that's how I come to find out, see. The bloke yow spoke to – 'eard me asking a sailor, see. And 'e said as 'ow they'd come to him only last night and asked for a place. Give 'im their name, see – and 'e told me where yow was stayin', so I come straightaway.'

The cab rattled through the crowded streets as he spoke. 'I reckon 'e'll be wantin' another sovereign for 'is trouble.'

'I'll give him five if this is true,' Matthew said. 'And you too, Micky.' He stared anxiously out as they approached the docks. 'Please God it isn't too late – do these ships ever sail early? Will they let us aboard as late as this? Can't you go any faster, driver?'

They arrived at the jetty to find all the commotion of a departure taking place. Sailors were like flies in the rigging, sails were being unfurled, small tugs were fussing about near the prow. On the dockside, men were standing by the great bollards to which the hawsers were fastened, ready to let go. On the decks burly men were ready to hoist sail, and in the few spaces left passengers stood gazing down, some excited at the adventure ahead of them, some in tears as they waved goodbye to friends and families.

'My God,' Matthew groaned, 'the gangway's up already.'

'The aft one's still there, mister.' Micky grabbed his sleeve and pointed, then scrambled down from the cab and scampered off towards the ship's stern. Like a monkey, he was up the narrow way and Matthew saw him arguing excitedly with a sailor standing at the top. Hurriedly, Matthew tossed a few coins to the cabman and told him to wait.

'I told 'im yow were comin',' Micky exclaimed, hopping from one foot to the other. 'Says it's too late – 'e can't go searchin' through the passengers now. Wants us to get back on shore.'

'I can't do that!' Matthew turned to the man and spoke urgently. 'I've got to find these two. It's vitally important. They came on board at the last minute, you must have some idea where they are. Pagnel – *Pagnel* – does the name mean nothing to you?'

The sailor shook his head slowly and Matthew realised that the man was almost an idiot, only half understanding what was said to him. Exasperated almost to desperation, he looked round and then, to his relief, caught sight of the officer he had spoken to yesterday.

'Hey, you! You told this boy the couple I'm searching for are aboard this ship. Is that true? I won't leave until I know the answer!'

The officer came over to him. He looked anxious, almost frightened.

'Look, you'll have to go. We're just about to sail, can't you see that? If your friends are aboard they'll just have to wave goodbye like all the rest – we haven't got time for fancy leave-takings now.' He glanced around nervously. 'Everything's ready. I can't –'

'Uncle Matthew!'

The shout sounded above all the commotion of departure. Hardly able to believe his ears, Matthew turned and stared along the deck. And there, coming towards him, were Daniel and Lucy.

He stared at them. He had not seen either of them for over eight years. They had been children then, Daniel a serious boy, Lucy a giggling girl from the schoolroom. Now, young though they still were, they were unmistakably mature, man and wife.

'I told you it was him!' Lucy said to her husband, and then ran forward to fling her arms around his neck. 'We couldn't believe it. How do you come to be here? How do you come to be in England?' She drew back and looked into his face. 'Are you really looking for us?'

'Of course I am!' Matthew exclaimed. 'Why else would I be scraping about these docks? Everyone's been searching for months – you must have known they would.'

Daniel looked slightly shamefaced. 'We were going to write when we reached America,' he said. 'We . . . wanted to be safe.'

'Well, you're safe enough now,' Matthew told them. 'No one's going to question your marriage – yes, we know you're married – and there's a welcome for you back in Kidderminster. And your mother, Daniel, is frantic with worry.'

'Is – is she married now?' the boy asked with difficulty, and Matthew nodded. 'I thought she might have waited . . . well, it's done now. But we can't come back, Uncle Matthew. Not now.' There was a slight commotion at the bottom of the gangway, the sounds of men shouting, and Matthew was aware of the officer pulling his arm. 'We're going to America. It's all planned. And we've spent almost all our money on the passage.'

'That doesn't matter. Another passage can be arranged – yes, I'll pay for it myself if you still want to go. But for God's sake, come home with me now. You don't know how much she needs you.' He gave Lucy an apologetic glance. 'The marriage isn't happy, I'm afraid. She really does need you, Daniel. Both of you.'

The two looked uncertainly at each other. And then the argument that had been going on for some minutes at the bottom of the gangway rose to a furious pitch and Matthew heard feet running heavily up the wooden planking. He turned, and saw two heavily built men coming towards him.

He had seen them before, he thought in vague surprise

They'd been coming into the hotel as he stormed out that morning. He had taken their cab. But not only that, he'd seen them before today. Not in the hotel, not in Liverpool. Somewhere else . . .

He turned back to Daniel and Lucy. But now the officer's agitation had overcome him. With a terrified glance towards the poop-deck, he grabbed his two passengers and tried to force them away. He was stopped by the larger of the two new arrivals.

'I'm sorry, sir, but you'll have to hold up the ship until we get this sorted out.' He fixed Matthew with a hard eye. 'Am I right in thinking you're Mr Matthew Farrell of Kidderminster in the county of Worcestershire?'

'Yes, I am,' Matthew said, surprised. 'But why should you –'

'Then I hev to ask you to come along with me.' The man ignored the rest of the little group and cleared his throat. 'I'm Sergeant Amos Bragg, and this is Constable Rummer, of the Kidderminster Borough Police Force. We've come to arrest you on a charge of murder, Mr Farrell. The murder of Mr Vivian Pagnel.'

'Mother . . .'

Rebecca, sitting by the fire and gazing into its flames, lifted her head slowly, as if called by some long-forgotten voice. Almost reluctantly, as if fearing what or whom she might see, she turned.

'*Daniel!*' She half rose, gripping the arms of her chair. 'Daniel – is it really you?'

He came swiftly across the room and held her as she swayed forward into his arms. 'Mother, sit down. Rest your head a minute . . . I should have warned you – I should have sent Polly in to tell you.'

'I would hardly have known whether to believe her.' She gripped his hands, staring into his face. 'But how do you come to be here? I sent Matthew to look for you. He surely can't have –'

'He found us,' Daniel said quietly. 'We were just about to sail for America. Another half hour and he would have been too late.'

'*Matthew* found you?' Her face lit up, then grew grave again. 'But he didn't know – you can't know – unless Polly –'

'Polly didn't need to tell us. We know about Uncle Vivian.' Daniel paused, and Rebecca moved her hand quickly, as if in self-chastisement.

'Oh, poor Lucy! She must be with you – and to come home to that, poor child. Where is she? Is Polly taking care of her? I must go to her. And Matthew – where is he?' She caught her breath suddenly, and her face whitened. 'Daniel, he must be warned! He's in danger – the constables are looking for him. They – Daniel, they think he killed Vivian. They believe Matthew shot him!'

Daniel held her hands closely. Rebecca looked at him and saw the new maturity in his bearing, in his face. And she saw something else; something more terrible yet.

'Daniel?' she whispered.

'The police have arrested Uncle Matthew,' he said gravely. 'They've brought him back to Kidderminster. He's to stand trial, Mother, and it seems as if he has little hope of defence – unless the real murderer comes forward. And that doesn't seem very likely to me.'

The silence was that of a tomb, long deserted. Rebecca's eyes moved over her son's face. Her lips were bloodless. She shuddered. 'Not again,' she breathed. 'Not again.' And then she frowned. 'But what about Tom? Didn't they arrest him too?'

'Tom? You mean Uncle Tom?' Daniel shook his head. 'Why should they? Uncle Tom didn't come to Liverpool, anyway.'

'But he was with Matthew'

'No. At least, Uncle Matthew never mentioned him.' Daniel gave her a puzzled look. 'Are you telling me that Uncle Tom killed Lucy's father? But if that was so, then why –'

'Daniel, I don't know who killed him. There were enough, heaven knows, who bore a grudge. But Tom disappeared the same night, the night Matthew set out for Liverpool. Everyone thought they were together.' She stared at him. 'Daniel, if Tom didn't go with Matthew, where did he go? And where is he now?'

They allowed Rebecca to visit Matthew in the borough jail, before he was taken away to Worcester. Once again she had that feeling of having lived through this before. But then she had been with Francis; this time it was Daniel who came to support her.

Matthew looked up as the door opened and then rose to greet her. His face was drawn and haggard. He too must have this dreadful sensation of having been through it all before, she thought, looking up at him. And this time, the ending might be even worse.

'Rebecca, you shouldn't have come.' He looked round at the grimy walls, the filth on the floor. 'This is no place for you.'

'It's no worse than many I've been in,' she retorted, although in truth it was. Even the weavers' hovels had never been like this. 'And I had to see you, Matthew.' She laid her hands in his and looked up into his eyes. 'Matthew, they can't keep you here.'

'They won't. I'm to go to Worcester tomorrow.'

'I don't mean that. They can't keep you at all. You're innocent. You never killed Vivian.'

'I could have done,' he said soberly. 'By your own account, he was shot only minutes after I left. Or after you thought I'd left. I could have hidden nearby – lurked behind those bushes near your front door. I could have shot him and then got away while you were discovering him. My carriage was at the bottom of the hill – my driver will vouch for the fact that I was in a desperate hurry.'

'Matthew, what are you doing?' she interrupted. 'Acting as your own prosecution?'

'I'm merely presenting the case as the prosecution will do – and it's all true, Rebecca. How is a jury going to think when it hears this? How can they do otherwise than find me guilty?'

'If only someone had seen you down the hill *before* Vivian was shot,' Rebecca said desperately. 'If only Tom had been with you. But we don't even know where he is. He's completely disappeared. And they think he was as guilty as you, anyway – they believe you were together out there.'

Matthew shook his head. 'I never saw Tom after I left my house. I gave him orders to look after Polly. The last time I set eyes on him, he was in my hall.'

'And nobody's seen him since. Even Polly doesn't know when he left the house – your housekeeper went in to take care of her and everyone seems to have forgotten about him.' Rebecca shook her head sadly. 'He's been doing this lately anyway – wandering off for days at a time. We'll simply have to wait until he chooses to come back.'

'And even then,' Matthew said, 'there's nothing he will be able to tell you.' He took her hands. 'Rebecca, we have to face the fact that this looks bad for me. The shot that was fired could have come from one of my pistols – one of them is missing. Perhaps Tom took it, who knows? Perhaps someone else came into the house later and stole it, intending to make it seem that I'd fired the shot.'

'If so,' Daniel said, 'whoever it was must have known it was there.'

'Quite a lot of people knew that. I kept the case handy, to remind me how lucky I was to be alive. To remind me never to be so reckless again.' Matthew grimaced. 'A hellish foolish thing to have done, especially when the guns were kept loaded. My servants knew – they could have told anyone. It was no secret.'

'So the only chance,' Rebecca said, 'is to find someone who actually saw the murder committed. And as far as we know, nobody did.'

'And that,' Matthew said quietly, 'means no chance at all.' He looked gravely as Rebecca. 'My love, do you understand what this means?'

She nodded and covered her face with her hands. He bent forward and took them gently away, then held his palms to her cheeks and touched his lips to hers. Rebecca wound her arms around his neck and clung to him. For a long moment they stood embraced.

'I won't give in,' she whispered when he took his lips gently from hers at last. 'I'll fight to the end. I *know* you're innocent, Matthew.'

'And so do I,' he said wryly, 'but it's going to be a devil of a job proving it.' He glanced at Daniel. 'Take her home and look after her well. And pray she has no more shocks, for she's had too many already in her life.'

The house on Mount Pleasant was a sad and silent one these days. With Matthew committed for trial at Worcester and Tom still unaccounted for, there was little heart for rejoicing over Daniel and Lucy's return, thankful though Rebecca was to have them with her again. But the family was gathering around her for a sadder reason now. Vivian's funeral had been arranged for the twenty-first of October – the thirty-fifth anniversary of the Battle of Trafalgar, his birthday and that of Rebecca herself, who had been born as the battle was being fought.

Did it have to be this day? Rebecca wondered as she dressed herself for the second time in the mourning black of a widow. The curtains were drawn at all the windows and she moved through a twilit world, her mind as dark as the gloom within doors. And the darkness was increased by the dismal fog that hung over the town and slunk like a thickly befurred animal through the narrow, twisting alleyways. It was as if there were no light to be found anywhere, nor ever likely to be any again.

She sat in the chair beside her bed and looked at the pillows where she and Vivian had lain together during their short marriage. It had been so different from what she had expected. The excitement that he had been able to light within her, that burning need of which she had been half afraid, had been quickly extinguished by his brutal treatment. But would he have behaved like that if Matthew had not returned? she thought. If he had not seen the way she and Matthew looked at each other, as she came out of the church on their wedding morning, would he have been a gentler lover, a more considerate husband?

She would never know. And she had not only Vivian to mourn, but Matthew too. For nobody had been able to suggest who else might have fired that shot, and she knew that without positive evidence he must be judged guilty. And she knew too, though she dared not speak it even in her mind, what his fate must be.

No judge would transport Matthew a second time. And for a murder such as this, there could be only one sentence passed.

She heard a light tap on the door and looked up to see Polly enter the room. The housekeeper too was dressed in heavy black, and came over and sat beside Rebecca, putting her arms around her as Rebecca began to weep. They sat together, rocking gently, without speaking until Polly produced a handkerchief and gently mopped Rebecca's tears.

'Just get yourself through this day,' she said, 'and you can cry all you like.'

'There'll be nothing else for me to do then.'

'There'll be a lot for you to do,' Polly said firmly. 'Ent there still a business to run? A bigger one that you bin used to, for certain, but you done it before.'

'Run the factory?' Rebecca shook her head. 'It's no use, Polly. I don't have the strength any more. I'm tired – too tired to start all over again. I've done it too many times, only to be dashed to the bottom again. No, this time there'll have to be a different answer.'

She saw the dismay in Polly's eyes, but could not even summon up a reassuring smile. Who was there to give her reassurance? For all her comforting words, it wasn't Polly who would have to take up the reins, start working at ledgers and designs, make decisions. It wasn't to Polly that three hundred men and more would look for work. She closed her eyes, visualising those men, seeing their wives and children looking over their shoulders. All looking to her – and she could not even decide what to have for breakfast!

She opened her eyes again and dragged together a tattered shadow of the reassurance that Polly wanted. There was no other course, she knew. Somewhere, she would find the strength.

'I'm sorry, Polly. I daresay you came to tell me that the carriages are here.'

'Yes, I did.' Polly's voice was subdued. 'Oh, Becky . . .'

Rebecca shook her head. 'Don't start me off again, Polly. And why I should weep for him, I don't know. He made my life miserable enough in the past few months. But he *was* a good friend to me, over the years. And if he did do it all for his own reasons – if he did always have an underlying motive . . . well, he was a comfort to me just the same, at times when I needed comfort, and I'll always remember that.'

It seemed that everyone in the borough was in the streets to watch Vivian's funeral cortège pass by. Rebecca, in the black-draped coach that followed the hearse, looked out from under her heavy veil and saw faces that she recognised from her childhood right through her life, as well as many others she did not know at all. She knew that behind her in the slow procession were a hundred others, friends, relatives, business acquaintances and even rivals. All come to pay their last respects to Vivian. Yet how many had truly loved or even liked him? How many had been his friends?

After the service, funeral meats were served in Pagnel House and Rebecca moved slowly and with quiet dignity amongst the mourners. She spoke to every one, accepting their condolences. She knew quite well that they were all wondering what would happen to the business now, and she was not surprised when one or two of the other manufacturers approached her and murmured that they would be glad to wait upon her sometime in the next few days.

'Certainly,' she said in a noncommittal tone and, with a sigh, 'I shall be at the factory a good deal, I suppose.'

Whether they were shocked by this or not, she had no idea. Nor did she care. 'Unfitting', as she had so often remarked, had been a word that had followed her throughout her life and she had no doubt that it would go with her to her grave. Indeed, she thought wryly, she might well leave orders to have it engraved on her headstone.

But the thought of gravestones brought Vivian sharply back into her mind and she felt a sudden wash of grief. It was true, as she had told Polly, that she had little to mourn for as a husband – but he had been a good friend, even though it seemed now that he had always expected some return for his friendship, and it was to this that she must cling.

But she had suddenly had enough of all these people. Few of them had had any love for Vivian, after all; most of them had come simply out of curiosity, or for convention's sake. She wanted to be rid them, all of them.

She found Daniel. 'I'm going to retire now. I've a headache. Make sure that everyone has enough to eat and drink, will you, and thank them for coming.'

He glanced at her and nodded. 'You look pale, Mother. I'll get Lucy to look after you. But – there's someone who says he wants to talk to you. He says it's important.'

Rebecca made a face. 'A manufacturer, I suppose, frantic to get his oar in before any of the others. Well, I'll not talk business today, Daniel – no, nor tomorrow. At least let poor Vivian cool in his grave before we let the vultures gather. Not that there will be any pickings for them!'

'I don't want pickings,' a voice said in her ear, and she wheeled to face the man who had come up behind her. 'I have to speak with you, Rebecca. Please. It's very urgent.'

Rebecca stared into the face of the man who was probably the only real friend Vivian Pagnel had ever had. A man she had never really liked, but had thought weak rather than bad. 'And what can you have to say to me, Ben Messinger?' she asked. 'What is it that's too urgent to wait?'

'It's about Vivian,' Ben said. He spoke quietly, glancing about him to make sure he was not overheard. 'It's about Vivian – and Matthew Farrell.'

Chapter Twenty-two

Ben Messinger followed Rebecca into the library. A fire had been lit earlier but had now burned low. He watched as Rebecca picked up the tongs and took some coal from the scuttle to bring it back to life. Rumour had it that she and young Francis Pagnel used to meet here in the early mornings, when she was just a housemaid. He wondered what memories the room brought back to her.

'Well?' Rebecca turned to face him and he looked at her small, straight figure with admiration. She'd always seemed to him to have something extra – something most women didn't have. Steel, built into that slight figure somewhere. He knew it was what Vivian had seen in her too, and wanted so badly to bend to his will. 'Tell me what it is that's so urgent,' she repeated and sat down, motioning him to a chair.

Ben sat down. Now that the moment had come, he did not know how to tell her what he knew. The news must come as both a joy and a pain. He wanted to give her the joy but he knew he could do nothing about the pain. He looked down at his boots and wished he hadn't come. Even more, he wished he hadn't been walking up the drive that night, a week or more ago.

Rebecca made a movement. He looked up, tried to meet her gaze, failed and tried again. This time he succeeded and somehow that direct, dark glance helped him to find the words.

'I've been dithering for the past week,' he said. 'I didn't know what to do. Whether to tell you this or let it lie. But I reckon I can't keep it to myself any longer. I can't sleep for thinking of it. And it's not going to hurt Vivian now – nothing's going to hurt him.'

'Tell me what?' Rebecca demanded. 'Mr Messinger – Ben – what are you trying to say?'

'Look,' he said unhappily, 'I know you don't believe Matt Farrell killed Vivian. But you can't prove it. And neither can he. Not without a witness.'

'That's right,' she said. 'We need a witness who saw Matthew down the hill, away from the house *before* Vivian was shot.' She leaned forward suddenly. 'Did *you* see him that night? Why haven't you come forward to say so before?'

Ben shook his head. 'I never laid eyes on Matt Farrell. I came the other way that night – I wanted to see Vivian and I walked over the fields. So if Matt was down the hill, I wouldn't pass him, you see.' He held up his hand as Rebecca began to interrupt, knowing that if he didn't get it all out now, he never would. 'Rebecca, it was someone else I saw. Someone with a pistol.' He stopped and then said unhappily, 'I saw him shoot Vivian.'

Rebecca leaned forward eagerly. 'You *saw* Vivian's murderer? You actually saw it happen? But – why haven't you said so? Why let an innocent man suffer?'

'I never meant to,' Ben said desperately. 'I didn't think they'd arrest Matt. I thought – well, even if they did, I thought he'd have an alibi, I thought they'd let him go. But they haven't and now he's going to go for trial and –'

'And he'll hang,' Rebecca said quietly, then more forcefully, 'he'll *hang*, Ben. You can't let that happen. You've got to speak out.'

'I know. That's why I came.' He stopped and looked at her helplessly and she frowned.

'But why come to me? Why not go straight to Mr Merrefield? They must arrest the murderer at once. Ben, you must tell them – and if you don't, I will. Matthew can't take the blame for yet another murder he didn't commit.'

She stopped suddenly, halted by the look in Ben's eyes. He saw her face change, the realisation begin to dawn only to be rejected. She shook her head and her face turned pale. 'No,' she whispered. 'No . . . no. Tell me it's not true, Ben.'

'I'm sorry,' he said miserably. 'But I saw it, plain as day. It was your brother, Rebecca. Tom Himley. It was him shot Vivian that night.'

They found Tom's body the next day, hidden in a thicket away across the fields. The pistol was still in his hand and it was clear that it had also fired the bullet that had killed Vivian Pagnel. They brought him back into Kidderminster and laid him to rest quietly, without fuss, in a corner of the churchyard, the vicar having agreed with the coroner that Tom Himley had been of unsound mind ever since he had lost his wife.

Rebecca travelled to Worcester alone next morning, refusing the company of either of her sons. She stayed at the same hotel where she and Francis had stayed when they had attended Matthew's trial nine years ago and, heavily veiled, she went to the court where a special hearing had been arranged. Nobody noticed or recognised her.

It was quickly over. There was no evidence to present, and it was obvious that Matthew was innocent of the charge brought against him. He walked from the court a free man, and found Rebecca waiting for him.

'Matthew!'

She flung herself into his arms and clung to him, regardless of onlookers. The bells of Worcester Cathedral struck midday above them and they barely heard them. On the narrow pavement, the crowds swirled past yet they felt themselves alone.

At last Matthew drew back. He looked down into her tear-drowned eyes and said gently: 'No more weeping, Rebecca. The time for sadness is coming to an end. There's nothing but happiness to look forward to now.'

Rebecca gazed up at him and hoped it was true. But could anyone say that with confidence? Wasn't there always something lurking round the corner? Wasn't there always a pain waiting, for those who loved?

If there was, it must be accepted. And when happiness

came at last, that too should be welcomed and not sullied by memories of the past. As Fanny Himley had said, the past was gone and could not be changed. The future was a mystery. All you had was the present.

'They're tears of happiness,' she said, and her face crumpled again. 'Oh, Matthew, I've waited so long.'

'And so have I,' he said as they walked down the street together. 'Ever since that morning when I stood at the door of your house in Unicorn Street and saw you coming up the hill towards me. And perhaps even before then. It seems to me I've always been waiting.'

They went back to Rebecca's hotel, where the carriage was waiting. But instead of going back to Kidderminster, they ordered the driver to take them out into the countryside. They drove through the Worcestershire lanes, bronze and golden with autumn leaves, and into the little spa town of Malvern, climbing up its round green hills. And there they stopped and walked up a steep little lane that led, Matthew said, to a place called Happy Valley.

'It's rightly named,' Rebecca said as they looked down on the little town and the wide, flat chequerboard of the Severn Plain beyond. 'Happy Valley, for one of the happiest days of my life.' She turned and looked at him, suddenly serious. 'But we mustn't forget our responsibilities, Matthew. I have so much to think about. The factory – the children. I'll have to make some decision about Daniel and Lucy. He can hardly go to Oxford now – he doesn't even want to. And I have a feeling he still hankers after America. I can understand it. They want to make a fresh start, and they're young enough for adventure. But America? What do you think, Matthew?'

'I think I have a better idea,' he said thoughtfully as they wandered along the softly rolling ridge. 'Why not send them to Australia? The voyage is getting safer and faster all the time. And I have friends there. I have a farm! Simeon and Rose would look after them, and if they didn't settle they could come home again. The experience would do them no harm.'

'Australia,' she said thoughtfully. 'It's a long way away,

Matthew – but I think it might be the answer. And we could go and visit them later, couldn't we? I've always had a hankering to see Australia.'

'Not by the means I did, I hope!' he said with a smile. 'But transportation is coming to an end, Rebecca. There'll not be many more men and women sent there to slave for the rest of their lives for some petty offence. And the country is beginning to be taken seriously as a colony in its own right. It could be a very good venture for a young man like Daniel.'

'You don't think you'll want to go back yourself?' she asked a little wistfully. 'You've travelled so much, Matthew. Kidderminster must seem very small and narrow to you now. Do you really want to spend the rest of your life as a weaver?'

Matthew stopped. He took her by the shoulders and turned her to face him. He looked down into her face and spoke very gravely.

'Rebecca, everything I want or have ever wanted is in Kidderminster now. Or, to be more truthful, is on top of the Malvern Hills.' He looked around. A golden mist had crept up the valley and hidden the town in its glimmering folds. The sun shone from behind them, and as Rebecca gazed down she caught her breath.

'Matthew! Look – what is it?'

The sun threw her own shadow on to the mist, and around it shimmered a halo of rainbow colours. It lay there as if on a carpet of softly brushed new fleece, moving when she moved, flowing like a pattern to take her shape.

Matthew stared down with her. 'It's a glory,' he said in a low voice. 'I've only ever seen such a thing once in my life before. It's like your own personal rainbow, Rebecca, thrown by the sun through the mist.'

'Why don't you have one too?' she asked in awed tones, and he came close and stood with his arms about her.

'Each person can see only his own,' he said quietly, 'but see – if we stand close enough, we can make one to enclose us both.'
They gazed down as the iridescence changed shape and made

an outline of opal colour about their combined shadow. It grew bright, so clear that each of the seven colours could be clearly seen. And then, slowly, it faded so that the edges were blurred and the shades merged gently together.

'It's an omen,' Rebecca said softly. 'An omen of happiness.' She turned in his arms and looked up at him. 'I would like to design a carpet like that. To celebrate this moment – the moment when we begin our new life together. And I shall give it a name, so that it will become famous.'

'And what are you going to call it?' Matthew asked as he bent his head towards her.

'The Weaver's Glory,' Rebecca said, and lifted her lips to his.